OUR
LONDON
LIVES

Christine Dwyer Hickey

Atlantic Books
London

First published in hardback in Great Britain in 2024 by
Atlantic Books, an imprint of Atlantic Books Ltd.

1   3   5   7   9   8   6   4   2

A CIP catalogue record for this book
is available from the British Library.

Hardback ISBN: 978 1 80546 132 6
Trade paperback ISBN: 978 1 80546 133 3
E-book ISBN: 978 1 80546 134 0

Printed in Great Britain by CPI Group
(UK) Ltd, Croydon CR0 4YY

Atlantic Books
An imprint of Atlantic Books Ltd
Ormond House
26–27 Boswell Street
London
WC1N 3JZ
www.atlantic-books.co.uk

To Denis, with all my love

By this, and this only, we have existed
Which is not to be found in our obituaries
Or in memories draped by the beneficent spider
Or under seals broken by the lean solicitor
In our empty rooms

T. S. Eliot, The Waste Land

PART ONE

1. Milly

1979

THAT FIRST TIME, she barely saw him at all. There was a glimpse when he came through the main door, and then again later, when the girl was crawling all over him. She hadn't been in the job all that long – two maybe three weeks in, and still finding her way around the place: the various bottles and taps, the big curved counter in the main bar, the compact lounge out the back. Beyond all that, the four flights of stairs, one darker than the next.

She'd been polishing whiskey glasses. The glasses didn't really need polishing but Trish had told her that Mrs Oak didn't like her barmaids to stand still or show idle hands. 'She thinks it makes the place look like a church,' Trish said, 'and who wants to drink in a church?'

Mrs Oak was still in hospital at the time, recovering from her car crash, and so they hadn't even met. But it felt like she was getting to know her anyway, because whenever Trish told her to do something, it always began with 'Mrs Oak, she likes it done this way' or 'Mrs Oak, she don't like that'.

It had been a boxing-club night – so a Tuesday or Thursday – and Trish had been standing at the end of the counter, leaning against the opened flap, talking to some man named Jackie. 'He's got real promise,' the man was saying, 'needs a bit of work, a bit of hardening up. But with the right handling . . .'

At first, she'd thought they were talking about a greyhound. The man had the look of someone who might keep greyhounds, with the sheepskin coat on him and a hat that seemed too small for his head. But then Trish had asked, 'How old is he anyway, this young boxer of yours?'

'Oh, he's not mine. Not yet. Not with that Shamie flapping around like an old mother hen. He's twenty, nearly twenty-one. Been better if I'd got hold of him a bit earlier but still, plenty of time. I mean, you just got to look at the condition he's in.'

'Oh, I've seen him, Jackie,' Trish said. 'Believe me, I've seen him.'

There was something about the way Trish had said that.

By then, it would have been about an hour before closing time. The boys from the club were starting to come in, by twos and threes. You could nearly hear the energy jangling off them and their voices seemed to electrify the room. He came in last, with Shamie. They hung back for a few minutes in the alcove just inside the main door, and his face was in shadow. Shamie, standing with his back to the room, hand on the younger man's shoulder, appeared to be doing all the talking. She knew who Shamie was, because on her first day of work, he'd gone to the trouble of introducing himself. 'I run the boxing club down the back lane,' he said, 'so you'll be seeing a lot of me. My boys give you any trouble, you let me know.'

She'd thought he had a nice face even if it was a bit battered-looking, and had hoped the bit about the boys giving trouble was a joke.

Within seconds, Trish was down at the till, pinging her way through the boxing-club order. She put the whiskey glass back into its little nest, folded the cloth, and followed her. The lads from the club were lined up at the counter. A whiff of aftershave and recent sweat, not at all unpleasant. On her first night here, she'd heard Trish call it a pong. 'You boys don't half pong,' she'd said. 'What happened – crate of Brut fall off the back of a lorry or something?'

She'd had to bite her lip to stop herself laughing out loud when Trish said that.

The next time she looked, the alcove was empty. She could see Shamie all right, now in the centre of the floor, his low profile and nose sitting close to his face. The lads from the club pushing around him like children looking for attention.

While she waited for a pint to settle, she scanned the room: the two leather booths to her left; the long seat under the main window to her right; the row of high stools by the shelf on the back wall. But she couldn't see the young boxer anywhere.

And then, just before Trish called last orders, she spotted him. He was sitting in the recess behind the cigarette machine, the girl beside him blocking the view. She had noticed the girl earlier on, and had thought she was beautiful, even if she looked a bit mad. Like someone out of a circus or a presenter on a kids' programme on the telly, maybe. Her hair, long and jagged, had bleached streaks all the way through it. She was wearing a short tartan skirt and a big red fluffy jacket; her wool tights had coloured stripes on them and her legs were long and skinny. She had felt sorry for her really, sitting there on her own for over an hour, gulping cider and smoking long cigarettes, her head going up every time the door opened. She didn't seem too nervous now though, slobbering all over him, her two arms clamped hard around his neck.

Behind the girl's shoulder, a dark brown crown of hair. Around the girl's waist, a man's large hand. One shoulder in a navy-blue

5

jumper, one denim leg. The other hand came into view, lifted a pint from the table and for a second there was a chink of forehead, the edge of a nose. But she couldn't see enough of his face to really know what he looked like. At the same time, she felt she would know him again.

When she came here first, it was mid-October, just as the weather was beginning to turn. London was much warmer than the village she'd left in County Louth, although the nights came on early and fast. But at least here, you could still go outside during the day wearing only a jumper, which was just as well because her coat had gone a bit snug on her since the last time she'd worn it. She had thought to try for London because it was big enough to lose herself in, and had decided on bar work after she'd heard a man down in the yard talking to her grandfather about someone he knew who had found work in a London pub. 'They're crying out for bar staff over there,' was how he had put it, 'and hasn't he a roof over his head, at least?'

She had felt the work might suit her because she knew her way round the only pub in the village, where her grandmother worked as a cleaner. And when she was a little girl, the owner would lift her up to the Guinness pump and allow her pull the handle and then tell her to take a mineral off the shelf and open it for herself. And when she was older, he gave her a part-time job as a lounge girl, Saturday nights when a man from Dundalk came in to play guitar and on Sunday evening when the old farmers came in for their sing-song. She knew the bite of a bottle-opener in her hand anyway, the weight of a Guinness tap. And she knew how to clean out a slops tray too, and how to sweep up the sawdust.

Mrs Oak's had been the last place she'd tried after a day of wandering in and out of pubs all over this part of London. The barman in the place up the road had tipped her off. She thought he might be from Belfast or somewhere up there.

'Try the pub across from the tube station,' he said. 'Landlady's in hospital, barman's packed it in, and there's poor Trish worn down to the balls of her feet with only a couple of part-timers to give her a dig-out.'

He'd given her an orange juice on the house, had taken his time with it too, holding on to the bottle for a while before finally taking the cap off and then lighting up a fag for himself. She didn't mind really – it was a chance to sit down, her legs singing from all the traipsing around.

'It's a good shop,' he said as he finally poured the orange. 'You'll not find better in Farringdon, nor Clerkenwell either. I drink there myself. But it does be fierce busy at times. Not like this hole. Nawthin' doin' here after six. But up there, you see, they go in after work, then all's they have to do is fall over the road for the last tube home. In fact, this might be a good time to catch her.'

Then he leaned across the counter and lowered his voice. 'One thing though – don't let on you're from the North.'

'I'm not from the North,' she said.

'You're not?'

She could feel the orange fizzing up like liver salts inside her belly and had to hold back a belch as she told him. 'I'm from Louth.'

'Aye, well, you should be fine so,' he said, sounding a bit disappointed.

The barman's name was Gerry. He didn't tell her his name; she heard a customer call out to him as she pushed the door back out to the street.

A few minutes later she was edging her way through a crowded pub. Voices chattering above and below one another. Other sounds too, pings and gurgles and chinks and chimes. Like they were all inside a clockwork machine and someone was turning the handle. She waited for the room to settle. Anything like the amount of people then! Their clothes and different colours of skin. A man the spit of Bob Marley with hair like a slab of carpet underlay resting on his back; another fella wearing a turban. And a girl with hair cut like a soldier's, eyelashes out to her nose. She tried not to stare. To keep her eyes fixed on the woman behind the counter. The woman's face bulging with the strain, hands moving so fast you'd swear she had three of them.

'Excuse me – are you Trish?'

'I'll be with you in a minute.'

'I was just wondering if—'

'I *said*—'

'Gerry sent me, Gerry from up the road, you might be looking for staff, he said.'

'Gerry sent you?'

'That's right.'

Without taking her eye off her, Trish laid a full pint on the counter, then picked up an empty glass, tilted it and began to fill it. 'What are you, Irish?' she asked.

'Yes.'

'North or South?'

'South.'

'Got a reference then?'

'A reference? Sure, yea. It's in the end of my bag there.'

'Can you pull a pint?'

'Yes, yes of course I can.'

'Pull one for me while you're at it!' a voice shouted out behind her.

'And me and all, I've grown a beard I'm stood here that long.'

'Well, what are you waiting for?' Trish snapped at her. 'Leave your stuff here under the counter, you can sort it later. Come on then. Chop-chop.'

And that was how she became a London barmaid.

She was eighteen years old and had known few people in her life so far. There had been her grandmother, her grandfather; the come-and-go farmhands who helped out on their smallholding; the occasional student at harvest time. There was a vicar until the parish church closed down and a handful of children from the small Protestant school that had also closed down, the year after she finished going there. There was a Catholic priest from a parish 12 miles away, who came into the pub to get drunk and sing songs. Once there had been a mother who still wandered into her head from time to time.

She knew the girl in the shop where she bought her grand-father's snuff and his weekend newspapers. She knew the owner of the pub and his sour-faced sister who ran the post office. She knew the bus man who waved at her from his big green bus that brought people up to Newry or down to Dublin city where she sometimes accompanied her grandfather in case he fell off the wagon and needed someone to help him get back on the bus.

There was the main street and the river, the church spire and the dairy. There was the hairdresser in the front room of a cottage where her grandmother got permed once in a while. There was the old haybarn that sold second-hand tractor tyres. The green postbox on one corner and the cream and green phone box on the other. The big blue statue of a holy Mary on the fork in the road, a wreath of dirty plastic roses at her feet. There was the graveyard on the hill at the side of the big Catholic church. And the small graveyard behind the closed-down Protestant church where, if she turned her head sideways to look through

9

the railings, she could see her mother's name etched into a pale grey stone.

There was no sawdust on the floor of Mrs Oak's pub; the ceilings were much higher, the rooms way wider and the array of labels on bottles seemed to go on forever, even in the compact back lounge. The village pub with its low ceiling and squinty windows had once been the centre of her world. Yet, no sooner had she stepped her foot in here than it began to shrink in her mind. Within a few days, hardly anything remained, apart from the memory of sound or sensation. An old man's spit as it hit the fire, or the lazy sound of the ticking clock and the shushing of her grandmother's sweeping brush. She could remember the feel of the owner's big hairy arm digging into her belly when he lifted her up to the pump, and the grunt he gave when he did that, and the musty smell of him behind her. And she remembered, too, the gush of the porter as it made its way out and the lazy way it curled around the inside of the glass and how, if she stared right into it, for a few precious seconds, everything disappeared.

There was too much light in the main bar of Mrs Oak's pub. It came at her no matter which way she turned. In the morning when she folded back the shutters from the big front windows, it fell on top of her in a great big slab. In the evening it bounced out of the backdrop mirrors and speared down from the chandelier. All day long it zipped and winked along the rows of different-shaped glasses that she polished and re-polished with her constant hands.

And there was too little light everywhere else. The further back into the house you went, the dimmer it became. By the time you went past the small lounge, the office and store room, down the long corridor to the porch that brought you out to the yard, you could hardly see a stim in front of you. The same thing with the stairs – the first flight was fine but after that the light diminished. Until the last flight when the stairs narrowed up to her room into a wedge of solid darkness. There were light switches on the walls of the landings – she had felt them with her hand – but they had all been taped over. Even in the middle of the day it rattled her nerves to go up there.

She counted the stairs and used the doors that she passed as markers. On the first floor: Trish's bed-sitting room, the kitchen and a staff sitting room that no one seemed to bother with. On the second floor, a big empty room that used to be for club meetings and another room just for toilet rolls, buckets and brooms. On the third floor, the big junk room filled mostly with old bar furniture, tables and small stools clasped together or the dartboard with the darts still stuck into it, cracked down the middle like a broken heart. And once, when she stepped in to take a peek inside, a stand-up chef with a blackboard in his hand gave a little wobble and nearly frightened the living daylights out of her.

Mrs Oak's flat was also on the third floor. The door to the flat was like a door you'd see outside on the street. There was a Yale lock on it and a bell to ring and a mat outside to wipe your feet and, right beside it, a tall narrow bin with a picture of a flamingo on it and inside it a man's black umbrella leaning to one side.

At first, she'd been terrified of Trish, the questions she could ask, the things she might say. After a while, she became more used to her. She loved listening to her anyhow, the way she seemed to cut up her sentences and skim them across the counter at customers. Trish liked to do all the talking and that suited them both. Every morning, except Sunday when the pub was closed, they had breakfast together. In the kitchen everything seemed that bit too big: pots, pans, even the kettle. There was a deep fat fryer like you'd see in a chipper and a slicer for cutting ham that belonged in a grocer's shop. And a big teapot that put her in mind of a baby elephant's head. Just standing there made her feel like Alice after she's eaten the mushroom.

For her, a scoop of cornflakes from a big steel container and bread from a giant sliced pan. For Trish, two cups of coffee and a fag on the side, while she put on her makeup and talked.

Mrs Oak was a widow, Trish told her. Her dead husband's name was Terry. She'd broken her leg and cracked her pelvis in the car crash. She had a sister called Martha who lived in Hove. 'A piece of work' was what Trish had called her.

Mrs Oak had been on the way back from visiting the piece of work when the car skidded and went off the road. She'd been in hospital for weeks but would be discharged soon. After the hospital there would be a nursing home, and after that, she would go to stay with her sister because she had a bungalow. She'd be back for a visit in mid-January and then, all going well, she'd be back for good by the end of the month.

'And I tell you what,' Trish said through the mirror, one big made-up eye, one small bare one, 'this place better shine then! Because Mrs Oak, well . . . she likes things done her way. She's all right, really she is, so long as you're straight with her. Just don't try pullin' the wool over her eyes. She can see right through you, can Mrs Oak, right into the back of your skull. Believe me, I know.'

There was a wedding photograph on the wall of the office. When the door was left open, she sometimes stopped to look in at it. Mrs Oak and her dead husband holding a long knife over a tall cake. Mr Oak had a heavy face with the jowls hanging off it. Mrs Oak looked like a clever schoolgirl, playing dress-up.

For the first few days, she fumbled her way up and down the dark stairs. Until one afternoon, when the cleaning lady, Mrs Gupti, happened to be climbing ahead of her and each flight lit up as if by command. The light only lasted a few seconds, but it allowed her to see a thick round button placed just below each defunct light switch. All she'd had to do all along was push the button, and a ration of light would be released, enough to take her safely from one flight of stairs to the next.

She could have asked someone about the dark stairwells. She could have asked a lot of other things too, but there were only so many questions she could ask without looking completely stupid.

Trish had said: if there's anything you want to know, just shout.

But whenever she did ask Trish a question, the answer shot back at her so swiftly that she sometimes missed the half of it. She didn't bother with the live-out staff because she knew there was no point. Silent Muriel who only came in for the lunch-time service and never looked anyone in the eye. And as for that Brenda one with the sneery mouth on her who frowned anytime she said a word as if she'd been speaking Chinese or something. 'Sorry, what? I don't know what you're on about do, do I? What? *What?* I can't understand a word she's saying.'

And so mostly, she just watched and listened and at night worried herself to sleep in her bed at the top of the house, in a room that seemed way too big for her.

She worried about Mrs Oak looking inside her head. She worried about what she might see there. Day by day, the anxiety increased. She could feel it like a tightening screw inside her chest. The smallest thing began to play on her mind. A scrap of ham left in the mustard pot, an incorrect order, or a jot of blood on the crust of a cheese sandwich after she'd cut herself on yet another broken glass.

The lights in the bar were beginning to give her headaches. The headaches were giving her a sick feeling in her stomach. And there was something else, too, something she couldn't quite put a finger on. It was there anyway, a shadow in the corner or behind her on the stairway. It was there at the end of her bed when she woke in the morning. It followed her into the toilet and stood with its back to the door, waiting.

And then she worried about the men in the bar, the love names that they called her: sweetheart, my lovely, my darling, gorgeous. Gorgeous! She nearly laughed out loud when she heard that one. Her grandmother had warned her about such men, endearments dripping off their tongues. 'They'll tell you anything, *anything*, just to get their way. Men who chew young girls up and then spit them into the sawdust.'

She was afraid that she might have been too familiar with the men in the bar, that she was coming across as someone like her mother was said to have been – flighty and a bit too free in her ways. But she hadn't made free with anyone. She had been polite, shy even. She had hardly opened her mouth at all. The shame of her accent had seen to that – a shame she had not been expecting.

And then she was afraid that maybe that was what men liked. Someone who barely spoke and went bright red every time they were spoken to. She wondered if maybe she should try it Trish's way, give them back answers with one lowered eyelid and a raised lip.

She practised being Trish in the mirror. She said:

'I'll give it to you all right, my love, across the back of your head.'

And then:

'In your dreams, mate.'

And then:

'Me? You're asking me out on a date? Tell you what, love, if I ever go blind and deaf and lose my sense of smell, I'll be sure to give you a shout.'

But even when she was alone in her room, her face turned puce and the words went limp in her mouth. Besides, the men didn't speak to her the way they spoke to Trish with her black eyelashes and bright blue eyelids and her spongy pink lips.

Watneys, Whitbread, Worthington E, Carling Black Label. Watney Red. Best Bitter. London Pride. Draught Bass. Glenfiddich and Haig. Irish. Black Bush. Macallan, Glenlivet. John Jameson's, John Smith's, Johnnie Walker. Jack Daniel's, Jim Beam and someone else.

She began to know the rhythm of the day. From the slow, lonely air of Monday to the frantic farmyard sounds of Friday night, each day had its own way of working. She knew the sewing-factory girls would come in on Friday at lunchtime and that the bingo crew were on Monday nights. The boxing-club lads came in a few times a week although some came in more often than others. Monday to Friday, the printers and market men dropped in and out. The journalists were there every morning, noon and night.

The sense of chaos began to settle down in her mind, the feeling of being trapped on a crowded platform and not knowing where the edge lay. In the moments before sleep took over, she saw it as a human jungle. She saw some bodies in shadow and some close up. Sometimes she only saw bits of them. The sleeve of a meat-market coat bruised with old bloodstains; the glint on the wrist of a Hatton Garden jeweller; the shape of old Mrs Rogers' hat. There were lights from the jukebox and lights from the cigarette machine. There were mouths floating around in the dark, opening and closing like the mouths of fish. She saw hands shooting into the air and heard the sound of her name being called over and over.

Martini Bianco, Martini Rosso, Campari and soda. Dubonnet

and white. G and T. Gin and orange. Gin and lime. Vodka and everything. Or 'vodkar', as some people called it over here.

The next time she saw him was about a week later, first thing on Monday morning. She couldn't say how she knew it was him, she just did. The doors had only been open about ten minutes, and old Mrs Rogers was screwed down into her place on the long seat under the front window, sucking on her morning milk stout. There were two market men at the end of the bar, drinking coffee, hissing at each other over a pile of dockets and receipts. The place so quiet she could hear the traffic out front and a distant twang of announcements from the train station across the street. A cold morning in early November, a crust of ice on the window panes and him with no coat on his back. He walked straight by her to the far end of the counter where Trish was pouring coins into the open drawers of the till. Without stopping he put a note down on the counter and growled something. Then he sat down. He took a newspaper from under his arm and opened it out. When Trish came over and placed his drink in front of him, he didn't lift his face, but a few minutes later she saw his head go up. She was curious to hear what his voice sounded like, to see if he had nice manners or if he'd give her a tip. She'd been bracing herself to go over and serve him. But then, he stood up and walked towards Trish, catching her attention with a single sharp rap of a coin on the counter before going straight back to his seat. Trish brought the second whiskey over to him and it seemed like only a moment later that the glass was empty and he was gone, leaving a small pile of change on the table and the newspaper thrown on the seat.

Trish turned round and looked at her. 'A young man drinking like that on his own,' she said, 'Monday morning, whiskey too?

A bad sign, in my experience. Good-looking bloke though, eh? We'll give him that.'

'I didn't really notice.'

'Not half, you didn't,' Trish said.

Over the next few weeks, she saw him often. Sometimes the girl was waiting for him when he came in from the boxing club. Sometimes he came in on his own. Nearly always he carried a gym bag on his shoulder and usually, he had a book with him. He sat in the same spot behind the cigarette machine unless it was taken, and then he sat on one of the high stools at the back wall. But he never drank at the bar. Now and then, he might go out to the hall to make a phone call or he might go the other way, out to the gents. At lunchtime, he often came in with Shamie.

One day he came in with a man she hadn't seen before. They did and did not look like brothers. The man was shorter and his face was fuller, and he had long fairish hair, but they had a similar expression about the eyes. The man was carrying an odd-shaped case, oblong and dark brown leather with the initials 'N. D.' in gold on the side of it, and when he asked Trish to put it behind the bar for safekeeping, Trish said:

'What's in it then – a machine gun?'

'No,' he said, 'a trumpet.'

'Oh yeah – blow it yourself, do you?' Trish said.

'Ha ha,' he said. 'Like I haven't heard that one before.'

When he came in with Shamie, he never drank; he had soup, two sandwiches and a pint of milk. When he came in with the girl, he drank pints of lager and, if they stayed till closing time, a couple of Jack Daniel's. When he was alone, he'd sit reading his book or maybe a newspaper. When he was in company, he'd stand up.

For her, he stood out because he stood still. The rest of the lads

17

from the club were all fidgety feet and twisting shoulders, tipping each other on the arm as they spoke. And mouth, of course, plenty of that. She thought there was a calmness about him, or a quiet strength anyhow, that belonged to a much older man.

She longed to hear what his voice sounded like, but so far this had escaped her. One evening, she got a notion to find out for herself. She hovered near to his table, emptying ashtrays and giving nearby tables a rub. But all she could hear was the voice of the girl. She felt that for such a good-looking girl, her voice let her down. It was like listening to the sounds coming out of her grandmother's hen-house: a constant, demented rumble with an occasional squawk darting out.

She waited until they were getting ready to leave, then moved to take their glasses off the table. 'Oh no you don't,' the girl screeched, hugging her glass to her chest like it was in some sort of mortal danger. 'That's the best bit, that is. Tell her,' the girl said, nudging him, 'it's the best bit.'

He told her nothing; he just picked up his empty glass and handed it to her.

For a second their eyes caught. She felt the blood rush to her face and almost dropped the glass, she was that busy trying not to touch him as it passed from his hand to hers.

She was shaking when she got behind the bar and didn't know what to think or why she would react that way. She was afraid of him, she decided. That must be it. And why wouldn't she be? Someone who bashed people up for a living was bound to be dangerous. Someone like that could probably kill a man. Even if he did have very nice eyes.

By now, it was December, streels of red tinsel all over the bar, Christmas lights blinking through the mirror, and a permanent whiff of sausage rolls hanging all over the house. As soon as the doors opened in the morning, customers came tumbling in, and when they opened in the evenings, they were queuing outside. Even in the daytime there was a wildness on the air, strangers losing the run of themselves, joining one another's company, shouting and singing and sucking the faces off each other under the plastic mistletoe. She had to give Mrs Gupti a hand with the toilets because they needed to be done out so often, and had to sluice the vomit off the path outside because the man from the brewery had complained that he'd slipped and nearly broken his snot.

By closing time, she felt as if she'd spent the day eating candy floss made out of cigarette smoke. Her eyeballs were itchy and red and there was a constant low-level heat in her head. She couldn't get rid of the smell; it stayed on her hands, even after four or five soapy washes. She could smell it off her clothes and her hair; she could smell it off her dark yellow wee whenever she went to the loo. She found the food sickening. Too much plastic ham, she decided, too many deep-fried sausages. She longed for a proper dinner, something with parsley sauce or something with gravy. She found a truckers' café off Charterhouse Square that did all-day service and for a while she took to eating there during the afternoon break. But the portions were huge and left her feeling sluggish and bloated. She thought her face looked like a bowl of porridge and her eyes had a piggy look to them. She was getting fat for the first time in her life, could hardly breathe when she closed her coat now and even had to buy a man's V-neck jumper just so she could leave the button of her skirt opened at the top.

She remembered walking home from the village with her grandmother one day after they'd been to see her mother's grave. Her grandmother crying, small tight sobs all the way down the lane that led to the house. At the gate she had pulled herself together, blown her nose and wiped her tears. 'Consider it a blessing,' she had said, 'that you're nothing to look at. It may keep you out of harm's way.'

Oh, but the tree, at least, was beautiful.

They'd had to remove a section from the end of the long seat just to make room for it, and it had taken herself and Trish a whole Sunday afternoon to set up and decorate. All through the day, she glanced at it, but at night when the clearing-up was done and the house lights were switched off, she sat for a while in the darkened room and stared right into it. She sometimes thought of her mother then, on a wintery evening not long before her death, begging a neighbour to give them a lift into a nearby village because she'd heard there was a tree put up outside the Catholic church. She was only four years old then, but her mother had been even more enthralled by the tree than she'd been. It was a scrawny old thing, really, with a few sad lights on it and holy pictures pinned to the branches. And now here was Mrs Oak's tree, plump and magnificent, glistening with light. She could feel a rush of love for it, as if it were a living thing. Her mother so young. More like her big sister, was what the neighbour had said as he drove them back home. 'Your poor parents,' he'd said to her. 'You must have their hearts broken, you and your fatherless child.'

Her mother's face when he'd said that.

One day, Trish said she was looking a bit peaky. 'You need to make time for a walk every day, drag a bit of air into those lungs of yours. The pub is just one big boiling pot of germs this time of year, and Mrs Oak, she wouldn't want you getting poorly, now would she?'

And now she felt she had to go out.

She would have preferred to do what she usually did, which was to take a leftover sandwich from the bar, bring it up to her room and see the afternoon through. She liked being in her room anyhow, the slope of the ceiling and the way she could see a good spread of London's rooftops through her two small windows. She had an armchair where she could sit reading magazines and a small round table and a mantelpiece to lay her few bits on. She had a makeup bag stuffed with cosmetics that someone had left behind them in the ladies' toilet.

Sometimes, she spread the contents of the bag across the mantelpiece and practised putting on makeup using a face from one of the magazines to guide her. She kept it on while she ate her lunch and tidied around, stopping now and then to look at herself in the mirror. But she always washed it off before Trish rang the bell for the evening shift.

On dog-tired days, she lay down on her bed and spent the afternoon break sleeping.

The names of the streets all around: Cowcross and St John; Briset and Benjamin. The names of the little cut-throughs that helped her to find her way home: Passing Alley, Jerusalem Passage, Turk's Head Yard.

She had gone on a few messages for Trish already – or ran errands, as Trish would say. The post office, the dry cleaners, the chemist when Trish needed something for her dodgy stomach. And once Trish sent her to Hatton Garden to collect a bracelet Mrs Oak had left in for repair before her accident, and a jeweller with girl's eyelashes said, 'Hello, pretty, and what can I do for you today?'

On the street, people nodded at her. They beeped at her out of cars and rapped at her through shop windows. It was like being back in the village where she'd been reared, the way everyone seemed to know her name and who she was. But at least here, it wasn't for any shameful reason.

Some people she recognised straight off: shopkeepers and friends of Trish who were to be found occasionally at the kitchen table, like Vera Greene whose father owned the chemist shop. There was Mr Hart, the sewing-factory owner; Mr Wells who was an accountant and who always made a point of sending Mrs Oak his special regards. She knew Maggie, who sold newspapers outside the train station, and Tony Agnesi, who ran the café. She knew Fred Darlington, who was in love with Trish and who owned the sheepskin shop on Leather Lane with the smell of death coming off it.

Even so, the neighbourhood felt too big for her. She was afraid of getting lost too and coming back late for work, or maybe straying into some dangerous place and not coming back at all.

She saw him one day, out on one of these walks. She saw him and he was coming out of Peter's Lane with the gym bag over his shoulder. She ducked into the doorway of Agnesi's across the street and stuck her face in front of the menu in the window. She could see a few seconds of him through the glass pane, the red and black squares of his jacket. She gave him a minute and then she stepped out of the doorway and followed. At Smithfield market, he crossed over the road and disappeared behind a line-up of trucks and vans. She didn't follow him across but positioned herself where she had a clear view through a gap between two vans. She saw him turn and cut through the markets. It was afternoon and there was hardly anyone around so she could watch his lone figure walking through the arcade, under the butchers' signs and past long hanging torsos of beef. She could feel the iron-hard beat of her heart. At the same time, she noticed an absence of fear inside her. She felt she could follow him all the way home and not even care if he turned around and saw her. But when she glanced at the clock over the market entrance, she saw it was time to go back to work. She waited until he had walked the length of the arcade and was pulled into the archway of light at the far end of it. She thought the jacket he wore might be called a lumberjacket, and that his legs were slightly bandy.

That night she went out to the yard during her evening break.

She sat on a beer crate, drinking her mug of tea. She could hear the sounds of the boxing club coming over the big grey wall, the grunting of men and the dull pounding of fists, like the sound of time passing. She wondered if he was in there, if his fists were helping to make that sound and what sort of clothes he was wearing and what sort of expression was on his face and if his hair was damp with sweat. When she closed her eyes, she could see his red and black jacket hanging on a hook on the wall.

You would be safe with a man like that on your side, she thought; a man like that would protect you.

A few days before Christmas, Trish said she wanted a word. She felt sick with worry as she followed her across the floor of the bar, down the corridor and into the office. There was a fur coat on the rack behind Mrs Oak's desk, black and plush, and she stood at the door, arms folded low over her stomach and stared right into it while she waited for Trish to speak.

Trish lit up a smoke and then took a couple of drags. 'I wanted to ask you something,' she said, then, 'I mean I was just wondering, you know. I was just – have you made any plans for Christmas? Were you thinking of going home or what?'

'Home?'

'Yeah, to Ireland, were you thinking of going home?'

'Oh no. No, I wasn't thinking of doing that.'

'Oh. Well, you see, it's just a friend of mine asked me to go away for a few days and I – I was going to ask if you'd mind keeping an eye on things here?'

'On my own like?'

'Oh, you wouldn't have to work or nothing. We close the afternoon of Christmas Eve and don't open again till the evening of the thirtieth. I'll help you clean up a bit and lock up shop, and then all you have to do is let yourself in and out the side door and make sure the place is safe. The thing is . . . well. Look, I'd really like to go; it's a lovely little hotel – well, according to the brochure it is, course you don't know till you get there, do you? Some of these places, they can be very photogenic. And this friend of mine . . . well it would be nice for me, that's all I'll say. You'll be all right, love – I wouldn't ask if I thought you weren't up to it. Any problems and you can call on Vera Greene. You got somewhere to go on Christmas Day? Relatives in London or something?'

'Relatives? Oh yes, yes I have.'

'Who's that then?'

'Well, my aunty. And, and my uncle. They live . . . Oh God, I can't think of the name now, it's the other side of London. My uncle is collecting me.'

'Will you be wanting to stay with them, do you think? Because I wouldn't like to leave the place—'

'Oh no! I mean, they wouldn't have room for me so I'd say I'll be back early enough.'

Trish jabbed her cigarette into the ashtray and gave a little smile. 'Well, that's settled then. Great. I owe you, I do. And I'll be putting a good word in for you with Mrs Oak anyhow. I'm sure she'll keep you on. When I tell her how you saved my bacon and how well you've been doing. One thing though, love – if you don't mind, that is. Could we keep this between ourselves? Mrs Oak – I mean, it's no skin off her nose or anything, but she doesn't really approve of my friend. Thinks he's . . . Well, never mind what she thinks, eh? I'd just as soon she didn't know. Is that okay then, can we keep it between ourselves? Thanks, Mill, thanks a lot.'

On Christmas Eve Trish sent her to help Brenda out in the back lounge. Mr Hart had left money behind the bar for the sewing-factory girls and they were all rightly langered now, even though it was only gone half past one. The room rattled with noise. Chattering, shouting, laughing voices. She could hardly hear the orders being roared across the bar at her.

On the jukebox 'Brown Girl in the Ring' started to play and the women had linked arms and were rocking side to side *tralala-laing* along to the music. And she'd been thinking that it was an odd song for this time of the year and didn't fit with the pretend snow squirted into the corners of the window panes or the Santa hats that seemed to be plonked on top of every other eejit's head. And she felt so happy suddenly, she had to stop herself from opening her mouth and joining in. It came as a bit of a shock to her, this feeling of joy, because she couldn't remember ever experiencing anything quite like it before. Joyful, she supposed was the word for it. Full of joy. It must be the music, the happy faces, the fact that for the first time since coming here, she didn't feel unwell: no headache, no sick feeling in her stomach – nothing. But then something else rushed through her. It came up from her belly and right into her chest. She could feel it going down her arms and pulsing in her neck. She had to hold on to the side of the counter for a moment to steady herself up. A surge of fear.

So that she was joyful and fearful all at once.

For the first time the words began to form themselves in her head. And now it felt as if they were screaming at her.

There's a baby inside you. A baby. A real baby inside you.

Oh God. Oh God, what am I going to do?

She carried Trish's bag to the taxi. Trish climbed in and the window began to roll down, bringing a half-view of her face followed by a gentle gust of gin and perfume.

'There's plenty to eat,' Trish said, 'ham and pickles, all that. Bread on the table and in the freezer, chips too. You know how to use the fryer? Course you do. And don't bother cleaning up till Boxing Day, but do check there's no food lying about – we don't want no little long-tailed visitors, now do we? And here, I've left a few goodies for you on the table and one of those new Baileys gift-box sets for you to take to your aunt's tomorrow. Mrs Gupti will be back Wednesday morning. I'll be back Friday. Have a nice day tomorrow. Any problems and Vera's on standby – and remember, if Mrs Oak rings, just say I'm gone out, you don't know where. I'll give her a tinkle in the morning anyhow, wish her happy Christmas and that, so she probably won't bother. And thanks, love, I'm ever so grateful for this, I really am. Well, that's me then. Merry Christmas!'

The window rolled up again and the cab pulled away, then looped back past her. She gave a little wave as the cab drove past, but Trish was staring straight ahead and didn't seem to notice.

She went in through the side door, reopened the bar and plugged the Christmas tree lights back in. She stood looking at the tree for a while and then went behind the counter and helped herself to two bags of salted crisps and two bottles of fizzy orange, which she then packed into a take-out bag. She made sure everything was safely locked up before turning all the lights off again. As she passed the office, Mrs Oak's fur coat caught her eye; she stepped in, lifted it off the rack and laid it gently over one arm.

Upstairs in the kitchen, she began her Christmas preparations. She made three ham and cheese sandwiches and wrapped them in separate foil packages. She put them into Mrs Oak's shopping basket along with the box of Mr Kipling cakes and the Baileys gift box that Trish had left out for her invisible aunt. Next, a carton of milk, a few teabags, a cup, a plate and a knife went into the basket. She filled the electric kettle and unplugged the radio.

Nervy and breathless, she did two runs up and down the stairs and then looked into the kitchen one more time. Three Christmas cards, out of their envelopes, were thrown flat on the table. She took the cards, a box of matches and a squat red candle she had seen earlier in one of the kitchen drawers. Now ready, she switched the light off before changing her mind and switching it back on again.

On the way up to her room, she stopped off at Mrs Gupti's cupboard and took a toilet roll and a bucket.

She locked the bedroom door behind her and waited for her heart to calm down. Then, at the side of the wardrobe, she set up her own little bathroom with the bucket and toilet roll. She set up her own little kitchen on the dressing table. She laid the Christmas cards out along one end of the mantelpiece, then lit the candle and put it on the far end. Finally, she plugged in the radio. A voice spoke out to her:

'It's past eight o'clock on Christmas Eve. *Ahhh* . . . but are all the little boys and girls tucked up in bed?'

The two electric bars glared out at her from the heater. But it was cold in the room and so she pulled Mrs Oak's fur coat off the bed. The coat seemed to pour itself over her like cool water, chilling her skin, but that quickly passed and soon she felt embraced by it. She opened the Baileys gift box, removed one of the little glasses and the bottle. She opened the lid, sniffed into it and poured some into the small round glass.

Now sitting at the window, eating her sandwich and crisps, sipping her drink, she gave herself over to the salty bulk filling her mouth, the warm milky liquid rolling over her tongue, crawling down through her throat and spreading into her chest.

After a while she stood up and looked down through the window. She imagined how she might seem to a passer-by: a woman in a fur coat standing in a window. That's what Gerry the barman might think, if he looked up – a woman, not a girl. And the boxer? He would be reminded of a woman in one of the books he carried around in the pocket of his lumberjacket. She turned her head and looked into the hushed railway station. Beyond the station and over the rooftops was the city of London. Parks and squares, shops and theatres, bridges and a river. A real palace. Places she hadn't been to yet but knew them from something seen on the television, or on the picture postcard carousel outside the newsagent's. Beyond London, a whole country lay.

Soon it would be 1980. Mrs Oak would be back; she would look at her with her all-seeing eyes and know everything there was to know about her and the baby. She might well throw her out on the street. But for now, at least, she was home. Everything she could possibly need was here with her in this room. For the next few days, all else could be put out of her mind.

She heard a car pass along Turnmill Street, and then the soft sound of bells from a distant church. Voices on the radio continued to talk; now and then, a Christmas song played, and sometimes she sang along with it.

2. Pip

2017

March

WHEN HE COMES out onto the street, he finds spring is waiting.

He had noticed it all right, these past few days, through the various windows. Or coming at him over the wall of the long back garden: buds and stretched evenings and the dawn chorus of course, adding another hour onto an already overlong day.

Earlier that morning, when the nurse told him that in two days' time it would be April, he had said, 'Yes, I suppose it must be.' But still, it catches him off guard – the warm air, the light, the whole sense of renewal.

He can remember waiting for snow. There had been warnings on the news, and in the garden, that peculiar silence. He had been looking forward to viewing it anyway, from a warm, safe distance. Glancing up now and then from his ringside seat overlooking the garden. Into the feathery maze. Coming back to his book then, and turning a page with warm, moveable hands. Beauty without pain. That would have been back in January. As it happened, the snow had barely lasted the night, and since then, he has had little or no sense of the weather beyond a vague impression of grey and rain, broken with an occasional shot of milky sunlight.

'A good time to go home,' the nurse had said. Broad smile and small, happy eyes. He thought she might be from the Philippines. The other staff members called her Tracey, but he doubted that was her real name.

'And where is your home?' he had asked by way of a little conversation while they waited for Dom to arrive.

'Oh, many, many miles away.'

'How many?'

'Thousands. Ten thousand.'

'Do you get to go back much?'

She didn't answer that one, just gave a little shrug. Her hand soothing the cover on the end of his bed. After a few seconds she flipped the question back at him. 'What about you – where is your home?'

He wanted to tell her that he had no home, that he hadn't had one – not a proper one anyhow – since he was ten years old.

But it had seemed a churlish thing to say to a woman who'd probably left it all behind – husband, children, even her name – just to keep the wolf from the door.

'My home, for the moment anyway,' he said, 'will be my brother's house.'

'Ah, nice, and where?'

'Notting Hill.'

'Ah, *very* nice then.'

'It's a nice house, right enough,' he had said, 'so far as I can remember.'

Soon after that, the receptionist had appeared in the doorway and beckoned Nurse Tracey out. Low voices in the corridor and then, the nurse turning back in, nervously passing the message on. 'Your brother, is not possible. So sorry, he says.'

'He says or his secretary says?' he asked.

'Oh, I don't know about that,' she said, handing him the receptionist's note.

Stuck in rehearsal, quicker to meet at house, be there by 5.

'Your brother, he is famous trumpet player? Sister Margo told me,' she says.

'So I believe.'

'You want a cab now?'

He stood up, pulled the bag off the bed and said, 'That's all right, I can find my own way there.'

Then he'd turned his face away in case she could see the relief written all over it.

Three nurses seeing him off. He stands on the street and looks in at them waving out at him from the hallway. A blaze of white against a dark interior. One brown face, one black, one pale Irish. Already he feels it, fragments of time falling away. The life in there, the other life waiting out here. The two-way mirror that divides one from the other. Moments ago, he had been standing in the hall while they fussed over him like he was a little boy going off to school. Now he is out here in the searing light, wondering how a day in March could be so warm, and trying to decide which direction to take.

The Irish nurse had walked him to the door. Then, standing on the step for a few minutes, she laid down the law in a crisp country accent: 'Now. Your brother said he won't be long. There's a café down the road from his house, he said – you can wait there if you prefer not to be standing out on the street. Eat something because you didn't touch your lunch. Remember, don't let yourself get hungry. Or thirsty. I put a bottle of water in the bag.'

'You forgot to say resentful,' he said.

'Sorry?'

'I'm not supposed to let myself get resentful. Hungry, thirsty, resentful. It's one of my triggers.'

'And is there need to remind you of resentment already – no? Good. So, your pills and prescription are in there. You've three days' supply – make sure you don't run out. And your discharge pack – don't lose that now, whatever you do, all your phone numbers are in there. As soon as you get your new phone, put them in – and don't forget, you can call your sponsor any time, day or night, any hour. Will we get you a taxi?'

'No, really, I'd like to walk, I can pick up a new phone on the way.'

'Well, if you get tired, hop into a taxi. The next few weeks will be crucial. Take it day by day and before you know it you'll have April behind you.'

'The cruellest month.'

'Why do you say that? It's a lovely month. Enjoy it. Just be careful, that's all. Have you sunglasses – no? Well, better buy yourself a pair so before you do anything else.'

'I'm not even sure the sunglasses work, to be honest.'

'Well, get them anyway,' she said.

The Irish nurse disliked him; she felt bad about it too, he could tell. The puzzled, guilty look on her face as if she was trying to figure it out: why do I dislike him?

He could have told her: it's your ancestral memory, love, that's all, recalling all the useless drunks that your foremothers would have had to put up with.

He could have told her, too, that he'd never had a better nurse, nor one that was so thorough.

She nodded at him a couple of times. 'Well, good luck then. And no offence or anything, but I hope we never meet again. Now, what have you to buy first thing?'

'A nice pint of Guinness and a whiskey chaser?'

She cocked her head to the side, gave him a look.

'Sunglasses,' he said.

A slap on his arm, then a warning finger. 'And you behave yourself now, do you hear me?' she said.

And he'd smiled as she turned to go back inside and thought: God, I just love Irish women.

He crosses to the shaded side of the street, his mind flicking through the parks of London, as it always does, whenever he needs to locate himself. Park to park, railing by railing; a tangle of concrete miles in between. He knows he is in the area of NW1. So that's: Regent's behind him, Hyde below him. Green Park and St James's to the left.

Something moves over the skyline. Grey, odd-shaped, slightly laboured. A heron. He stops to watch its short, inelegant flight blundering over the chimney pots. Coming from Regent's Park, he reckons, like himself, heading south-west.

He wonders what time it is now, and he's about to turn his wrist to check when he remembers: there is no watch there. The imprint of the watch has long since faded, the hairs it once flattened sprung back into place. You lost it. Or pawned it. Or gave it away. You may even have allowed it to get stolen. How many times do you have to be told? You stupid bastard, your father's watch is no more.

A young woman gets out of a car up the way, pips it shut, then begins walking towards him. He could ask her – do people still do that? Ask for and give the time – stranger to stranger? He can't recall the last time anyone asked him. But then again, they probably wouldn't be so inclined. As she nears, he sees her phone pinned to her ear and decides not to disturb her. She toddles right past, uncertain on heels, so close to him now that a whiff of her perfume slips into his mouth, startling him. He had been expecting her to give him a wide berth. Why hadn't she given him a wide berth?

Because you are not that man now, he tells himself. Now you are somebody else.

At the corner, he turns onto a long straight road, an afternoon lull hanging over it. Hardly anyone about that's not tucked into a car, van or bus. Bar an elderly couple on the far side, and on this side, a lone figure in the distance. Although that could be a tree either. Two rows of traffic: southbound, sluggish; northbound a little more fluid. He reckons it's somewhere between half past two and three.

If he could arrange it so that he's barely there before Dominick has to go out again. Even better, if there was just enough time to pass each other in the hall, one coming in, one going out, with a pause in between for essentials: key, alarm code, whereabouts of bed. That way, he could be fast asleep by the time Dom comes in tonight. And then, first thing tomorrow, be in a rush to go out. Where, though? The chemist, the social, the physio. But no, tomorrow is Saturday so physio and social are out. It doesn't matter – the thing is to get out early. By the time he comes back, Dom would probably have gone out to work or a concert. Sunday morning, he could say he has to rush off to an AA meeting. By the time he comes back, Dom would probably be off at one of his poncy Sunday lunches. And so on, for the first few days anyhow. If he could just manage to engineer that bit of distance, things might work out between them, or long enough anyhow for him to find his own feet. But he knows Dom will not be avoided, that at the very least, he will not be denied his 'Ground Rules' speech.

Ahead of him he sees a row of shops. He begins to move

towards them, testing the air. The seaside smell of frying fish and, now, the hot sweaty tang of a dry cleaners. Both smells contained in their own little pockets, both identifiable – just as he likes them to be.

There's a clock over the fish shop. He steps out onto the road to view it better. Five minutes to three. Still a fair bit of time to kill. He could stop off at Queensway, stretch it out a bit while he looks for a phone and sunglasses, maybe get a bite to eat. Stretch it out again with a slow walk back. He steps back onto the path and continues on the straight. The road widens.

He had not been looking forward to the journey back to Dom's house, the two of them capsuled in the back of a cab, worming through the slog of afternoon traffic. The bag on the seat like a barricade between them and Dom running through a few neutral topics in case the taxi driver might hear their business. The rehearsal he'd just left, the concert tonight. Brexit, probably. Poor Theresa May, Jeremy fucking Corbyn – the usual. A little light bragging about his son. A few low-key but well-aimed jabs at the mother of his son, Monique, and the hardships incurred by his second divorce.

He'd been training himself in advance, the better to endure it. All he had to do was to make sure he was wearing his listening face. A few agreeable nods, a smile or frown as the need arose, and to remember to keep the fingers of both hands screwed tightly together to stop himself from jumping ship.

He had done it before. Once even from the back of a cab – what the circumstances were, he can't quite recall now. Dom had just bailed him out from a cop shop out Hoxton way, drunk and disorderly then. They were stuck in crawling traffic on the Euston Road and Dom, who had not yet featured on Radio 3, had been less worried then about what the taxi man heard and had been giving him a right bollocking. Until, without even thinking about it, he'd pushed the door of the taxi open and stepped out of the cab onto the road – right into the middle of the traffic. The sounds erupting around him like a herd of frightened cattle, honking and lowing. Voices roaring out of car windows. Oy! Oy you! You facken idiot. *Mor*-on!

He knew Dominick's voice would not have been among them, that at most, his face would have blown up and reddened, his body stiffened and then a sharp 'drive on' for the taxi man. Not that they would have got very far, with the traffic going that slow. And so Dom would just have had to sit there and listen to the symphony of outraged horns brought about by his younger brother.

Not that he'd cared. He was thirty-four years old or there-abouts and had stopped giving a fuck about most things by then, or maybe he just had nothing left to give a fuck about. He'd a few notes left in his wallet and pocketsful of silver after three days of trawling from one bar to another. Otherwise, no wife, no kid, no boxing career, no home. Nothing. Eyeballs on fire and his tongue like a filthy doormat. He could feel the poison swimming like a rat through his veins. A short while earlier, when the copper had woken him to tell him his brother was outside, he'd thought he could never sink lower. Had he been in crawling distance of the Thames he would have gladly rolled himself over the wall. But oh then, those few moments of glory on the Euston Road! Wading through the fumes of early-morning traffic. He could have stepped into any ring, one hand tied behind his back. The faces craning out of bus windows knew it, the baying voices all around. Dom's taxi driver, and even Dom himself – they all knew it. He was indestructible; he was unbeholden to any man.

He had kept his arms raised high above his head as he weaved in and out, putting one lane of traffic and then the other behind him. And when he got through to the other side, a vanload of navvies cheered and whistled. He kept walking along the pavement through the early-morning crowd, in his beer-stained shirt and his piss-splashed trousers, until he had walked himself off the street and under the ground where he found himself standing under a big destination board, looking up at the flickering possibilities.

He could do it again, just disappear. Like he's done so many times before. And it didn't always have to be on account of Dominick either. All those mornings he'd woken with restless feet and an unsettled mind, and had walked away from whatever bit of a life he'd managed to tack together since last time he'd done a runner: a key to put in a door; a sink in the corner; a woman, a bed with two sheets, sometimes a job. He could easily do it now.

He stops, removes his jacket, loops it between the handles of the bag and rolls up his sleeves. If he disappeared now, he would be well prepared. Everything he needs is here in this bag: his meds, clean clothes, a wallet with a few quid in it, thanks to Dom. He could go into Paddington, jump on a train, revisit one of the old haunts, get away from London and this overheated day in spring, months to go before the real summer gets started: dust-coated streets and parks stuffed with people. He could end up anywhere; Wiltshire – the Downs, maybe. The Downs would be glorious just now. Or Scotland, right up to the Highlands. Or he could go the other direction – to Devon, relive the couple of summers he spent there all those years ago. Camping out in a field, carrying his home like a snail, on his back. Passing himself off as just another country rambler. But you could do that sort of thing back then, when everyone looked a bit scruffy. He remembers bits of it: a field of wild ponies; a rash of poppies across a sloped meadow. Big ancient stones that took on the form of large animals in the dusk. And he remembers, too, hooking up with groups along the way, students and school teachers on holidays; campfires and girls with long hair; joints passed hand to hand, bottles of cider; hunks of cheese and pickled onions to take care of the munchies. And that moment of acceptance, when a bottle or a joint was passed to him with a smile; when faces turned to him to listen to whatever shite he was talking – that warm feeling of *I belong*. And then almost at once, not wanting to belong, wanting to just get away from their stupid temporary surrogate families, knowing that sooner rather than later he would fuck it all up.

Wiltshire would be a better bet; the Ridgeway, white road winding ahead mile after mile, no sense of an ending, alone and yet never feeling alone. In Wiltshire, you never hook up with anyone.

He stops, suddenly aware of his shortening breath. The air hot and tight around him. He leans forward, hands on his thighs. Oh, you could all right, he thinks, just hop on a train to Devon or hitch up to Scotland. Or you could stick one of Dom's trumpets up your arse and blast yourself off to the moon.

There's a low brick wall a few steps away, a squat concrete office block a few yards behind it. He perches himself on the edge of the wall near to the entrance gate. A security man in his little glass box lifts his head, eyes him for a second and then goes back to whatever he's doing or pretending to do. He lays the bag down and takes a few four-square breaths. He is too old now for running away, a sixty-year-old man with a raggy liver, a gammy knee and dodgy hip. Too old for nesting down in a doorway or under a hedge. Besides, on a strange road, it's so easy to fall. And the next fall will be his last. He knows that – he knew it even before the man in the white coat sat down on the side of his bed, crossed his little fat pin-striped legs and, with a smile in his eyes, told him so.

He has lasted a day under Dom's roof and he has lasted a few weeks. He has slipped out of back doors in the middle of the night or he has just gone out one morning and failed to return. On a few occasions it has been his brother's idea. Get the fuck out of my house. Get the fuck out, you prick, and don't come back. But one way or another, sooner or later, it has always ended the same way. Apart from the first time. That house on the Goswell Road. But they had been young then, he just over from Ireland and Dom keen to guide and support him. A lively house, people always passing through who acted as buffers: musicians and other friends of Dom's, posh girls who made the first move. He'd had a girl himself – a mad one from over near Smithfield. Dom ended up having to call the police for her one night. It didn't matter though; nothing mattered. They were brothers who had been living in different countries for a long time. And now they were reunited. He'd been proud of Dom then and had liked to drop it into the conversation: my big brother who won a music scholarship to a school in Hertfordshire. My big brother who'd just graduated from the Royal Academy and already nabbed himself a job. My big brother who could make the trumpet talk to you. And Dom too, in his own way, had been proud of him. How many times had he heard him say it: my kid brother – better not mess with him; on his way to being a champ. You should see him dance in the ring. There was three years between them, and they spoke with different accents, but they were getting to know each other again. And for a while at least, they had been on equal terms. Late-night rashers and eggs at the kitchenette table when Dom came in from a gig; a kitty in the cupboard for bread, milk and bills.

And now here they are again, after more than ten years without so much as a word, apart from a few squeezed-out conversations in the safety of the clinic's visiting room. Dom does his best, his dutiful best, and always has done in fairness. But the thoughts of living together again, of being beholden to him at this time of his life . . . it's not that he doesn't love his brother, it's just that he can't fucking stand him.

He reaches into the bag, pulls out the bottle of water, opens it and takes a long gulping swig, resisting the urge to down it in one. Then he rolls the side of the still-cool bottle across his hot forehead and replaces the lid. He is gasping for breath, shirt stuck to his belly, his two feet boiling inside his heavy shoes. He could do with losing a bit of weight, no doubt about that. Get himself fit again, come up with a plan. He has turned into a bit of a slob. All right, a fat fuck. But nothing that can't be fixed. Step by step, mile by mile. A bit of discipline, that's all it takes.

He puts the bottle back into the bag. As he does so, his eye is caught by a small packet wrapped in plastic. His *mea culpa* letters. Shit but he'd almost forgotten about them. He edges the stack out, removes the plastic wrapping and holds them in the spread of his hands.

The best part of three weeks it had taken to write these letters and even longer to persuade him to try. Doctor Sunita had brought him around in the end with her toffee-soft eyes and her mouthful of immaculate teeth. A way to seek forgiveness, she had said, 'without which you simply cannot move on. A step towards repaying your psychological and emotional debts'.

'So, what about the financial debts then – will I be let off them?'

'Afraid not,' she said with her sad little smile.

In the end he had believed her; had occasionally become a bit emotional as he wrote and re-wrote, day after day, flinging crushed balls of paper into the bin in his room, like an old-fashioned Hollywood writer. Until finally he hit his stride, after which he began to enjoy himself. Doctor Sunita had been right, it was a cleansing process. A way to prove to himself that he had accepted responsibility; that he was capable of change, of making amends. He had been quite proud of his finished letters, had treasured them even, wrapping them in plastic to keep them clean and stashing them on the floor of his bedside locker, never reading them again, although sometimes taking them out of the wrapper just to hold the envelopes in his hands.

And now, standing here on the street, he can no longer see the point of them – unless to make him look soft in the head. He is ashamed of his slobbering sentimentality, the passive-aggressive tone he had used – forgive me, or else I'll never be sober. And even if they did forgive him – what next? Would they write back to him? Would he have a pen-pal situation on his hands, based on the common bond of his drinking-related sins. Or worse – what if they wanted to see him, to grant their forgiveness in person? Standing before him, with arms open wide, 'Come here to me, you . . .'

Six envelopes in all. He wonders, why only six? Is it based on the average number of lives that an alco fucks up in the course of his drinking life? Because he could have easily come up with a dozen more. And the rest of it.

He shuffles through the envelopes: Lorraine. Angie. Shamie. Bob. And Milly – of course. Milly. He even has one for Dom, which seems a bit ridiculous – what's he supposed to do, say, 'Here, I have a little something for you,' and hand it to him with a knowing wink? Or maybe draw a little stamp on it and throw it down on the mat and hope he thinks it came in with the rest of the post?

He has no idea where Angie lives now. Or Lorraine – although one would probably lead to the other and then on to Shamie. Last time they actually spoke, Shamie had been talking about getting out of the East End. In fact, the only address he's completely sure of is Milly's. And she is the only one who is likely to forgive him. He feels the weight of the letters in his hands; the burden of having to deliver them, of having to stand naked in public until the verdict comes in, with the shit running down his legs.

He could always tear them in half, then tear them again, keep tearing until all that he has is a handful of confetti to throw all over the road. Be rid of them. Be free. He taps the envelopes off the palm of his hand a few times. Then he rocks himself on his heels, gives his shoulders a few rigorous shrugs and lets out a long, loose sigh. 'Ah fuck it,' he says, then slips the letters back into the plastic wrap.

He opens the bag out and looks inside. His AA handbook looks back at him. Behind it, the Palgrave's *Golden Treasury* with the sticker on the front: First Prize, English, 1969. He slots the plastic wrapping in between them.

'Make no rash decisions,' he says. 'Later – you can decide later.'

He picks up the bag, rezips the gaping mouth of it. 'And stop talking to yourself in the street,' he says, 'there's a good man.'

He comes to a corner, sniffing the air. He can smell something new: nutty, a touch of liquorice. Spice or a mixture of spices. Spices and hot oil. He looks around but can't locate the source.

On the far side of the road, the sound of a construction site trundling away. No houses or food shops within sight. A familiar low-level anxiety begins to stir. But then he reminds himself: just because he can't see the source, doesn't mean he's imagining the smell. This is London, there's always a smell of spice. It's on the breath of the city; it's coming out through the pores of its skin.

The construction site is surrounded by hoarding, big faces painted all along it. A multicultural statement of grins, like one of those ad campaigns from the seventies. The hoarding promises so much more than a place to lay your head. It promises a whole life. Friends. A balcony to put them on. A space to plug in your car or park your bike. Work your whole life to pay for the privilege, just try not to let the words 'glorified tenement' slip into your head.

And now, a different hoarding begins to edge into his mind – one with the faces of animals on it, instead of grinning people. The zoo. London Zoo. Standing across the road from it, holding Lorraine's small hand in his, hoping the tremors wouldn't pass from one to the other.

He had gone on the piss the night before and had woken up on the wrong side of the city, with just enough time to pick her up in a taxi. And standing across the road from the zoo, holding her little hand, his drinking mind had started to connive: he didn't have to bring her inside, did he? He only had to *convince* her that she had been there. He could make up a game, point out each animal on the hoarding, give it its own little story, put it into her head. Then they could walk around the periphery of the zoo, listen to the sounds of the animals coming through. Tell her: that's Leo the lion roaring for his dinner – remember we just saw him? That's Sammy the seal barking for a bit of fish, I showed him to you a few minutes ago – what does Sammy say? That's right. Good girl. And the chimps – hear them fighting? What are they fighting about?

And that's exactly what he did. He could have got a job on *Blue Peter*, he did it so well. In fooling her, he had almost managed to fool himself. She was only a child – what difference would it make to her? A shy child at that, who would hate it in there, crowds closing in on her, all that pushing and shoving. She would probably prefer to have her daddy all to herself for the day.

The more he had thought about it, the better his idea had seemed. He could buy her chips, get her a video instead of throwing money away on overpriced tickets and an overpriced lunch, spending the afternoon edging along, queue to queue, just to see some poor old animals locked up in cages.

He would come to think of that weekend as the Last Weekend. The last Friday night that he'd fought to England Boxing rules; the last time he'd had unsupervised access to Lorraine; the last time he had fooled himself that he hadn't got a problem. Last few quid in his pocket, no one left in the world to put the squeeze on.

The darkened room; a blade of sunlight through the side of the curtain. The child kneeling on the floor in front of the telly, an aura of cartoon colours about her head. Under the table a growing congregation of empty lager cans; above the table, hidden under a towel, the diminishing stash.

When he woke up it was dusk and the television screen was blank.

The bottle of Coke he had bought her on the floor, still a quarter-way full with the straw sticking out; a scatter of sweet wrappers. She was gone, the door to his bedsit wide open. He was reeling when he got on his feet and nearly broke his neck in the stumble to get down the stairs. As he landed in the hall, still calling her name, the door of the flat beside the staircase creaked open and the old dear who lived there poked out her powdered face. 'If you're looking for the little girl,' she said, 'her mum's been to collect her.'

'She couldn't have,' he said. 'She doesn't even know where I live.'

'The little girl, she knocked on my door. She said, I want to go home, can you phone my mummy please. She knew her own number.'

How many years ago was that now? Does Lorraine remember any of it, he wonders. The shitty flat, the painted animals outside the zoo? The fact that they didn't get the chips in the end and the reason why – because he hadn't got the patience to wait in the queue, not while he had a full bag of cans winking up at him? Or does she remember standing in the hall at dusk, knocking on the flat of the powdery old woman? Even if she did forget, her mother would have reminded her, filled in all the gaps.

Why had he not made more of an effort with his daughter? He'd wanted to, but the pain just became too much to bear. The first sight of her, the saying goodbye. And now, the idea of sending her a letter of apology. An insult, that's all it is, to the woman who was once his beautiful child.

Oh remorse, he thinks. Christ, what use is it to any of us now? Remorse or even forgiveness – no amount of it will wipe out the damage, or bring back the years. Don't you dare fucking cry, he says to himself. Don't even think about it, you bastard, you hypocrite.

Across the street, the grinning faces on the hoarding slip in and out of view through the passing traffic. Peep-o, peep-o. He watches for a while and then, with a swing of his bag, turns away from the sight and passes into a narrower street.

A bit more to see here at least. Foal-legged black boys kicking a ball. Outside a discount store, two women in saris sitting on kitchen chairs, knitting. More dodgy shops this side of the street, most of them with the grating pulled down over the windows. A group of ashen-faced teenagers crouched on the ground. Boarded-up windows in a block of flats. Smashed bottles,

crushed glass and small silver canisters that look like spent bul-
lets, glinting on the road.

He takes his wallet out of his back pocket, slides it around and
slips it down into his front pocket. It's something he has always
liked about London, the little warps you can sometimes slip
through: one minute walking through a wasteland of respect-
ability, next minute wondering if you're about to be jumped.

A bookie's shop comes into view: big, blue and brash. It spreads
itself all the way round the corner, allowing an entrance from
both streets, so that no one with an itch can get by. A busier end
of the street ahead, people coming towards him in the middle
of the road, coats over arms, jumpers tied around waists, bewildered faces looking around, as if to wonder, where's this bloody
heatwave come from? The crowd is coming from the far side of
a row of parked vans and estate cars. He's about to make his way
down there when his eye is distracted by the pulsing green cross
of a pharmacy.

Inside, an absence of aromas. Pharmacies don't smell like they
used to: disinfected, medicinal, fragrant. Reassuring. He went
to school with a boy in Ireland whose father owned a pharmacy
in the centre of Dublin. A chemist shop, as it was called then.
The boy, pigeon-toed and extremely clever, wasn't in his class,
nor was he in his dormitory. The only connection had been the
chess club where they'd played against one another a few times.
He neither liked nor disliked the boy, simply because they didn't
really know one another. He had been puzzled when, one day,
the boy had looked across the chessboard and asked him home
for the mid-term break and he could remember the boy looking
surprised and even somewhat alarmed when he'd accepted the
invitation. They lived above the shop, and he could remember the
sound of footsteps and buses through the open window, extracts

of passing conversations. He'd loved the way you could smell the shop all over the house, and the way, any time a customer came in, the bell gave a gamey little tinkle.

No bell in this shop anyway, just an automatic door, never quite closing, never fully open, giving a nervy little gulp anytime someone passes by on the street.

He puts down his bag and stands by the carousel of sunglasses, one lazy hand turning it every few seconds.

The parents were decent people. As soon as he met them, he understood why the boy had taken him home. 'This is my best friend,' he'd said and they both had beamed with something like relief.

The father took off his white coat and hung it on the back of the kitchen door before he ate lunch. The mother wore a pink fluffy jumper and made apple tarts. He'd been looking forward to running all over Dublin city, the shops, the pictures, just rambling around looking at things, but then, all he had wanted was to sit in the kitchen, peeling apples for the mother, listening to her tweeting on about nothing and looking at her fluffy jumper. The boy (what's this his name was?) was not impressed.

Eileen and George, the parents were called. There had been an innocence about them – something their son didn't inherit. Christ when he thinks of what happened to them.

A voice calls out, startling him. 'Can I help you, sir?' He turns and sees a girl behind the counter, looking in his direction.

'What? Yes, yes, that's right,' he says, 'yes, I'm looking for sunglasses, but you've probably guessed that. Blue ones. I'm looking for blue ones.'

The girl comes around the counter and stands beside him. A smiley, pretty face looking up at him. She's wearing a badge on her white coat. He thinks it could say 'Trainee' or maybe it's

'Trinny' but he'd have to peer right into her chest to know for certain.

'Blue ones? Well let's see now. Oh yes, what about these?'

She extracts a pair of glasses, points their little arms at him.

'They're not blue.'

'Oh, they are, look,' she lifts them to the light, tilting the frame.

'I meant the lens has to be blue,' he explains. 'Blue-toned, that is – not the frame.'

'The lens? Oh. All right. Well, what about these? These are nice, more silver really, but they have a bit of a blue tone. Like to try them on?'

He lowers his voice. 'I'm on Epilin, you see, the light affects me, especially in this weather. So you see, the blue—'

'You're on what? Sorry?'

The owner of the shop comes out of his little hatch. The girl turns to him. 'Mr Mills,' she says, 'do you know if we have any sunglasses with blue lenses? The gentleman says he's on – what was it again?'

'Ah, don't worry about it,' he says, 'I'll get them at the optician. You don't have them, I can see that.'

'Oh,' she says. 'Oh but . . .'

He steps back out onto the street, the door gagging behind him. He can hear the girl's voice explaining: 'But I couldn't hear him, Mr Mills, he was whispering, you see, and—'

In the middle of the road, through the oncoming crowd, he walks and wonders, why didn't I just say it? Just come out and say it? To think that even after all these years, unexpected moments of shame can still arise; moments when I simply can't bring myself to say it. 'I'm epileptic. That's right, sweetheart, I'm an epi-fucking-leptic.'

As he nears the row of white vans, he begins to make out the tops of canopies and tents, like a Bedouin camp in the distance. He edges through until the tents begin to separate and the road splits into two sides of a market. Eamonn, of course. The boy's name. Throw a stone in that school and it would bounce off an Eamonn.

He'd had his first fit that weekend. And then, for years there'd been nothing. A good place to have it really. The father cleaning the blood from his bitten tongue, the mother hugging him to her fluffy bosom. 'Bless you, oh God bless you,' when he started to sneeze into it. Later feeding him ice cream from a spoon.

Less than a year on, and the parents were dead. Went up in a fire, chemist shop and all. It had been in the newspaper. A day pupil had sneaked it in to show him.

From the study hall window, he'd watched Eamonn go off to the funeral, a priest each side of him in the back of a taxi. 'Hey,' he'd felt like shouting out the window at him, 'what about *me*? I thought I was supposed to be your best friend!'

At the end of that term, Eamonn left the school. For those few weeks, he had seemed completely normal, going about his pigeon-toed business, collecting his usual As, no sign that he'd even been crying. While in a dormitory on the far side of the school, he'd hardly slept. There were nights when he'd had to bite into the pillow, he became so distraught. The visions of the flames, the white coat, the jumper.

Years later, a therapist asked if he'd wished they were his parents. He'd been thrown by the question. But then again, he'd been in prison at the time and been thrown by a lot of things.

'Are you asking me if I wish my parents had died in the fire?'

'No, of course not. I mean, would you have liked them to be your parents?'

'Did I love them – is that what you mean?'

'Well, did you?'

'I suppose I did,' he said. 'For that weekend anyway.'

He moves along the row of market stalls, banners of cheap clothes fluttering overhead. Below, an array of carefully organised crap spread out on makeshift counters. A wall of novelty baseball caps behind one of the stalls – the man fronting it wears one of the caps, a cloth dick sticking out of the front of it, the word 'dickhead' printed over it, in case you didn't get the joke. The dick wags as the man's fussy hands arrange and rearrange his display of sunglasses. He wonders if he should chance them? But the glasses on a market stall? And even if they did have the ones he needs, supposing they were fake or he had to return them? Sorry, mate, it wasn't me, mate, you didn't get those here, mate. Must have been the other dickhead who coincidentally looks like my identical twin. The man glances at him. 'All right, mate? Got some lovely Ray-Bans just in, if you're—'

But already he's moved on to the next stall.

Kitchen utensils, bolts and nuts, ironing-board covers. Jockey shorts, two a fiver, knickers to fit a giant panda. A sign now and then that says *No Knives Sold Here*, which probably means the opposite.

His mood lifts. He has always loved markets, since he was a boy. Saturday mornings on the Portobello Road, Dom and himself with their pocket money. A big discussion all the way up Westbourne Grove. I think I'll get this, or I think I'll get that. Then he'd jump on the first trinket to catch his eye and whatever sweet-tasting crap he could ram down his neck in the shortest time – candy floss, usually, or a big greasy doughnut. While Dom, still clutching his ten-bob note, walked up and down and considered his options.

Men with dark hands shifting goods around; women with

brown hands decorated in *mehndi*. Fat white hands wearing too many rings.

He had a thing about hands when he was a kid. Always seemed to notice them, especially in shops and markets.

Once or twice, he'd been seized by a longing to run up and down the row of stalls, reach in, touch and even kiss the hands, tell them that he loved them. But of course, it wasn't the hands he loved, or the people attached to them, it was the market itself; the smell of plastic and hair oil and sweat. And endeavour. That's what it was – what he loved then, and what he loves now: the relentless toil of human endeavour.

He sniffs the air again. Then begins to follow his nose to the opposite side of the market. Finally, he has located the aroma of spices. It's coming from this stall and that stall and the one after that. A Venus de Milo of brown sweaty meat rotates on a stake. Next, a woman with yellow-stained fingertips drops pinches of turmeric onto a flat, sizzling pan, her lovely face framed by a hijab. Milly thought they were nuns when she came over here first and couldn't believe how good-looking some of them were and that they were allowed to wear makeup. She'd gone all red when he put her straight. But he couldn't help laughing some-times, the things she came out with. 'Sorry,' he'd said, 'I don't mean to laugh at you.'

'That's okay,' she'd said. 'You've a nice laugh, you should use it more often.'

For a minute, he sees her young face; the big smile, the startled blush.

At the tail end of the market, he finds a coffee van. One remaining chocolate muffin crouches under a plastic dome at the side of the counter. A cup of coffee was just what he needed now, maybe that muffin to keep it company. He could start thinking about the diet tomorrow. It would keep him going anyway, until he found somewhere to sit down in comfort.

A beefy girl on the far side of the hatch. He thinks there might be something wrong with her eyes, but doesn't like to stare at her.

'A coffee,' he says and looks away.

'What sort you want?' she asks, bored or exhausted, or both.

'Eh, large, with hot milk.'

'Flat white is it?'

'Yea, that's fine.'

'Two shots or one?'

The girl stands, cardboard cup poised, waiting.

'I don't know, two I suppose,' he says. 'May as well go mad, what?'

She turns away, the coffee machine growls and spits into the cup.

An old woman steps up beside him, waits a few seconds and then says, 'It used to say milky coffee on the menu boards in caffs. It used to be written up in little white letters that stuck onto the board. They were always crooked or falling off. Nobody minded.'

'That's right. I remember.'

'Course, nothing's straightforward these days. Everything so complicated. No, not complicated. Convoluted. That's what I mean to say. Flat white – what does it mean? Such nonsense.'

Her face is loose-skinned but strong, plastered in brown makeup. Her eyes greyish blue. A blonde once, he thinks, possibly Russian, strains of an old accent clinging to cockney.

She takes a sip from her cardboard cup, grimaces, puts it back down and looks at him again, a wildness in her eyes. She's wearing a coat with a dirty fur collar on it, and appears to be missing one earring. A woman who could do with a drink by the look of her.

He pays the girl, holds his hand out for his change, lets a coin fall into a cup enthusiastically marked 'Tips!!!'

He forgot to ask for the muffin. The old woman distracted him and now the girl has disappeared back into her little cave.

The old woman is still talking: 'Who'd want to be young? Who'd want all that? Everything such an ordeal. So much worry, even coffee is a problem. Then they photograph it, can't do nothing without broadcasting it. Oh, look at me, I'm drinkin' a coffee . . . oh, look now, the coffee cup is empty. Not even a real cup. Drink it walking along the street. Not even sitting down to talk. When I was young, we sat, we talked. Conversation – you know? But I wouldn't be young now, not if you paid me. I mean – who'd want all that?'

I would, he thinks, I'd be young again. Would I do anything different, though? I would, I'd do everything different, just for the hell of it, and probably end up in the exact same spot, listening to some mad old woman with a missing earring and the makeup melting off her face.

'What they gonna do, when the real problems come along?' she says. 'I'd like to know.'

'I think you've lost an earring,' he says.

'What you talking about?'

'Your earring, you seem . . .'

She lifts one hand to the empty ear. 'Oh, that. That went fifty years ago. I put it down. On shelf in my boyfriend's house, thinking it bring me back to him.'

'To Russia?'

'Lithuania,' she says, lowering one disdainful eyelid. 'And she gave me tepid tea.'

'Sorry?'

'Her in the caravan with the hedges stuck on her eyes – does she think we think they're *real*, those eyelashes? Who'd want to wear such things, I don't know. So ridiculous. And I can't abide tepid tea. I just can't.'

The old woman drops her head slightly and gives him a sidelong look.

He takes a coin out of his pocket and raps it on the counter. The girl turns and peers out at him through her hedges.

'Give this lady a hot cup of tea,' he says.

'Are you hungry?' he asks her. 'Would you like something to eat?'

'Like what?'

'All's left is that,' the girl says with a nod towards the muffin.

'I'll take it,' the woman says, a little too quickly.

'And give the change to the lady,' he says to the girl, laying a tenner down.

Then he picks up his cup, nods at the old woman and walks away.

A few years ago, he would have stayed for a chat. She was just the sort of old bat he got talking to when he was drinking, even when he was a young man. Probably would have ended up going to her local with her. An afternoon spent surrounded by oddballs, listening to all their old stories. The corner of a dusty dim pub on a bright sunny day, lager glistening in pint glasses, later the tawny glow of whiskey – I mean, who'd want all that?

He comes out onto Edgware Road and takes a sip of coffee. Lukewarm piss. If this is his only alternative, walking around sipping shit coffee from a cardboard cup, then he could be looking at trouble.

He imagines the old woman pecking at the muffin with her broken fingernails, suspicious eyes darting about. He finds himself longing for the muffin now. The muffin or a biscuit, anything sweet really.

It's always the same when he gives up the gargle. A yearning for sugar. In rehab, they did nothing to discourage that. He can feel it too, after a few months of three squares a day and all the snacks you can shove into yourself. The trousers Dom bought for him are grabbing him by the balls. And when he looks down, the buttonholes of his shirt are like a row of stretched eyes looking back up at him.

That will all have to change now. And at least he's getting a good walk in today and he *didn't* eat the muffin, so he's off to a good start.

First thing tomorrow, he'll set out a training programme, step by step, mile by mile. Cut out sugar, absolutely. Eat no shite.

He brings a discreet hand to the button on the waistband, releases it and . . . better. Then, changing the bag to the other hand, he crosses the junction.

Now standing in the gloom under the Marylebone Flyover, he finds a moment of respite. The soothing rhythm of overhead traffic, the cross-breeze cool on his face. His eyes ease into the broad shadow; he closes them for a few seconds and gives the bridge of his nose a rub. When he opens his eyes again, he notices a man sitting on the ground with his back leaning on one of the concrete supports. He walks towards him.

A biscuit-tin lid is placed on the ground between the man's feet, a few coppers spread across it. He considers taking his wallet out and dropping him a fiver but, deciding that this may not be the best place for an open display of generosity, he reaches into his too-tight trousers instead and pulls out a few coins.

'Not much in the way of footfall here,' he says to the man.

The man shrugs, turning his pink eyeballs upwards for a second. Young, hardly more than a lad – eighteen, nineteen at most, and only starting out on his decline.

On the road outside, three buses creep by, casting a red hue into the grey shadow. He notices, now, a large drawing etched into the grime on the concrete pillar. The young man leaning into the drawing as if he's part of a cartoon: a tree to sit against, a bird overhead, a fox looking up at him. He can't remember if the etching existed last time he was here, a long time ago. He can't remember much about that night, except that he'd followed a bottle of vodka into the underworld and had ended up who knows where.

'Would you know what time it is?' he asks the lad, who looks pained, as if he's just asked him to do a few cartwheels and spin on his head. Reluctantly, he produces a phone and holds it up.

He looks at the boy on the ground and thinks, you have it all in front of you, son. Then he drops the coins onto the lid.

Just gone half past four. He stands at the kerbside and looks down Edgware Road. He has always liked this stretch of road. When he was a boy, his father would sometimes bring him down here during school holidays, to act as his little helper. He hadn't really understood what his father's job was then, except that he worked for a wine merchant. Dropping into pubs and restaurants, talking to landlords, taking notes in his big ledger, showing pictures of wine-bottle labels. His father was a teetotaller, apart from the few drops of wine he took to wet his lips while making a sale, and that one time in Ireland when Father John gave him a glass of whiskey. But the way he talked about the wine! He loved to watch him open a bottle, the few hushed words beforehand; the tilt, the deep twist, the creak of the cork releasing. The glug before the wine finally let itself fall into the glass. The lingering aroma. The glass then held up to the light, before his father invited the landlord to sniff and taste. He often wondered since if this little ritual had been the start of his trouble. If it pushed him towards alcohol. The way the ritual of the Eucharist pushed other boys into the priesthood.

They travelled all over London, sometimes in the car, sometimes by bus or tube. They took the car when he was delivering samples. Edgware Road was always his favourite stomping ground: the curly writing over the shopfronts, women in veils and long dresses, the whole un-British feel to it.

He would like to walk the length of it now, to follow the straight line of it from here to Marble Arch. Past the gaudy window displays and the dim shisha cafés, taking in the sweet breath of hookah pipes on one side of him, the traffic fumes on the other. Maybe sit in a plush corner of a Turkish café, drinking tea and eating cake so sweet it would skin your teeth.

He crosses the road, drops his cup of unfinished coffee into a bin attached to a bus stop. He feels the strength draining down through his legs and into his feet, and then his feet beating against his shoe leather. He squints into the distance. The number 23 is stuttering up the road. He should drop into Queensway, buy a new phone and that pair of sunglasses. But he's too tired now and just wants this journey to end. He steps onto the road and puts his hand out. God, but he could murder a bar of chocolate.

3. Milly

1980

IT WAS MID-JANUARY before she finally met Mrs Oak. A dull, damp Sunday morning when the pub was closed. That way, Mrs Oak won't wear herself out talking to customers, Trish said.

'She'll only stay an hour or so, then she'll bugger off back to her sister in Hove, leave us in peace for a few weeks more.'

Mrs Oak arrived for the visit an hour early. When the side-door bell rang downstairs, Trish had been in her dressing gown, bleaching the stains from teacups.

'I don't believe this, I just don't believe it!' she said. 'What am I talking about? Of course I believe it. She's always the bloody same. Well, what are you waiting for? Let her in, Milly, for God's sake let her *in*.'

And then Trish sprinted upstairs to her room, reefing electric rollers out of her hair.

It took her a while to find the keys. She could see Mrs Oak's silhouette on the glass panel at the side of the door and called through the lock at it. 'I'm sorry about this, but I have to find the key.'

Mrs Oak didn't reply; she just stood there and waited. A good five minutes it must have been, before the key to the side door was found, the door unbolted and then, finally, unlocked.

'I'm sorry to have kept you,' she began while Mrs Oak walked right by her, down the narrow hallway and in the back way to the bar.

'You must be Milly,' she said over her shoulder. 'How are you getting along?'

'Fine, thank you.'

In the bar, she put her handbag down on the counter and looked at her. 'That's good,' she said and then began walking around. She did a couple of tours of the bar on both sides of the counter. First, she moved stiffly, but bit by bit she began to loosen out. Then she went out to the office and then on down the corridor towards the porch. After a few minutes, her footsteps returned, paused at the end of the stairs and then began to climb them.

'Are you sure you can manage, Mrs Oak?' Milly called, rushing out to assist her.

'We'll soon find out then, won't we?' Mrs Oak said.

She stayed up in her flat for about an hour, although once or twice it sounded like she was moving around in the junk room. She looked drained when she came back down to the kitchen, sat at the table and nodded yes to Trish's offer of a coffee. She stirred the coffee for what had seemed like a long time, considering she didn't take any sugar. It was like she was enjoying the sound of the teaspoon irritating the inside of the cup. Then she told Trish that she had decided not to go back to Hove after all, and that she would send for her things in the morning.

'You sure that's a good idea?' Trish said. 'Didn't they say you should wait till the end of the month? I mean, all those stairs – you sure you're up to it?'

'It's either that or I strangle my sister.'

Trish had been right when she'd said that the wool couldn't be pulled over Mrs Oak's eyes – although it had taken a couple of weeks before she found out about the baby, or at least till she decided to mention it. At first, there had been a few sidelong glances. Then, over the course of a couple of days, an occasional question – never more than one at a time.

'How long have you been in London, Milly?'

'What brought you to London, Milly?'

'Have you got a boyfriend, Milly?'

'Did you have a boyfriend, Milly, before you came over here?'

Then, one morning at the end of January, she called her into the office and simply fired it at her. 'Are you by any chance pregnant, Milly?'

She answered that particular question with an explosion of gulping sobs. The racket she made brought Trish running into the office. While Trish fluttered around trying to calm her down, Mrs Oak just sat there and waited.

A week or so later, Mrs Oak told her about the mother and baby home. And three weeks later, to the day, she gave her the suitcase. 29 February. A leap day, Trish called it.

The suitcase belonged to Mrs Oak's dead husband.

'That thing,' she said, pushing the case ahead of her into the kitchen, 'is better travelled than I am. Cheltenham, Epsom, Scotland. It's even been to Ireland a couple of times. And Paris once. I went along to that one, let me tell you. Can't think of the name of the racecourse now. I thought he'd said Chance something – a good name for a racecourse, I said. But of course it's not that at all, is it? It's just how they pronounce it.'

Then she wiped the buckles and straps with a damp cloth and turned the hoover on. She was embarrassed to see Mrs Oak cleaning the suitcase on her behalf and reached out to take the hoover from her a few times. But each time, Mrs Oak brushed her away.

Mrs Oak had fought her way through the junk room on the third floor just to get at the suitcase. She had to drag a load of old mirrors and bits of broken furniture and boxes loaded with all sorts, just to find it. Downstairs, if a beermat had been laid down crooked, Mrs Oak would notice. She ironed tea towels and polished her shoes like a soldier. She would cop the smallest smear on the highest corner of a mirror and think nothing of sending you up after it. Poor Mrs Gupti had to pull the fridge out to clean behind it and she even had to go round giving the plugholes and plugs a wipe. That's how fussy she was. And yet, she allowed the junk room to exist. Right across the landing from her flat, too, and with the door left open to let in the air, so that every time Mrs Oak came out onto her landing, she was greeted by an eyeful of junk.

The junk room was only one of the many things that surprised her about Mrs Oak.

All morning, on and off, Mrs Oak had been talking to her. And on and off all morning, she had been quietly crying, while Mrs Oak pretended not to notice.

At the same time, she was struck by the number of words coming out of Mrs Oak. Up till then, she had seemed to be a woman of so few. Or at least, when it came to her staff she was. She went about her business in a quiet sort of way. She gave out her orders in the morning and then read the daily papers at the kitchen table because, as Trish explained, she liked to know what her customers were on about. During the day, you wouldn't even see her all that much, unless they were short-handed. She usually stayed upstairs or worked in her office. In the afternoon break you could sometimes hear the sound of her radio upstairs and late at night, the hum of music playing.

But come evening, Mrs Oak turned into someone else as soon as she stepped behind the bar. She talked and she laughed and looked just like a film star with her fair hair all done up, her beautiful clothes, her makeup just right, and her fingernails pink and pearly.

Before meeting Mrs Oak, she'd heard a few comments. She'd heard her described as a real lady. Another time, as a classy bird. Mr Hart from the sewing factory said: 'She's a good solid head on her shoulders the way she turned this place around after Terry's shenanigans.'

Vera Greene's father said he was confident that she'd make a full recovery. 'Once a fighter', he said, making a fist of his small hand.

The only people she'd heard use her first name were Shamie, Mr Greene and Mr Wells. 'How's Dora doin' – okay?' Shamie asked Trish one day, and with Mr Wells it was always, 'Next time you're speaking to her, do give Dora my best regards.'

Dora Oak. It seemed like such an old lady's name. And that was the biggest surprise about Mrs Oak – how young she was. For a widow, anyhow, and for a woman who owned a whole pub to herself.

When Mrs Oak was cleaning the suitcase, she wore a pinny with two patch pockets over her aerobics gear, and a pair of bright green leg-warmers. Her hair was pulled into a high ponytail, and on her feet she wore a pair of pink furry slippers. Every time she thought of something else to say, one of the slippers smashed down on the hoover to shut it up.

'Nobody knows about this, Milly, bar me and Trish, and we're not going to breathe a word, not to anyone.'

'I told Vera Greene,' she said.

'What did you go and do that for?' Mrs Oak said.

'I was sick and she guessed, to be honest.'

'Well, she would, I suppose. She was training to be a midwife once upon a time. Don't worry about Vera. She won't say a word. Not even to her father. I'll make sure of that.'

Then she stamped the hoover back on, and toed the lid of the suitcase open. There was a bookie's docket caught in the inside strap and the squiggle of a brown shoelace in one corner. Mrs Oak picked both up and stuck them into the pocket of her pinny. She turned the hoover off again. 'You'll be all right, Milly, you'll see. You're young. You don't know how young you are. I tell you what though, it's bloody unfair, what men get away with. It's *sickening*.'

Then the slipper came down on the hoover again, and the nozzle went poking and slurping over the shell of the suitcase.

A minute later, she stamped the hoover off again, turned around and looked straight at her.

'My heart goes out to you, Milly, it really does.'

When she said that, the sniffling turned into sobs. She couldn't bear Mrs Oak to see her that way again, all snot-faced and breathless, and so she turned away and ran upstairs to her room.

A few minutes later, she was mortified to hear Mrs Oak dragging the suitcase up the narrow stairs. And even more so, when she saw her coming into the room and sitting on the edge of the bed.

'Come on, Milly, you have to be brave,' she said, 'and at least you're not going to one of those convent places. I wouldn't do that to you. I mean my eldest sister, she got in trouble just after the war, and the way they treated her. She was never the same after it. Where you're going, it's lovely really. A house, you know, a proper house, not an institution, with a lovely garden to sit in and you'll be in a small town where you can come and go as you please, more or less. You'll be neither judged nor punished, I've made sure of that. Look, I was annoyed with you when I first found out but that was because I felt you'd pulled a fast one on me, coming here to work when you were expecting. Pretending you lost your reference and everything. I felt the responsibility had been dumped on me, to be honest. Anyway, we've been through all that. I wish we could keep you, I really do, but you're beginning to show now and I can't have that, not in front of the customers. Goodness knows why, given the carry-on of some of them. But that's just the way of things, Milly. At least this way you'll get to keep your job. We'll just tell everyone that you had to go home to Ireland to look after your sick gran, all right? When you come back, it will be like none of this ever happened. Now dry those tears, pull yourself together, there's a good girl.'

Then she stood up and gave the room a look-over.

'You've made it very nice in here, Milly, I must say – very homely, with the plants and cushions and everything. I've laid some things out on the kitchen table for you. Towels folded and ready to go in. And I got you a washbag with a few bits in it, a couple of magazines to read. Sorry I have to ask you to work tonight, especially when you've got an early start tomorrow. But I'm short-staffed, you see.'

'That's all right, Mrs Oak, I don't mind.'

'Right, I best be off, I'm already late for my Jane Fonda class. You have a rest. We can finish packing later.'

'It's all right, Mrs Oak, I can manage myself.'

'I won't have you carting that thing downstairs, not in your condition. Call me when you're ready, I'll give you a hand.'

At the door Mrs Oak stopped and looked at her. 'You know

what my Terry said to me when I told him about my sister? He said, "Bad girls don't have babies. They get rid of them." And you're a good girl, Milly. Don't let anyone tell you any different.'

That last night was such a busy one. A boxing-club night as well as the fortieth wedding anniversary of a couple she'd never seen before. She'd been working hand over fist, glass after glass, money in, change out, since the doors opened at five o'clock. She was glad of it, too; it stopped her thinking about the next day, where she was going and what might happen to her when she got there.

The funny thing was, only a few seconds earlier, he'd been on her mind. She hadn't seen him in weeks and had been wondering what had happened to him – if maybe he'd moved to another gym or gone away to one of those training camps for boxers that she'd heard someone mention. And she'd been half thinking that it might be nice to see him one more time before she went away to a strange house in a town she didn't know, and whose name just wouldn't stick in her head beyond the fact that it began with M and had sounded downright ugly. When there he was suddenly, standing on the other side of the counter, slightly off to her right.

She was serving one of the black lads at the time. The Rastas, Trish called them. The Rastas made a thing out of her pulling the Guinness because she was Irish and she made a thing out of letting it settle before topping it up. She felt it made her look as if she knew what she was at, anyhow, and thought it more impressive than the pull-slosh-and-slap-it-up method that they used over here.

She didn't even have to look up to know it was him. She knew the shoulder squeezing into a space a customer had just pulled out of, and she knew the hand now turning a beermat over and over on the counter. She felt as if the skin could lift off her body

65

and fly away on its own, just knowing he was there. An arm's length away. If she reached her hand out, it would touch him.

The Rastas always called her 'Irish' as if it was her name and she didn't mind that in the least. 'I only want Irish serving me pint' was what they always said, and now the man she was serving was saying it too in his deep, rich voice: 'I don't mind waitin' so long as Irish is doin' the pullin'.'

But he didn't like it. From the side of her eye, she could see his shoulder pull back and the beermat stop moving. Then his voice: 'Her name isn't Irish.'

The Rasta man looked at him. 'Sorry, what?'

'I said, her name isn't Irish.'

'Well, I know that . . .'

'Yea? Well, why call her Irish then?'

'I was only—'

'And what's *your* name, if you don't mind me asking?'

'My name?'

'Yes, what do people call you? What do your mates call you? Do you, for example, have a nickname? What did your mother call you?'

'My mother – you asking me about my *mother*?'

For a minute she thought there would be a fight. The other customers noticed it too; the sudden tense silence.

But then he softened his tone. 'Look, my name is Philip, some people call me Philip. Some call me Phil. My mother called me Pip. I'm just wondering what people call you, that's all.'

'Well, Jerome, I'm called Jerome. Jerry sometimes.'

'Okay Jerome, Jerry sometimes – how would you like it if people went around saying hello, Jamaican. Good morning, Jamaican. Pass the salt there when you get a second, Jamaican – instead of Jerome? What would you think of that?'

66

'I didn't mean no insult!' Jerome said, a startled catch in his voice and the stain of a blush spreading under his dark skin.

'Good,' he said. And then, skipping poor Jerome in the queue, he'd asked for two pints, a vodka and tonic and a double whiskey.

'I've no trays left,' she'd said to him when she had the drinks ready.

He put the note down, poured the tonic into the vodka, knocked the whiskey back in one go, then settled the two pints and the vodka between both hands and lifted them from the counter.

'I'll get your change,' she said and he shook his head in a way that told her not to bother.

So, he was Irish himself, she thought, as she smiled at the shame-faced Jerome. But not like the other Irish lads that came in. Surly mumblers, some of them, who wouldn't have a word to throw to a dog until the drink hit home, and then you'd have a job getting them to shut their cake-holes. Or the other type, always trying to show how clever they were and sneering at the English. Nor could she imagine him cramming into a sweaty dancehall in Highgate where Brenda said she went once with an Irish girl who used to work here and never again, shuffling around with the Saturday-night herd, having them pull lumps out of her. Three times she'd heard Brenda tell that same story, and each time she'd felt a bit more ashamed.

At the same time, she was glad to know that he was Irish; she found it comforting somehow.

At closing time, she was by the front door with old Mrs Rogers. When Mrs Rogers had a few drinks on her, she always needed help getting her long thin arms into her tweed coat.

She could see him standing in the middle of the bar, putting on his jacket. The boxing-club lads all around him. She had a quick look about as she held Mrs Rogers' coat open. There was no sign of the girl. There was no sign of *any* girl, anywhere near him.

Shamie, shiny-eyed, was telling a story, clapping him on the back now and then, while the rest of the boys listened in. He must have won a fight or done something to make Shamie that proud.

Mrs Rogers was telling a story of her own, about the lovely masses they gave in the Italian church on Clerkenwell Road, and she was pretending to listen.

'They often give you a little something afterwards,' Mrs Rogers said, fixing her pudding-bowl hat onto her head. 'Christmas Day it was coffee and this funny cake, oh what's this they call it? Panny something or other.'

And now he was walking straight towards her, raising an arm to wave goodnight to someone across the bar. In a moment he would be right beside her.

Mrs Rogers blocking the doorway, still going on about the cake. He waited for her to move out of the way. But Mrs Rogers wasn't budging. 'At Easter,' she said, 'they have a different sort of cake. Nicer than the Christmas one, not so dry, and that one's called . . . oh, let me see. Yes, Columbo cake, same as the detective, you know.'

She drew Mrs Rogers towards her so that he could get by, but almost at once the old woman stepped back again, narrowing the gap. He began edging his way behind her.

'Sometimes they say the mass in Eyetalian and I don't know what they're on about. I don't in English either, to be honest, but you know? People are ever so nice afterwards. You can have a chat.'

It had been so long since she had seen him. It would be even longer before she saw him again. She thought: maybe I'll never set eyes on you again. Maybe when I'm away you'll become a big-shot champ and won't ever bother with this backstreet pub again.

If only he would look at her. Say something, nod his head – anything. The smallest recognition, she felt, would ease whatever might lie ahead. But he was looking forward, to the door and the street outside. Another couple of steps and he would have edged his way past Mrs Rogers and then he would be gone.

Without thinking about it really, she lifted her face and, raising her voice over Mrs Rogers' head, shouted: 'Goodnight now – safe home!'

Mrs Rogers gave a little jump.

He looked at her for a long second and then said, 'Oh hello, Irish.'

'Hello Irish yourself,' she said, and then he smiled, or at least almost smiled at her.

It kept her going, those few words, that almost-smile. In the mother and baby home, she clutched it with both hands and pressed it into her head, her heart, the growing drum of her belly. In the hospital, it soothed the pain, the shock of the contractions. While she waited for the next one to slice through her, she went over every inch of the awkward scene with Jerome. And then she ran through his every move in the bar at closing time. The shy way he had listened to Shamie's praise. The sleeve of his lumberjacket going up his arm. The way he had hung back waiting for Mrs Rogers to move, before carefully edging his way behind her.

And later, too, during the six weeks spent in the post-natal home, feeding the baby in the dead of night, she looked out into the dimmed corridor and imagined him stepping through the front door out onto the street. The final turn of his head. Maybe because some movement through the doorway of the bar had caught his eye, or maybe because he was looking back at her.

Philip, Phil, Philly.

Millicent, Mill, Milly.

Pip, Pip, Pip.

4. Pip

2017

April

HE LISTENS FOR a moment to his agitated heart. Then, reaching for the water bottle on the bedside locker, takes a few frantic gulps.

'For fuck's sake,' he hears himself say, 'for fuck's sake, what brought all that on?'

Not a dream, because he wasn't really asleep. Not even one of those half-awake dreams where random memories hook up to make a story. It had all seemed so real, *they* had all seemed so real. His mother, her eyes; his father, his voice. Dom's white fringe – he'd forgotten how white it once was.

He feels overwhelmed, pinned to the bed. At the same time, he has to ask – how come he has trouble recalling events from last week when these little scenes from the past can just pop up in his head, perfectly formed, not a detail out of place? All the way back to 1961.

The movement under his feet – weightless, and at the same time dense. And the queer lightness in his stomach when his father lifted him into his arms. The sea then – the immense unexpected sight of it.

'Wave bye-bye to Dublin, Philip.'

'Byebye, Dubnim, byebye.'

They were on the boat. The boat coming over. The first and last time they would make that journey as a complete family.

He sits up, then lies back again, pushing his breath down into his lungs and filling them sideways. Then, drawing everything together – his breath and his thoughts; the past far and near; the room itself – he slowly blows it all out towards the ceiling. He is not on a boat. He is in Dom's house. He has been here for three weeks to the day. It's a long time to be in Dom's house. Dom no longer of the white fringe. Dom no longer of any fringe at all.

In the clinic, they warn you about this carry-on; the past sneaking up on you when least expected. You're told: face it, deal with it, stay sober, move on. There are probably a few snippets in his AA handbook to tell him about these little forays into the past. From the corner of his eye, he sees the dark blue cover on the bookcase where he left it last week. But he hates his AA handbook now as much as he has ever hated any thing or any person in his life. And yet he can't seem to bring himself to throw it away. When he moved in here a few weeks ago, he was all over it. He followed the steps; swallowed the Serenity Prayer for breakfast, dinner and tea; traipsed around AA meetings all over west London. From the sweat-scented room above the dry-cleaners in Portobello to the church of jittery shadows off Moscow Road, he has listened to the jargon, drank the pissy tea, scoffed his way through a hill of cheap biscuits. He has forgiven the unforgiveable, in the hope that he, too, would be forgiven when it came to his turn to stand, his heart held out in his hands, blood dripping all over the floor.

He hasn't laid a finger on that book for well over a week. Nor has he been to a meeting. He pretends to go, of course, like a kid skipping school, just to keep Dom happy. Dom and his other custodian: Colin, his well-meaning but dim-witted sponsor.

The truth is, he feels it does him no good, all this talk of drink and suffering; wild nights and waking in gutters. What it does is serve as a reminder of what he could be missing. That's what most people don't realise about alcoholics, he thinks: we are cursed with eternal optimism. Once we start to feel better, the bad times retreat and the good times edge forward. Maybe that's why the AA meeting was invented, so we can remind one another of the horror.

The narrow bed groans, and then groans again as he turns from his side onto his back. Hands behind head, he regards the mound of his belly under a lilac-coloured sheet. Underarm, a whiff of sweat, slightly repellent but comforting somehow: the smell of himself, alive and humming. On the chair by the door, the white folds of a naked duvet. The cover for the duvet was all he needed last night, all anyone would ever need in this small, airless room, where the centre of the ceiling has been punched out to make way for a skylight and the surrounding area, lined in pine, gives the room the look of a garden shed.

He wouldn't mind if it *was* a garden shed – if it was his own garden shed, that is. Somewhere to duck in and out of as he pleases. He is a man well used to small places, from the cubicle in boarding school to a shop doorway here and there. In between, there have been recovery rooms, not to mention the occasional prison cell. Nor has he ever been all that fussy. At most he requires: a bed, a place to have a wash and go to the jacks, a box to keep his few things in, a lamp to read by, or even a torch. Somewhere to boil a kettle is always a bonus.

Every few days, he makes a vague plan to leave here. But he reminds himself that this is London, where the smallest kip costs an arm and a leg. And so, until he can think of a way to start making money, here he is stuck. It's not the worst place to be. The door closes behind him and only opens when he turns the key, and there's the convenience of having a bathroom right next door – even if he has to fold himself in two to get under the dinky little shower.

He has stayed in this room once before, years ago, not long after Dom moved in with wife number two. But he can hardly remember the occasion now. Apart from the lambs on the wallpaper. It used to be a nursery, or at least he can remember ending up there after a party and waking up with a thick head to find a baby looking out at him through the bars of a cot. It had frightened the shit out of him: a baby – presumably Max – staring out at him, with all the judgement of the world in its eyes.

After the nursery years, it became a room for au pairs. He seems to remember that the turnover was pretty high. Dom's French wife Monique had been a fussy cow. One of the au pairs was sacked for sneaking a bloke up here. Monique was outraged, which was a bit of a cheek on her part, now that he thinks of it.

The night he arrived from the clinic he went through the room. He found a brand-new percolator still in its box on top of the wardrobe; behind it, three unopened identical bottles of duty-free perfume.

He had been particularly interested in the bookcase, painted an eggshell blue with a few books grouped here and there. French books for kids; a couple of outdated London guidebooks. A few other books, unread and forgotten – at least until he had arrived. A copy of *The Trumpet-Major* – presumably a joke aimed at Dom, along with books that had obviously been gifts to welcome Monique into the fold. *To Monique with warm wishes.*

To Monique, a flavour of what we Brits have to offer . . . affection-ately yours.

Monique, obviously not impressed by the selection, had exiled the books to this room: three Dickens, two Hardys, a *Mrs Dalloway* and a *Waste Land*.

He has come to look on the room as a sort of holding-pen for unwanted things; things it hadn't seemed quite right to discard, which could be the reason he feels quite at home here.

On the far side of the Velux window, splats of bird shit and dead moths. The impatient light of a late April morning, pushing to get going. He reckons it's between five thirty and six.

When he was younger, he liked to be out at this hour. Coming home from somewhere just before or after sunrise, a club or an all-night café; somebody's party or some girl's bed. Not drunk, just slightly electrocuted from alcohol. That low-level buzz he used to enjoy as a young man before the hangovers turned vicious and began biting the hand that fed them. Wandering the empty streets, through the silence of parks that had only just opened, or finding his way down to the river. His footsteps and the chuckling seagulls. Hardly meeting a soul, unless a shift-worker. Or the small heaps of humanity asleep in doorways, less common then than now. Maybe crossing paths with another homeward-bound drinker, exchanging a nod of battle-weary recognition.

And even when he wasn't drinking, but in training, he loved going for his run at this hour. Sunrise over the Thames; the build-ings and bridges falling away; the buckle of river water alongside him, Westminster to Blackfriars. On murky mornings, he could see ghosts moving through the mist. Even on the darkest of days, he had always found some sort of hope in the grey light of the river.

Hauling himself out of the bed, he sits on the side of it and studies the downward view: droop of man-boobs, hairy plop of belly, lolling flute just visible behind it; bony knees, loose, flat thighs, crooked feet. Something else nobody thinks to mention about growing old, the little knobs that start growing out of your feet.

Feet of Christ, Monique had once called them, that time she came home late with a few drinks on her and found him standing barefoot at the kitchen sink.

His father had the same feet. Long-toed, curved and white. Later, with little knobs on them. Towards the end of his life, they had looked like two hunks of raw meat. Another thing to look forward to. The older he gets, the more similarities he finds between himself and the old man. The knobs on the feet, the preference for being out of doors, the ability to whittle a whole life down into one cardboard box.

He slides the drawer of the locker open, sticks his hand in and pulls out his new pill dispenser. Flipping the lid back, he looks inside. The nurse in charge of meds at the clinic gave him this dispenser, filling the little shells up, telling him how much easier it would be to remember what was what. He flicks the rest of the compartments open and gently runs his fingers across them. Some of them are relative newcomers – sometimes he still has to look at the packet or bottle they came in to remember their names. Although he does at least know what they're for: choles-terol, blood pressure, liver, stomach, bones. Most of them are round and white – he has to put on his glasses to tell them apart. Except for the Epilim and Mysoline, of course – those he could find in the dark.

His father had taken months to die. Hanging on with all the tenacity of the true atheist who knows he's got nowhere else to be. And yet, when it came, his death had seemed a bit sudden. He happened to be with him at the time – not intentionally of course, it had been more a question of bad timing on his part, thus opening a right can of worms.

Afterwards, as he'd left the nursing home, the matron trotted out after him with the box in her arms.

He hadn't wanted to take his father's box, the responsibility it seemed to imply. He felt certain there must have been a mistake. Dom was the one who had taken care of everything: had found the nursing home, attended doctors' meetings, forked out whenever anything was needed.

He tried to say as much to her, but she'd insisted. 'Your father was quite clear on the matter: he wanted *you* to have it' was what she'd said.

To think him and Dom had nearly killed each other over that stupid box.

He puts on his glasses, organises the pills into their compartments and studies the dispenser again: colour-coded and each compartment labelled: *Morn, Noon, Night, Backup*. Like something you'd give to a child. Today is Friday, an indigo day. With a flick of his finger, he releases his two old reliables from the compartment marked *Morn*.

Now that he thinks of it, it wasn't 1961 when they first came to London. It was '62. He had always presumed it was '61 because he knew that he was three years old when they'd come over. But it was January '62, as he had discovered when he found the passenger ticket stuck into a book in his father's box.

He swallows the pills down, puts everything back into place and then, leaning his forearms on his knees, he stares up at the lambs frolicking up the wallpaper.

*

The cold air on his face and the gulls ranting and raving as they chased after the boat. He could feel the vibration of words passing from his father's chest into his small arm. People stepping away from the rail, ducking through a low door to get back inside. The gulls, losing their grip on the wind, beginning to fall away. And then only the sound of breathing: father's, son's and the big gasping sea.

Inside the boat, they made a happy little group. His mother easing a package out of her basket and placing it on the table. The same wrapper as the loaf bought from the shop near where they lived, the same letters on the side. Dom reading them out, finger skipping along, one word to the next.

'Johnston Mooney and O'Brien.'

He, pointing at words his arm couldn't reach: 'Jonon moonon eyebry.'

'That's not reading,' Dom said. 'That's just copying.'

'He's only three,' his mother said.

'I'm twice his age,' Dom said.

'That's right, you are. And you'll never be twice his age again.'

Dom frowning under his white fringe, mumbling sums, looking for a way to contradict her.

She opened the wrapper and there was a little house made out of sandwiches. He clapped his hands when he saw it. His mother, laughing, said he was a good boy. 'Good boy, Pip!'

Dom with a gap where his two front teeth had been, chewing his sandwich, humming to himself while he ate. His heels kicking the board under the seat: banga, banga, bang.

His father's voice asking: 'Are you not hungry, Phil?'

His mother's voice: 'Pip? Pip?'

Her worried fingers on his face.

'Hmm?'

'You were miles away – what are you thinking about, the serious little face on you?'

He shrugged, then smiled and crammed the sandwich into his mouth.

'Not the whole thing! Not at once – you'll choke.'

Putting her hand out so that he could spit the bread into it, emptying the small wet heap into a tissue and dropping it into the bin at the end of the table. 'Now,' she said, 'let's start again, slowly this time. Greedy bum.'

'Greedy bum!' he shouted. 'Greedy bum!'

'See – now, he's copying you,' Dom said. 'He's always copying off someone.'

'I'm only three!' he said.

His mother wiping the corner of his mouth with her hand. 'Salad cream,' she said and sucked it off her knuckle.

Dom, putting down his sandwich to speak, said, 'When we were in Dublin, Dad sounded different to everyone else. But when we get to London, *we* will sound different to everyone else, and Dad will sound the same.'

'True,' his father said. 'But we are all the same, all people are the same. We might look different and sound different but we are all—'

'Even the poor ones,' Dom said.

'Oh yes indeed, even the poor ones,' his father agreed.

There were poor people everywhere. He knew because his mother was always pointing them out. 'Oh, look at that poor woman!' Or 'Those poor children' or 'That poor unfortunate man.'

There were poor people on the boat. She said it as soon as they sat down: 'Oh, some of those poor young lads – they don't know what they're getting themselves into.' Or 'Look at the poor woman over there, John, did you ever see anyone so bereft? I bet she's been home for a funeral.'

The poor men sitting on the floor and drinking from brown bottles. Some lying on coats, spread out on the floor.

'Why are they sleeping on the floor, Dad?' Dom said.

'They probably have to go straight to work once we land.'

'They work so hard,' his mother said, shaking her head. 'Poor men.'

Then she began wrapping the sandwiches back up.

'No!' he shouted.

'Surely you're not still hungry, Pip? Here, do you want another?'

He looked at the sandwich she was holding out to him. But he didn't want the sandwich; he just wanted the little house to stay, even if it was smaller now and no longer really looked like a little house.

'That's not fair!' Dom said.

'What's not fair?'

'He's had three already – if he has another one, then he'll have had more than me!'

'Well, here, you have it then.'

'I don't want another one.'

'What are you carrying on for, then?'

'Because it's not fair!'

Dom dropping the crust of his sandwich down on the table, folding his arms tight to his chest.

'We'll keep them for the train so,' his mother said, wrapping them up, 'and I hope you know, Dom, they don't allow sulking in London. It's against the law.'

'No it's not!' Dom said, shaking his fringe, looking away. 'That's just stupid.'

His mother lifting her handbag, unfolding herself from the seat.

Brown wavy hair. Red skirt, dark blue coat, her hand pressing into the table, long fingers and one gold ring. He touched the ring. She didn't notice. She was going away from him and she didn't notice. He put his mouth down and kissed her hand. There now, she noticed that.

'I'll be back in a minute,' she said to him, combing his fringe with her fingers. And then she was gone.

He made a bowl of his two hands and whispered into it, 'She'll be back in a minute.'

Then he looked at the poor men again. One of them smoking a cigarette, eyes shifting side to side, watching people walk by. The man had a hole in his shoe. And the ends of his trousers were raggy. His face was all dirty! Dirty and full of lumps. But his eyes looked new and bright, shifting, watching, waiting for something to happen. His eyes came to their table, then stopped at him.

'He's looking at me,' he whispered into his hands. 'The man with the dirty face is looking at me.'

When he peeped over his hands, the man winked.

He began to edge his way around the seat towards his father. He wanted to tell him about the man with the dirty, lumpy face. He wanted to tell him about the wink. But his father was too busy. He was drawing something on a piece of paper for Dom. He couldn't see what it was because Dom's arm was in the way, his hand squeezing his pink cheek up to his pink ear.

Dom asking questions and his father's voice explaining. He grew tired of listening to all that; tired of looking around at the poor people on the floor. He wanted his mother.

The seat tilting, like a see-saw but not so high. The men lying on the floor tilting, and the people walking around. Two girls laughing, holding on to one another, rocking from side to side.

He remembered the sea. And wanting his mother and wanting

the sea, he wriggled down off his seat, ducked under the edge of the table and ran.

He ran calling out for the sea, past coat hems and legs, the corners of suitcases, the hard edges of handbags.

'Sea! Sea!'

He ran past the feet of people asleep on the floor, sideways around a red cigarette tip and then with a leap over a bag someone had left on the floor.

'Sea, sea, sea!'

His mother's voice behind him. It was there and then it was gone and then it was back again. Louder and stronger and now every word of hers chasing behind him. 'Excuse me, oh excuse me, Pip! Come back here this minute! Pip! Excuse me, I'm so sorry.'

'Sea, sea, sea, sea!'

His mother chasing him. The sea outside. He is giddy with the idea of having the two things he wants most in the world coming together: his mother and the sea. He runs laughing across the busy floor, twisting his body this way and that; he runs, keeps running, runs, runs, until a big glass wall jumps out in front of him then – splat. It stings his hands as they slap right into it, and – dunt. It hits him quick and sharp on his forehead.

Outside only darkness and the shape of a man, coat flapping around his legs, one hand holding his hat down on his head. He can see yellow lights melting in the glass, and black and grey swirls moving through it, and long drops of water falling down along it. He can see the shape of a little boy with his hands pressed against the glass and the blur of a round white face looking back at him. Chin and hair; mouth and sticky-out ears. But he can't find his eyes.

He wants to take his hands off the glass, put them where his eyes should be. But he's afraid in case he finds nothing there but those two black holes showing on the glass of the window. No eyes! He feels a sob rumbling in his chest. He opens his mouth ready to howl. But then, the glassy shadow of his mother comes up behind him, gasping for breath, laughing.

And laughing as she turns him around: red skirt, dark coat, handbag.

'I should murder you,' she says. 'You can't keep running off like this. Not where we're going. It's too big a place and if you get lost, I might never find you and what would I do then?'

He tells her: 'I can't find my eyes.'

'What?'

'I have no eyes.'

'Course you have.'

'I haven't.'

'You have so. Look: one two, lovely brown eyes looking up at me.'

'But I can't see the sea.'

'That's because it's dark outside. It's way past your bedtime and you're still up. What do you think of that now?'

He begins to whimper, 'I want to see it, I want to—'

'Oh, but it's so cold out there. It's even cold in here. Isn't it cold? Look at your little cherry nose,' she says, tipping it with her finger.

She stoops, her face down level with his, her red skirt and dark coat spreading out on the floor.

'Your eyes are brown,' he says to her.

'Yes, like yours.'

'Not like Dom's?'

'No, not like Dom's.'

'Not like Dad's?'

'No, not like Dad's. They have blue eyes.'

'Only like mine.'

'Yes, only like yours.'

He throws his arms around her, clinging to her neck, wiping his face in her hair. 'Mammy,' he says.

'Yes, Pip?'

'Mammy. My mammy.'

'Yes, my pipsqueak, my little lamb.'

PART TWO

5. Milly

1982

THE ASSISTANT LAID the third little dress down on the counter.

'Now, this one,' she said, fanning the dress out to show, 'comes with a matching bonnet.'

She flipped the dress over to reveal a pink sunhat pinned to the back of it. 'What d'you think?' she asked.

The assistant was around her own age, twenty or twenty-one. She was slight and had one of those shaggy perms; it made her small face look as if she was drowning in brown seaweed. It was hard not to stare at her eyes, all smothered in glittery purple.

'That's seersucker, that is,' the assistant continued. 'Go ahead, have a little feel. Ideal for summer. And baby. On account of it don't show the creases so much. Hold on, though, is she potty-trained?'

'Well, let's just say we're working on it.'

'You're going to love this.' The assistant turned the hem of the dress back. 'Ta-da!' she said. 'Matching knickers! Lined with plastic to keep her nice and dry. Look, they've got frills on and all. Pity she's not with you, though, we could have had a little try-on.'

'Yes, it is.'

'You don't live round here then?'

'No.'

'You were in last year – am I right? Bought a little green pinafore. Mrs Hadley served you. For her first birthday, was it?'

'I can't believe you remember!'

'We don't get that many younger customers, to be honest. It's all christenings and bar mitzvahs in here, godmothers and grans, know what I mean? I get that bored! Can't see it lasting much longer, to be honest, not with all the cheap baby clothes you get now: Marks, BHS – all the biggies. Well, you know what I'm talking about. I mean the stuff in here, don't get me wrong, it's all top quality. But pricey. Mrs Hadley, she'd kill me if she heard me talk that way to a customer. Always on at me to be more refined, she is. Says I talk too much too, but how can I talk too much when there's no one to talk to? That's what I say. Well, to myself, not to her. I wouldn't dare say it to her! She's old school – pre-war, more like. Pre- both wars, I sometimes think. Can't see her lasting much longer either, come to think of it. Could you bring her in Saturday?'

'Sorry – what?'

'Your little one. Could you bring her in Saturday?'

'Oh, no. The party's on Saturday.'

'Well, that's no good then, is it?' She peered into the collar of the dress. 'She's, what, two now? This says "2–3 *ans*" – see? That's French for years. But they're smaller over there, aren't they? It's the food, I reckon. Kiddies' portions for everyone, I'm told. Would you say she's big for her age or small?'

'I suppose, average.'

'You could always bring it back. I could give you a credit note, though I wouldn't delay using it, if I was you. Where do you work then?'

'Me? Oh, out near Chesham.'

'That's a bit of a trek. Live out there too?'

'That's right.'

'What brings you to this neck?'

'I was delivering something for my boss.'

'What you work at then?'

'Me? Oh, I'm a typist.'

'Oh yeah? I should have done a typing course. More options that way. Know what I'd really like to do, though? I'd like to work on a makeup counter in Debbie's or somewhere. You know, Debnams?'

'Oh yes, I know it.'

'That's my dream. Trouble is, you need qualifications, don't you? I'm thinking of doing one of those beautician courses at night, but they don't half cost. Are they nice, the people you work with? Is there a social life attached?'

'People go for a drink after work, I suppose.'

'See that's what I need. Any eligibles?'

'Eligibles?'

'You know, available men. Because the love of my life, he ain't walking through that door any time soon, now is he? So, what d'you think?'

'I suppose you could meet him anywhere really.'

'No! I mean the dress, what d'you think about the dress!' She barked out a laugh then stopped suddenly and cocked her little head. 'Do you hear that? Is that the phone – it is, isn't it? Back in a jiff.'

She began to hurry down the long narrow space behind the counter, heavy shoes clopping off the wooden floor.

'You take another little look there,' she shouted over her shoulder. 'All three are lovely really, the yellow's very nice and as for that gingham . . .'

Then she opened a door set into the panelled wall and disappeared, taking her opinion of the gingham with her.

Alone in the shop, Milly turned from the counter and began to wander around. She liked the old-fashioned look of the place. The light was dim and had a greenish hue to it, and there was a dull, soft sheen to everything: the wood on the counter, the parquet floor, the thin brass rails with little bootees hanging from them. Along one wall, clothes were arranged in batches: whole outfits, from shoes to hat – as if waiting for a child to climb up there and squirm its way into them. On a corner shelf, a family of teddy bears sat with empty porridge bowls on their laps. And pictures of fat, rosy-cheeked babies from another era looked down from the wall at the other end. She moved along the counter, looking through the glass top at the displays: layers of tiny vests, thin and white; then sunhats and dainty socks; bibs and folded baby gowns, all white or pale cream or yellow – everything laid on trays like pastries waiting to be put into the oven.

A box sat on the end of the counter. Christening robes, she saw now, each one wrapped in its own package. She placed her hand on the top one and began to gently pluck it. It calmed her, the feel of the cool soft plastic, the stiff cloth beneath it, the occasional touch of beading on her fingertips. Outside, the sun's light pressed down on the narrow street, and she could hear the muffled sound of traffic pushing and shoving to get out onto Marylebone Road. Beneath the green half-mast blinds, a selection of bare arms and rolled-up shirtsleeves passed by. She let the light wash over her, the silence. I wish I could stay here all afternoon, she thought. I wish I could stay in this shop just looking at things, touching the clothes, not thinking about anything.

But already she could hear the returning clip-clop of the assistant's shoes. She drew her hand away from the christening robes, straightened the top packages and hurried back down the counter.

'That was madam checking up on me,' the assistant said, her face all flushed and vexed. 'I told her I was with a customer but she was too busy moaning to listen. You need to try harder, she says, but what's she want me to do, run out on the street dragging people in, force-feeding them bleedin' baby clothes? I tell you, I'm that close to telling her where to stick her job. And the sun won't be shining there neither. So, what's the verdict then – have we decided?'

She nodded, cleared her throat and said, 'Yes, I'll take it. The pink. The one with the bonnet.'

'I knew you would. I just knew it! She's a lucky little girl, your – what's her name?'

'The baby? Oh, it's Flora.'

'What a lovely name. Will you be paying cash or cheque? We don't do credit cards. They're not trustworthy. According to you-know-who.'

'Who?'

'Mrs Hadley, of course.'

'Cash, I'll be paying cash.'

'Lovely. Well, do you have the right amount, I wonder, because otherwise I'll have to go out and start looking for change?'

'I think so, yes.'

'Well, let's see then, shall we . . . ?'

The assistant turned the price tag round, widened her eyes and said: '*Ouch!* Tell you what I'm going to do. I'm going to let you have my staff discount, if it's any help. That's ten per cent off.'

'Well yes, I mean if you're sure you don't mind?'

'It's not as if I'm ever going to use it, is it? I mean I don't really know anyone with kids. No one I'd bother spending a week's wages on anyhow.'

She began to layer the tissue paper on the counter, then she folded the dress down into it.

'What colour's her hair?' she asked, then, 'Brown, is it – same as yours?'

'No, it's lighter. Sort of reddish-brown.'

The assistant opened a drawer, took out a spool of dark blue ribbon, pulled a length of it free and snipped it. She rolled the ribbon between her fingers and placed it on top of the parcel. 'People always go for green with a redhead. But I think blue, dark blue like this, is *way* more classier. Now, you tell little Flora that's a birthday gift from her Aunty Tina.'

'I will. Thanks very much.'

'What's your name by the way – mind me asking?'

'It's Milly.'

'Flora and Milly. They don't sound like Irish names,' she said, pressing the lid down on the box and turning a thin piece of pink ribbon around it. 'You are Irish – am I right?'

'Yes.'

'Hubby too?'

'Yes, him too.'

'People say all sorts about the Irish, you know with the bombs and that. But I don't think that's fair, really. I mean you can't blame a whole country for a few loonies, now can you? Things seem a bit quieter now. Thank *goodness*, eh? Let's hope that's the end of it. I mean can you imagine, Milly, say you're waiting on a bus or something, or had little Flora out for a walk and . . .' She lifted her hands mid-air and with a loud, sharp clap, shouted, 'Bang! That gave you a start, Milly – look at you jump. Can you imagine what the real thing must be like, eh?'

She went back to the parcel, fixing a small neat bow into the ribbon. 'I used to work for an Irish woman, lived in a big house in Chelsea,' she said, edging the package into a carrier bag. 'I used to be her cleaner.'

'Well, I hope she was nice to you.'

'I wouldn't go that far!' she said, and then they both laughed as if she'd said something really funny.

She counted the exact amount onto the assistant's hand, notes first then a few coins.

'Call in again,' the assistant said, closing her fingers over the money. 'It's nice having a chat with someone your own age for a change. It can get a bit lonely in here, to be honest. I'm on my own every Friday and Saturday. Mrs Hadley, she gets her bit of hair done on Fridays, and her lot, they don't work Saturdays, do they?'

She passed the carrier bag across the counter. 'Don't lose that, whatever you do, after what you paid for it – eh? Enjoy the party. And you take care now, Mill, you hear me? Bye now. Bye-bye.'

Back out on the street, she felt shocked somehow; shocked and a little sick. Everything seemed exaggerated – too loud, too bright, too sharp – the way it always did after a sleepless night. A lie-down was what she needed now, but she couldn't bear the thought of going home just yet.

Last year she had taken a sandwich and a packet of crisps in her handbag and after she had bought the green pinafore had gone into Regent's Park. She'd thought it a stroke of luck finding an empty bench by the small pond in Queen Mary's Gardens. Somewhere to have her lunch and read her book in peace. She must have been sitting there for a good few minutes before she realised the bench was empty only because it was raining. That sly drizzle you sometimes get in summer. She had stayed, though, because she couldn't think of what else to do. She liked Regent's Park anyhow and sometimes went there on her day off. She found it a peaceful place to be. The lake and the strangeness of the herons out on the island. The small birds bobbing around on the grass. The different sounds of water. In summer, there were picnic rugs and deckchairs laid out on the grass, and although she was usually shy about eating in public – even when she knew no one was minding her – here it didn't seem to matter so much. Most people sat facing the lake anyhow, or the bandstand, and as long as she did the same, there were no eyes to meet hers. The Broad Walk was no good, though – she had tried it once but felt too exposed, as if she'd been sitting on a hospital corridor waiting to be called in for bad news. Old men passing by, slyly glancing. But walking around was good enough too, just looking at it all: the people, the boats on the lake, the deckchairs and picnics. Listening to the chatty voices or the music coming out of radios as you passed by. When there was a band playing, she would lay her jumper out on the grass, sit down on it and read her book. Sometimes she would just eat an ice cream and pretend to herself that she was somebody else: a girl on holiday maybe, or a student between lectures. Or even an office girl who just wanted a little time on her own.

But last year! Last year the deckchairs had remained folded and chained, the drizzle of rain never let up, and even though she had wrapped her jumper around the carrier bag, she was afraid the baby's pinafore would be destroyed. And so, in the end, she had eaten her damp sandwich with wet fingers and then headed home, sitting on the tube like a drowned rat.

And here was today, a perfect day – you couldn't ask more from it really – and yet she couldn't bring herself to go near Regent's Park. Nor could she face the return journey. Moving with strangers through endless corridors, gliding with them up and down escalators. Nobody saying a word, the echoes of foot-steps and breath all around her, as if she was walking among the dead. Well, she didn't want that. And she didn't want the park. She didn't know what she wanted really, and so she just kept walking.

She was too annoyed to do anything else. Annoyed and disappointed because of that one working in the shop. Making her privy to her little swindle – and, worse, thinking her stupid enough not to notice that there'd been no receipt. And how could there have been a receipt, when she hadn't even put the purchase through the till? All that guff about feeling sorry for the Irish. It was exactly her type that sat around telling Paddy the Irishman jokes in the pub. She'd probably put a bit by for her beauty course – as if they'd let her work in Debenhams, the head on her. Or maybe she'd have a night out on the proceeds, treat all her pals on the money she'd sneaked into her pocket. She could imagine them now: sitting over their lager and limes, peering at one another through their shaggy perms, blobs of purple gunk all over their eyes – 'A whole week's wages on a dress for a bay-*bee*. And I says to her, I says, tell you what, I'm going to let you have my staff discount! The poor Irish cow only fell for it, didn't she?'

She'd a good mind to tell on her. To drop in when the owner was there, say, 'I bought this dress last week from your assis-tant, but she forgot to give me the receipt. I didn't notice at the time because she was talking so much – and quite frankly I was shocked at how unrefined she was . . .'

At the corner, she stopped. The streets were beginning to fill up with the lunchtime people. They were queuing outside snack bars or ducking into pubs and cafés. She stepped aside and stood in front of a jeweller's window. She could see the dark stamp of herself on the glass hovering over the display; the handbag on one shoulder, the cord of the carrier bag with the baby's dress in it on the other. A blur of gold and silver on the far side of the window, a few twinkly bits in between. She opened the handbag, slipped her hand in and rummaged around till she found a tissue. Then she blew her nose and wiped the hot, angry tears from her eyes.

She had wanted to buy the dress, to *pay* for it with her hard-earned money. Money that she had been putting aside in dribs and drabs since Christmas. She had wanted a receipt to put in the keepsake envelope. That had been the whole point of it. And now that little shaggy-headed wagon had spoiled the day. Well, that was the end of that. She would never, *ever* step set foot in that shop again. Not even to rat on her. Besides, if Gerry was right, then there was no use complaining about anything these days. 'Once they cop you're Irish,' he said, 'they don't want to know. It's all – go back to your own country then, if you don't ruddy like it.'

But Gerry was from Belfast and they saw things differently there. Sometimes it annoyed her, the way he talked to her as if she was from Belfast too. 'See us,' he'd say. Or 'It's different, so it is, for the likes of you and me.' When he started that, she sometimes wished he'd just stayed in his own pub, behind his own bar, and left her to get on with her work.

She liked Gerry and was grateful to him, too, for tipping her off about the job when she'd first arrived over. But that didn't mean she wanted to be lumped in with him. He took the whole business of being Irish so seriously, she'd been afraid to tell him that she wasn't a Catholic. And the way he sulked that time she wouldn't go to the Irish club with him. Some people were like that, others you'd hardly know they were Irish at all, apart from the accent maybe. Like Pip. How long was it before she even copped he was

Irish? He just got on with it. But at the same time, he wouldn't let anyone look down on you for being Irish. That incident with Jerome, for example, and the way he sometimes referred to his brother as 'my English brother', as if he wanted the difference to be noted.

She gave her nose another blow then popped the tissue back into her bag.

In the window, a cuckoo burst out of a clock. Half past twelve. She could hear a faint chiming coming from other clocks perched on the side walls of the display inside. She waited for the cuckoo to fly backwards home and then moved on.

Through the railings of Portman Square, she could see small happy groups seated on the ground and, as she reached the end of the street, there were office workers perched on the steps outside a building, girls with their faces turned to the sun, men in white shirts, darting crusts at the pigeons. At that end of the street, a crowd shifted towards Marble Arch and Hyde Park. A group of small children and babies from a nearby nursery were headed towards her. She didn't want to find herself caught up in all that so she turned her head and looked down the opposite end of the street. A quieter, shadier stretch, the buildings had a faded look about them that would be gentle on the eye. She could wander up there, find a turn-off that would take her into Oxford Street, maybe buy herself an ice cream and take the slow way home.

A few steps on and she began to feel the need for a wee. Since the baby, she couldn't seem to hold it in as well as before and the urge came on more suddenly. She peered up the street but couldn't see a pub or anywhere she might easily slip in unnoticed. There was some sort of movement ahead, the coming and going of taxis. She thought it might be a small hotel with the black wrought-iron canopy over the entrance. As she got closer, she saw a few lone people standing outside, as if waiting on someone. A couple turned and went under the canopy, followed by three old ladies all chatting at the same time. There was an A-board standing on the pavement outside the building with photos of musicians pinned onto it and she saw now that it was some sort of concert hall. Her eye was stalled by one of the photos – two men and a girl. One of the men was holding a trumpet. She stooped to take a better look at it. Was it? She hadn't seen him in a while but it looked like him all right. Or at least like a dickied-up version of him with the hair brushed back Dracula-style. 'Distinguished' was the word that came to mind. She moved to the other side of the board where a different photo showed him face-on, holding the trumpet across his body, one hand cupped over the mouth of the bell. And yes, it was him. Definitely. Pip's English brother, Dom. Or Nick, as it said under the photo. It gave her a lift to see someone she knew – someone people paid money to see. How nice it would be to have a friend with her, to be able to say out loud to someone, 'Oh, I know him. Yes, that's right. His brother is . . . His brother is a friend of mine, actually,' she could probably say by now.

It occurred to her then – what if Pip was going to his brother's concert? She could turn around and bump straight into him. That would be lovely all right – the state of her hair and her eyes all scaldy from crying. But she remembered then that he was abroad with Jackie at a boxing tournament, and probably wouldn't be back for another few weeks.

There was a queue of people going through the door; she was in the way standing here in the middle of the pavement. A man just inside the door seemed to be giving directions. A big man, dressed in black. In the shadow of the canopy, his hands looked too large and too white, as if he could be wearing gloves.

He disappeared from the doorway then and she wondered about going in. She could easily blend into the crowd, and once inside, ask someone about the loo. You would probably have to say 'lavatory' in a place like that, or 'powder room' maybe. But supposing the concert began while she was in the loo and when she came back out there was nobody around except for the man in charge? He would want to know what she was doing if she wasn't going to the concert; he would hear her Irish accent and think the worst. He would search her bag and pull the baby's dress out, poking around the bonnet, the frilly knickers with his big white fingers. He would ask her all sorts of questions: where she lived and if there was anyone who could vouch for her? Then, he would probably call the police.

She turned away from the hall and crossed over the road, deciding that she could hold it in until she at least got to Oxford Street.

And after all, the tube had not been in the least bit uncomfortable. Between the long breeze through the open windows and the soothing movement of the train itself, she'd had a hard job keeping awake. And now this! As soon as she stepped out of the station, it hit her: the hot, woolly air.

The station clock showed a quarter past four. She'd spent far too long wandering about, in and out of air-conditioned shops along Oxford Street until, finding herself at the top of Piccadilly, she'd decided to go down and take a look at that bookshop Pip had mentioned and, again, spent too long wandering up and down its dark brown stairs, trying to look at every book on every shelf.

She felt a headache prowling in the back of her skull and anything like the thirst! She regretted now that bag of crisps as she walked down to Green Park station, the dry, sour taste it had left in her mouth. So much for having a cup of tea and washing her hair before work – at this rate, she'd be lucky to squeeze in a few moments of baby-time.

The paper boy was calling out – something about the Israeli ambassador, was it? Somebody shot him, did he say? Oh, surely not the IRA? Why would they pick on him, of all people? Lenny Wiseman had just come back from his holidays in Israel. He'd been telling her all about it only last night. He'd be upset, the poor man. The homeland, he had called it, tears standing up in his eyes.

A noise growled overhead: an airplane or maybe thunder. The paper boy was shouting in her ear so she couldn't work it out. The Dorchester, did he say? He was shot in The *Dorchester*? You'd imagine a place like that could keep you safe. But nowhere was safe now. Poor Mr Wiseman. He'd come to England in a special train when he was a boy, a *Kindertransport* he had called it, and she had thought, what a lovely name for a trainful of children – until she remembered the circumstances. She liked Mr Wiseman, enjoyed the little chats they had from time to time and hoped he wouldn't be funny with her now, like some were whenever a bomb had gone off. As if she'd personally given the command.

The noise again (thunder or an airplane?). A muffled sort of sound, but there was a force behind it too. And now she remembered something else Belfast Gerry had said to her a few weeks back, after there'd been a bomb in Chelsea Barracks and a customer had started abusing him across the bar just because he was Irish.

'It takes them back to the war, you see. Oh aye – as far as the Brits is concerned, we Irish, we're the new Nazis, so we are.'

Oh God, she thought, please, please, *please* not another bomb.

She glanced across the street. The main doors to the pub were still shut, but the grille had been pushed back from the entrance. The front lights hung hazily over the top of the stained-glass windows and she could see shadows moving about inside. Mrs Oak and Trish must be in there already, getting ready for the busy night ahead. She couldn't face a conversation now, no matter how well meaning. She would go in the back way and slip up the stairs.

In the back lane, there was no one about. Not even a speck of light from the boxing-club basement. She could hear the sound of a telly through the open window of an upstairs flat in one of the houses, and further down the lane, an Italian conversation in full spate coming out from behind a van outside Piccardi's delivery entrance.

She glanced up at the back of the pub. Over the high stone wall, she could see the top three floors: gutter pipes, windowsills, open windows. But no sense of life came from behind the limp net curtains. She took her keys out of her handbag and opened the steel door into the yard.

The yard was empty and all clear inside, through the porch and along the corridor. The door of the windowless office was open but the light was off. The lounge was still locked. She stayed by the wall until she reached the bottom of the stairs. Now she could hear the familiar sounds of preparation coming from the bar: the crunch and tumble of the new ice machine and the clink of bottles being loaded onto shelves. They were in there – she had made it. She would not have to answer any questions or speak to anyone; she would have her few moments in peace.

She was halfway up the stairs when she began to hear voices. Another couple of steps and she could make the voices out. Three in all. Mrs Oak first, then Trish.

Oh Christ, she thought, it must have been Brenda in the bar. Brenda and that new muttery barman Mylo, or whatever his stupid name was.

The third voice was coughing. The third voice belonged to Vera Greene. The kitchen door was always left open. Unless they all happened to be standing looking out the front window, she would never make it past them. She took another few stairs and now she could hear every word.

Mrs Oak saying, 'Well I did tell her take the day off but she would only agree to the morning – I mean, what else was I supposed to do?'

'You couldn't force her, could you?' Trish was saying.

And Mrs Oak again: 'I could hardly force her, now could I?'

And now Vera: 'People do as they please, don't they? I think she's better off working, to be honest. I mean, if I was her, I must say, I think I'd . . . Don't get me wrong or anything, but at the same time . . .'

'At the same time what, Vera?' Mrs Oak said.

'Well, we've all had our little heartbreaks – that's what it means to be a woman. We just have to get on with it. She's not a kid any more.'

'Twenty-one next month,' Trish said.

'Well, there you are. Think of what it was like for us at that age. You were a married woman, running a bar. I was doing my midwifery exams whilst nursing my dying mother and helping my dad in the shop. Trish was – what were you doing, Trish?'

'Me? I was running MI5 and teaching Mother Teresa how to suck eggs,' Trish said.

Mrs Oak laughed. 'But she's young for her age, Vee,' she said then. 'Really, she is. She'll be all right. We'll throw her a little party for her twenty-first. I'll get her a nice cake from Terroni's.

Remind me to order one, Trish. We can buy her a little bracelet or something. You'll come, Vee, won't you?'

'Course I will. She's lucky to have you, she really is. Doesn't she have anybody else, family or friends or that?'

'There was talk of an aunt when she came here first,' Trish said, 'but she seems to have vanished into thin air.'

'Oh, I see.'

'She's entitled to her privacy,' Mrs Oak said.

'Did I say she wasn't? And where is she now – hiding up in her room as per?' Vera asked, and then started coughing again.

'I have no idea,' Mrs Oak said. 'Would you like a glass of water, Vee? Trish, fetch Vera a glass of water, would you? Vera, can't you get your dad to give you something for that cough? I don't know how you can bear it, I really don't.'

'It's the hay fever. I can't help it, can I?'

She could hear Trish's chair scraping off the floor and now the sound of running water. She thought she would die of shame standing on the stairs, afraid to go back down, afraid to carry on. But she couldn't stay here forever, frozen mid-step until someone came out of the kitchen or up from the bar and caught her.

She took a few careful backward steps down the stairs, then ran up them again, this time slapping her feet on the linoleum.

A pause and then Trish's voice calling out, 'That you, Milly?'

'Yes. Yes, it's me.'

'Would you like a bite to eat or something?'

'No thanks, I'm fine.'

'A cuppa then? We're just having one.'

She came to the doorway and stopped. 'No thanks, I'll go on up. I won't be long.'

'It's very warm out there,' Vera said. 'Have you heard the thunder?'

'Thunder? Oh yes, I did. I heard it. Well, I better . . .'

'Take your time, love,' Mrs Oak said. 'Take the evening off, if you want.'

'It's Friday night, Mrs Oak.'

'We'll manage. Tell you what, have a little rest if you like and you can come down later.'

'Did you buy some books, Milly?' Trish said, nodding at the bag with the Hatchards signature on it. And then to Vera, 'Our Milly is a right bookworm these days. Since a certain young boxer started making recommendations. What was that one he gave you, Milly? She was so moved by it, I just had to borrow it. But too much dilly-dallying in it for me. I didn't know what they were on about it. I like a good romance, one that gets straight down to business. Harold Robbins, that's my man. What was it, Milly?'

'*The Great Gatsby*,' she snapped. 'And I read because I like reading. It's nothing to do with him.'

'All right, all right, I'm only having a little joke.'

'Oh look, she's gone all red,' Vera said.

'Leave her be,' Mrs Oak said. 'You go on up, Milly. Come down whenever you want.'

Vera began to crane her neck towards the baby bag. 'What else did you buy, Milly? Something nice for yourself?'

'What? Oh, not really. Just a nightie.'

'Good for you,' Vera said. 'You do right to treat yourself, today of all days.'

She nodded, then turned away from the kitchen and began up the stairs. She could hear Trish hiss at Vera, 'What you have to say that for?'

'What? What did I say?'

'We don't mention it, do we? And now she knows we've been talking about her.'

104

On the top floor, she stopped at the little bathroom at the end of the corridor. It was a run-down room, with a wobbly geyser and brown streaks on the bath. The lino curled at the edges and sometimes when she was sitting on the loo she saw queer little ridge-backed bugs crawling out of it. There was a long chain on the toilet that didn't always work, and no amount of bleach could get rid of the crust of ancient stains in the gullet of the bowl. If fussy Mrs Oak ever bothered to come up here, she'd probably have it renovated. Or she would make her move to one of the rooms on the second floor and share a bathroom with Trish. But she didn't want that. Any more than she wanted a load of workmen wandering around up here fixing things up. No one came up here except herself. Even Mrs Gupti had stopped since she'd told her that she'd do the cleaning herself. And now all of it – the bathroom, the corridor, the stairs, the bedroom, the entire fourth floor – belonged to her and nobody else.

She washed and dried her hands slowly. Then, turning her mouth to the cold tap, she began to suck on the flow of tepid water.

In her room, she sat on the bed and eased the box out of the bag. She untied the ribbon, lifted the lid away and parted the tissue paper. She removed the blue ribbon that shaggy-head had given her and flung it into the bin by the door. Then, unfolding the little dress, she spread it out on the bed. She unpinned the bonnet, then took the frilly knickers from the little plastic hanger and first gave the frills a little flounce, then put her hands in through the legs of the knickers and stretched them out a little. She picked up the bonnet, pressing her knuckles around the inside of the crown before placing it a few inches above the dress on the bed. Kneeling down, she reached under the bed and pulled a big brown suitcase to her. She unbuckled the case and pushed the lid back as far as it would go. She felt her breath catch. After a moment, she took the few things out, leaving only the keepsake envelope behind.

She held the little white nightgown like a book, on the flat of both hands. The nightgown was made of flannel and there was a row of tiny embroidered pink flowers across the chest. A small yellow stain sat on the shoulder and there was a tiny splatter of it over the sleeve. She lifted the gown to her face and sniffed as hard as she could. Last year she had cried when she found the smell of baby vomit had disappeared, but since then, she had grown more used to the idea.

She took the small baby brush out of the case and sat still for a moment. Then, glancing up, she caught sight of the mirror over the mantelpiece. She stood and walked to it. Without looking at her face, she swept the brush across her hair, the bristles so light and soft that she could barely feel them. She looked at the birthday card she'd put there this morning, with a picture of a lamb on the front of it and a big pink number two on the right-hand corner. Through the mirror, she read her back-to-front inscription: *To my darling daughter Flora, with all my love.*

When she came back to the bed, she arranged the clothes along it with a few inches gap in between each item: the new pink dress first, then the green pinafore, and then, close to one another, the nightgown and vest. She placed her right hand on the vest, her left on the nightgown, then after a few seconds she lifted them away and placed them down on the green pinafore. She moved on to the new pink dress then, putting one hand on the bonnet, the other on the dress. She did that again, working her way up the line. She said, 'First you were this size. Then you were this size. And now? Now you are this size.'

*

After she folded the baby clothes back into the suitcase, a tiredness came over her. She saw it as a presence wandering through a big house, switching off lights. Even in her sleep, she could feel it holding her down whenever she tried to drag herself awake. When she opened her eyes again and looked over at the alarm clock, it was twenty past seven, the evening shift more than two hours in and the first time she'd been late for work since she'd started. She imagined herself jumping up, running down the corridor to the loo, giving her face a splash, her teeth a frantic brush. Then darting back to the room, grabbing at clothes, hairbrush, shoes, before falling over herself to get downstairs to the bar, stair by stair building up excuses in her head. But then the stairs seemed to disappear from under her feet and she felt herself glide upwards for a delirious moment, before rolling back to sleep.

The next time she looked at the clock, it was ten minutes past nine. She heard herself shout, 'Oh Christ!' and pulled herself upright, but almost at once, slumped down again. There were voices passing below on the street and the rumble of trains coming and going from the station. But from the house itself, there was nothing. Downstairs, the bar would be heaving by now but she wouldn't hear a squeak of it, not until she reached the first-floor landing anyway. Nor would they be able to hear her. It had something to do with the way the room was positioned. She could be screaming her head off tucked away up here and no one would be the wiser.

It had taken a while to get used to the quietness of this room again. In the mother and baby home, there had always been something: voices, movement, footsteps in the night, the flushing of a chain. Now and then, a girl crying into her pillow.

But it had been a happy place, despite everything. Each girl basking in her few months of peace before it all came crashing down on top of her, knowing how lucky she was to have shored up here. Some of the places – the stories you'd hear . . .

She missed the home, the bit of hope it had allowed her to clutch on to so long as she was in there. She missed Anneka the cleaner, and Mrs Cranston the housekeeper, and Mrs Bruel who owned the place. She missed Nurse Ryan zipping in through the gate on her little moped. And the companionship of girls her own age, which was something she'd never really known before. Everyone in the same boat, never more than eight or nine at a time, so it hadn't felt like any sort of institution. And even though they were doing the most grown-up, serious thing you could do, at times they had behaved like kids themselves. The trick-acting that went on when it was Mrs Cranston's day off, water-bombing one another on the stairs. Laughing and running wild around the house and garden, and for her, that too had been something new.

She missed going for walks – their daily waddle, as Nurse Ryan called it – through the quiet English town and down by the river, or on Friday to the local shops to buy sweets for watching television that night. Even if, too often, the walk had been spoiled by local schoolboys whistling and heckling or following them up the road making crude gestures. *Here comes the puddin' club!*

Give us a go, girls. Ah come on, what difference will it make now?

When this happened, the girls would dive into sudden conversation with one another and carry on as if nothing was happening. But she knew they had felt it, as she had felt it: like a sharp, angry pain in the heart. The fact that twelve-year-old boys could shout at them like that, and there wasn't a thing they could do about it.

But in the house anyway, nobody judged you – Mrs Oak had been right about that. There had been a general lightness on the air. Except for those mornings when a social worker or the woman from the Christian Crusade might arrive, and a girl was called into the office. Then, a sort of wariness would settle over the home that sometimes lingered for the rest of the day.

She missed the talk most of all. Evenings when there was nothing much on the telly and they would end up sitting around the fire, while the dark spread out behind them. Faces in the firelight: Hilary, Sadie, Janice, Marie. Nell, Carrie, Esther, Mary. Trusting their fears, their little secrets, to one another.

Two years on and her memories of that time had jumbled up in her head, so that she sometimes had difficulty recalling who owned which secret or what name belonged to what face.

And yet, she remembered the nun so clearly – even if she still wasn't sure if she'd been real or some sort of an apparition.

A sickly smile on a wan face, drawing the screen around her hospital bed. The screen, dark grey behind her; her clothes and veil all black. A board in her hand, white form clipped onto it.

She hadn't been able to hear what the nun was saying. Beyond a vague hiss whenever her teeth had hit on an 'S' sound. She decided to ignore her, to look straight ahead at the speckled light through the high-set windows, the tree branches wagging in at her, hoping that sooner or later, the nun would get fed up standing there hissing to herself and go off about her business.

Sounds all around: clattering dishes in the distance and the muffled chorus of crying babies from the nursery down the corridor. The flick of magazine pages turning. The greedy sound of suckling on the far side of the screen. And Kate Bush on a radio going: *wowowow, wowawowa wow*, as if riling up the wailing babies.

She had heard all that. But not what the nun was saying.

'I can't hear you,' she admitted finally. 'I'm sorry, I just can't . . .'

109

The nun leaned her white face in. A full mouth of curved teeth. Grey eyes.

'I'm Sister Clare,' she said. 'Can you hear me now?'

'Yes.'

'She will go to a good Catholic family.'

'Who will?'

The nun hesitated and then began to whisper again. 'A family who will give her everything she could possibly—'

'What are you talking about?'

'Sister, you call me Sister.'

'All right. What are you talking about, Sister?'

'I said,' the nun took in an impatient breath and began to repeat herself, 'she will go to a—'

She cut the nun off. 'No, no, I'm sorry, there's been a misunderstanding. I'm not—'

'But you decided. I was told that you'd decided.'

'No, Sister. Excuse me, but—'

'You don't mean to say that you're now thinking of keeping her?'

The nun had shifted from foot to foot, then pressed the edge of the clipboard into the bed and began chopping it on the mattress. 'You don't mean to say that you, a mere girl . . .'

The nun, biting her lip, had looked away. She waited a moment before speaking again.

'There are two very good people who expect you to sign today. *I* expect you to sign today. We were told that you were giving the baby up.'

'Oh, I see,' she said, 'I get it now. It's because I'm Irish. Of course. That's why they sent you. They presumed. And now, you're confused.'

'But why would I be confused?'

'You presumed—'

Again, the nun cut her off. 'You want the best for your baby. Isn't that so?'

'Yes. We're going to the post-natal home in a couple of days. The two of us. Six weeks, we'll be there – I'm breastfeeding, you see, and when you breastfeed your baby, well you're allowed to stay together for six . . . Six weeks is a long time, anything could happen.'

'Like what? If you don't mind my asking.'

'My boss might help me to—'

'Your boss? Is he the—?'

'She, she's a woman.'

'And you think she's going to help you keep the child?'

'I don't know. Maybe. I'm calling her Flora, after my mother.'

The nun lifted the clipboard. On the top of the form, the word 'CONSENT' loomed out.

'Be that as it may, I'd like you to sign today. This couple, you see . . .'

'But I am not one of you, Sister,' she said, pulling herself up in the bed. 'Can't you understand what I'm trying to tell you? I am not a Catholic. I'm a Protestant.'

'Are you sure?' the nun said, lifting the clipboard close to her face, peering at it, trying to find the mistake. 'But it says here, it says right here. Look.'

The nun's finger pointed at the form, pushing it towards her.

She thought of all the stories she'd heard in the home of how they steal babies, these pale-faced nuns, making you sign forms, whisking the baby away before you have time to think.

'You are *not* getting my baby,' she said. 'You keep away from my baby. Mrs Breul, she said, she said we're going to the, you know, the . . . For six weeks. You keep away now. Away.'

'You're one of Mrs Breul's girls?'

'That's what I've been trying to tell you.'

'I see. Well now. Well.'

The nun lifted her clipboard, turned as though to leave, but then stepping back for a moment she hissed straight into her face, 'For the sake of whoever does get your baby, miss, I sincerely hope that she hasn't inherited your manners.'

Six weeks had seemed like such a long time. Forty-two days, eight to ten feeds a day – who knows how many nappy changes? Anything could happen in six weeks. Any small miracle.

In the post-natal home, she had signed papers she didn't fully understand and there had been a long chat with a social worker. But that didn't mean she had given up her baby. Her baby was taken. Out of her arms, she was taken, and brought into an adjoining room where, through the thin walls of a skimpy office on a glorious day in mid-July, she heard a woman say, 'Oh she's so beautiful, oh do look at our baby, David, isn't she the most *beautiful.*'

Nobody had told her that she should leave the office and so she'd sat on, hoping that the baby would be brought back to her. Or that, at the very least, the woman would ask to meet the girl who had carried and given birth to the baby who, from now on out, would belong to her and a man named David.

When the nurse came back in, she'd been surprised to see her. 'Oh, you're still here then, Milly?'

'I thought they just wanted to meet my baby. I didn't realise that it was, you know, today. I didn't understand.'

'You're free to go now, love,' the nurse said and patted her arm.

The nurse had held the door open, and walked her down the corridor and waited while she collected her things. Then she saw her to the front door.

'If you want my advice,' she'd said, 'keep it to yourself, tell no one. It's a terrible thing giving your baby up to another woman. But still, I shouldn't tell a soul, if I were you. People only think less of you.'

Then she was standing at the bus stop, Mrs Oak's dead husband's suitcase on the ground beside her. There was a dragging sensation between her legs and her hands felt as if they belonged to somebody else. Her blouse was soaked with milk. She watched the traffic push towards and away from London. She watched people appear and disappear as they made their way home. And then she climbed onto a bus and sat among them, as if she was just like anyone else.

6. Pip

2017

May

HE HAS SURPRISED himself by how easily he has settled in, even if, at times, he feels like a cross between Dom's butler and his wife. All of which he has brought on himself. Day by day, bit by bit, so that neither he nor Dom seem to have noticed that he's been making himself useful. Maybe even indispensable.

From that first morning at the end of March, when he came downstairs, opened the fridge and found it empty. The big double-doored fuck-off fridge, the size of a small caravan – was *empty*. Give or take a few out-of-date jars, a half-pint carton of milk and a tub of margarine.

The previous time he'd been in this house, the fridge had been like something out of an upmarket deli, all neatly arranged wedges and rounds, fragrant mysteries wrapped in wax paper; an international array of jars; bottles of premier cru and rosé lying on their sides, and always a snipe of champagne ready to pop at the slightest excuse. But there had been a wife back then, and a French wife at that.

Marjie's fridge in Paddington had been a cosier first-wife enterprise. Small and compact, but it had nothing to be ashamed of either. A block of cheddar, a few slices of decent ham, mustard, milk, eggs and leftovers sensibly stored in plastic containers. To think that this was how Dom – always fond of his grub – had ended up.

He'd felt he had no choice really but to buy a few groceries. He thought it might be a good start – make it look as if he wasn't going to be a complete freeloader anyway. His first full day back in the big sober world and he hadn't felt up to negotiating the supermarket with its rush of colour and noise, so he'd asked a woman at a bus stop if there was a grocery shop nearby and followed her vague wave up to the top of Westbourne Grove.

It had seemed like a calm, wholesome sort of place. A modern grocery shop that, like himself that morning, was brimming with good intentions. Happily, he stepped inside. From the grocery section, a few wide steps led up to a café, and he had thought to do his bit of shopping, then treat himself to a decent cup of coffee and maybe just the smallest of cakes. He filled up a basket with the makings of a breakfast for when Dom – always a late riser after a concert – finally surfaced. Marmalade, a box of eggs, streaky rashers, a small slab of butter. He found a loaf of bread with so many seeds in it you could hardly see the dough. The milk came in a pouch. He hadn't been sure that it was milk at all and had stood for a moment holding it in his hand and examining it, until he sensed someone was watching him. A woman who looked as if her face had been cling-filmed. And he realised then that he'd been squeezing the pouch like it was a big tit. He'd been embarrassed but at the same time found it funny and thought he might throw it into the conversation with Dom later, as a bit of an ice-breaker. He finished his shopping: small tin of tuna, packet of sugar-free biscuits, even though he felt sugar-free biscuits rather defeated the purpose.

Finally, he picked up a small fruit cake to go with his coffee later on.

When he handed the girl a fifty-pound note, she came back with a Colgate smile and a handful of change.

'Sorry, love, I gave you a fifty,' he said.

'Yes, I know, sir. Would you like a receipt?'

'Well, I'd certainly be interested to see how *that* came about,' he said, balking at the few coins in his hand.

He'd moved to the side, put on his glasses and looked down at the receipt. Nine quid for a tin of tuna that could sit in the palm of your hand. That little loaf of bread cost a fiver?

He would in his bollix be treating himself to a coffee here, he had thought; nor would he ever set foot in the place again.

When he came out, he walked down the road and stopped at the crossroads. On the far side of the roundabout, his eye had been caught by the large gleaming window of an estate agent's office. He crossed over.

For a minute, he had thought it could be his eyesight, that maybe his vision had doubled the zeros on the end of the rental prices. And so he'd put down his messages, stuck on his glasses and, shielding his eyes with both hands to block out the light, peered in again. He'd nearly laughed out loud. Who in their right mind would even consider paying those prices? And for what? A small, and it had to be said fairly ordinary-looking, flat on Ledbury Road? A bedsit, in fact, re-branded as a 'studio residence'.

He looked down the road – a road they used to run amok on when they were kids. Dom had a pal who lived down there, in a flat squeezed in with several others into a ramshackle house. It had been a rough and ready sort of street then, mothers roaring at their kids, music barging out of windows, old men shuffling along; young men out of work, sitting on steps or hanging round the corner.

Out of curiosity, he'd picked up his bag of messages and began to wander up Ledbury Road. There had been nothing familiar about any of it; not the smooth white houses or the sterile shops that seemed to specialise in various body parts: brow bar; nails; face gym – whatever that was supposed to be. Outside the various cafés, expensive-looking women sat smoking and drinking coffee. And overhead, the sun quivered at him through carefully curated trees. Reminding him of the sunglasses.

He'd been thinking about Dom's friend as he'd wandered up the road, Derek . . . something. He'd been unable to find the house and decided that, like many others around here, it had probably been demolished. A small window on the first floor. At least he could remember seeing Derek looking out the window, buck teeth and the glint of his old-man glasses. He'd lived with a gin-swigging mother who'd barred Dom from the flat when she found out that his mother was Irish – never mind that she'd been Irish enough to give the boy his dinner when his own mother was too drunk to feed him.

It had been one of the few times in his childhood that he'd seen Dom upset, which could be the reason he remembered it so well.

As he walked along, he began to notice that he was feeling quite well – or not too bad, anyhow, for his first day out of the clinic and the start of his sojourn with Dom. He'd been putting it down to a good night's sleep, or maybe the novelty of his surroundings, or the sun on his shoulders as he turned into Chepstow Crescent. But then, he felt himself jolt. Just a few feet ahead of him, on the opposite side of the street, was a burned-out car. It was the last place he'd expected to be hit with such a reminder. Two policemen were standing by, and a tow truck was waiting to remove the car. The emergency lights on the roof of both truck and cop car only added to the memory. A whoosh of flames came into his head along with the smell of petrol and fear, the taste of blood. He almost dropped the bag from his shaking hands while his mind reached out for a shot of whiskey. But instead, he stood his ground, steadying the bag in his arms, looking at the shell of the car crouched on the side of the road, the policemen, the lights – the lot. He stayed rooted for a while, then, turning around, retraced his steps. Past the shops with names that sounded like nursery rhymes: Sweaty Betty, Wolf and Badger. Past the cafés with the women still smoking outside. And then, suddenly, he was on the far side of the crossroads and halfway down the road. His heart calmer and his hands almost steady. Closing his eyes, he let the relief run through him. He had faced it, dealt with it, stayed sober, moved on.

He never got round to telling Dom the story about the milk pouch, but Dom had been so pleased to see a bit of food in the fridge that it had started something. Before he knew it, little notes began to appear on the marble counter: *If you're passing a shop would you mind . . .* Or *I need this suit for concert Friday. Dry cleaners at back of launderette on Porchester Road do best deals.*

And now it has become part of his daily routine.

Not that he minds all that much. It puts a bit of shape on his day, running Dom's errands, collecting his dry cleaning, organising his bins, doing his shopping. It gets him out of the house. There's the twice-weekly trot up to the butcher's shop on Golborne Road and the evening wander around Waitrose with the shabby genteel, all trying not to look as if they're there for the six o'clock bargains. Sometimes, he goes further afield: the music shop near the Old Kent Road where Dom gets his trumpets serviced. Or to various box offices to collect or leave tickets, and a couple of times he's been dispatched to the Royal Academy to deliver, or to collect, something Dom has forgotten. And now there's this new Airbnb carry-on to add to his long list of duties – again, all his own fault.

For the first couple of weeks, they didn't see that much of one another. The notes did the talking. Inevitably, there was a crossing of paths, usually in the kitchen and usually on Sunday when Dom – or Nick as he was known in the music world, or even, God help us, Niki – liked to get a few things off his chest. Things he couldn't allow to come out in his day-to-day working life.

Nice guy Nick, the talented conductor, the man equally at ease in concert hall or jazz club. Loved by his students, fancied by their mothers, respected by their fathers. He wore his charm like a well-cut cashmere coat. In the privacy of his own kitchen, he tore it off and let rip: the mechanical arseholes who played music like robots; the witless morons in charge of the various academies. Jeremy and Theresa usually got a few kicks up the hole. The council, the taxman, the dry cleaners who failed to get the truffle oil out of his best dress shirt. And then there were the expected gripes of the twice-divorced man: ex-wives and alimony, lawyers, in-laws, headmasters and various other mentally deficient pricks. And he'd been glad to see that his brother was still a champion curser; nobody swore better, or more elegantly. It was something he had always admired about Dom.

It hadn't taken too long to notice that Dom was not as flush as he used to be. He had always been a generous man – at times overly generous. A fact that he could throw in your face when least expected. But now, when he did remember to leave money out on the counter to pay for his messages, it was either not enough, or just about enough, or even a scribbled – and usually unfulfilled – promise to fix him up later.

There was the recurrent use of certain words in the notes: cheap, bargain, cut-price. There was the morning spread of bills and final notices on the floor in the hallway. There was the vacant fridge and the absence of staff: both cleaner and gardener.

He'd known the old gardener slightly, and had seen him a few times working in the gardens at either side of Dom's house. A little older now, a little more stooped over his lawnmower as he pushed it straight past Dom's gate. When he stayed here a few years back, he'd sometimes bring him out a cup of tea and stop for a bit of a chat.

One day he made it his business to bump into him again.

'You're still at it then?' he asked the gardener.

'For my sins. Haven't seen you about in a while.'

'Ten years, nearly ten and a half.'

'Ten? Bloody hell. How are you then?'

'You know – older, fatter. And you?'

'Oh, you know – older, thinner. Like this lawnmower, held together by screws.'

'You don't do my brother's garden now?'

'I don't do work for nothin', if that's what you mean.'

In the end he'd simply asked Dom: 'I can't help noticing,' he began, 'that you're not, you know, as flush as you used to be.'

'Why – you looking for a loan or something?'

'No. I just wondered.'

'Since when did my financial affairs become any of your fucking business?' he snarled and walked out of the kitchen.

A moment later, he came back in.

'She didn't go quietly, you know,' he said. 'I had to buy her out. Have you any idea of what a house like this is worth, what it costs to maintain the bastard? I'm up to my bollix in it, seeing as you're asking.'

'I wish I could help you out.'

'But you can't, can you?'

'No. But I do have an idea.'

'What's that?'

'Have you ever thought of Airbnb?'

'And why would I want to do that?'

'No, I don't mean stay in one; I mean, do it here. Do Airbnb here.'

'Strangers all over my house – is that your great idea?'

'You're away a lot of the time, as far as I can see, or you're always out anyway, apart from the Sunday.'

'And where do you think I'd find the time to—'

'I could manage it for you.'

'You? Don't make me laugh.'

'Look, Dom, I've been sober since January.'

'You were in hospital in January. Then you were in rehab. You're only out, what, a couple of months? As far as I'm concerned, you're only sober since you got out.'

'Hear me out at least.'

'How would you even know anything about it?'

'Well, let's just say I looked into it. I was thinking of staying in one, you know, instead of coming here.'

'Oh really – and what made you change your mind?'

'The cost.'

'And there was me thinking it was brotherly love.'

'Look, even in a fairly downmarket area, it costs a packet. In an area like this? Well . . . And I can do it. Sort the whole thing out – manage it for you. The money would go straight into your bank account. No, listen, listen to me – you have two en suites here, right?'

'Yeah, but one of them is in my room.'

'You could move into the room on the first floor – you know, beside the main bathroom. You'd be right beside your music room.'

'Fuck off. I'm not—'

'And if I cleaned out that playroom or whatever it is looking out at the back garden, there's a toilet and shower right beside it.'

'I said, there's no fucking way I'm moving out of my—'

'Okay, fine, okay. It's just an idea. Three rooms, in a house like this. You could make four, five hundred quid a night – that's all I'm saying. You wouldn't even have to pay me. They pay extra for cleaning – I'd take that.'

'I said, no fucking way.' Dom huffed off up the stairs into his study.

Twenty minutes later, he was back again. 'Five hundred quid, did you say?'

'At least. More if you get good reviews.'

'A night? Not a week?'

'A night, if you use the three rooms. We could have it up and running by the middle of the month.'

'What about Max, supposing he comes home?'

'Is he likely to anytime soon?'

'He's on a gap year. I just wouldn't like him finding out.'

'I can block out the days with a bit of notice.'

'What I mean is, I wouldn't want his mother getting wind of it.'

'You bought her out, why is it her business?'

'If there's even a whiff of money, that French conk of hers starts twitching. And these guests, how do we know they're not nut-jobs?'

'You can check their reviews. If you're not happy, don't take the chance.'

'We'd need to buy a bed for the garden room.'

'There's a bed up in the spare room.'

'That's in bits. I keep meaning to throw it out.'

'I can fix it. It just needs a new mattress.'

'There's a damp patch on the ceiling.'

'I can fix that too. I used to be a builder's labourer – remember? I picked up a few things on the way.'

'You used to be a lot of things, Phil.'

Dom stood for a moment, staring into space and tapping his teeth with his thumbnail. Then he said, 'Okay. So now you can add Airbnb host to your skill set.'

Since then, Dom no longer wastes much time on his Sunday rants. They have a meeting instead, going over figures and forthcoming visitors. They read reviews from former guests and try not to look too pleased. Afterwards Dom makes coffee that comes out of a pod and they sit and chat for a while. Dom, calmer now that he has a few quid coming in, can be surprisingly good company. For the first time in years, they start getting along.

One Sunday, Dom tells him he's thinking of getting the gardener back.

'Don't bother,' he says, 'I can do it. I need the exercise. You don't need to pay me, it can cover my keep.'

'Don't tell me – you used to be a gardener too?'

'In prison, I helped in the—'

'Don't talk about prison. It's the past, it's over, it's done. I don't want it mentioned in my house. I don't want it mentioned anywhere near me.'

Another Sunday, Dom invites him along to a colleague's house for lunch. 'He lives in Kensington Gardens; we can walk there. There's usually about ten or twelve people. His wife's a good cook; what do you think?'

He thinks it sounds like his worst nightmare, sitting around a table, listening to Dom's colleagues having their Sunday fun. For a moment he goes into a blind panic until he realises that all he has to say is: 'Well, I'd love to go, Dom, I really would. But I'm not supposed to . . . you know, put myself in the way of drink.'

'Yes, of course not – oh fuck, what was I thinking? *Fuck*,' said Dom. 'Sorry about that. How is that going, by the way? The whole, you know, not drinking thing?'

'Good, yea.'

'Still going to your meetings?'

'Yea. I am, yea.'

'How do you find them – do they help?'

'Honestly? Well, I'd be lost without them.'

There are advantages to this new, busy life: the tiredness at the end of the day, the easy sleep, the extra money – Dom, now clearing a good lump of cash every week, has become generous again, insisting on giving him a bonus on top of the cleaning fee. Apart from that, all the running around has meant his weight has finally begun to shift. And, he has stopped thinking about drink in his usual obsessive manner.

He hasn't forgotten about it, of course – he would never be so callous – but it no longer sucks every moment out of his day. Along with his other worries – his future, his health and his stash of undelivered *mea culpa* letters – it's around somewhere, out of sight, if not quite out of reach.

7. Milly

1982

AT THE END of July, she was coming out of Finsbury Library when she walked straight into him.

She nearly died at the sight of him standing there, right in front of her. She thought the skin on her face would split, she blushed that hard.

He said her name, 'Milly?' as if he wasn't quite sure that it was her. Then he gave her such a smile.

'You've been away awhile,' she said.

'Yea, a few weeks. Got back about a fortnight ago.'

'And you haven't been in to see us – have you found a new local, then?'

'No, I'm off the sauce.'

'Oh. Oh right.'

She looked straight at him then. 'It suits you,' she said. 'You look fit.'

'Thanks very much.'

'Healthy fit, I mean,' she quickly added, in case he thought she meant handsome.

'Yea, I know.'

She waited for him to say something else, but he just stood looking at her, grinning. In the end she had to ask him what was so funny.

'I'm not laughing.'

'No, but you look as if you'd like to.'

He put his hand on her arm then. 'It's just so great to see you, Milly, that's all.'

They were standing at the pillar under the concrete canopy, the traffic a blur of red and grey over his shoulder. And then, a sudden gaggle of small children seemed to sprout around them. A nursery teacher, wide-armed, attempting to herd them through the library door. He leaned in to take a look at the books she was holding. She could smell his skin.

'How did you get on?' she asked. 'Did you win?'

'Mostly.' He pointed at one of the books. 'Have you read him before?'

'Only the one where he fancies the young one,' she said. 'The dirty old pervert.'

He laughed and pointed to the second book. 'That one there won a big prize last year.'

'You enjoyed it though?'

'I haven't read it yet.'

'No, the tournaments, I mean, the fights?'

'Oh, it gets you around, you know? I'm off to Berlin in ten days. If I do well there, I may go on to Italy. I wouldn't mind Italy. Not that you get to see much.'

'Why not?'

'Between the fights and the training, Jackie keeps me going. That's why I'm off the gargle really. You can't train at that level and drink.'

'But you're glad you went with him?' she asked.

'Well, he's different to Shamie, I suppose. Jackie – he follows the money.'

'So, are you rich now?'

'I could buy you a cup of coffee, if that's what you're hinting at.'

She laughed. 'I am not!'

He turned, moving his hand as if to bring her along. 'Well, come on,' he said. 'I might even throw in a bun.'

'Are you not going inside?' she said.

'Not now, I'm not.'

As they turned onto Percival Street, he began to talk. There were roadworks going on at the top of the street, the sound of a jackhammer shattering his words mid-air. But she loved the fact that he was talking to her; just to glance up at him now and then and find he was looking down at her, his hand moving through a story she could only barely get the gist of. And the way he guided her across the road so that she didn't have to bother checking to see if it was safe or not. And then, as they came along King Square, three right looking yokes stepped out of the park, swigging large bottles of cider. If she'd been on her own, she would have been terrified. He put his hand on the small of her back and, without breaking his stride or his story, edged her slightly ahead of him. She felt the power of him then, the physical confidence. When she glanced back at the trio with their hair standing up like horns on their heads and their chalk white faces and the nappy pins dangling off them, she thought they just looked like big stupid children dressed up for Halloween.

On the side streets there was hardly anyone around. The sound of his voice over the stillness. He was telling her about the boarding school in Ireland. The library – the Priests' Library, he called it – and how he had been allowed to use it for some reason. You'd be surprised, he said, at some of the books they had

127

there. The priest, Father John, he called him, was a friend of his father's.

'He encouraged me to both box and read; he took an interest in me, I suppose you could say.'

She smiled again. She was aware that she was smiling too much. It was like someone had rammed a shoehorn sideways into her mouth. Stop grinning like a simpleton, she told herself. *Stop.*

After a while, she began to sense that he was faltering. Knowing that it wasn't in his nature to do so much talking, she was afraid that soon he would run out of words. Or worse, he would lose interest in talking to her. She tried, but could think of nothing, absolutely nothing, to say.

And so she began asking questions. One after another, she fired them at him. He must have thought she was a right nosey wagon.

So how was his brother?

And how was his father?

And where was he living?

And did he like his brother's fiancée – Marjorie, wasn't that her name?

He said he'd been staying with his brother and his fiancée, who was indeed called Marjorie or Marj.

'I saw his picture a few weeks ago, outside a concert hall at the back of Oxford Street somewhere,' she said.

'Yea? Oh, you mean the Wigmore – did you go in?'

'No, I wanted to. But no . . .'

He said Dom and Marj were living in the upper part of a house in Paddington, not far from where he'd lived when he was a child. His brother was giving trumpet classes in one of the rooms; Marj gave singing classes in another. Dom's first solo was coming up, in that new place, the Barbican. He was up to ninety practising for it. Between that and his students, the noise at times was frankly brutal. The neighbours were up in arms over it. Banging down the door, posting notes through the letterbox. The bloke next door took his revenge by blasting Led Zeppelin out in the middle of the night.

'I wouldn't blame them either,' he said. 'Jesus, at times it sounds like there's a herd of scuttery elephants let loose in the jacks.'

He made the sounds of the scuttery elephants then and she went into fits.

And now she was laughing too much. Calm down, she told herself. Calm. Down.

'Sorry,' she said. 'Sorry, it's just been so long since I heard the word "scuttery".'

'That's okay.' He smiled. 'Anyway, we had a row, so I'm not there any more. I'm staying in Jackie's place.'

'His house?'

'No, no, a bedsit in one of his properties – near London Bridge. He lets it out to a gang of nurses. I'll be getting something a bit better when I come back next time. The nurses, well they can be loud enough too; mad parties and that. Still, they're quiet during the day.'

'Where will you move to?'

'Oh, I don't know. Jackie said he'd sort something.'

'You rely on him a lot,' she said and was instantly sorry. 'I mean,' she began, 'I mean, it's good to have him there.'

'It's all right, Milly, I know what you mean.'

They walked in silence for a few moments and then he began to tell her about Shamie, how hard it had been to leave him. He still had sleepless nights over it, he said.

'I probably wouldn't have even kept up the boxing, only for

him, you know. I'd probably be teaching English and Geography somewhere in the arsehole of Ireland. I used to do a bit of boxing in school and then in college I joined the club just for something to do, really. Shamie brought a team over to Dublin and I ended up fighting his lad. Afterwards he pulled me aside. He said to me: maybe you prefer to get your degree? Why, I said, do you need a degree to box in London? You need a lot of things to be a good boxer, Shamie said, but a degree ain't one of them. Good, I said, I'll be over in a couple of weeks. And that's what I did.'

'You left college?'

'I was glad to be out of it, to be honest; I was looking for an excuse, I suppose. Let's just say I didn't really fit in.'

'Well, I don't think Shamie would begrudge you success,' she said, 'but yes, I know what you mean – no one would like to let Shamie down.'

'Oh Christ,' he said. 'I wish you hadn't said that.'

After a while, she began to notice that she'd stopped worrying about who was speaking or what she could, or should, say next. Now they were just two people walking along a street in London, talking.

At the corner of Bath Street, he said he needed to make a call and they had to try three different phone boxes before they found one that worked. She sat on a low wall across the road and pretended not to watch him. She examined her fingernails, then carefully turned her shirtsleeves over her elbows. He moved his head from side to side and rolled his shoulders a couple of times. His hand pressed against the window. His back was to her, yet she felt certain that he was talking to a woman. But that was fine. In a moment, he would step out of that red box, cross the road to her and they would walk away. They would enter the door of the café at the same time and sit down at the same table. People would assume they were together. But they were together, sort of. Or at least something between them had changed.

In Bunhill Fields cemetery she almost told him about the baby. He had been showing her around the graves as if they were at a party and he was introducing her to dead people. At the gravestone of the man who wrote *Robinson Crusoe*, she felt the words pinball down from her brain and into her throat. But he started telling her about the real Robinson Crusoe and then he was quoting from a poem some Irish poet had written. He said the name Alexander Selkirk and she wasn't sure if that was the name of the sailor, or the name of a poet.

He could see she was puzzled. 'Come on,' he said, 'it's Kavanagh. You must have done it in school?'

'Oh yes, of course! I think I remember it now.'

She didn't like to tell him that she hadn't been to secondary school because the only school for miles around was run by nuns and her grandparents had neither the money nor the inclination to send her to a Protestant boarding school.

When they'd finished looking at the graves, they sat down on a bench. It occurred to her that this was the first time she'd really seen him up close in broad daylight. His eyes were darker than she'd thought. His nose had slipped a fraction to the side. She loved the shape of his neck.

He stretched his arm out behind her. Not around her as such, but along the back of the bench. If she moved a few inches . . . that's all it would take.

He said, 'So how does it feel to be twenty-one?'

'The same, I suppose.'

He said, 'Sorry I missed your party last week.'

'There was nothing to miss.'

'What, you didn't enjoy it?'

'I mean, there was no party. Mrs Oak cancelled it.'

'Why would she do that?'

'The bombs in Hyde Park. They went off the day before.'

'Yea but – what had that got to do with you?'

'Mrs Oak. Well, she said . . . she said it was unseemly to have a party after that.'

He gave a puzzled laugh. 'She said that?'

He was quiet for a moment and then, 'I wonder how fucking unseemly it would have been now if you were Welsh or Scottish?'

She was startled by the way he growled that out.

'Oh, I didn't want her stupid party anyway,' she said.

'Yea, but I'm sure you must have felt it.'

She shrugged. 'It was fine.'

She didn't tell him how she thought she would vomit every time it came on the news, the whole pub with their eyes raised to the television up in the corner. Or about the overwhelming sense of shame for days after the event. Or how, when Mrs Oak had said in front of a crowd of customers: 'The Queen's Cavalry horses? I mean, what sort of barbarians would do a thing like that?' Brenda had answered, 'Why Irish ones, of course,' and then turned and looked straight at her.

She didn't want to tell him that when she closed her eyes at night, she could still see the horses lying on the ground. The beautiful dead shape of them.

'What did you do instead?' he asked.

'I took the day off. Went for a walk. Had an early night. Read for a while. It was fine.'

He put his hand on the ball of her shoulder then, just for a second. 'Fuck them, Milly, that's what I say.'

She felt the words line up again: I was away having a baby and not looking after my grandmother, that time I was supposed to be in Ireland. I was in Surrey in this mother and baby home, you see. She was two last month. I called her Flora, after my mother.

She began, 'I was . . .'

He looked at her waiting. 'What?'

'Oh nothing.'

'No go on, what – you were what Milly?'

'I was just wondering, is it – is it hard to punch someone in the face?'

He looked at her, then his head went back and he laughed. 'Sometimes, I mean, it feels you know? But then again, sometimes it can be very easy.'

He stood up then. 'Come on, let's get that coffee. I wouldn't like you to think I was all talk.'

A couple of days later, he came into the pub, walked straight up to the counter and stood right in front of her. Mrs Oak was on one side, pulling a pint, Trish on the other, taking an order.

Mrs Oak said, 'Well, look what the cat's just dragged in. Hello, Philip, what can I get you?'

'I'm not staying,' he said. 'I'm here to see Milly.'

And then in front of everyone, he said, 'I was wondering if you'd like to come to the Barbican – you know, that new place up the road I was telling you about? Tomorrow night, my brother's playing. We could go somewhere afterwards, if you like, or maybe for a drink with Dom and his mates.'

Then with a glance at Mrs Oak, in a pointed way, he added, 'Call it a belated birthday celebration.'

Mrs Oak's eyes dropped for just a second. Then she resumed pulling the pint and making small talk with the customer.

She wasn't able to move, she was that mortified; standing there looking at the counter with her stupid big red face. Until Trish said, 'Well answer the chap, Milly, can't you?'

She nodded her head twice and then walked away.

Trish insisted she wore one of her dresses and a pair of her sandals to the concert and then insisted on helping her with her makeup. The dress was too big; the makeup too much. To spare Trish's feelings, she slipped into the ladies' toilet downstairs on her way out and wiped most of it off.

For some reason the Barbican had made him cranky. He was fine on the walk there, but once they were inside, something in him seemed to turn.

She said, 'It's nice in here, isn't it?'

He said, 'I think it looks like a big bus station, people walking around looking bewildered. It looks nothing like a theatre.'

'I wouldn't know,' she said, 'I've never been in one before.'

There were small bar counters set up here and there, everything out in the open, and this had seemed to annoy him too.

'You can't even sit down in comfort,' he said, 'it's a ridiculous set-up.'

She said, 'I'm happy enough to stand.'

He was restless and kept looking around. He went off to buy a programme, a glass of wine for her and a Coke for himself. He was clumsy with his bottle and glass, letting the Coke fizz over, and then he had the whole thing gone before she'd taken more than a sip.

He left her standing there on her own while he went to the loo, and when she went to the loo, she came back to find him pacing up and down like a lion. When they finally sat down in the auditorium, he seemed to relax a little. She was holding the programme; he leaned over and pointed out his brother's name: Nick Dawson. 'And who's Telemann?' she asked.

'The composer.'

But when his brother stood up out of the orchestra and began to play, he tensed up again. Throughout the solo, she took a few sneaky peeks at him. She thought he looked nervous, then she thought he looked proud. Mostly, though, she thought he looked sad.

Afterwards they waited for Dom to come out.

Almost at once, he said, 'Come on, he's not coming.'

'Give him a chance,' she said, 'we've only been here a couple of minutes! Does he even know you're here?'

'I left him a note. I'm telling you now, he's not coming.'

They waited for another few minutes and he still didn't show. She said: 'Maybe we could follow him to the pub?'

'I'm not his fucking puppy dog,' he said. 'Come on, we're going.'

They were walking back through a tunnel, the traffic edging beside them, long ugly fluorescent lights overhead, when she began to recognise his agitation. She had seen it in her grandfather many times, and sometimes when a customer had been on the dry, there was a restlessness about them just before they jumped off the wagon. She felt he was sorry that he'd told her he was off the drink because now he felt he couldn't drink in front of her. In fact, he probably couldn't wait to get rid of her, so that he could go on a bender.

Her feet were sliding around in the sandals. The strap of the dress kept slipping off one shoulder. She was having trouble keeping up with him. She must have hoisted the strap back up once too often, because by the time they got to Aldersgate Street, he'd clearly had enough. He stopped suddenly, flipped back his jacket and found an old dry cleaners' docket pinned onto it. 'Here,' he said, 'fix yourself up before the fucking thing falls off you.'

She snatched the pin from him and then blurted out, 'Why did you ask me to come tonight? Was it just to show me how rude you can be? Or . . . or maybe you felt sorry for me because you think I'm such a child that I'm fretting over a stupid birthday party? Mrs Oak won't talk to me now, I hope you know, because she thinks I went whining to you. Get me a taxi, I'd rather go home by myself. Go on, get me a taxi and fuck off, you cranky bollix.'

Then she let the pin fall.

He picked the pin up and handed it to her. But her hands were shaking and she couldn't manage it. He said, 'Oh here, give me the bloody thing,' but he said it gently, taking the pin from her and then, drawing her over to the streetlight, he fixed the pin into the strap.

'But such language, Milly, I'm surprised at you . . .' and then he laughed.

She burst out crying.

He said, 'I'm sorry, Milly, I am really. It's my brother, I don't know, he just . . .'

And then he was holding her and saying it into her hair, 'I'm sorry, Milly. I really am. I'm sorry.'

And then he was kissing her.

They walked back to his bedsit near the river. She couldn't remember anything about the walk, what they talked about or who or what they saw on the way. They were on Queen Victoria Street before she noticed that his jacket was around her shoulders and he was carrying the sandals in his hand.

Afterwards, he fell asleep straight away, in a narrow bed pushed to the wall. She was on the inside and had to wriggle down the length of the bed to get out. She gathered her clothes and sneaked into the bathroom down the hall.

Her plan was to be gone when he woke up. She did not want to see his look of regret, to watch him squirm while he searched for ways to tell her that he wanted to 'just be friends'.

She was halfway dressed when she realised that her knickers were missing.

For several minutes she sat on the side of the bath wondering what to do. Overhead was a lattice of washing lines, the legs of nurses' tights dangling from them like jungle vines. There were nursing caps and half-slips and blue puff sleeves hanging to dry. There were no knickers. She could go home knickerless, if needs be – the knickers weren't the issue. What she didn't want was him finding them the next day and thinking she was trying to leave some sort of message.

She had been on her knees, arm stretched under the bed feeling around, when she heard him say: 'What the hell are you doing, Milly?'

'I'm looking for something. Go back to sleep, I'm just getting dressed.'

'Why?'

'To go home,' she said.

'It's the middle of the night.'

'I know.'

'Do you want to go home that badly?'

'I don't want you . . .'

'You don't want me what?'

'I don't want you to think that I'm hanging on hoping for something. And I can't find my knickers.'

He sat up in the bed, leaning on his elbow. 'Jesus, Milly,' he laughed and then, reaching out, he put his hand on her arm. 'Tell

137

you what, why don't you come back to bed and that way you won't need your knickers.'

In the morning, he gave her a navy-blue jumper to wear over Trish's flimsy dress. It had been just after dawn when they came onto a narrow street. There was a church with a clock jutting from its portico that said a quarter to six. They passed under the portico and the lanterns were still burning. She could see the light from the river bouncing off a black wall.

He walked her to Cannon Street tube station. She thought she might never be down this way again and that she might never walk beside him on a street again and so she tried to remember every step, every turn, the name of each laneway.

At the station he kissed her cheek and said he'd be in touch.

'It's fine,' she said. 'Really.'

'Jesus, Milly,' he said, 'would you stop?'

Then he squeezed her hand.

She watched him walk away; he was in his running gear. He was like a horse, she thought, barely able to contain itself before reaching the open field.

The next morning at breakfast, the new extension phone blasted into the kitchen. She could hardly hear what he was saying over the thud of her heart.

'Do you fancy going away for a few days?' he asked.

'When?'

'Today?'

'What do you mean today – are you mad? I can't go today.'

'Course you can. Tell her something's come up, that you want a few days off your holidays.'

'She's not here, she's gone out.'

138

'Well, is Trish there?'

'Yes.'

'She's beside you?'

'Yes.'

'All the better, tell her and she can pass on the message. I'll wait for you at Paddington station. By the ticket desks, five o'clock. Don't let me down now.'

She put down the phone and when she looked around, Trish was watching her through her makeup mirror. 'You got a problem, Mill?'

'I don't know. What time will Mrs Oak be back?'

'She'll be here for the evening shift. Why?'

'I don't know.'

'Well, I can't help you then if you don't know, can I?'

'I was going to ask for a few days off.'

'Oh yeah? How many days?'

'Three, I think?'

Trish had turned round in her chair then and looked at her. 'You know he's been seeing someone else?'

'Who has?'

Trish gave her a long look.

'No, I didn't know.'

'You want to know who she is?'

'No.'

'But you want to go with him anyway?'

'Yes.'

'You sure about that?'

'I am.'

'You go on, love. I'll get Mylo to fill in for you. You get yourself ready. I'll sort Mrs Oak out, don't worry.'

'Are you sure, Trish?'

'Yeah, go on. We all deserve a chance at a broken heart, don't we?'

He took her to a small hotel in Reading. It seemed to rain for the whole time they were there, not that it mattered. In the mornings, he went out for his run. Then he brought breakfast to the room on the way back. She loved the sight of him standing there holding the tray, his hair damp and his face flushed. The heat that came off his body. On the third night they hadn't slept at all, just stayed awake and talked. He told her that he'd been seeing someone else but that he was going to finish it. 'I'd have done it before coming here,' he said, 'but she's in Scotland training to be a physiotherapist. I'll phone her before I head off to Berlin. It's been fizzling out, to be honest. I don't think she'll mind all that much.'

And then she told him about the baby.

It had been late on Sunday night when they came out of Paddington station. Dark and grim and lonely. There was hardly anyone around, bar a drunk staggering down Praed Street and a woman in white boots standing in the doorway of a Coral bookies shop. Through the open door of an all-night grocery, an Indian man sat on a high stool and stared at the ground.

He held her hand in the taxi, and when they got to Marble Arch, he put his arm around her and said, 'You know that girl I told you I was seeing? It's Angie. Angie Brennan.'

'Shamie's daughter? Ah, not Angie. I really like her.'

'It'll be all right, I'll phone her tomorrow. I promise.'

'But how could I have not known that?'

'Angie wanted to keep it quiet, the way things are between me and Shamie – it's another reason I've stopped going in. Look, we weren't seeing each other very long and for most of the time

Angie was up in Scotland training. It wasn't what you could call serious, and Angie—'

'Please,' she said, 'stop saying her name. I don't want to know. I just don't want...'

She put her head on his chest and looked out the window. He kissed the top of her head and said, 'I'll call you when I get back from Berlin. I'll call you from there if I can. Don't worry. Everything will be okay.'

It had started to rain. She could feel his words ringing in his chest, the strength of his arm around her. She watched the long drops rolling down the window, the lights from the West End curdling behind them. 'If I die here,' she had thought, 'I will die happy.'

It would be eighteen months or so before she saw him again. New Year's Day 1984. He walked into the bar with a child in his arms. A little blonde head, next to his dark hair. Grandad Shamie beaming beside them.

She had known about the child. She had known that shortly after he came back from Berlin, he married Angie, and that six months on, a baby was born. She had heard it from Trish; she had heard it from Mrs Oak; she had heard it from Shamie. Soon enough, she'd been hearing it from every second punter who had walked through the door.

She would have heard it from him too, but by the time he phoned, it was old news and she had refused to take his call. And when a couple of weeks later his letter arrived, she refused to touch it and told Trish to throw it on the fire.

'We don't have a fire,' Trish had said.

'Well tear it up then, throw it in the bin.'

'What do you mean?'

She'd snatched the letter out of Trish's hand, torn it in half, then torn it again. 'This,' she said as she continued to rip it into shreds, 'this is what I mean. This, and this. And this.'

'Feel better now, do we?' Trish asked.

'Yes, as a matter of fact, we do.'

Whatever about Angie, the child had been a different matter. Carrying her into the pub like that. A little girl, too. And she had thought, really, you would come in here, with your daughter in your arms: after all I told you about Flora, you would do this to me?

She had to put down the glass and go outside.

She was struggling with the lock on the back-yard door when Mrs Oak came out after her. 'You don't walk away from an order,' she said, 'ever. You don't do that. Are you listening to me, Milly?'

'I know. I'm sorry.'

'If this is about him in there . . .'

'It's not about anything. I just need some air.'

'Eating your heart out for the likes of him, really, Milly. Now you get yourself back in there. Tell him his little girl is a princess and ask what's her name. Then ask how his wife is. I'll give you ten minutes and then I'll be in to let them know children are not allowed on my premises. And before you do that, wipe your eyes and tidy yourself up a bit. There's a makeup bag on the corner of my desk.'

8. Pip

2017

June

HE GOES INTO the en-suite bathroom, runs the spray-head around the shower and lifts the damp towels. He hunkers down beside the toilet and washes it like it's a beloved child: behind the ears, under the chin, seat up, seat down. He rolls a squirt of blue-tinged bleach down its throat, then cleans the piss from its porcelain neck.

Last night, a family of Germans departed. The day after tomorrow, a Swiss lawyer and two French couples arrive; the Swiss for three days, the French for a week. He runs through the list in his head. He has laundry to collect, and he needs to give the room the German kids stayed in another quick going-over. Although Germans, so far anyway, are inclined to leave the place in better nick than they find it. The French, on the other hand . . . But the French have been pleasant to deal with, gracious even, admiring the house, leaving thank-you notes and little treats behind them. Even if Dom can barely tolerate the idea of them under his roof – as if everyone born on French soil is somehow responsible for Monique.

Seven o'clock in the morning, and already he feels the heat

of the day and wants to get his jobs out of the way. Between preparing the house for Airbnb and dealing with the flurry of guests, it's been non-stop for the past five weeks. For the next couple of days, there are no arrivals and, with Dom in Glasgow until late tonight, he has the house to himself, at least for today. Maybe he'll do a bit of gardening – guests like to sit in the garden and have a drink on warm evenings. He may sit in the garden himself, read for a bit, have his lunch out there. Later, go to the bank with his newfound earnings, maybe even get a haircut while he's out and about.

He draws the dirty sheets from the bed and drops them in the corner. He pulls the bag out of the dustbin and plonks an empty bottle of mineral water into it. He gets down on his knees and peers under the bed.

A screwed-up tissue, a few sweet wrappers and what looks like a boarding pass. As he reaches in, he feels the old shadows moving around him. It can happen, sometimes for no reason, while he's going about his daily routine. Or it can happen, too, for a good, solid reason – like when he finds himself kneeling on the floor, boarding pass in hand with the words 'TXL/Berlin' printed on it.

He gets up, rolls the dirty sheets into a ball and stuffs them into a black plastic sack. He unpeels the cases from the pillows and he thinks of Berlin where it all went belly-up. Then, he thinks of regret: what melts away and what sticks. After the humiliation and pain had subsided, after the disappointment had finally settled – what had he been left with? Only the circumstances and that one searing image. He would have preferred it to have ended any other way: a knock-out or maybe a narrow decision. A disqualification, even. Nearly thirty-five years down the road and that's the only part that still sticks in his craw.

144

He pulls down the sash windows. Then, dragging the bag of laundry out to the landing, he sees himself as he was then, dropped to the floor before the first punch was even thrown. A twitching mess on a 20 x 20 elevated stage, like something crawled out of the sea to die.

On the way over, Jackie had paid for the flight. A few days later, he was handing him a bus ticket: Berlin to London. No discussion, no explanation: he had done his duty, paid a doctor, had a specialist look him over. And now it was clear, he couldn't wait to see the back of him.

'You should have told me, simple as,' Jackie said. 'Keeping a thing like that a secret, you might have been killed.'

And then, as he slipped a twenty-pound note and thirty Deutschmarks into his hand, 'These Jerries, they know their stuff, no point arguing with them. You just got to accept it, Phil, your boxing days are done.'

On the bus, he turned his head to the window and watched Jackie walk away. Then he pulled the hood of his sweat top over his face and silently wept. But then, somewhere on the long, lonely trip back to London, he had looked out over the darkening lowlands of Belgium or Holland or wherever the fuck they were, and thought, I'd lost the heart for it anyway, and then he thought, had I ever really got the heart for it in the first place? Apart from that first time – the only time he had gone at it with anything like a killer instinct. The only time, too, that he had really wanted to cause serious damage. There had been a pure – perhaps even spiritual – element to his aggression: an elation that he had hoped for, but had failed to find since.

He trawls the hoover up the stairs, releases the cord and plugs it in.

Passing the hoover over the floor of the en suite, he reminds himself that he was a nine-year-old boy that first time and that his mother had just died. He unplugs the hoover and with a gentle kick sends it gliding across the floor into the bedroom. Coming back to the bathroom, he chooses a can from the box of cleaning gear on the floor. He stands at the mirror above the wash-hand basin and looks at himself. Then, with a clockwise squirt of foam, he deletes his own face.

He'd had no idea that she was going to die. She had been feeling a bit poorly and needed to go into hospital for a little while, his father said. Even Dom, at twelve years old, and knowing absolutely everything, hadn't considered death. In fact, he had decided she must be in hospital because she was having a baby. 'Disgusting carry-on,' he said. 'I'm never speaking to either of them again.'

He, on the other hand, had been chuffed to think they would have a new baby for Christmas. There had never been any religion in their house and this sometimes made him obsess about it. It wasn't that they didn't believe in God. God was everywhere, his father said – he was all over nature, he was in the love we showed to one another, the pity we felt for our fellow man. He just wasn't a whole person up in the sky. There was no heaven, and there was certainly no hell. His father didn't tell lies; he couldn't even lie to them about Father Christmas. Like Jesus and God, he was a story made up to make children behave. On Christmas Day they didn't receive toys, just an envelope with money in it, as a reward for good behaviour.

But he had a feeling about this new baby – it was fed by things he'd seen and heard all through December. It was everywhere, on the radio and the television. It was all over the school and in shop windows. He only had to look down from the number 23 bus and there it was: Christmas. New baby. Love. Comfort and joy. They would have a holy baby; there would be a yellow arc of light over its bald little head.

Dom went off the baby idea after a bit. 'Something's not right,' he said. 'Something's wrong.'

Then he sent him up to the attic to look for evidence.

He lay on his belly and looked down through the hatch at Dom looking up from the landing.

'Can you see any baby things – a cot, pram, something like that?'

'No.'

'Well, that's it then. There is no new baby.'

When he looked down into the hall, he could see the hood of his mother's brown coat on the stand, the belt hanging from it. He could see her walking shoes on the floor. He could see part of the clock on the wall. It was something past three and they were still in pyjamas because she wasn't there to tell them what to do, and their father spent most of his day at the hospital.

'There's lots of other things up here, though,' he said. 'Christmas presents wrapped up all fancy with our names on labels.'

'What – actual *presents*?'

'I could see what they are?'

'No.'

'There's a *really* big one for you—'

'No, I said. Get down now before he comes back. There's something wrong, I'm telling you. There's something not right.'

And then she was dead. They were brought up to the hospital and made to sit in a room that smelled like an ashtray. People walking by on the corridor looking in at them. His father's voice: 'We must be brave because she was so very brave . . .' And he had felt a rage churning inside him. He had to keep everything clenched: mouth, hands, feet, stomach, bumhole, just to keep it from bursting out.

How could his father – always going on about the truth – have told them so many lies? And as for his mother – how could she have sneaked off one day when they were at school, without even saying goodbye?

The nurse said to Dom, 'Would you like to kiss Mummy goodbye, Dominick?'

And Dom's voice, high and screechy: 'But she's dead already, isn't she? She's already dead as far as I can tell she is dead so why kiss a dead person if she's already dead is my point?'

When the nurse turned to him, he couldn't speak. He thought of the presents in the attic, carefully wrapped. Their names mis-spelled on the labels. And it seemed so obvious then – someone who worked in a shop had written them. His mother had prob-ably ordered them on the phone before she went into the hospital and had forgotten to tell the salesgirl the correct way to spell their names. Philip with only one l. Dominick with a k.

Why couldn't he have just taken a minute to think about that? He wasn't stupid. He wasn't as clever as Dom in school, but he knew how to work things out. Why couldn't he have been the one to say, 'Something is wrong, something's not right.' Instead of getting all excited about a baby that had never even existed.

The funeral had been in early January. After the graveyard, there was a lunch in a nearby hotel. He couldn't eat his lunch and two women he didn't know kept fussing around him. The man who lived in the basement under their house brought him out to the car park. Mr Moyse was his name. Dom called him Mister Mousey.

'What are you, Phil, left-handed or right?'

'Left.'

'A southpaw then. Good. Now, left is number one. Right is two.

So when I call, you hit – one, two. Well come on then. One, two, that's it. Put a bit more oomph in it, come on. That's more like it.'

He looked around at the rows of cars, the slabs of concrete in between. A man was sitting in a van eating a sandwich, looking at them.

Mister Mousey, in his dark suit with the flat of his hands held up.

'Why are we doing this, Mr Moyse?'

'I'm going to set your punchbag up in the garage. It's as well to get a bit of practice in before you begin.'

'But the bag's not mine.'

'You got it for Christmas – didn't you?'

'That was a mistake. It was meant for Dom. I was supposed to get the trumpet.'

'You've lost me, son,' Mr Moyse said.

He had thought of the day in the kitchen when his mother asked him if he'd like to learn an instrument. He'd been doing his homework, humming along to music on the radio.

'You like music, don't you, Pip?'

'I suppose . . .'

'If you were to learn an instrument, which one would it be?'

'That one,' he said, pointing to the radio.

'The trumpet? You'd have to practise. Every day. You'd have to take lessons. Could you do that?'

'Maybe,' he said, then making barp-barp sounds out of the side of his mouth, he went back to his homework.

'The labels were swapped,' he said to Mr Moyse.

'Swapped? What do you mean swapped? Who swapped them? Speak up, Phil, I can't hear you.'

'I did.'

'You did, Phil? Why would you do that?'

149

'I don't know.'

'But you must have had a reason, son.'

'Dom's present looked bigger.'

'I see. Well, never mind now, eh? Say nothing, is my advice. There's been enough upset in the house as it is. You'll do better than your brother with it, I shouldn't wonder. Leave him to his bugle, eh? What did you say you were again – left-handed or right?'

'That sow thing you said.'

'Southpaw, that's right. Now give me one, two, one two. One, one, one. Two, two. Again. That's it . . . good. That's good, Philip, very good.'

A couple of days later, he went into the garage, took the new gloves out of their bag and screwed his hands into them. Then he looked at the bag that Mr Moyse had hung out of the rafter. He threw it a punch. It gave a little wobble. He punched it again and it swung back at him and hit him on the side of the head. He threw a few more digs at it. He grabbed it around the middle with his right arm and beat his left fist down on it: one, one, one, one.

But it wasn't enough. He needed something more. But there was nothing more, only his nine-year-old self and a lifeless bag stuffed with sand, dangling from the shadows.

He looked at the two big leathery puffs on the ends of his arms. He looked around at the old tins of paint, bicycle bits, the striped cord on a broken heater, the rusty garden rack, the rows of dusty wine bottles that his father had forgotten to deliver. He looked at the cold concrete wall. Then he opened his mouth full-hinge, put up his hands and, screaming like a savage, ran at it. Fists, head, feet, everything.

He didn't remember Mr Moyse coming into the garage and dragging him out. He could remember him patching his face up all right, holding his injured head while he studied the damage. He could remember the way his nimble fingers dabbed and cleaned and stuck plasters on his forehead. In years to come, whenever he sat in the corner and watched the cutman's hands at work, he would think of Mr Moyse and wonder what happened to him.

Mr Moyse put a mirror up to him and told him to take a good look at his face. But it wasn't his face. It was a much older face with a fat lip and a bulge in the centre of the forehead, and long scrape marks at both sides.

'How did that happen?' he'd asked Mr Moyse.

'You were whacking your head off the concrete wall and chumping yourself in the face. You'll end up in the looney bin with that carry-on. Promise me you won't do that again. Can you do that, Phil? Can you promise? Because otherwise, I'm going to have to tell your dad.'

'I promise.'

'We'll say you were climbing that wall out there and you took a humpty and landed on your face. I'll clear up that mess you left in the garage so he'll be none the wiser. I doubt he'll be asking too many questions, the state he's in. You'll be all right, Phil. It'll pass. It will all pass. Does your head hurt something rotten?'

'No.'

'Well, it will do – here, swallow this.'

He picked the tablet off Mr Moyse's open hand and swallowed it down.

'How do you feel now?'

He felt his brain rattling around, searching for pain. And then the exhilaration. And then the excruciating pain, and then the relief.

'I feel okay now, thank you, Mr Moyse.'

*

In the room Dom calls the conservatory, he lies on an Indian rug and puffs his way through a few press-ups. He is vaguely aware of a noise out on the street – a large, lumbering sort of commotion. At the same time, he is considering having another go at that meditation carry-on recommended by the nurse in the clinic. The idea – as far as he can make out – is to turn your mind into a river, let the thoughts drift along like leaves. The last time he tried, his thoughts showed no interest in drifting; they preferred to jump up and be counted. He ended up with a pain in his head and a glut of memories to contend with for the rest of the day.

He decides that instead of meditation, he will have a nice leisurely breakfast. Recalling the few sausages left in the fridge and the four eggs waiting to be scrambled, he flops down on his belly and stays gasping for a moment. He lifts his head to a long view of the dining table, and beyond it, the expansive kitchen. On the back wall, a trio of clocks: New York, Tokyo, London. The London clock is out of order. But he knows from previous dealings with these clocks that if it's five in the afternoon in Tokyo and four a.m. in New York, then it has to be nine in the morning in London.

Under the island counter, a slab wrapped in plastic puzzles him for a second. He stares at it until it settles into a package containing bottles of water – of course. His last Airbnb review mentioned the extra little touches: the water, the tissues (does he need another box of tissues?), the *Time Out* magazine on the dressing table. The good-quality toilet roll – better check the bog-roll situation before he goes shopping.

He turns on his back, bends his legs, puts his hands behind his head and gets ready to aim an elbow at the opposite knee. He waits and listens. That racket outside still going on, and now he notices a hissing within it, and with irritating regularity, a dull beeping sound. And slicing through all that, in a long dry grunt, is the sound of a doorbell ringing.

He opens the door to Max and a girl. Behind them, he finds the source of the noise. A truck with the word 'Rotterdam' painted on its trailer is inching back and forward, hissing and beeping, while a hot-faced driver grapples with the wheel as if steering a boat through a storm.

He hasn't seen Max since he was a kid and would have passed him by on the street. Max, on the other hand, has no trouble identifying him, and even calls him Uncle Phil. In the hallway, he waits while Max unharnesses himself from a hefty backpack. And now here he is, upright, long, thin, piano-fingered: Dom must be pleased with that much, anyhow.

The girl tells him that they've been travelling all night, having hitched a lift – or a ride, as she calls it – from the truck driver in Rotterdam.

'We must look like a right pair of hoboes,' the girl says with a touch of pride and Max fires her a look as if to shut her up, making it clear that he knows about his uncle's time on the road. And what if he does?

He leaves them in the hall and, barefoot, picks his way down the granite steps and the garden path, out to the road and the sweating Dutchman, trapped between two rows of tightly packed cars. He guides him out backwards.

The Dutchman leans out the window to thank him.

'Sorry about that,' he says. 'They could have got out at the top of the street.'

'Yes,' the Dutchman agrees. 'But of course, they did not!'

Then he gives him the thumbs up and his truck waddles away towards Westbourne Grove.

When he gets back into the house, they are in the kitchen

sitting up at the counter, baggage sprawled at their feet. The girl, a cockney by the sound of her, is not introduced. And he remembers Dom telling him that Max's girlfriend was – as he put it – 'a bit of rough', before quickly adding that it was a fashion these days, middle-class girls pretending to be rough. This one seems genuine enough to him. She is probably about Max's age. Slim, very pretty, slight touch of danger about the mouth.

Max says that he's been travelling for the past few months. 'We've just come from Budapest,' he begins and then stops, sighs and, combing his long hair with his long fingers, says, 'Sorry, up all night, tell you all about it some other time.'

'Maybe he don't want to hear all about it,' the girl says then and he thinks, clever girl. Too clever for Max, maybe.

'I'm whacked to be honest. Don't know what day it is,' Max says.

'It's the thirteenth of June,' the girl tells him. 'Tuesday. My cousin's birthday – remember?'

'Oh yeah,' Max says and then, 'Anything to eat, Uncle Phil?'

'Well, there's sausages – that is if you're not vegans? In which case I can scramble a few eggs.'

'You're stereoing us, Uncle Phil,' Max says.

'Am I? Sorry.'

'And even if we were vegans, we wouldn't be eating eggs, now would we?'

They sit there looking at him, making it obvious that he's expected to cook and then serve them. While they wait, Max mills his way through a sliced pan.

'So, I hear you're off to Oxford, Max,' he says as he lays the sausages out on the pan.

'Uheh,' Max says around a bread-stuffed gob and then after a moment, 'We're going to Devon for a few weeks – I told him this.'

'He mentioned Oxford. I just presumed.'

'Oh, he just likes talking about it. I suppose he said I was going "up to Oxford"?'

'No. He just mentioned Oxford.'

He is surprised to find himself covering for Dom, who did indeed say 'up to Oxford.'

'Where is he anyway?' Max asks.

'Glasgow. He should be back this evening.'

'Won't be here this evening, we're going out,' Max mumbles and then, stretching across the table, pulls another slice of bread from the wrapper. 'Do you think I look like him?' he asks the girl, then, 'Mum says I do.'

'Like who?'

'Him, my uncle.'

The girl lifts herself slightly off the high stool and examines him, up and down. She shrugs. 'Maybe. There's a lot more of him than there is of you.'

'How is your mother anyway?' he asks, trying not to look down at or hold in his stomach.

'All right. *She* thinks I'm like you. At least she does when I do something to piss her off. She says, "Oh, but you're so like your *Oncle Philippe*." We moved from Hampstead – did you know?' Max asks then, holding the bread on the palm of his hand as he begins plastering the butter onto it.

'I didn't know you were there in the first place.'

'Oh, we didn't own the flat or anything, we had a landlord. A Russian geezer. Dad paid the rent, I'm sure he's mentioned that.'

'Not that I recall,' he says and then, catching Max's eye, they both laugh.

'Yes, he did,' Max says, pointing the knife at him. 'He bloody did. He never stops talking about how much she cost him. Anyway, she's gone back now.'

155

'To Paris?'

'Once the Brexit shit hit the fan, she panicked. You'd think they were going to break the windows, drag us out and chop off our heads, the way she went on. I said, "*Er no-oh*, actually, it's only you frogs do that sort of thing." She's working in an art gallery – I'm not supposed to tell Dad that, by the way. Going out with some big rich fat cunt named Herman.'

'Language,' the girl says. 'Talking that way in front of your uncle.'

'He doesn't mind, he was a boxer.'

'Now who's been stereoed?' he says and feels sorry then when Max blushes.

He turns back to the frying pan, rolling the sausages around.

Behind him, the girl speaks. 'How come you sound Irish?'

'Because I am – well, half Irish anyway.'

'Which do you identify as?' she asks.

'Identify?'

'Yeah, you know, which would you rather be: British or Irish?'

'Neither,' he says and Max laughs.

'You don't sound like Max's dad. What'd he do – go to elocution classes or something?'

'Maybe I was the one who went to elocution classes?'

The girl laughs. 'You're cool,' she says and then to Max, 'You never said you had such a cool uncle.'

He goes to the fridge, roots the eggs out and begins to explain.

'After Max's grandmother died, we were both sent to boarding school in Ireland. His dad only stayed two terms and then he got word that he'd won a scholarship to study music over here. I stayed till the end. I didn't come to live here full-time till I was around your age, Max – a bit older, probably. And then back in the mid-nineties, I was back there for a few years. I came back to London again maybe ten years ago.'

Max looks away from him, embarrassed. So he knows about the prison stint too, he thinks and begins cracking eggs into a glass bowl.

'So Max,' he begins, 'what will you do in Oxford?'

'You're supposed to say "read",' the girl says. 'All the nobs, they say read.'

'No you're not,' Max says. 'You can say whatever you like. English. That's my subject.'

He listens to them argue behind him while he watches over the eggs. Then he lifts the pan, brings it over to Max and drops three sausages onto his plate. 'You must be clever enough, all the same,' he says.

'Don't sound so surprised, will you?' Max says. 'But no, I'm not. Not really. I just studied my balls off. Anything to avoid finding myself stuck in Paris. I'm still a British citizen, Brexit or not.'

'But you speak French?'

'Only if I have to.'

'Anyway, you're off to Oxford. So you won't be stuck in Paris.'

'Yeah, after Devon. If Dad gives me the money, that is.'

He walks around the island to the girl, drops three sausages onto her plate.

'I used to go to Devon when I was younger,' he says.

'Did you go sailing?' the girl asks.

'Sailing was not on my agenda,' he laughs.

'We're going sailing, with some nobs he knows. I can't stand sailing.'

'How can you not stand something you've never done?' Max asks, raising two exasperated hands in the air.

'I bet I'm seasick, you wait and see.'

'Good, I hope you are.'

'It could blow back in the wind and hit you in the face. That's

157

what happened to my little brother once on the chairoplanes in Southend. Someone in front hurled, and then everyone behind, they all got it in the face. And give over eating all the bread, Max. I want to make a sausage sarnie. You'll have the lot gone, if you don't stop.'

She stands up and pulls the bread towards her. She takes two slices out and, placing them on the marble countertop, daintily begins constructing a sausage sandwich. He spoons the eggs onto their plates, then goes back to the sink and holds the kettle under the tap. He can hear the girl's voice over the clatter of water.

'Were you really a boxer?' she says.

He plugs the kettle in. When he turns round, she is still waiting for an answer.

'A long time ago,' he says.

'Were you famous then?'

'Not in the least.'

'Why not?'

'I didn't stick at it long enough. Or maybe I just wasn't good enough.'

'Yes you were,' Max says. 'He was, he was in the papers.'

'How do you know I was in the papers?'

'We have cuttings upstairs.'

'What – you mean your dad kept cuttings of my fights?'

'No. My grandad. They were in a box I found upstairs before we moved out. Those are serious sausages, Uncle Phil – where'd you get them, Waitrose?'

'No, a butcher's shop on Golborne Road.'

He watches them eat with dirty hands; the girl a little more reserved in her manners.

'There's a couple left . . .' he says.

'Yeah, great,' Max says.

He lifts the pan and flicks a sausage down onto Max's plate then he brings the last one over to the girl.

'Were you pro?' she asks, widening her eyes up at him.

'Pro what?'

'You know, professional. When you was boxing?'

'For about five minutes.'

'Cool,' she says, flashing a tooth stud as she gave him her best smile. 'Why'd you stop? Did you kill someone? Is that it?' She gazes up at him hopefully.

'No that's not why I stopped.'

'Why did you stop?'

He doesn't want to say it was because he threw an epileptic fit in the ring, so he decides he may as well ride on his reputation. 'I just found something I liked better.'

'Like what?'

'Drinking.'

'Drinking! Oh, that's brilliant, that is.'

He thinks of Milly suddenly, not because the girl in any way reminds him of Milly. They have nothing in common. Unless, a time when he sat at the kitchen table with her in the middle of the night shortly after he came back to London after a summer spent on the road. Like Max, he had been scruffy, but unlike Max, he had been ashamed of it and had at least washed his hands before eating. He could remember looking up at her, just as the girl was looking up at him now, as the sausages rolled from the tilted pan onto his plate. He was salivating like a dog and hardly able to hear what she was saying, he was that hungry. It had been a real hunger the sort that never knows when and if it's going to end. Milly ended it that night. She ended everything. Afterwards, they had sat talking in low voices until daylight, while Mrs Oak slept upstairs. Milly holding his hand, weeping. 'Oh Pip, why can't you be, why can't you just be . . . ?'

He turns away, busies himself at the sink for a moment and then says, 'I'll let you have your breakfast in peace. Maybe see you later. Oh, and if you're taking a shower or going for a kip, will you use the old playroom?'

'The playroom?'

'It's a bedroom now.'

'What's wrong with my own room?'

'Your dad has people coming to stay the day after tomorrow. And he's sleeping in the room beside his music room.'

'He's what?' Max laughed.

'He'll explain later. Just, if you can stay out of your old room.'

'What do you mean my old room? It's still mine, isn't it?'

'Yea, of course it is. He'll tell you about it later.'

'Did he leave me anything?' Max asks.

'Like what?'

'Money? Did he leave me any money?'

'Not that I know of. Was he expecting you home today?'

'Not exactly. I mean I texted we wouldn't be back till next month, but then we ran out of money, you see, and . . . my mate Will asked us to Devon and so . . .'

'He should be back tonight.'

'But we're going out. We can't go empty-handed.'

'I'm sure your friends will understand, Max.'

'I can't go out if I'm skint.'

'Text your dad then, let him know you're here. He might get an earlier train.'

Max pulled out his phone. A flutter of thumbs and fingers and he put the phone down.

'Did you miss it when you stopped?' the girl asks.

'What – the boxing? No.'

'Still, it must have been dead exciting. Did you meet what's-his-name, that Ali bloke, Muhammad, whatever?'

'Before my time.'

'What about that other one, Mike Tyson, did you meet him?'

'After my time.'

'You don't give much away, you!' the girl laughs.

Max's phone pips. He picks it up and reads the message.

'Right, that's it,' he says to the girl, 'we can forget it now.'

'What's he say?'

Back late, don't wait up. Welcome home. Sleep in playroom. What is this with the playroom all of a sudden? Like what am I – six?' Max lifts the phone to his face and scowls into it. 'Thanks, Dad,' he says. 'Thanks a fucking bunch.'

He's turning to leave the room again when the girl pipes up, 'It's my cousin's twenty-first, you see. We wanted to buy something for her. We can't go with no pressie. What would they think? My aunties, all my cousins? They'd be ashamed of me, they would.'

He stops and looks back at her. She's sitting on the edge of her stool now, simpering at him. He waits to see what she'll come up with next.

'We're meeting in a pub on Bramley Road. It's called the Pig and Whistle – you know it?'

'Yea, I know it.'

'My cousin, she's just moved into a flat on the estate behind it; she's got a baby I haven't even seen yet. She's on the top floor. She calls it the penthouse, but she's just joking – it's council so it's probably a dive. You know where I mean? The towers.'

'Yea, I know where you mean.'

'That's where the party is. We need to get something for the baby. And Max was going to buy me a pair of shoes. Nothing fancy, just, you know?'

She lifts her foot to show a hole in the sole of her runner.

'And I need a dress. One of those throwaway things from Queensway will do. You know, something that looks okay for one night but there's no point in washing it cos it just falls apart. I don't want to let myself down, do I? You can come if you want – to the party, I mean. Or just the pub, if you don't fancy the party.'

'I don't go to parties or pubs.'

'Why not?'

'I'm an alcoholic.'

She gives a little gasp, laying her hand on her breast. 'Oh yeah, of course, the drinking.'

He walks back across the kitchen to his sulking nephew.

'I can give you fifty quid, Max.'

'Oh, thanks.'

He takes out his wallet, pulls a fifty out and then after a second, takes out another fifty. 'Consider it a down payment for all the birthdays I missed. Just one thing, though.'

'Yes, Uncle Phil?'

'Clean up this mess when you're done.'

'Sure, yeah. Absolutely.'

'And stay out of your room and your dad's old room.'

'Yeah, I know. Keep to the playroom like a good little boy!'

In his room, he looks up at the Velux window, a square of taut blue with a bird floating across it. He gets up, takes the hooked pole from the corner, curves it onto the catch and gives it a push. A release of morning air, like warm breath on his face, the startled flutter of wings departing. He can smell cut grass from a neighbouring garden and new bread from a nearby bakery. The gurgling drone of pigeons, the sound of a bus in the distance.

He gathers his things: glasses, pills, bottle of water. He drops them into a Sainsbury's bag and then looks at himself in the mirror. Yes, he mutters, you'll look like an old man barrelling around with your Sainsbury's bag, but at least you're less likely to lose anything.

He checks his back pocket for the list of messages Dom left on the counter yesterday. He'd better double – no, triple – the quantities with that pair of hoovers down there. He takes his wallet out of his back pocket and slips it into the bag. He takes his phone from the top of the bookcase and slips it into his pocket. Now he's nearly right. If he's going to loiter around the park and have lunch out, he'll need a book to keep him company. He stands for a moment, running his eye over the bookcase before deciding on the copy of *The Waste Land*.

It's four o'clock in the afternoon when he gets back to the house. The waft of dope hits him in the face as he opens the hall door. The whine and thump of some sort of music coming from an upstairs room. He goes down the hall and takes the few steps down to the kitchen. The breakfast mess hasn't been touched – if anything, it has been added to. Crisp bags, chocolate wrappers, a cardboard six-pack of beer, four of them now empty, sitting in the middle of the island, surrounded by dirty dishes. He opens the fridge door, another box of beer inside. Quickly, he puts the messages away and decides to leave the mess as it is.

As he climbs the stairs, the whining music increases. The door of Dom's old room is open – the room he spent an hour cleaning this morning. Dirty clothes now heaped on the bed and he can see a trail of wet towels on the floor of the en suite. The music is coming from behind the shut door of Max's old bedroom. He gives the door a thump.

'I thought I asked you not to go in there?'

The music stops. A brief silence. Then a giggle and a snort.

'And I thought you were going to clean up the mess? Do you hear what I'm saying to you? Clean up that mess, Max,' he says, 'because I won't tell you again.'

'Is that a promise?' the girl says and then they both start choking with laughter.

'You little prick,' he mutters.

As he reaches his own room, the music starts up again. He can't hear it as such, just a loud thump-thumping that makes it sound as if the house itself is having a heart attack. He stands for a moment and considers going back down. But then he realises that Max is Dom's problem, not his, and best avoided till he heads off to Devon. He takes off his shoes, lies down on the floor and sticks his earplugs in. A woman's husky voice tells him to breathe in and out. Then she tells him to follow his breath, 'as if it's the first breath you have ever taken.'

She's just got to the river of drifting thoughts when he hears the front door slam. The pounding has stopped. He gets up, tears the earplugs from his ears and goes down one flight to the landing window. They're at the gate. The girl, in her metallic bum-freezer, skinny little legs dangling on spiky heels, looks like an iridescent bird. Max looks about the same as he did at breakfast, only cleaner. He watches them for a moment, walking away down the street holding hands; Max running his fingers through his newly washed hair, the girl pulling at the arse of her dress. Ah, good luck to them, he decides – he should have locked the Airbnb bedrooms anyway. And that's exactly what he will do now, as soon as he's cleaned them out again. Lock the doors and hide the keys.

Once again, he looks forward to the evening ahead: an empty house, a steak for dinner, feet up on the couch in front of the telly with a good strong cup of tea.

He only seems to have been five minutes in bed, when he finds himself waking up again. There's a smell of burning in his nostrils and he feels as if he is on the edge of something. He thinks he could be about to have a fit. But when he opens his eyes, he feels steady enough and the smell is real. He thinks: fuck, there's something on fire, that pair of fucking dope-heads came back from the party and left something on the hob.

He turns on the light, jumps out of bed and runs down to the kitchen. But the kitchen is calm and in darkness. He sniffs his way back up to the hall. Dom's trumpet case is on the floor by the wall, his overnight bag beside it. He checks out the music room. Then the room where Dom now sleeps. He finds the keys to the Airbnb rooms and opens each door. He checks every room in the house. No Dom. Max and his girl are still out.

As he makes his way back up the stairs to his room, the smell of burning reaches down to meet him and, when he steps into his room, he realises that it's coming through the open Velux window. In its frame, a halo of orange against black. He comes back downstairs and opens the patio doors and now he can see, somewhere over Lancaster Road direction, a huge ball of fire against the wall of the sky. A plane, he thinks, a terrorist attack. But the fire is shooting upwards not down, reaching out in long, muscular flames. He can hear the sound of screeching sirens now, the noise multiplying by the second. Voices nearby – on the far side of the house. He can't make out what the voices are saying but even so, he can sense a collective feeling of dread. He goes back through the house and opens the front door.

And for the second time in twenty-four hours, he finds himself standing barefoot out on the road. This time, he is surrounded by neighbours usually only seen from a distance, caught between the opening and closing of a front door or climbing in or out of a car. Most of them are in nightclothes; some, like him, in bare feet. All with their faces turned towards the top of the road, where ambulances and fire engines tear past, screeching. Some people are looking at the screens on their phones. One man behaving as if he is a news reporter. 'It's going up, yes going up, it won't be contained. The whole tower, it would appear. It looks like they're carrying people out. Unbelievable scenes I'm looking at here.'

'What's going on?' he asks a man standing beside him.

'I'm not sure. A fire.'

'Yea, but where?'

'Those towers, you know, over that way.'

'Near Bramley Road?'

'I don't know Bramley Road. I've never been down there.'

A woman in a hijab holding a toddler in her arms turns around and says, 'Grenfell, it's called. Grenfell. How could you not know that?'

And then, somewhere between hearing the woman say the name of the tower and imagining his nephew and the girl going up in flames, he feels his mind cleave. He can hear his own voice: 'What time is it, do you know?' it asks a woman in a red dressing gown standing nearby, hand clamped to her mouth. He can hear his voice ask her a second, then a third time, until she turns to him without unclamping her mouth and says, 'I don't know, I told you. Three a.m. maybe, something like that.'

A man beside him, holding a phone, is also in bare feet. The man has a shirt on, open down the front. He can see a blue fire on the fuzz of the man's belly. He looks down at the man's toes. Then the slippers of the woman standing in the red dressing gown beside him. Then his own lumpy feet. The woman in the hijab puts the baby down. The toddler looks up at him. Big black curls and a languid face. He is holding a bottle in his mouth with one hand; with the other he's twirling a curl around his index finger. Soft eyes blinking a message at him as he sucks away on his bottle. This is how you do it. This is all you really need.

'Was there a party?' he says to no one in particular. 'You know, a party in the tower?'

'Sorry, mate?' the man with the open shirt says. 'I don't know how it started.'

'No, no, I'm not asking if it started at a party, I'm just wondering do you know if there was a party in, you know, that tower, if you heard anything about that?'

'Sorry, mate,' the man says again and goes back to his phone.

He tries the woman in the red dressing gown again. 'It's three in the morning, did you say?'

She looks at him, aghast this time. 'Why do you keep asking me what time it is?'

'I don't know,' he says.

But he does know. He's asking because he's trying to figure something out. What, though? Where to get a drink, that's what. Where to get a drink at this hour of the night. He wants a drink. No, he *needs* a drink. Really, really needs one. Not a pub drink either; none of this waiting at the counter while a barman faffs around with bottles and glass and money. Something swift and continuous, that's what he needs. Something instant. He wants to dive in. He wants to fucking drown in it, from the inside out.

'Three o'clock, did you say?' he asks her again, and she glares at him before sidling away.

Spinning lights belt across the top of the road. *Screeeeching* sirens. His mind shifts. He looks at the toddler again. He feels like pulling the plug on his bottle, jerking it out of his greedy little mouth and flinging it over the bushes into one of those gardens because he needs, *really* needs, to feel the weight of his own bottle in his own hand, right now.

Shadows around him, somebody crying. The self-appointed, on-the-spot reporter still at it. 'I don't know if that's a person I'm looking at jumping over the side, or a bit of the tower breaking away.'

Someone is saying: fuck, oh my God. Fuck oh my God. He can't tell if it's coming from a phone or from someone standing behind him.

Fire throbbing over North Kensington into an already over-warm night. He begins to think: it could easily find its way down here; it could come after us. Walls of rolling flames, street after street, larruping through the gaps in the houses. 'We need to get out of here,' his voice says. But no one is listening or no one can hear him with that incessant fire-engine shrieking. Voices on the phone, the child suck-suck-sucking on that fucking bottle.

He imagines himself tearing his rooted feet from the ground, turning and running. Running towards Talbot Road, taking the back route to that off-licence up near the library. Running like he used to do when he was a young man, the push of his feet on the ground, the fuh, fuh, fuh of his breath on the air. The off-licence would be closed but the owner? Surely he would be up, with all that noise, those flashing lights outside? He could bang down the door anyway. Offer a tip. Twenty quid on top of the purchase price. More if he wants – fifty, you want fifty? No problem. Plus the cost of a bottle of Jameson's. Make it two bottles, just to be on the safe side.

It occurs to him then – I have no money. I have to go back into the house for money. For shoes to run in. But if I'm back in the house, why bother with the off-licence at all? Why not just . . . ? He nearly laughs out loud.

And now he sees himself, charging up to his room, packing his stuff, putting on his shoes, down to the music room where, before his arrival, Dom had discreetly relocated the contents of the cocktail cabinet. Down on his knees pulling out bottles, sticking them into the bag, one, two, as many as he can fit. And then run like the clappers.

Leave the street behind, go south towards the river. Away from the smell of burning fumes and the screaming sirens and the crying women and the small rectangles of lit-up phone screens, beaming out visions of hell. Away from Dom's face.

Dom's face when he begins to realise that his son is missing, presumed dead – because at this moment, he feels, he truly feels, that the boy and his girl are dead.

Dead. Because he gave them the money to go out and get stoned and pissed and without that money, Max and the girl, whose name he doesn't even know, would have sat in sulking for the night and driving him mad, but at least they would still be alive. He looks down to find the child has moved right up beside him; nappy hanging down to its knees: ammonia, shit or the smell of burning. All the different smells of burning. Max's long hair, her cheap little dress. The white chemist coat of Eamonn's father. Fumes of perfume, medicine, wool, flesh. And for fuck's sake – no! The blue and yellow flames blasting through the windows of a Volkswagen Polo.

All of this occurs in a matter of moments, because the woman in the red dressing gown is still weaving away from him through the crowd, throwing wary looks back over her shoulder at him. Beyond her, he notices a shape beginning to form at the far end of the road. And there they are suddenly, emerging from the chaos. The only ones moving or facing this way: Dom in the middle, holding each by the hand, as if they are little children. And then

169

he feels the fragments come together again, and with a single sharp sob exploding in his chest, he comes back to himself.

The sight of them staggering down the road, Dom's large frame buckling slightly. The girl sobbing while Max's face seems to glide like a death mask under the streetlight. People stepping aside to give them space, presuming – as he has done – that they have been rescued from the fire.

He rushes to meet them.

'They're okay, they're okay,' Dom says, 'let's just get them inside. Take her, will you?' He lets go of the girl's hand and puts his arm around his son as he guides him through the gate.

He takes the girl by the elbow, then half carries her into the house.

He sits her down on a chair in the kitchen, and rushing up to the Airbnb rooms, pulls duvets off the beds and drags them downstairs to wrap around their shoulders.

Max is shaking so much that he has to place his hands over his, in case he drops the cup of sugary tea. He watches the rise and fall of both pairs of hands, his large and rough over Max's slender white fingers, and listens in the background to Dom's laboured breathing.

'Did you have them checked out?' he asks Dom.

'Checked out?'

'You know, did the paramedics check them?'

'Why?'

'Their lungs, the fire. Poisoning?'

'They weren't in the fire.'

'Where were they then?'

'Bramley Road – they were just standing there, watching the whole sorry scene. I'd only just got home; was just in the front door when Max texted.'

'What about the party?'

'What party?'

'They were going to a party.'

'That's the first I've heard of any party.'

The girl is shivering – he can hear the soft tapping of her teeth from across the room. He goes over to her. 'Are you all right, love?'

He hunkers down and looks into her face. 'Look at me, look at me. Are you all right – what *is* your name, by the way?'

'It wasn't really a party,' she says. 'It was just a piss-up.'

'That's okay.'

'It wasn't even her birthday. We just said it was, so you'd give us some money.'

'That's okay. As long as you're all right.'

'Jenny,' she says and then, throwing her arms around his neck, she begins to sob, 'My dad used to call me Jenny Wren.'

'Should I give them a drop of brandy, do you think?' Dom asks.

'I think they've had enough,' he says. 'Better stick to tea, water, wash out their system. You should have one, though.'

'You won't mind? I mean, it won't make you, you know, want a drink?'

'Me? Nah. Of course not. It wouldn't even cross my mind.'

After they finally get Max and Jenny Wren to sleep, he comes out to the front door, mug of tea in his hand. He doesn't know how many hours have passed or if that blue haze over the road is the light of dawn or if it has something to do with the fire.

The street is quieter now, the sound of the emergency services subdued and more distant. There are lights on in windows in the houses across the road and there are still a few people loitering outside, moving around like ghouls. He sniffs the air and is surprised that he can't smell anything now. For a minute he wonders if he's lost his sense of smell, but then Dom walks out behind him, bringing a drift of Rémy Martin.

'What the fuck was that,' Dom asks him, 'the nine circles of hell? You should see the coverage on the television.'

'I don't want to see it.'

The woman in the red dressing gown comes across the street and stands at the gate. 'I'm sorry,' she says, 'if I was a bit . . . you know . . . earlier on.'

'That's all right, love,' he says. 'I was a bit, you know, myself.'

'There's soot all over my friend's window,' she says. 'My friend, she lives off Lancaster Road you see, and, well, she's found bits of this black spongy stuff in her garden.'

The woman stands there turning her head left to right as though looking for something. 'I'm Kim, I live across the road,' she says, 'though we've never spoken.'

She begins to move away from the gate, but then she changes her mind and comes back to it.

'It's not done, you know,' she says, 'it's still going on. Pouches of fire in some of the windows – you can see them, apparently. My friend, she says, well, a lot of people . . . a lot of them are . . . you know?'

They stand looking at one another for a moment.

'Could you do with a cup of tea?' he finally asks.

The woman thinks for a moment. 'I don't know, I suppose,' she says, stepping through the gate before stopping to tighten the belt of her dressing gown and touch her tear-stained face.

'I'll stick the kettle on,' Dom says.

PART THREE

9. Milly

1989

SHE WAS LINKING his arm, keeping steady on heels, as they crossed Bayswater Road. He was getting anxious about the time. She could tell by the choppy movement that had come into his step, the stiffness in his arm as he firmly drew her along. But it wasn't yet twilight; the last of the sunshine flittering down through the plane trees. They were *not* short of time.

Outside Kensington Gardens, some of the artists were already packing up. Others stood around chatting. One man, alone, was sitting on a canvas chair, staring into his own paintings. She had seen this man on a few occasions, always sitting in the exact same way, a flask on the ground beside him, Sunday newspapers rolled behind his back. He wasn't young. His pictures looked faded, as if they'd been painted a long time ago and had never sold. Once, because she had felt sorry for him, she stopped to take a look. But she'd been aware of the man watching her. And there had been an awful moment of when and how to walk away. Now, whenever she came to his section of the railings, she quickened her step and looked the other way.

Past Lancaster Gate, the last painting on the railings caught

175

her eye. It was of a narrow street down by St Paul's, the back view of a man disappearing into it. She thought at first that there was someone walking beside the man, but when she looked again, it was only a shadow. She paused to take a better look but felt a resistance from the arm hooked onto hers, pulling her along. She wanted to say to him: Oh, will you please stop fretting about the time! Why not just enjoy the walk, the first chill of autumn? Let me look at the bloody painting!

He was annoyed because his shortcut had ended up being the long way round. When they'd left the restaurant in Queensway, she'd been certain she'd heard the waiter tell him: turn right, and *then* left. He had been more than certain that it had been the other way round. He'd seemed set on it anyway, and so she let him at it. Besides, she quite enjoyed walking streets she'd never been on before, guessing at the lives behind windows. And some of those houses, the way they leaned into the curve, they were only . . .

She'd said it to him: 'Aren't these white stucco houses only lovely?'

'Stucco – is that what you call them? Glorified tenements, they look to me. All the bells on that door. How many sardines can you squeeze into one can, eh?'

He was not, she was beginning to notice, a man who liked making mistakes.

'J. M. Barrie used to live along here,' she said, just to get a bit of conversation going.

'Who?'

'You know, your man who wrote *Peter Pan*?'

'Oh, right,' he said and then, 'We better step it out a bit, Mill.'

The sky became suddenly dull and now dusk was coming on, the lights from the traffic wobbling towards Notting Hill Gate.

She was wobbling a bit herself. The new shoes. Or maybe it was that last bottle of lager. Special Brew, of all things. Mrs Oak called it rocket fuel and said if it was up to her, it would be banned.

But the restaurant had run out of ordinary lager and she'd thought, what the hell? At least it would help the food go down – he'd ordered such an almighty heap of it!

The restaurant had been recommended by his twin sister Grace, a big bruiser of a girl who had a reputation for 'knowing her grub'.

She had been shocked when she saw the amount of food, the table filling up with plates and bowls of God knows what.

'It's an all-inclusive, Milly,' he'd said. 'Might as well take what we pay for, eh?'

After ten minutes, everything had started to taste the same and she'd stopped eating. She drank the gluey lager and watched him horse his way through the rest.

That was something else she was beginning to notice: when Grace was with him, he didn't eat much and then she leaned in to his plate, helping herself to his leftovers. But when Grace was absent, he milled all around him and left not a scrap behind.

The streetlamps were lit up and she hadn't even noticed them coming on. And now her head was feeling a little light, her bladder a little heavy and her shoes had tightened their grip. Her thoughts were running amok. She would have to rein them in. She turned her head and looked across the road to the window of a café: a white rectangle. Above and beyond it, smaller yellow squares of light chequered across the red-brick buildings that skirted this part of the road. The windows on the house they'd passed a few moments ago should be filled with light by now – a discreet cream colour, she imagined, just enough to show off the blue badge pinned to the wall outside – J. M. Barrie once lived here.

Did he look down from an upstairs window at twilight, she wondered, and, catching sight of a stray flicker from a lamppost, get the idea for Tinker Bell? But of course there would have been different types of light back then, carriage lamps and street-lamps, all lit by gas. She turned to him and almost said it – do you think the idea for Tinker Bell came when . . . But the puss on him! Moving her on with a determined eye as if they were being followed or something. God, she thought, I am a bit drunk. Tinker Bell? Oh, he'd love that all right!

But he knew who Peter Pan was; the first time they'd gone on a walk together, she'd taken him to Kensington Gardens. He said he'd heard the name all right, but had neither read the book nor seen the film. He'd thought it was only hilarious that she'd gone to see the film on her own, as an adult. He'd said: with not even a kiddie in tow, Milly?

She had pitied him that day for the boils on the back of his neck and the lemon-coloured polo neck he'd been wearing which she took to be an attempt to disguise them. They had sat on a bench just before the park closed. He was a nice enough kisser, she had thought, if a bit dribbly.

The boils were gone now – if not the polo necks – she'd asked Vera to recommend something for them because he'd been too embarrassed to ask for himself. He was still thin as a rake but more wiry than puny now. Carting crates up and down the cellar stairs and changing all those barrels, probably. He had a handsome face – well, quite good-looking anyhow – and he was much more self-assured than he used to be. The way he talked to customers or to Mrs Oak even, who had come to rely on him to help with the accounts.

They even discussed ways to improve business and once, when she was passing the office, she heard him say, 'If you were to cut the ham a bit thinner, Mrs O., it should stretch an extra few days. Over the course of a year, you'd see the saving.'

'Do you know what that's called, Mylo?' Mrs Oak had said. 'That's what's known as a false economy.'

She still pitied him sometimes. She pitied him now. All upset because he thought they were going to be late. He was nervous about the job in Kent, probably. About giving in his notice, if he did get it. But he would get the job – she was certain of that. He'd probably send her a card at Christmas or give her a call on his day off. They might even meet once or twice. Then that would be it. One day he would own his own pub. In ten years' time, she would remember him only as someone from Sheffield she'd gone out with for a few months. That is, if she remembered him at all.

Past Kensington Gardens, he stopped short; she felt herself sway a little.

'Are you all right?' he asked.

'My shoes, they're new. It feels like they're chewing my feet.'

'They're *what*?'

'They're too tight.'

She waited for him to ask, 'Well, what did you wear them for when you knew you'd be walking?'

But he just stood there, frowning at something. They were standing at an archway made of white stone. The word 'IN' was painted in black on the side of it. Through the archway, she could see a sort of hut in the middle of the road with a barrier on both sides like you'd see in a car park. There was a weak light on in the hut, although it appeared to be empty.

'Is this the way?' she asked.

'I'm not sure,' he said, frowning at the 'IN' sign, 'but the bloke in the restaurant said we could go straight through and then . . . but what's that hut about, I'm wondering now?'

'There's nobody in it,' she said.

'It looks a bit official though, don't you think?'

'Come on. We might as well try it.'

And now it was her turn to drag him along.

On the other side of the archway, she forgot everything: her feet, her bladder, the ridiculous thoughts wandering round in her head. 'What is this place?' she asked him.

'The bloke in the Chinese, he said if we walk straight through, we can—'

'But it's such a lovely road,' she said.

He squinted into the distance and said, 'It's bloody long enough anyway.'

There was a row of old-fashioned lampposts on both sides; she could see the space on the ground between them as they crossed over the road and began to walk along. At the top of the posts, a glow pushed through the lanterns, filling the clefts of darkness with a long yarn of wavering light. Yes, she thought, J. M. Barrie could easily have seen a creature dancing around in there.

'Are they gas lamps, would you say?'

He sighed. 'Milly, I really wouldn't know.'

Behind the light, different-sized mansions were set into careful gardens, each one elaborate in its own way. Yet they all seemed to be surrounded by the same ghostly silence. She found it hard to believe that real people were living inside. At the same time, she felt as if she was being watched. It was all a bit spooky, she thought. The misty lights, the watchful houses – even the way the leaves were drifting down from the trees, as if they were creatures sniffing the air.

'Are you listening to me, Milly?'

He was speaking.

'Of course I am.'

'I wouldn't like us to be late, is all.'

'We won't be.'

'I just feel it might seem, you know, a bit—'

'A bit what?'

'You know, disrespectful. And I heard they don't let you into these things if you can't be bothered to arrive on time.'

'Disrespectful?'

'To Mr Wiseman, Milly. After all, he gave us the tickets.'

A glint of brass on the pillar of a house caught her eye. She broke away from him and walked over to read it.

'We could get a taxi, I suppose,' he said, 'but what would that cost?'

'Look at your watch,' she said. 'Tell me the time.'

'Twenty to seven.'

'What time does the concert start?'

'Yes, I take your point. But we don't know how long it might take us to get there is all I'm saying.'

'See those houses across the road, Mylo? Well, Kensington Gardens are just behind them. I know where we are now and I promise you we won't be late.'

He was standing just behind her now, silent for a moment and then, 'You look very nice tonight, Milly,' he said. 'I'm sorry if I'm a bit . . . It's just . . .'

'I know,' she said. 'It's okay.'

She could smell the sweet-and-sour sauce of his breath coming across her shoulder. And now she could taste it, as he turned her around and kissed her.

She pulled away gently, patting his chest. 'These are embassies,' she said. 'See the flags? The brass plates? This is the Norwegian embassy. Isn't it just . . . ?'

'Oh God,' he said, 'are we even supposed to be in here?'

'I'm sure they'd have arrested us by now, Mylo.'

She took his arm and they started walking again.

'I never knew this place existed,' she said. 'How many Sundays have I spent wandering around Hyde Park and Kensington Gardens, and I had no idea . . . Ten years in London and I never even heard of it.'

'You can't see everything, Milly. It's a big city.'

'It's such a lovely road, and yet . . .'

'What?'

'It feels haunted.'

He laughed. 'You say the oddest things sometimes.'

'Do I? I can't say that I've noticed.'

'Well, I bloody 'ave!' he said, and laughed again.

The kiss appeased him. He was in better form now.

'I could take my shoes off,' she said, 'speed us up a bit?'

'Along here? I don't think so, Milly. They'll think we're proper gypsies. Anyway, I can't have you walking the streets in bare feet.'

An image came into her head then: her bare feet moving down a street near the river; a man's hand beside her, carrying her sandals, his jacket square on her shoulders.

'Milly? What are you thinking about?'

'I wasn't thinking about anyone,' she said. 'I mean anything. I was just wondering what the concert . . . what it will be like, that's all.'

'I've never been to one before, have you?' he asked.

'I have. Once.'

'Oh, but not the Albert Hall, I hope?'

'No. Not the Albert. The Barbican.'

'How come?'

'Oh, a customer was playing. You know the fella comes in

sometimes with the crowd from the Barbican on Friday? He plays the trumpet?'

'I know who you mean. He never brought you to a concert, Milly – the trumpet player? Was it a date?'

'God, no. Somebody I knew had a spare ticket and I tagged along.'

'Oh, I see. Well, I hope tonight lives up to it.'

'I'm sure the Albert Hall will be much swankier,' she said, squeezing his arm. 'We'll have a lovely time. And look, Mylo – look ahead up there. We're nearly at the top of the road now. When we turn left, we'll be on Kensington Road, it's only about fifteen minutes from there!'

They came to the gate of the Romanian embassy.

'You have to admit,' she said, 'that it looks a bit spooky. Do you think Dracula lives there?'

'Milly?' he said.

'Do you think he's looking at us through the side of one of those windows? Or standing under those trees there.'

'Milly? Milly, would you think of marrying me?'

'What did you just say?'

'Would you marry me, do you think?'

She gave a little laugh. 'Well, that's a bit sudden, isn't it?'

'Sorry. I didn't mean to spring it on you. I meant to wait till Christmas. Sorry, Milly. Sorry, I've given you a shock.'

'No, it's just . . . It's just I wasn't expecting—'

'We could make a good go of it, you and me. Get our own place. You know that interview I went to for assistant manager for the place in Kent? Well, they have another pub in a village nearby. The couple that runs it want to retire. Me and Gracie went to look at it last week on my day off.'

'You brought Grace to see it?'

'For a second opinion. A woman's view, if you like, before I spoke to you and that. She thought it was right nice. She said you'd be well chuffed with the place. It's a proper village, not too quiet you know. Pond and a green and a few small shops. Tea rooms. And I noticed a cricket club too.'

'Do you play cricket, Mylo?'

'Well, no, I meant for business – they'd come in afterwards, wouldn't they? I think you'd like it, Milly. We'd be our own bosses.'

'Yes, but that's hardly a reason to get married!'

'Ah no, that's not why I'm asking you, Mill. You know it's not. You must know how I feel about you. But look, think about it anyway, would you? I mean, you'd make a great landlady. Sorry. I mean . . . I just find it hard to say these things but I'm mad about you, really I am. I do love you, Milly. You know that. And I don't see the shame in saying that I think we make a good fit.'

'Okay, that's enough now,' she said. 'I'm not thinking straight. I drank a bit more than I'm used to. That Special Brew! My God. Let me think it over. I swear I had no idea. I'm flummoxed here, that's all I can say. I'm just . . . I can't . . . I just can't think.'

'We won't say another word about it for now. But I do hope you say yes, Milly.'

She pulled herself together. 'Okay, thanks, I'll do that. I mean, I'll think about it and that. Anyway, we better get *moving*. Or we really will be late. Come on then. We don't want to miss the start.'

Her hands felt a bit shaky as they climbed the steps to the entrance and followed the crowd into the hall. She could not speak, nor could she look at him when they got inside. As they began to climb the stairs, she caught sight of him in a mirror, his face drawn and his eyes alarmed, as if he, too, was in some sort of shock. On the second staircase, they lost one another and she was glad to feel the press of strangers around her. She noticed red at her feet, mahogany at her hand, the glitter of light overhead. She saw programmes tucked under arms or flapped at sides, or sticking out of the pockets of men's jackets. But she felt absent somehow, as if she had left herself behind somewhere on the way here.

He was five or six steps ahead of her now. She could see her coat in his arms and the turn of his head every now and then, checking to see if she was still behind him. But she could not bring herself to meet his eye to let him know – I am here, it's okay.

When she reached the second floor, he was standing at the wall facing the stairs, the coat like a bride in his arms. She lifted her hand and pointed to the queue outside the ladies' toilet at the far end of the corridor.

When she finally came out, he had moved up the wall and was waiting to greet her.

He said, 'All right, Mill?' and then, 'There's a piece of loo roll stuck in the back of your shoe, by the way.'

'Yes, I know,' she said, 'my heel is bleeding.'

She hung back as their tickets were being checked, allowing a couple to walk ahead of her, and again, she was glad of the distance.

Her sore heel slowed her up as she made her way down the slope of the auditorium and she felt a touch of vertigo as she tried to find her bearings. Mylo, by now, was quite a few steps ahead of her, she could see him down there, looking at the tickets then studying the seat numbers at the end of the row. There was an old man just ahead of him. She didn't notice much about the old man at first, other than his position, until she saw his hand reach out as if he was going to grab onto Mylo's arm. And then his knees gave a sort of buckle and his whole body swayed. Behind the old man, a woman who was just about to turn into her row of seats dropped her handbag and tried to stop the fall. But the man slipped her grasp, and then he was down, his head hitting the side of the step. The woman was kneeling by him now, saying, 'Oh, oh my goodness. Are you all right? Are you all right?' And then, 'You'll be all right; you'll be all right. Just don't move, stay easy now.'

The man was trying to get back up, but his legs failed him. The woman, who was slight and not that young herself, couldn't manage the man, anyone could see that.

She looked down at Mylo, expecting him to at least go to the woman's aid. It was obvious that he had seen the incident. But Mylo had turned the other way and was sidling along a row of seats. A small group formed around the fallen man and someone was helping the woman to her feet. Then a voice came from behind, asking to be let through. A manager appeared, followed by a man and a woman dressed in a St John Ambulance uniform. In a moment it was all over, the old man was being led away and the manager was assuring everyone that he would be all right and asking them to take their seats.

She watched as the old man was guided back up the steps, a uniform on both sides. A handsome old face, a small comma of blood over one eyebrow.

'Are you with someone, dear?' one of the uniforms was asking.

'No, I came alone – my wife, you see, she's . . .'

'Of course, dear, that's all right. We'll take you into the light where we can have a good look at you. All right, dear? Don't you worry, Norman here has a hold of you. That's it, dear. Almost there.'

When she sat down beside Mylo, he said, 'That was a bit unfortunate. Think he'll be all right?'

'Yes,' she said, 'I think so.'

'I didn't know whether you'd want a programme or not.'

'No, it's all right.'

'I can get one, if you want,' he said, looking around as if finding a programme would be such a difficult task that it would hardly be worth the hefty price of it.

'No, really, it's fine.'

'Terrible thing to happen, that. Poor old man, eh?'

'Yes, terrible.'

'Are you all right, Mill?'

'Actually, I need to get a plaster. For my heel.'

'Where you going to get that, this hour of the night?'

'I can ask one of the usherettes.'

'Oh? Well, don't be long then. You don't want to miss anything.'

'No. I won't be long.'

She hobbled past the door to the ladies, her shoe gnawing on the broken skin of her heel. Then, continuing along the curve of the corridor, she stopped now and then to look at one of the photographs hanging on the wall: old stars who would always be famous, others she'd never even heard of. There were few people around now and the usherettes were less busy; she made her way down to the last entrance to where one of them was idly standing.

'I was wondering if by any chance you would have a plaster?' she asked, turning her heel to show.

'That's a nasty one,' the usherette said. 'You wait here, my love, I'll get you something from first aid.'

She took off her shoe while she waited. The stinging sensation eased a little and the tightness passed as she unclenched her foot. It was so quiet now, just a few busy steps from staff members making last checks or the odd crackle from a nearby walkie-talkie. Then the sound of a bell ringing.

A couple came running up the stairs, breathless and laughing; the woman about her own age, the man a little older.

'We made it,' he said, grabbing the woman by the waist.

'No thanks to you and your "one more will do no harm",' the woman laughed, slapping him on the shoulder. And then, laughing again, they slipped into one of the entrances, giddy with love, giddy for one another.

When the usherette returned, she asked her about the old man.

'Oh yes, he had a tumble, poor dear. They put him in a box. Oh dear me no, I should probably rephrase that,' she laughed, lowering her voice. 'I mean one of the theatre boxes – easier for him to come and go, poor love. He's all sorted now. Patched up and comfortable. I think it was the fright, more than anything else. It's the embarrassment, isn't it, when something like that happens? He's having a nice cup of tea in there now. Pleased as punch he is. And thank goodness, eh?'

'Yes, thank goodness.'

She kept walking. She could feel the usherette looking at her, wondering what she was at, limping up and down the corridor when the concert was about to begin. The bell rang again, a longer, more persistent ring. She could put it off no longer; she would have to go back in and take her seat beside Mylo.

At the top of the stairs, she watched the last of the stragglers make their way down the steps of the auditorium, then spread out and edge along the rows to their seats. The place was full: a huge bowl of heads and faces. She could see the couple that had come in late picking their way down the steps in search of their seats just under the stage and, on the stage itself, the organ like a golden skyscraper rising behind them.

She didn't know the number of her own seat and couldn't see Mylo anywhere. What if she couldn't find him at all? What did he even look like? And who was he anyway – what did she actually know about him? That he was from a village somewhere near Sheffield. That he had a twin sister called Gracie who ate off his plate. That he was reliable, hard-working, diligent and inclined to be stingy. That he wanted to marry her for reasons that may or may not have to do with love. And finally, that when it came to it, he couldn't be bothered to help an old man.

And then Pip came into her head. Not like a memory, or a half-forgotten hurt. But like a force punching through from her chest and exploding into her mind. Pip would have caught that old man. He would have put out his hand and at least tried. He would not have turned away and pretended not to notice. He would have stayed with the man, too, talking to him, reassuring him until the St John Ambulance people came along.

The lights faded. She was alone here in the shadow above the auditorium. The players were beginning to come out, one by one, settling into his or her place. And now she could hear the sounds of the orchestra tuning up, as if clearing its throat. She had no idea what to do, which way to turn.

Then she saw it: a sky-blue polo-neck jumper rising from the crowd, and from it, a man's arm frantically waving.

By the time they got out of the Albert Hall, she was limping so badly they had to take a taxi. Like two big silent lumps of lard, they waited in line, surrounded by the chatter and laughter of people still waving their 'Land of Hope and Glory' flags.

In the back of the cab, they sat apart and in silence. She thought they were like a couple at the end of, rather than at the beginning of, something.

At Holborn Viaduct, there were roadworks ahead and the cab slowed down. He leaned across to her suddenly, and without thinking she recoiled, pressing her forehead against the taxi window.

Under the streetlight she could see the four statues standing along the balustrade of the bridge. They looked like four big housewives, she thought, caught at the front door in their night-dresses, taking in the milk.

A song came on the radio then: *If you don't know me by now.*

And Pip was with her again, sitting beside her in the cab while Mylo was standing with the statues out on the bridge, in his sky-blue jumper, watching them drive away.

As the cab reached the winged lion at the end of the bridge, Mylo touched her on the arm, and when she turned around, she had to stop herself from saying, 'Mylo – what are *you* doing here?'

'I've something to say to you, Milly,' he began.

'Yes?'

'I'm going to stay out of your way. In so far as I can do, given that we work together. But outside of the work situation, I'll leave you in peace. Can we say a week at most? I wouldn't like to have to wait any longer than that. I want you to make the right decision; we neither of us need to make a mistake. Let's be honest about it, Mill – you and me, we're nearly thirty and—'

'Excuse me,' she said, 'I'm twenty-eight.'

'Of course, I didn't mean to— I'm sorry, Milly, I'm just a bit . . . Well, you know, nervous. I don't want to crowd you, that's all.'

She felt sorry for him then, his forlorn face washed by the lights of the passing traffic; the way his voice sounded, like a frightened little boy.

For the next few days, she pushed through the hours. She couldn't bear the idea of being in the bar with Mylo after closing time, watching the finickity way he lined up the ashtrays before wiping them; the way he counted the beermats with his lips moving.

She told Trish she was feeling run-down and asked if she could knock off at ten o'clock for a few nights to catch up on her sleep.

She told herself she needed time on her own to think about Mylo's proposal, and did her best not to think about Pip.

She had no idea where he was living now. It was nearly six years since he'd last walked into the pub with his little girl in his arms and since then, there had only been rumours. He was living in Glasgow. He was single again. He was back in London. He was gone again. He had stopped boxing. He was still boxing, but only in hotels on the dinner-and-fight circuit or in other unlicensed bouts where they made up the rules as they went along. He was working as a labourer for a builder in Kilburn. He was staying with his brother and doing a bit of sparring on the side. He was living with an Australian girl in Shepherd's Bush. He was gone again. He was back again. He was bare-knuckle fighting with the gypsies in Epsom.

It could still leave her on edge whenever she heard he was in London. The idea of him being in the same city. When she went out, she would sometimes find herself wondering, what if he comes around that corner? Or walks out of that pub? What if I see him coming down the escalator in King's Cross station? But by and large, she felt that she had weaned herself off him. Although the odd time, he would still come into her head – a smell or a sound, or if she saw someone who bore a slight resemblance to him, that could trigger it too. His brother, who sometimes came in on Friday night with Marj after the Barbican. Or his father, who occasionally accompanied them. The brother, she thought, looked more like the father, yet there was something

about the father's head, his quiet way of sitting, the way he sometimes placed his hands flat on the table before he said something.

Five years was too long a time to hold either torch or grudge
for any man. It embarrassed and even irked her to think of that
time now, all the tears she had shed. But she wished him no harm;
she didn't have to – from what she'd been hearing, he brought
enough of that on himself.

Mylo's proposal was like a hump on her back – she was worn out
carrying it around. It was beginning to affect her work. She was
making mistakes in the orders and when customers were talking
to her, she could hear the words but couldn't always get the
meaning. Trish had started giving her funny looks and she could
only be grateful that Mrs Oak was in Malta with her bridge club
ladies. Every time she lifted an eye, Mylo's worried face seemed
to be hovering in the background. She did not believe that he
loved her. She believed he was confusing sex with love. They had
done it a few times already. It was fine. It was nice. It was manage-
able. The first time she'd sneaked him up to her room he'd been
a bag of nerves. She'd thought he was just afraid of being caught.
It didn't take long, though, to realise he was nervous because he
hadn't done it before. Although he never let on. In fact, he tried
to play the experienced but considerate man, asking her if she
was all right every few seconds, so that in the end, she'd felt like
saying to him, Oh, just do it, for Christ's sake. Just hurry up and
get it over with, will you?

Afterwards, he couldn't keep the grin off his face. He called her
'Pet' and asked her a few times what she was thinking, as if he
expected her to say, 'Oooh, I think I'm in heaven, Mylo.' When all
she was thinking really was that he had balled his socks together
before he got into her bed.

Her thoughts kept coming back to his sister. He had discussed it with Gracie as if he'd been thinking of buying a second-hand car. She could imagine the pair of them talking it over on the way home on the train, Gracie munching through a large bag of Maltesers – 'Oh, but she's a scrawny old thing really, Mylo – could you not do without till summat better comes your way?'

'But I love her so much, Grace. She's a real grafter; and a good steady hand, too, for shaving wafer-thin slices off the back of a ham.'

Besides, she was a city girl now. Concrete and glass and fumes made up her landscape and she had no wish to go backwards to hedges and grass and the smell of cow shite. The idea of living in the country! Village life was village life, no matter how prettily it presented itself. It would have the same hardness, the same unforgiving nature, as the village in Ireland where people had nothing to do but watch one another. And no escape either, even going for a walk along a deserted lane or crossing somebody's field – in the country you're always noticed. Here, all she had to do was close the door behind her, get on a bus and within five minutes, she was looking down at a world of strangers going about lives that she didn't have to care or know about. When she walked among them, she was invisible and at the same time part of something. She loved everything about her life in London: the buildings, the shops, the statues, the people. And the way there was always somewhere new to discover – like that eerie road with the embassies on it. She loved her work, too: always, she had someone to talk to or have a cup of tea with at the end of the day. She was respected and also protected by Mrs Oak and Trish, even the customers.

Could she give all that up, she wondered, for Mylo and – let's face it – Gracie?

*

In the end she said yes, though she wasn't sure why. She followed him out to the yard on Friday morning and told him. He kissed her behind a stack of beer crates, then he ran inside to phone Gracie with the news.

They decided to wait till Christmas Eve before making the announcement. He would inform the people in Kent that they would be ready to take up the position as soon as the present incumbents retired which, he reckoned, should be around the end of January.

'I doubt Mrs Oak will mind if we hang on a few weeks. Give her a chance to replace us. 1990, eh, Mill? What a start to a new decade! My own boss and a married man. Could I ask for anything more?'

The minute she accepted she was filled with dread. She would become Mrs Mylo Martin. She would spend her holidays in Yorkshire with his maiden aunt. She would share the same Christmas table with Gracie, year after year, after year. Until one of them died.

At the same time, there was an element of relief. She was sleeping again, her head, if not her heart, felt easier. She had removed all other possibilities – she had freed herself from Pip.

That Sunday, Grace invited them to her flat on Ladbroke Grove for a slap-up dinner.

'We can go for a walk after,' Mylo said. 'We'll need to after Gracie's Yorkshire puds. We can discuss the wedding, maybe go window shopping for a ring in Hatton Garden on the way back? We can talk about our future.'

And she felt happy enough after they left Gracie's, holding hands with Mylo as they walked up Ladbroke Grove. Mylo slightly tipsy beside her, cracking his little jokes.

And then she saw him. He was on the other side of the road, waiting to cross over. A girl by his side.

She turned her head the other way and tried to keep Mylo talking. But Mylo had already spotted him. 'Isn't that him that used to be a boxer – that Phil?' he said. 'You know, the brother of the trumpet player?'

'No,' she said. 'I don't think so.'

'Pretty Boy, Trish used to call him.'

'Oh come on, leave them, Mylo. Please. I want to have a look at the rings before it gets dark. And I'd like a cup of coffee first.'

'You could have had a coffee in our Gracie's.'

'I know, but I fancy going into a café, just the two of us. I don't feel like stopping to talk. Ah, Mylo!'

But Mylo had already stepped up to the kerb and was waiting for them.

He was standing right in front of her now, while Mylo and the girl rabbited on.

'We just got engaged,' Mylo announced. 'But it's a secret, mind. Not a word to anyone.'

The girl squealed. 'Oh that's lovely, congrats! Ohhh, that's really nice to hear, you make a lovely couple. Don't they, Phil?'

'Lovely,' he said, leaning into her and kissing her cheek. 'Congratulations, Milly.'

She could feel him staring at her but couldn't bring herself to return the look.

'Come on, then,' the girl said, 'let's see the ring!'

'Oh, we haven't bought it yet,' Mylo said, 'we're going to stop by Hatton Garden on the way home, do a bit of window shopping. Get an idea of what we want before we buy. Because these blokes, they can push you into it, can't they, once they see you're keen? Hike up the price, or give you something they can't shift otherwise. And Milly here, she'll be wearing it a long time.'

The girl beamed – lovely teeth, a pretty girl, a blonde. But weren't they always? Milly thought.

'We're off for a drink,' the girl said then. 'Why don't you come along to celebrate?'

'We can't,' she said, 'we're in a hurry. But thanks anyway.'

'You still at the boxing?' she heard Mylo say.

'Not really, no. A bit of sparring now and then. Or stand-in.'

'What's that then?'

'You know, if someone pulls out of a fight.'

'Oh right. We're moving to Kent. Getting our own place, we are. Not a word, mind. We've not given in our notice to Mrs Oak yet.'

'Well, good luck with everything,' he said, and then to the girl, 'We better get going or we'll be late.'

'For what?' The girl laughed.

'Congratulations again,' he said and shook Mylo's hand. Then he took the girl by the elbow and pushed her through the door of the Ladbroke Arms.

'You know, I always liked him,' Mylo said. 'I mean he's a bit, you know, wild, I suppose. But a decent sort, I always found, underneath it all. Don't you think?'

'I don't really know him, to be honest.'

'Although they say he treated Shamie's daughter something shocking. I tell you what, though – he don't look so pretty now, does he? Trish will be disappointed.'

They went into a café down the road; she thought it might be a Turkish café or maybe Greek. It was winding down after lunch and they sat at a table at the front and ordered coffee. Mylo was talking about some training course they would have to take. Then he was asking her something about the pub in Kent, suggesting times and ways to go down to see it together. Then he was talking about Mrs Oak. Now and then, she heard herself say, Yes, all right. Okay. Why not? If you like. I don't mind.

At the far end of the café, people were standing up and putting on coats. Families saying goodbye to other families: girls in pink frocks, boys with hair slicked to the side, mothers with stiff hairdos, men in suits. The language of home slipping through their English accents: *guleh guleh guleh*, it sounded like.

Mylo was still talking. And she still didn't know what he was saying. Then he stopped suddenly and touched her hand. 'Are you all right, pet? You seem a bit . . . ?'

'I've a terrible headache,' she said. 'I hoped the coffee might help but—'

'It's not done? Maybe we should go back so you can have a nice lie-down?'

There was a glint in his eye as if he was including himself in the lie-down.

'I'll be all right,' she said, 'let's just go and look at those rings.'

On Tuesday morning she was coming out of Barclays bank and Pip was standing outside.

'What are you doing around here?' she said.

'Waiting for you.'

'Why?'

'I just wanted to see you, to talk to you, I mean.'

'Well that's a shame, because I don't want to talk to you.'

'Don't be like that, Milly. Look, I did try to tell you. I wrote and called but you wouldn't even talk to me.'

'What was the point? I knew, I got it. Angie was pregnant, you were getting married.'

'What could I do?' he asked.

'Is that what you want to talk to me about? That was years ago, for Christ's sake, I'm well over it. As you seem to be.'

'What? The girl on Sunday? I don't even know her. Have a cup of coffee with me, at least?'

'I can't. I have to get back to work.'

'They'll manage. Just for a quick cup. I just need to talk to you. Then I promise I'll leave you alone.'

He took her to a dive on the far side of Smithfield. They sat down the back, in a corner. The floor was sticky under her feet and there was a faded picture of a Page Three girl on the wall. He brought her a mug of coffee and a large whiskey for himself.

'If you're drinking,' she said, 'I don't want to hear *anything* you have to say.'

'It's only one.'

'It's just gone opening time, Pip. And you've already had a couple, I'd say.'

'Dutch courage,' he smiled. His eyes were raw and she noticed he was missing a tooth at the side. He was wearing a long coat, frayed at the sleeves. Either he'd lost a lot of weight or his clothes were miles too big for him.

He said nothing for a moment, just took short, quick sips from his drink, in between played with the glass. She was about to ask him where he was living now, when he said, 'You can't marry him.'

'*What?*' she laughed.

'You just can't.'

'Are you serious? I mean, are you seriously telling me who I can marry?'

'Milly, listen to me. You can't—'

She stood up then. 'What am I even doing here? Look, I'm going.'

'Sit down,' he said, 'please, just sit. You know I'm right. You can't marry him, Milly. You just can't.'

'You have no right . . .'

'Okay, okay. But let me ask one question. Can I? Ask one question?'

'What?'

'Did you tell him?'

'Tell him what – about us? I mean, that time in Reading?'

'About the baby. Did you tell him?'

'What do you mean?'

'You didn't, did you? Well, are you going to tell him?'

'Well, yes.'

'When?'

'That's none of your business!'

'Oh come on, Milly. Whether or not it's my business is irrelevant. The question is, will you tell him?'

She sat down again. 'I need a cigarette,' she said. 'Do you have a cigarette?'

'I didn't know you smoked.'

'Sometimes, yes. The odd one. Anyway, why would you know if I smoked or not?'

'What do you smoke?'

'Anything. Mild.'

He came back with two cigarettes in his hand and a box of matches. 'The machine's out of order; the barman gave me these.'

He took the box and the match from her hand and lit her cigarette. She noticed they both had a shake in their hands now.

'It happened before I met him. I don't have to tell him. Why should I tell him?'

'Why not? You don't think he would mind, do you?'

She took a couple of pulls from the cigarette and said nothing.

'Milly?'

'Of course he'll mind,' she said. 'You know fucking well that he'll mind.'

'Ah, don't cry, Milly. Please. I don't want to make you cry. But you can't marry a man who would judge you for that. You just can't.'

She swiped the tears from her face and smashed the cigarette out on the ashtray. She stood up and began edging her way around the table. 'I'm marrying him. And if he ever finds out about the baby, I'll know where to look.'

'You know I wouldn't do that.'

As she walked away, she heard him call out her name on a loud whisper. *'Milly!'*

She turned back around.

'He'll never let you be yourself. He's stupid. He's a stupid man who thinks he's clever – you don't want to marry someone like that.'

'At least he wants me,' she said. *'He wants me.'*

The day before they were due to visit the pub in Kent, she was serving a few of the older lunchtime customers in the back lounge. Shamie stuck his head in the door and announced: 'They've let them out. They've released the Guildford Four! Quick, it's on the news.'

One by one, the customers moved out to the front bar until she was left alone with one old man, an ex-soldier, sitting with his back to the wall, pulling the edges of his overcoat around his knees and staring into his half of bitter.

She could hear the bleating of the signal for the one o'clock news, the voice of the newscaster and then complete silence. She pulled back the flap of the counter and slipped out to the bar.

Some of the customers had tears in their eyes, others looked a bit shame-faced. She heard someone say, 'They're showing it again, they're showing it again.' And then a few shhhing sounds flew around the room, even though no one had been making a sound.

She looked up at the screen in the corner: a young man, wild-eyed, fist in the air, was coming through the crowd. He was handsome, with dark wavy hair; she thought he was not unlike Pip.

'Who's that?' she asked a woman standing beside her.

'Why that's Gerry Conlon, one of the Guildford Four – you know?'

'Oh yes,' she said, 'is that him?'

'It is, poor chap.'

She had not been expecting that face. The fire in his eyes, the untold grief. She looked across the room at Brenda, arms folded, leaning on the counter, with her mouth hanging open; she only wished that Mrs Oak hadn't been in Malta, but had been here to witness this moment.

The man on the screen was speaking now. 'Fifteen years I've spent in prison,' he said, 'for something I didn't do. I watched my father die in prison for something he didn't do.'

She had to turn away and leave the room.

Mylo found her sobbing in the kitchen.

'What the hell are you doing, Milly?' he hissed.

She could hardly speak through the sobs. 'That poor man – so young. Such an awful . . . How could . . . how could such an awful thing even happen?'

'Pull yourself together, Milly, for goodness' sake. Whatever will people think?'

'He's innocent, isn't he? I'm not the only one upset.'

'We don't know the full story yet, do we? He may have got off on a technicality for all we know. British justice is rarely wrong, you know.'

'What?'

'Anyway, that's not my point, is it?'

'And what is your point then, Mylo?' she asked, pulling herself free from his grip.

'You don't want people thinking that you're, you know – one of them.'

'But I *am* one of them, Mylo, if it comes to it. I am Irish.'

'I don't mean the Irish in general. I mean, you know, that lot.'

'He's innocent. He had nothing to do with the bombs.'

'Like I said, we don't know that for sure. I still have my doubts, you know; I'm not quite satisfied. British justice—'

'They've been released. The verdicts have been overturned. Or are you just too fucking stupid to see that?'

The next time she was alone with Mylo was during the night-time clear-up. She stayed behind the bar loading dirty glasses into the washer. She could hear him in the background making preparations for the following day: the sound of beermats slapping down on tables, and the gurgle from the pipes as he checked them over.

As she listened, her mind turned to the old man at the railings of Hyde Park. Week after week, tying his paintings to the iron posts, sitting on his chair, staring into his pictures of lopsided flowers and weightless horses, trees that looked as if they could float off into the air. Refusing to see what a blind man on horseback could see.

When her work was done, she walked around the bar. She could see he was still in a huff. 'Mylo,' she said, 'could I have a word?'

He wiped his hands slowly and put down his cloth.

'Well, if you've come to apologise,' he said, 'I'm willing to let it go. But I have to say, Milly, that I'm—'

'No, it's not that. It's not to apologise. Sit down for a minute, will you?'

He looked at her for a couple of seconds and said, 'Oh, Milly, you're never going to tell me you've changed your mind?'

'I'm sorry, Mylo,' she said. 'Truly I am.'

10. Pip

2017

July

THE FIRE HAS unnerved him. For the first couple of weeks, he finds it difficult to venture out. At the same time, he can't bear staying in. When he does go out, he always seems to forget something – glasses, sunglasses, money, pills – and then he has to turn back. More often than not, once he steps back into the house, he ends up staying put.

The fire makes him think about other fires. And not just the one that swallowed up Eamonn's parents either. He thinks of Lakanal House in Camberwell a few years ago, and further back, to King's Cross station. He thinks of the cage of fire in the little Volkswagen Polo in Dublin that had taken Bob's brother. And he thinks of the other fire in Dublin where all those teenagers died in a Valentine's disco. Hands pulling at the chains on the doors to get out, screaming, suffocating, burning. Their last moments of pain and terror as they cried out for their mammies. Burning people everywhere. For the first few nights, whenever he closes his eyes, they are waiting for him.

On the street, he finds himself throwing his eye over buildings, looking for fire hazards, and as soon as he walks into a shop or a café, he starts looking for exits. He thinks: how would I escape, how would I get out of this shop, this house, this bus, this street?

He begins to obsess about the victims of the fire, studying their faces in newspaper reports, remembering their first names. He scours the list of the missing and the dead for familiar surnames, and when he is satisfied that he knows no one, his thoughts turn to those he does know, all the possible disasters that might befall them. His daughter and even her mother; Dom and Max; Max and Jenny; Dom and Kim, the woman in the red dressing gown from across the road, who has taken to dropping in now on a regular basis. Shamie and his wife Beth. The boys from the old boxing club. And Milly – he thinks about her a lot.

One night he goes into the newsagent's on Queensway and, finding a standalone gas fire on full blast, eats the head off the Afghan bloke behind the counter. 'Turn that fuckin' thing off,' he says to him. 'It's dangerous, someone could tip against it, knock it over. Is that what you want – another fire?'

Later, he tells Dom about it. 'A warm summer's night and he had it on full blast. I don't know how he can breathe in there.'

Dom says nothing.

'What – you don't think I was right to say something?'

'No. You had a point, but . . . Well, he could have lost someone in the fire, you know? He probably knows some of the victims.'

And then, for days afterwards, he feels like a complete shit.

He goes through Dom's house, sticking his head in and out of windows, trying to figure out how they'd escape if the house went on fire. He takes notes and draws up escape routes. Dom would be all right – he could get down onto the flat roof of the extension. The Airbnbers at the back of the house could take the same route – so long as it isn't the extension that's on fire. The Airbnbers at the front would have to jump out the window.

They might break a limb, of course, but they'd survive. Max and the girl would get out the side window. They might even be able to make a break through the hall and escape out the front. A fire has its own mind, of course; it would all depend on what route it decided to take. Even so, he feels it's as well to be prepared.

Up in his own room, he climbs onto a chair, opens the Velux window and sticks his head out. He looks down on the haphazard range of rooftops and chimney pots and considers his options. He, on the other hand, would be bollixed – unless he sprouts a pair of wings and learns how to fly.

Even now, four weeks later, he is wary of enclosed spaces and rarely gets on a bus or takes the tube. And yet he can only walk so far without completely tiring himself out. When he walks to Bayswater, he sees people who look like some of the victims – or relatives of the victims anyhow. When he walks around here, there's the tower. And he hates the way it suddenly looms over the rooftops or, through a gap between streets, rears up to show its long, charred bones. He thinks of those who died and those who really should have been saved, and he is filled with a barely controllable rage. Then all he wants to do is put his fist through a wall or, better still, a window. There are days, too, when he senses the overriding depression in the area and feels so diminished by sadness that he's half afraid he might start weeping out on the street.

There is an eerie stillness around the tower. A presence. Even when it's not in sight, he can sense it. And he thinks of the Tower of Silence in Mumbai then, where the Parsi lay out their dead, and, looking up, half expects to see vultures wheeling overhead.

The fire has left him wide open. When Dom tells him to cancel the Airbnb for a couple of weeks because Max and his girl have decided to stay on for a while, he is more than relieved. The thought of having to grin at a load of strangers on holiday, answering the inevitable questions about the fire as if it was a tourist attraction.

The downside is the pair of them lying around the place all day getting on his wick; being forced to listen to their thumping music – or worse again, their conversation. And yet, he keeps remembering the night of the fire. The way he had felt when he wrapped the duvets around their shoulders or hugged the sobbing girl and helped Max to drink his mug of tea. And the following day, somewhere around noon, as he hauled a drunk and exhausted Dom to bed, listening to him mutter his way up the stairs, 'Thank God you're here, Phil, I don't know what we would have done without you. I really don't, Phil – you know? Family counts at times like this – am I right, Phil? Family counts – you know?'

The fear and emotion in the days that followed, the closeness. Eating together, sitting in the garden together, watching television together. The way the word 'family' had been bandied about.

In early July, he comes across *The Waste Land* again. He finds it in the bottom of a Sainsbury's bag under the stairs where he must have left it on the evening of the fire. He can remember bringing it with him earlier that day and sitting on a bench in Hyde Park, with the book in his hand. But he hadn't gone as far as opening the pages. Just holding it had brought him back to the mid-nineties and his time in prison and he hadn't felt ready to start thinking about all that.

The edition in the prison had looked more like a school copybook. There had been a flimsy, almost homemade look to it; at the back, a few pages of notes by the author. A brown shiny cover as he recalls, it had been in among a load of old books in the library that had been donated by a Quaker charity.

He had been sharing the cell with an older man at the time; a bald, white-faced blob, maybe the age he is now. The man barely spoke a word, except at night when he would lie face to the wall, whispering what he could only hope were prayers. The lack of conversation had been a relief, although there were times when the whispering spooked him.

As he lay on the top bunk, reading *The Waste Land*, he could feel a breeze passing through his head. The poem wrapped itself around him. Sometimes he had to get down from the bunk and stand at the small window to think about a line or a section he had just read. At dusk, a blue-grey light came off the stone walls and across the prison yard. The violet hour, he realised, comes on wherever you are. At dawn the light was more of a silvery grey. He felt the poem had helped him to notice such things.

He never wanted to stop reading it; he wanted to leave the last *Shantih* and go straight back to April. But in prison, he couldn't very well walk around clutching a book of poetry to his chest. Instead, he decided to carry it around in his head. Learning it off, he built it up slowly, each day adding another bit on, before going back to the beginning to consolidate what he had so far. He went over and over it, until four hundred and thirty-three lines later, he felt he had it right: every word and every silence.

He even learned the epigraph off, never mind that he had no idea what it meant, much less how to pronounce it.

It lifted the excruciating boredom of prison life. It awoke his senses and changed his attitude to everything. From the appalling stink of the morning slop-out, to the chorus-line clang of slamming doors in the evening, everything seemed relevant somehow; everything just as it should be. Nothing bothered him as much then. Not the desperate late-night yowling of grown men behind locked doors. Not even the whispering voice in the bunk below him. Everything he saw, heard, smelled or felt became the language of the poem he was now living through.

It got him past the first part of his stretch anyhow.

After the fire – two or three weeks after it – he does it again, reads it several times, then slowly begins to relearn it. The edition he has now – the one that was given as a gift to Monique – is more substantial, containing other poems along with pages of convoluted notes and a lengthy scholarly introduction. But he isn't interested in being educated, in reading someone else's guesswork. He wants this to be a private matter between himself and the poet. At the same time, it has to be, as it was before, a solo journey. Familiar in its strangeness, something that only he can experience for himself.

He is surprised at what he remembers and what he has forgotten. The lines that seemed to have been written for him when he read it in jail are still relevant nearly twenty years later – even if now, they have a different meaning.

I have heard the key turn in the door once and turn once only . . .

And he is surprised, too, at the recurrence of the word 'tower' rising out of the landscape of the poem, and falling. The blackened wall; the far-off cities leading to London. And the various tongues of fire, jumping from candle to hair into the final flames of purgatory. As though it was written weeks, instead of almost a hundred years, ago.

Everywhere in London he finds connections between the poem and the small coincidences that make up his day and all the other days of his life so far, in this unforgiving city. It brings to mind the Lithuanian woman he bought tea for, the day he was discharged from the clinic. And further back, a different mad woman, who stopped him on Ladbroke Grove one day when he was about six years old and asked his name. Her queenly voice following him all the way home: 'Ask Mummy, would you, Pheelip? Ask Mummy if she would like me to read her cards? Only half a crown to know what lies ahead – that's not so bad, now is it, Pheelip?'

In prison, when the chaplain came to say goodbye before taking up a new post in South America, he asked him if he could translate the epigraph.

The priest frowned at the page for a while before admitting, 'My Latin is limited, I'm afraid. Something is hanging, though, and eyes are mentioned. The bit on the end is Greek – that's all I can tell you.'

The next day, when he came back from the shower room, there was a note on his pillow.

I saw with my own eyes the Sybil at Cumae hanging in a cage, and when the boys asked her: Sybil, what do you want? she said I want to die.

He thought the priest must have made it his business to find out. He asked his cell mate, 'Did the chaplain come back with this?'

His cell mate didn't answer, just turned his pale face slowly to him, and gave a wet-lipped smile.

He decides to revisit his *mea culpa* letters. He can't say why, nor can he make the connection, but he feels the poem has led him back to them. Over the past few months, they have crossed his mind from time to time, but he has always managed to fob himself off with some excuse or another. He would get around to it – when the rain stopped falling or the sun stopped beating down or when he wasn't so tied up with these damned Airbnb duties. When the time was right, he would know it. But when was the time ever right for traipsing around London having doors slammed in your face? And then he would remind himself of the advice he received from Colin, his AA sponsor: go softly, take your time – the worst thing you can do is to take on too much, too soon.

'The time is right, now,' he tells himself one morning as he takes the letters from their plastic sheath and lays them out along the top of the bookcase. He wavers for a moment, reaching towards and away from the envelopes as if he's afraid they will scorch his hand. Then he snatches them up, wraps them back in the plastic and puts them into his Sainsbury's bag. He will start with the easiest and work his way up to the hardest. He won't think any more about it. Just get down the stairs, through the front door onto the street, one foot in front of the other. Not thinking, just walking.

It takes a good while to get there, trudging along, talking himself in and out of the task. He makes a few stops: coffee once; three times to go to the jacks. A short sit-down here and there, once on a bench in Hyde Park and then on the low wall of the flower beds in front of the Animals in War Memorial.

When he sits down, he pulls *The Waste Land* out of his bag and then, when he's ready to move on again, he drops the book back in.

In Shepherd Market he sits on a bench that encircles a lamppost. The bench is divided into single compartments. Behind the lamppost, a leaning tree provides a soft shadow. There are people to watch. He could sit here for hours, read for a bit, watch for a bit, let his mind wander. But he knows he's been here too long already because of the changeover of forearms on either side of him: dark brown under a blue rolled-up shirtsleeve, eating a sandwich. Young, tanned and sleeveless chatting to someone on her far side. Wobbly freckly white, guffawing into a mobile phone.

A few yards ahead of him stand a pair of phone boxes: regal-looking, freshly painted, completely ignored. There used to be queues outside phone boxes. Impatient knuckles rapping on windows if you took too long. The smell of piss in some of them. Others had their guts pulled out for coins, or just for the hell of it.

He remembers arriving from Dublin one time, for school holidays, and getting off the train in Euston. He would have been about fourteen years old and with little or no sense. He'd spent all his money on the slot machines on the boat coming over anyway, and had to call his father because he had no money to pay for the last leg home to Slough. The queues were so long in the station, he'd gone outside to look for a phone box. He could hear his father's voice accepting the reverse charges, his voice so strange after an absence of more than six months that for a second he thought he might burst into tears. But then he had begun to notice the postcards stuck behind the phone and on some of the windows. By the time his father had come on the line, he could hardly listen, he'd been that busy getting an eyeful: half-naked women with their arses cocked in the air. Suzie will . . . Fifi is all yours . . . Massage and anything else you fancy. And in the middle of all that, George the plumber would see you right.

'Now you're not to worry, Philip,' his father's voice was saying, 'I'm sending Dom to fetch you. Are you listening to me, Phil? Go back to the station and stand near a policeman, Dom will find you. Are you there, Philip? Can you hear me? And speak to no one . . . do you understand me? *No one.*'

People make calls on the go now, their whole lives squashed into their little phones. What they see, what they think, where they go, how they get there. What they remember – it's like they're carrying their brains around in their pockets.

He thinks: what I could do now is just phone her. What I *should* do now is phone her rather than just turn up out of the blue. Actually, that is what I'll do, I'll phone. He roots in his bag and takes out his mobile phone. But his charge is low and as this is a busy time for her, he could be left hanging on for a while. He dips into his pocket and pulls out a few coins. He'll do it the old-fashioned way. Yes, that's what he'll do. He gets up, takes the few steps to the phone box, puts his hand on the brass cap of the door, pulls it, holds it, and then lets it go. The door creaks back into place.

Oh fuck it, he thinks, just do it. You stupid bollix. Just go there, and do it.

He turns on his heel and heads north onto Curzon Street.

When he arrives, the shutters are down. It's a quarter to five on a warm Friday evening, office workers criss-crossing over the street. Girls with freshened faces trotting along; young men with hands in pockets, moving with purpose, laughing and talking, tongues hanging out for a drink. The buzz of a summer week-end all around. And yet the pub is firmly shut. He notices what appears to be a sign stuck to the main door.

Across the street, he lurks between the locksmith's and the tube station entrance, keeping a watch for any sign of light or movement.

He studies the ground floor, the windows and doors, but there's nothing. He brings his eye upwards: the windows face blindly out, not one of them open a crack. He can't see the dormer windows from here, just the edge of the frame that holds them, the little peaks at the top. But there is a dead-eyed look about the whole place anyhow. Crossing the square on the diagonal, he leaves

213

the pub behind and begins to make his way up Cowcross Street.

The last time he walked this street was maybe twelve, fifteen years ago. When he was a young man this whole area would have been his stomping ground. The boxing club, the pub, the walk through the markets to the flat where he lived at the time above a printer's shop on the far side of the square. All the places that no longer exist. On this side – the newsagent's, the barber's shop, the factory. On the far side of the street – the Wimpy bar, the butcher's, the unisex hairdresser. Back here, the pub where Belfast Gerry used to work. Vanished. Then replaced by new buildings. Not a hint that they had ever even existed. He had been expecting changes, but not complete annihilation.

But there's something else. He can feel it as he walks along the busy street. Slower than everyone else, older by a mile: he stands out. In fact, now that he has a closer look, there are no older people about, no schoolkids, no babies in buggies either, no women dragging shopping trollies behind them. No one who looks as if they might actually live around here anyway.

For a moment, he forgets where he is. He stops and tries to gauge his surroundings. There's a Starbucks right across the road, and he can recall slipping into a Starbucks earlier to use the jacks. Where was that again? And yesterday he bought his coffee in a Pret. And he has just passed a Pret with an identical face, further back along the street. It occurs to him then – it's not so much that the street has changed, it's just that it has become the same. He could be on any of several streets in London.

Ahead of him, the road opens out. On the far side, he can see the entrance to the markets, the open ironwork inside like the palate of a half-opened mouth. It's a relief to see that, from here anyway, it looks unchanged. Sturdy, majestic, grubby. If a lot less busy than he remembers.

He comes back down Cowcross Street on the opposite side, stops at the pub and puts on his glasses. He bends into the notice and reads. The sign is weather-beaten, covered in plastic that has steamed over with condensation. He can't really make it out beyond a few words or a phrase here and there. Notice is hereby given. Acquiring authority. Council. But one thing is clear, anyway: Dora Oak's pub is no more.

He decides to go around the back for a better look. Moving along the bend into Turnmill Street, he sees that a whole block has been erased. Whatever it once was, it is now a patch of razed ground lurking behind a wall of glossy panelled hoarding, with fancy logos of a construction company printed on it. He follows it to the corner and looks up the narrow side road. Poor little Benjamin Street is bunged up with scaffolding, and without the old shops and houses to guide him along, it takes a while to figure out how to get into the lane. Eventually, he finds a cut-through blocked off at the end by an old makeshift hoarding. He notices one of the planks is slightly off-kilter. He tugs on it for a moment and it easily gives. Through the gap he can see the laneway. It has a derelict, forgotten look to it, as if nobody has been down here in years. He can see the back wall of the pub, the broken door of a garage across from it, and now, the old boxing club. He gives the plank another push and then squeezes himself through.

Standing outside the old boxing-club basement, his knees level with the three low, vertical windows, he feels nothing much and wonders why. The windows are thick with grime and webbed at the corners. He gets down on his hunkers and peers through the first one. He can make out the apron of the ring and a snake of fallen rope. In the background on a hook, a pair of gloves hang like giant kidneys. He can see the doorway leading out to the changing rooms, and the shower and toilet he helped Shamie and

Tony to put in one summer. He remembers that he was happy here, even if he never felt as though he really belonged. And it occurs to him that if he's never regretted that part of his life, he's never really grieved for it either.

There's a poster on the wall: a shadowy figure of a fighter squaring up. For all he knows, it could be him.

He comes back to the locksmith's and steps into the tiny shop, relieved to see a face that may not be familiar but is at least middle-aged. The man's bald brown head is bent over a key, refining the edges in short, intense, ear-splitting movements.

'Can I help you?' he asks without looking up.

'I was just wondering if you know anything about the pub across the road?'

'In what sense?'

'I mean, has it been sold? Where the owner's gone? Or the Irish girl – do you remember her?'

'I'm a non-drinker, I don't pay much attention to pubs.'

'Well, did you happen to notice how long it's been shut down?'

'I couldn't say.'

'Okay. Thanks anyway.'

'I can tell you though,' he says, holding the key up to the light and blowing on it, 'a developer bought it maybe ten, fifteen years ago, something like that. Then he went bust and disappeared. The lady that used to own it – a good-looking woman, am I right?'

'That's right.'

'She passed away.'

'Mrs Oak's dead?'

'Was that her name?'

A curtain behind the counter flicks back and a woman in a sari, sewing at a small desk, sticks her head out. 'We don't know that she's dead! You can't go telling people that someone is dead when you are only guessing – he could be a relative of hers. Please, pay no attention to my husband. She's in a nursing home – which one, I don't know.'

'And what about the girl?'

'The girl?'

'Irish girl? Her name's Milly.'

'Hardly a girl!' the woman laughs.

'You know her then?'

'She helped me once when I had a fall out on the street.'

'Do you know what happened to her?'

The woman looks at him sideways, adjusts the drape of her headscarf and gives a little laugh. 'Oh, she married the developer.'

'Now who's guessing?' her husband says, inserting the key back into the machine where it gives a horrified screech.

'So far as I know,' the woman shouts at him and then lets the curtain fall back down.

He feels a bit dazed – disappointed and dazed – as he walks back up Cowcross Street. Milly married. Of course, the woman hadn't been certain. But still, she wouldn't have pulled it out of thin air either. She must have heard something. Milly a Missus Somebody. She could have been his Missus Somebody, if he hadn't been such a stupid prick.

And why shouldn't she be married? As long as he's good to her. He'd better be good to her. Because if he isn't good to her . . . ?

'Ah, fuck it anyway,' he mutters as he finds himself standing once more at the top end of the street facing Smithfield market, without the slightest notion of how he got there.

He sits down on a concrete bench and looks at his feet for a while. Then he lifts his head and takes in his surroundings. There's a café in front of him pretending to be French. Beside it, the door that used to lead to Vera Greene's flat, now painted in zebra stripes with a company brass plate fixed to the left-hand side of it.

He watches a variety of feet pass by: leather, canvas, painted toes.

Then he thinks about Shamie. The last he heard, he'd moved house but was still doing a bit of coaching in a gym on the far side of Charterhouse Square. A pair of yellow runners stop at a tourist map just to the right of him. When they move away, he stands up and shakes the pins and needles down from his arse through his legs and feet. Then he steps over to the map and looks into the cat's cradle of neighbourhood streets until he recognises the name of the lane. He puts his finger on the 'You are here' dot, and traces his route.

The gym is at the side of a new building, stone steps leading up to the entrance. He puts his hand on the door and thinks – what if Shamie is in there? What if I open the door and walk straight into him? He pushes the door open a fraction. And it's like he's listening to the soundtrack of his old life. The ticking of a skipping rope, the slap of gloves, the echo of voices and exertion. Somebody is counting; somebody else is giving instruction. He steps in.

A right little hive of activity inside. In the ring, on the ground, by the wall. He throws his eye around. Two blokes sparring in the ring; one black and rangy, the other white and built like a block. Over to the side, a man with the pallor of an ex-junkie is training a young boy. A lad of around eighteen, gleaming with sweat, is unlacing his boots while counting his mate through a series of military press-ups. At the far wall, a girl with a golden ponytail is punching the fuck out of a bag.

He studies the layout. It's a cleaner club than the old place, more compact too, without the catacomb of tiny rooms out the back that an old warehouse basement allows. The ropes not yet frayed; the punchbags still smooth; a whiff of recent paint on the air.

He takes a few steps towards the ring.

As he gets closer, the two sparring lads slip out and another pair stoop in. A middle-aged man and a skinny black boy who looks about twelve years old.

The boy is wearing a hat with a long neck-flap on it, like he's off to join the foreign legion. The man's arms are a blur of blue tattoos. He has a scar over his eyebrow, which lifts for a moment when he sees him walking towards the ring. Then he puts up his jab mitts and begins directing the boy in a dull steady voice. 'Jab, jab, hit, hit, elbows tight, that's it, keep 'em up. That's it. Come on now, let's have a bit of a dance then.'

'Take you back a bit, eh, Phil?' a voice behind him says.

He turns to see Christy Pavese standing behind him.

They both laugh, then shake hands.

'Where you been all this time?' Christy asks. 'Inside again?'

'No, not this time. At least it was a different kind of clink.'

'Huh?' Christy leans his head in, frowning.

'I was in a clinic.'

'Oh yeah? All better now, I hope.'

'Yea, not bad thanks.'

'So, what you think of this place? A far cry from the old dump, eh? I'd a permanent cold in those days. I put my arthritis down to it, like a bloomin' cave it was. Ought to be someone I can sue.'

'Still moaning then, I see, Christy.'

'Never lost it, son, it keeps me alive,' Christy says.

They turn and watch the boy dancing faster now, the flap on the back of his head fluttering with the movement.

'He's got it, that kid. You used to have it too. Remember?'

'I don't know about that.'

'Shamie thought so anyway. Jackie too. Oh well,' he sighs and then, 'Here, remember Fari? The Iraqi boy? Course you do. He knocked your lights out once, didn't he? He was in a couple of weeks ago with his little grandson. Now he really had the hunger, did Fari. Ended up inside a couple of times. Short fuse done him. Short fuse and women. He'd the hunger for them, an' all. Not a good combination – specially if the woman's already got a bloke, know what I'm saying? Pussy, pussy, pussy, that's all he could think about.'

He looks at the boy in the ring again. 'At his age, I could have sworn you had it. I mean, if you'd asked me to bet . . .'

'You didn't know me when I was his age. You didn't meet me till I was twenty-one.'

'Yeah? I swear, my memory . . . All the boys over the years – where do they go? What you think of our new club? Beautiful, eh?'

'Yea, very nice.'

'Bit small, do you think?'

'It depends on your numbers.'

'We don't get the numbers we had before. We don't get the interest. All this talk about brain damage, it puts the parents off, don't it? Here, I know what it was with you – it was the drugs, am I right?'

'No.'

'Drink then?'

'Epilepsy.'

'You're fucking joking me?'

'And drink probably had something to do with it too.'

'I never knew that. Did Shamie know?'

'Not at first, but yea, I told him.'

'Funny he never said.'

'That's why I'm here actually, I'm looking for Shamie.'

'What you want him for?' he asks, his neck jutting out defensively. 'We got all the coaches we need here, Phil. We got too many.'

'Don't worry, Christy, I'm not after your job. I just want to give him something.'

'What's that then?'

'A message.'

'I can give it for you.'

'Thanks, but I prefer to give it myself.'

'He don't come in much these days. His missus, she's an invalid now.'

'I'm sorry to hear that. Where's he living?'

'Oh, he don't like me to give out his address.'

'Fair enough. Right, I'll be off so.'

'Yeah, see you then. Mind how you go.'

He can feel Christy's eyes on him as he walks towards the door and pushes his way back out.

There's a boy sitting on the step outside, wrapping his hands.

He watches the boy cautiously cross the wrap back and forward, then pause as if trying to remember which way to go next.

'Tuck it in,' he says to him. 'You need a bit more padding on the knuckles.'

The boy looks up at him, then down at his knuckles. He nods and tucks it in, then looks at him again.

'I'd hook it around your thumb, he says, now back to your wrist.'

'Oh yeah,' the boy says.

'Would you happen to know Shamie's address?'

'I don't know his address,' the boy says, turning the last of the wrap around his wrist and fixing it into place.

'Would you happen to know if I gave you a fiver?'

'No really, I don't know the address. But I can tell you where the street is.' The boy reaches up, scissors his fingers around the fiver and gives it a little tug.

He hears Christy call out to the boy as he goes inside.

'I hope you didn't give him Shamie's address? He don't like people knowing his address.'

'I don't know his address, do I?' he hears the boy say.

He follows the boy's directions across Clerkenwell Road then over St John's Square and through Jerusalem Passage. Then he comes to a bullnose corner that straddles two streets. He steps to one side and considers the left-hand option. Down there, at least, there is something to recognise: terrace, railing, brick and gate. A man is pottering about in the small garden at the front of one of the houses. He is about to head down there and enquire about Shamie, but already the man has disappeared, leaving the clang of a slammed front door on the empty road. He can't seem to move. He feels unwell, his breathing unsteady, and all that walking has brought on the first twinges of pain in his left knee. The air is hot and dusty; he can taste it on his tongue. He's forgotten to bring a bottle of water and now there is a dryness in his throat that is making him feel nauseous. The rush of blood to the head that brought him this far has now deserted him. And then the long walk, along with the let-down of not having seen Milly. Or worse, of not knowing where or how to find her. And even if he did manage to track her down, the husband could object to her seeing him. She might even object herself, if she has any sense.

He reaches into his bag and, taking out his phone, checks the time.

He would have to take his pills soon enough. A sit-down was what he needed now, something to drink. A building appears in the back of his mind. A pub on a rounded corner, just like this one. The something Arms. Somewhere behind him. Not far at all, just a short way back down the road. Around here anyway. He had been in there once with Milly.

He decides to push on, taking the street where he spotted the man a moment ago. As he moves along, he begins to recognise these houses. When he was a young man, he worked as a roofer for a while with two older Irish men who had digs along here. The men left early in the morning and were encouraged not to come back until late – although not too late – in the evening. For years they had lived in a house along here, working themselves half to death, and little or nothing to show for it in the end. He went on the piss with them the odd Saturday. But you had to know how to drink with those boys. There was a wildness about them that he had always envied: in their music, their banter, the way they could stride across rooftops as if they were taking a walk across low-lying hills. Were they brothers or cousins? He can't remember now. From the west, anyway. When they wanted a private conversation, they sometimes switched to speaking Irish.

Years later, he spotted one of them, one Christmas Day, waiting in a queue for the charity dinner in that place by Trafalgar Square. He'd been one step away from the gutter himself and had been thinking of going in. But when he saw his old friend, he changed his mind. He had watched him for a while, toothless and thin, elderly before his time – standing in line, laughing and joking with the rest of the Irish, knowing full well that in a couple of hours they'd be back in a doorway or in a kennel that called itself a hostel. But that was the Irish for you, he had thought at the time, as he'd turned away bitter and without much pity: put them in a queue outside Auschwitz and they'd turn it into a fucking party.

And just look at this little street now, he thinks. Not a battle-axe landlady or rent collector in sight. One bell to every door, no trace of rust on the painted railings, brickwork all clean and repointed. One house running into another with not much difference, except for one – the house where the man had been coming and going – which he can now see, like a big throbbing thumb, sticking out.

The front of the house is festooned with dolls and teddy bears. He thinks it might be some sort of a nursery school but on closer inspection, sees that some of the dolls are hanging by the neck, and one of the teddy bears has a small penknife stuck into his eye. So not a nursery school then, unless run by the Addams Family. There are trinkets along the outside windowsills upstairs and down: old Dinky cars and empty milk bottles, jars and tins from long-ago larders. A statue of the Child of Prague with his head lopped off stands on the little shelf by the fanlight. And spiked along the railings, a sinister display of doll's clothes and a single baby sock.

The door opens. It's a sharp, sudden move as if the owner has been watching from behind it and wanted to give him a fright. A man steps out; slight, wiry, sharp-eyed, a full sweep of grey hair. Behind him, in the hall, hundreds of newspaper strips dangle from the ceiling.

'I was just admiring your house,' he says to the man. 'Is it an art gallery?'

The man doesn't answer. He tries again: 'I'm looking for someone who lives around here. He's called Shamie. Used to be a boxer and then he was a coach for many years over in the old boxing club near the station.'

'What club?' the man asks. 'No club round here.'

'Okay, well thanks anyway.'

'He's not blind though,' the man says.

'Who?'

'I can always tell. Even when I was a boy I could always tell. I'd say to them, I know you can see me. Blind people can always see me. No boys around here. No. They're all gone now. No boys live here. Only me.'

What the fuck is this? he thinks and, nodding his thanks, begins to turn away.

'And the spirits, mind. Mustn't forget.'

'No. Indeed.'

'There used to be boys and girls all over the street,' the man says, then taking a few steps forward and now leaning on the gate, 'we lived round the corner, tiny house. All in together. Mum, Dad, me, Stan, Vera, Albert. Billy, of course – it finished her off, bringing him in. Only me here now, me and the – well, you know.'

'The spirits?'

'That's right.'

'Okay,' he says. 'Well, I better get going. Good luck now.'

He has just reached the house next door when the man speaks out again.

'But I know who you mean,' he says. 'He lilts a bit when he walks. Got a nice baby. He says to me, he says, she's my baby and I wheel her around.'

'There's no baby.'

'There is. He said so. She used to make a cake for me at Christmas time. But now she's a baby, she don't do that no more. They live over there. In the flats where the school for the blind used to be.'

'Oh yes, oh yes, I see.'

'I know you do,' he said. 'I can always tell.'

Shamie doesn't invite him in. He puts the door on the latch and stays on the threshold. An old man now, though still bright-eyed and burly, he gives the impression that, if pushed to it, he could still handle himself. Over his shoulder, a folded wheelchair shows behind the coat stand and a long handrail runs the length of the wall.

He tries a little conversation, asks Shamie how he is, tells him that he's looking well. 'I was sorry to hear about the old club closing,' he says then.

'It was a long time ago.'

'What happened?'

'I handed over the reins to a younger bloke,' Shamie says. 'It closed a couple of years after.'

'Wouldn't have happened on your watch.'

Shamie frowns. 'Yeah it would. A developer bought it, and then he went under. So it rots, till another developer comes along. Why are you here?'

Behind Shamie, the kitchen door is ajar. There's the sound of a radio and, from another room, voices on the television.

'I wrote you a letter,' he said finally.

'A letter? I didn't get no letter. No letter came here.'

'No, I didn't post it, I have it here.'

He reaches into his bag and, pulling out the envelope addressed to Shamie, tries to explain. 'You see they tell you to write to people. You know, when you're in rehab.'

'Rehab? What, you a rock star now?'

'All right, drying out. Anyway, part of the programme is, you know, that you write a letter to people you may have upset.'

'Upset?' he asks with a short, bitter laugh.

'It's known as an amendment letter,' he says and holds the letter out to Shamie, who ignores it.

'Say what you have to say to my face.'

'I can't, Shamie,' he says.

'Why not?'

'I just can't.'

'All right then, don't.'

'I hear Beth's not so good.'

'What you want, Phil?'

'I want you to read the letter.'

'Fine, I'll read the letter,' he says, taking the envelope and moving to close the door.

'Shamie, hold on. Please.'

'What?'

'I just want to ask – where have they gone?'

'Where've what gone, Phil – the good old days? The boys from the club? Your wife and daughter? Look, I've gotta go. My wife, she needs me.'

'Shamie, please. I want to make amends, I do really.'

'Bit late for that.'

'Shamie, Angie's had two husbands since me. We were kids when we got married.'

'She brought your child up on her own. She made a good job of it too. Where were you then?'

'I know.'

'Time and time again, you let Lorraine down.'

'Yes, I know.'

'Angie's a good girl. She was a good mum.'

'I didn't say she wasn't. I'm saying she's well over me by now. Look, I know I fucked up. I'm not going to even try to justify it.'

'Well how could you, really?'

After a moment Shamie shrugs and says, 'Lorraine – she's done all right, considering. She's a teacher.'

'In Scotland?'

'No. Not in Scotland.'

'I'd like her address, Shamie.'

'Yeah, I bet you would.'

'Could you at least post these for me? One's for Angie.'

'Oh yeah, she'll love that all right.'

'Look, could you just post them for me? To Lorraine anyway. Could you do that? And my address is on there if she ever wants to . . . well, you know. Get in touch.'

Shamie waits a moment, then nods and takes the letters. 'I'll see that they get them.' He begins to close the door.

'Wait! What about Milly? Do you know where she's gone?'

Finally, Shamie looks him straight in the eye. 'Do something decent for once in your life, eh? Leave Milly be. She's got enough on her plate without you jumping on it. Is that it then?'

'Shamie, please . . . I'm trying, I really am. I haven't had a drink since January. I nearly died when I was in hospital, they didn't think I would make it. I was discharged back in April. And I haven't touched a drop since. I know you don't think it, but it's been tough for me too.'

'Is that right?'

'Yea, I'm . . . I'm doing my best. I really am.'

'Listen to me, now listen carefully. I don't want to know. I don't want to hear about you, or your sob story, or your sad little life. You know why? Because I don't give a fuck.'

Then Shamie steps back into the house and quietly closes the door in his face.

There's a sick feeling in his stomach as if he's taken a punch, and his heart is skipping along in tight little beats. He thinks about the pub again, as he comes to the end of the street. The something Arms. He can see it neatly framed in his mind's eye: yellow tiles on the outside wall, the colour of lager. Flower baskets hanging around the doorway. The comfort of the quiet dark corner. A sensation comes up through his chest, slithers into his neck and noses into the glands just below his ears. The sweat pushes against his skin. And he feels as if he's walking through a tunnel – the way he used to feel whenever he came out of the dressing room and began the dark walk down the corridor into the blast of savage light. No turning back.

If he went on the drink now, it would be the finish of him. A couple of months would be the most he would last. And would that really matter, he has to wonder? He'd be done with all this shit: the guilt and the regret, the constant struggle and worry. The loneliness – there, he's said it. Loneliness.

And then he sees it: the pub, just ahead on the corner. Swathed from head to foot – the entire building parcelled in sheets of thick plastic held together by scaffolding. The entrance is boarded up and he thinks – surely not another demolition order? But the sign on the door says *Closed for Renovations*.

He walks around the corner to the other side of the pub, just to make certain. At the end of the building, a flap of plastic has shifted, the socket of an empty window behind it. He pulls the flap aside. The place has been gutted; there's a short, squat machine chained up like a hostage in the far corner, a few empty mugs sitting on a plank at the side; a few empty paint tins with sticks poking out of them. Nothing to suggest that a pub had existed or was likely to exist. No memory of pleasure or warmth or refuge remains.

He stands as he is, breathing long and deep, until he feels the spike of adrenaline begin to die down.

Retracing his steps back down Jerusalem Passage, he comes into St John's Square. When he reaches the entrance to the Priory, he stops. Through the arch, he can see into the garden and the cloisters beyond. He remembers coming here with his father when he was a boy. They sat on a bench and ate cheese sandwiches. Later, when his father was old and sick, he had returned the compliment.

He climbs the four steps, then stands in the shadow of the arch. To go in there now, sit down in the shade on one of the benches, not to think or remember, just to rest his mind and his body, even for a short while.

He takes a step in but then sees a man coming towards him. Stocky, a few years older than him and, as he can now see, carrying a bunch of keys.

'You're closing?' he asks the man.

The man looks at him for a moment. A pleasant, outdoor face. 'Can I help with something?' the man asks.

'Oh, not really, I was just going to sit in the garden for a few minutes, that's all. I can come back another time.'

'You know the garden?'

'My father used to bring me here when I was a boy. In later years, I used to bring him.'

'Well please, of course you must come. I have a few things to do; I can come back to you maybe a little later. Sit, enjoy the garden. Can I get you something – a glass of water?'

'Water would be great, thanks. I have to take pills soon.'

He stands awkwardly in the middle of the courtyard until the man returns with the water. 'Please sit here, where you can't be seen from outside,' he says, beckoning him to a bench under the wall.

He sits and takes the glass.

'You are not well, I think?' the man says.

'It's not that; it's just, if I don't take the medication, I have fits.'

'Ah, you are an *epilettico*?'

'It sounds better in – what are you, Italian?'

'Yes.' The man smiles and begins to step away.

'Are you a priest?' he asks him.

The man lifts his head and laughs out loud. 'Oh, my wife, she's gonna love that,' he says as he walks away. 'I tell you what she will say – he's no priest, that one! He's a devil like all the men from Amalfi!'

He puts his hand on the faded wood of the bench and looks around. At his back, the wall of the chapel. Above his head, the big stained-glass window of the church. And there is the chalk-white Christ at the end of the garden, pinned to the wall of the cloister. He closes his eyes.

They had been listening to bees. He had heard the sound of them humming. A strong, steady sound – too steady and a bit too musical for actual bees. He'd suspected that it was his father who was doing the humming. He had thought it was some sort of a park – a dull park, with neither grass nor swings for him to play on. He'd been struck by the way anything that did grow seemed to come out in spurts through the flagstone paving. He can't remember now if the white roses were growing up the wall then, or if the dry, twisted tree was in the centre. The man hanging on the cross at the end, he does remember him.

'Was Christ his surname?' he had asked his father.

'No, not his surname.'

His father changed the subject, as he usually did when the conversation veered anywhere near God. Instead, he began to tell him about the crusaders and how this place had once been their headquarters. He loved his father's crusader story and as he listened to it had imagined a knight, pulling his gloves off as he strode through the garden, the forked cross of St John blazoned on his white mantle; the sound of a bridle jangling while a horse nodded and waited in the shadow of the archway. His father's story about the knights had been vague and there was a hint of disapproval in his voice. He hadn't wanted to answer any questions, to talk about where the knights had been or who they were or why they had fought. He hadn't wanted to talk about Jesus Christ either. He had just wanted to play his stupid bee game.

Later, years later, when his father had started to decline and Dom had moved him from his small flat in Holborn to the nursing home in Acton, he'd brought him back here. Stuffing him into a taxi and pointing out landmarks that had long since been deleted from his mind. Half drunk, he had tried to get his father to talk about the crusaders, to make him remember that day. He'd said, 'You told me about them, the day you pretended to be a bee.'

'A *bee*?'

'You were joking.'

'Oh.'

'St John of Jerusalem?'

'Who?'

'The Knights Hospitallers?'

'Oh, those chaps,' his father had said, and then just sat staring ahead, not appearing to look at anything in particular. He can remember, now, feeling a sudden hatred for his father at just that moment. It came on him out of the blue. Anger fired by resentment. He had wanted to stand up and walk away, leave him there, alone and demented sitting on a bench in this little enclave.

He'd been close to tears when he said it to him: 'Why do I hate you? I know there's a reason. There has to be a reason. *Why?*'

His father couldn't or wouldn't reply. He just kept staring into space, his lips moving convulsively as if trying to hold on to some long-forgotten prayer.

He sips the water the Italian has given him and picks his tablets from the palm of his hand: purple, orange, white. There is no wind in the Cloister Garden, and he can hear no sound from the outside world. Now that he thinks of it, he only came here once as a boy, and only brought his father here on one occasion. Yet, he had told the Italian that it had been a few times in both cases. Why do we always have to multiply when it comes to the past, he wonders; why is the truth never enough?

Shamie comes into his mind then, quickly followed by Milly. He feels himself moving backwards across a body of thick, black water. He feels completely adrift and suddenly afraid.

He takes his copy of *The Waste Land* from the Sainsbury's bag and flips it open. With a shaky hand, he reaches for his reading glasses and carefully fits them onto his face. He looks down at the page where the book has fallen open and reads. Then he closes his eyes and lets the words come into his mind:

> To Carthage then I came
>
> Burning burning burning burning
> O Lord Thou pluckest me out
> O Lord Thou pluckest
>
> burning.

PART FOUR

11. Milly

1995

ALL DAY, SHE'D been listening to talk about the gangster who had just died in prison, and on the news, they were showing photos of him and his twin brother like they were some sort of royalty. The pictures, taken in the sixties, showed pale faces and tight black hair, dark suits and skinny ties. She thought they looked like a couple of singers in a black and white film, clicking their fingers and crooning their way through a sugary song.

One of the photos showed them as teenage boys. They were learning how to box in that one; bare hairless chests and fists raised half-heartedly. They looked scared, soft even, the expressions on their faces seeming to say – don't hurt me, oh please, don't hurt me. And she wondered how they had got from that moment there, to the moment a few years on, when they were pinning a man to the floor and stabbing him in the face.

'And not just his face!' she'd heard Charlie Shaw say to Vera Greene earlier as she cleared empty glasses from their table. 'Chest, stomach, neck – ahem, privates. The works. They say it was all over in a few frenzied seconds.'

'Talk about making mincemeat of him!' Vera had gasped, eyes gleaming over the remains of her lunchtime cottage pie.

The machine for washing glasses had broken down again and Mrs Oak had put her in charge of what she called 'the glass situation', meaning her whole day would be spent collecting and washing. When she'd first started here, the glasses were always hand-washed – usually by her – and she hadn't minded in the least. Now, though, she was full of resentment. For the bockety old machine; for Mrs Oak's reluctance to upgrade to a newer model; for Brenda who *never* emptied the glasses properly before loading, causing all sorts to get stuck in the pipes. Collect, wash, rinse, dry, polish – no sooner back on the shelf than they were off it again and it was time to start over. She had forgotten what a pain in the arse it all was.

She looked up at the big window. Rain and wind flinging itself against the glass panes in small self-contained blusters. Beneath the window, an elderly man was settling himself into the spot where Mrs Rogers used to sit, a flop of shamrock hanging from his lapel. It was well into the afternoon by now and no sign of a lull. The weather had made people reluctant to leave; some of them hadn't even bothered going back to work, like that load of Irish builders down the back who had come in for soup and sandwiches and decided to honour St Patrick by staying put. And drinking till they dropped, by the look of them. Others seemed to have lingered just to talk about the dead gangster, the way people do when a relative or close friend has just died.

The door pushed open, breaking through the cigarette smoke that lurked ghoulishly in the alcove. A couple hunched under the shelter of a coat stumbled in. The man pulled the coat back, revealing a smiling girl, and a cheer went up from the advertising agency's table at the far end of the long seat. In seconds, the girl was surrounded by squealing women, her hand held out to display her diamond ring, while the men at the table rose to back-slap the groom-to-be. She knew the girl – Sandra was her name – or at least she had found her one night about a year ago, sobbing in the toilets after closing time on account of some Irish fella who was working around here at the time. And look at her now, engaged to a completely different man. They were not all that young. The girl, she reckoned, was in her mid-thirties, around her own age; the man maybe a couple of years older. They were not all that good-looking either. And yet a light seemed to come out of them. Standing there with their rain-tipped hair and shining faces, they looked as if they'd created themselves for one of their own advertisements.

'You'll meet someone else,' she had told the girl, as she pulled lumps of toilet paper off the roll and mopped up her tears. 'But I don't want to meet anyone else,' the girl wailed, 'and even if I do, I'll *never* love them the way I love him.'

She wondered if the girl had got over her broken heart, or if she had simply settled and, if so, did the brand-new fiancé have any notion that he was second choice? He was looking around now, craning his neck over the crowd, looking for service. Their eyes caught and she lifted her hand to indicate that she would be over to him in two minutes. He nodded solemnly, a frown jammed into his forehead. But the moment his fiancée took his arm, the frown dissolved and his whole face changed. It was as if her touch could cure him of anything. His arm around her waist now; her head leaning back on his shoulder. Just looking at them gave her a pang, of loneliness or longing or envy. Maybe a mixture of all three, she decided. She turned away, bringing the glasses to the huge caterer's tray she'd left balanced on a pair of high stools, then she emptied an ashtray into the plastic bag on the floor.

It seemed like such a long time since anyone had touched her.

After they had decided they were better off as best friends, Pip hugged her whenever they met, the hug ending with a double buddy-pat on the back, just to confirm the friendship. And Mrs Rogers, when she'd had one too many, sometimes used to lean her tall, thin frame down to give her a night-night-luvvie kiss on the forehead. But Mrs Rogers was gone now and it was ages since she'd last seen Pip. Apart from an occasional drunken show of affection from one of the customers, it was ages since she'd been touched in any way at all.

From the corner of her eye, she spotted Brenda behind a loaded tray of drinks, headed in her direction.

'When you're done there, Brenda,' she said, 'can you take an order for that ad agency crowd? One of them has just got engaged.'

'And can you hurry it up with those glasses?' Brenda snarled. 'Else I'll have to bring the bottles over there and pour them straight down their necks.'

'I'm doing my best, Brenda,' she said. Then, leaning into Mrs Pryce's table, she began plucking glasses up with her fingers.

'Animals, that's what they was,' Mrs Pryce was saying, her pudding-bowl hat wobbling with self-importance because she'd actually known the gangsters' family. 'We lived in Braithwaite House then – that's where the mother was, you know. We was all scared of them. My poor husband, he used to hide behind the door when the two boys were about, for fear they might ask him to do something. They took a good photo, mind,' she added, nodding her head towards a shot that had just popped up on the television screen, 'because in real life, they looked nothing like that. A couple of short-arses is what they was.'

'Well, they had that David Bailey do it, didn't they?' the man beside her said. 'He elongated them, you see. A trick of the camera.'

'Pasty-faced, too,' Mrs Pryce said. 'All they got going for them really was money.'

'Are you finished with that glass, Mrs Pryce?' she asked.

'Oh, well, I—'

'That's okay, you take your time.'

'She'll have another one, won't you, love?' the man beside her said. 'Go on, do. I want to hear some more about the terrible twins.'

'Oh well, I suppose one more . . .' Mrs Pryce said, holding out her glass.

'The usual, is it, Mrs Pryce?'

'Do you know, I might chance a gin and tonic. Just for a change.'

'Hold on a tick,' the man said, lifting his glass and larruping back the end of his pint, 'and stick another pint of best bitter in there for me while you're at it, love.'

She took the glass from the man and looked at the tidemarks clinging to the inside of it. 'When I came here first,' she began, 'I used to wonder at the way the English gave up their used glasses to be refilled – something you'd never see in Ireland where every drink is served in a fresh glass. I used to think it was a dirty sort of habit.'

'Did you?' Mrs Pryce said. 'My goodness.'

'I used to think you were missing an essential part of the ritual. You know, the sight of a clean glass filling up. I hated the feel of the dirty glass in my hand, pouring good drink in on top of dregs.'

'Oh, well . . .' Mrs Pryce sighed uneasily.

'Do you know what I think now, though, Mrs Pryce?'

'I haven't the faintest idea, my love.'

'I think it should be made compulsory.'

241

She took the two glasses and, pushing her way to the side of the counter, called down to Trish. 'G and T for Mrs Pryce. Pint of best for her new best friend.'

Then she moved on to Fred Darlington's table. Two girls were standing at the end of it talking. One of them, wearing builder's boots dyed bright blue, was telling her particular gangster story. Her friend, jumper under her dress, and her dress over a pair of jeans, had two scarves wound around her neck. She looked as if she hadn't been able to make up her mind when she'd got dressed that morning.

'My mum and aunt were in their company once in some posh restaurant in Mayfair or somewhere, and he kept saying, "Get the dearest, love – go on, it's all right. You get the dearest, I'm paying, it's okay." And my aunt, she says, "But I only want a bowl of soup" – she was a model, you see, and watching her figure. But he just kept saying . . .'

The overdressed girl turned then and saw her. 'Can you bring us some drinks here?'

'No, I can't,' she said, clawing a couple of glasses from the table and lifting them away.

'Well could you at least empty the ashtray?' the other girl said and then called out after her: 'It's *dizz*-gusting, that's what it is.'

As she walked back to the tray, she considered bringing Fred another pint, just to annoy the two girls. But she knew Fred would prefer to get up and go to the bar himself where it was acceptable to stand staring at Trish for as long as it took her to serve him. What is it, she wondered, that makes some of us pine for things we can never have, while others like that Sandra pick themselves up, and get on with things?

She began settling the new batch of glasses onto the tray. Soon, the after-work crowd would begin to drift in, sucking up whatever air was left in the place, dribbling their brollies all over the floor, swiping the sleet off their coats. Using up more glasses that would need to be washed. There would be no let-up until just before eight when the first commuters would begin to shuffle off half-cut, to fall asleep on the train, snoring and farting all the way home. Not for the first time did she long for the old days when they used to shut up shop for a couple of hours in the afternoon. At least you were guaranteed a bit of respite then – a cup of tea, a few minutes' lie-down on the bed with a book.

She closed her eyes. In the noise behind her, the voices of the younger Irish lads seemed louder than the rest. She didn't know how she felt about the Irish now. Even if she was Irish herself. These past few years had put her off some of the younger men anyhow. At least some of the ones from the building trade who came in here. Full of themselves most of them, compared to the older crew. She felt they were always letting themselves down and she was always having to clean up the mess. Rivers of piss and omelettes of vomit and floods of tears from girls crying over them. She turned around. But everyone was at it now, shouting and roaring as if the drink had made them all deaf. Not even listening to one another half of the time. Same thing every week, yapping on about nothing, round and round like the hands on a clock. How long had she been working here anyway?

She lifted the tray cautiously from the two stools, testing it. Then, slowly, she eased it up and stepped sideways. Almost at once, the vacant stools were pounced on by Jerome and his friend.

'You don't mind if we take these, Milly?'

'I couldn't care less, Jerome,' she said, stepping away.

Three men in suits grouped just ahead of her. She waited for them to step aside so that she could get through to the bar.

She could feel the glasses shivering on the tray, the delicate chime of them. She raised her voice towards the three suits: 'Excuse me, please – if I could just get through?'

But the three men were too busy shouting a conversation at one another. She decided to just stand there until somebody noticed that she existed; that the whole five-foot-four, eight-stone-two flesh and blood of her was standing here, like a little simpleton waiting to pass through to the counter so she could get on with her bloody job.

She could feel the anger bristling through her again – something else that had been happening on and off all day. And an odd sort of energy was tightening inside her. As if she was ailing for something. She felt roped in, physically trapped – pent up, that was it. The smoke was making her eyes itch. It felt as though she had a heat rash on her skin and yet when she looked up at the windows, there were spatters of sleet on the glass. Oh, to be out there, she thought, to be running up the street with her head thrown back and her mouth wide open, feeling the touch of cold sleet on her skin, her lips, her tongue.

The smell of old fag ends and sour beer shifted under her nose.

'Excuse me, please?' she said and then, raising her voice, 'Excuse me please!' and then louder again, 'Excuse me, for God's sake, *pleeease*.'

One of the suits turned and looked at her. A smooth-faced man, wearing a tie that looked like a strip of flocked wallpaper. 'Oh sorry, love,' he said. 'You trying to get by?'

'What do you think?' she asked.

He drew his arm out like a security guard, pushing his friends aside to make a pathway for her. 'Would you like me to take that for you?' he asked. 'It looks pretty heavy.'

'I can manage.'

She glanced at him as she passed – kind eyes, greenish. 'But thanks all the same.'

Sylvester Agnesi was standing behind the man, waiting to greet her with his stupid jokey Irish accent. 'Happy Paddy's Day,' he said, 'me ol' sagoshty!'

'I don't even know what that means, Mr Agnesi,' she said.

Sylvester dipped at the knees, then rising up, lifted his glass over his head. 'God bless the Irish. They're the best in the world, I don't care what anyone says. Colin's Hatch. Dan Patch, Kelly Mac. God bless you, every one.'

The man with the wallpaper tie now standing beside her. '*Who?*' he asked.

'Racehorses,' she explained, and then to Sylvester, 'You'd a good day then?'

'I had a terrific day, my darling.'

'That's great, Mr Agnesi. Now if you wouldn't mind standing aside?'

'I was supposed to be in Cheltenham today, Mills, but I looked out at the weather this morning and said, bugger that, I'll make do with the bookies, that's what I said. And see how it turned out!'

'I'm delighted for you. Now if you don't mind . . .'

'The gods, you see, Milly, they're either on your side or—'

He came at her sideways, putting his arm around her shoulder.

The tray lurched, the glasses wobbled, her heart stopped.

'Mr Agnesi!' she said. 'Will you mind the *glasses*?'

And then the man with the fancy tie reached out, took hold of the tray and lifted it from her.

'Sorry, my darling,' Sylvester said, pulling a wad from his pocket and peeling off a twenty. 'Here, you get yourself something nice.'

'I can't take that, as well you know.'

'Well, get yourself a little drink then. I can buy you a drink, can't I?'

'Tomorrow when I'm less busy.'

'I won't be here tomorrow, I'll be in Lingfield. And as I said to Mrs O, you've spoiled my Saturday nights with this early closing. I said to her, I'm put right out, I am. I used to look forward to my drink after a day at the races. We haven't all moved out of the East End, you know, I said to her, I said.'

'No use complaining to me, Mr Agnesi. I just do what I'm told.' And then to the man holding the tray, 'If you wouldn't mind leaving it down there on the counter, thanks a million. Just there above the sink, where I can get at it.'

'You're a lovely girl, Milly, you know that?' Sylvester said. 'I don't know why you haven't been snapped up a long time ago, I really don't.'

'Maybe I don't want to be snapped up,' she said, veering away from him and lifting the flap to get behind the counter.

She could hear Sylvester laughing behind her. 'Oh-ho! That's the spirit, Milly my love, that's the spirit!'

Behind the counter, she turned on the tap, her eye taking in her immediate surroundings. Mrs Oak to the right of her, pulling a pint.

Trish behind her, concocting a couple of hot toddies.

Shamie was seated up at the counter right in front of her, alongside his doddery Uncle George.

'Did you get the glasses?' Trish asked.

'Yes, I got the bloody glasses,' she snapped.

'Whatever's the matter with you, Milly?' Mrs Oak asked. 'You're like a cat on a hot tin roof these past couple of days, prowling around, all hot and bothered.'

'I'm trying to stop us from running out of glasses, Mrs Oak,' she said. 'The machine's broken again.'

'Yes, I know. So you said. Nothing much I can do about it just this minute though, is there?'

Ashamed of her little outburst, she kept her head down, watching the sink puff up with suds. Half listening to the conversation around her, she pulled the glasses down from the counter in twos and threes, and dunked them into the water.

Shamie's Uncle George was going on about the gangsters, talking in stops and starts, breathing down his bashed-in potato nose: 'They was wrong,' he said, 'I know that. You know that. We all know that. But they done a bit of good too – I mean, they gave to their own. Medical bills, funerals and that.'

'Medical bills! Funerals!' Trish said over her shoulder. 'They probably caused them in the first place.'

'Ah no, no. I take your point. But they gave to those in need, too, is what I mean. And there was no shortage of them, let me tell you. Look, all I'm saying is, they helped people out. The poverty, it was – what you call it, Shamie? What's the word I'm looking for?'

'Abject? Rife?'

'The poverty was everywhere. It was bound to produce their like sooner or later. And they didn't kill no – what you call them – civilians, I suppose you could say. Only their own sort, you know?'

'Thugs, you mean?' Mrs Oak suggested.

'Yeah well, life was different back then. Easy to be . . . to be . . . Easy to judge now. Life was *hard*. They weren't all bad, is all I'm saying. I mean, your Terry,' George said then, pointing straight at Mrs Oak, 'he would have known what it was like. He would have known the family, he would have known them well.'

'I can assure you,' Mrs Oak said, 'he most certainly did not.'

She placed the newly filled pint on the counter, put the flat of her hand out for payment and then walked off to the till at the far end of the bar and began serving customers down there.

'You hit a sore spot there, George,' Shamie chuckled.

'Oh dear,' the old man said and began to call after her, 'I didn't mean *that* way. Not *that* way.'

'Course you didn't, George – now sit down, will you? She'll be okay. I'll explain to her later.'

'I'm sorry if I upset her.'

'Don't worry about it,' Shamie said. 'Here, Georgie, do you remember the older brother?'

'The older brother? Oh yeah, yeah him, of course I do. I think.'

'He was a boxer, useful one too. He fought for the navy. Welter. Nice enough bloke, I came across him here and there. And as for the grandfather! Remember him? A right nutter, he was. Cannonball, they called him.'

'Did I fight him?' George asked.

'Nah, he wasn't a pro. He wouldn't have had the discipline. Nothin' he wouldn't do, mind you. Fight, eat glass, swallow a hot poker, sing, dance, fight some more, you name it. Gloves on, gloves off. Am I right, George?'

George looked as if he was about to cry. 'I mean, he was a gambler, wasn't he?'

'Who was?' Shamie asked.

'Her dad, Terry.'

'You mean her husband?'

'Oh yeah, her husband, Terry. They come across all sorts, don't they, these gamblers? I didn't mean . . . I get mixed up, sometimes. The words they, you know, they get jammed in the doorway.'

'It's all right, Georgie.'

'But I'm upset again,' George said.

'That's the old melancholia playing up on you,' Shamie said. 'Remember? The doctor explained. You put a smile on your face and it'll pass.'

'Like this?' George said, grinning like a maniac.

'Christ!' Shamie laughed. 'Tone it down, will you? You don't want your dentures falling out. Still, at least you made Milly smile.'

'I'm not smiling,' she said.

'Yes you are. You're laughing.'

'No, I'm not.'

'Yes you are,' Shamie said. 'Look at her. She can't keep it in. I see you.'

'All right, I am,' she laughed.

'Now that I think of it,' George said, 'there was a rumour. A whisper is all it was. No one round here would believe it, I think. Old Terry, he was a good sort. But he was a gambler. They're different, that's it. My brother, Artie, he hid a load in his work-shop. Not for what's-his-face on the news there. Someone else. Money, was it? No. For money he did it. Televisions? Nah, it couldn't have been televisions because he hid it in the sawdust, and you'd never have enough sawdust for that, would you? Diamonds, maybe. Yeah, that could be it. He got away with it too. We forget that, how many get away with it. And then he blew it all. Two flies going up the wall, he was. And Terry, well . . . ? He were a two-flies-going-up-the-wall man and all. They questioned him, now that I think of it. Terry, they did.'

'Probably best to shut up now, George,' Shamie said.

'Oh they didn't charge him or nothin'. Just pulled him in for—'

'Tell you what, why don't we go and sit down over here, eh?'

Trish turned around carrying two hot whiskies cloaked in

paper napkins. 'You have a nice little sit-down over there, George,' she said. 'It'll be more comfortable for you.'

'But it's mine next. I have to, you know. Shout.'

'Milly will come over in a few, won't you, Milly?' Shamie said.

'I will, of course. Just let me dry a few of these glasses.'

In the background, she could hear the faint sound of the phone ringing into the hall.

'What have I done?' George said. 'Have I said something about Artie?'

He was looking at her, his squashed nose all red, the folds of his face draped around it.

'Did you know him?' he asked her, wiping his tears with the back of his hand.

'No. No, I'm afraid I didn't.'

'He was my brother.'

Behind her she could see Brenda pushing through the crowd and then her voice shouting over George's shoulder, 'You're wanted on the phone, Milly.'

'Be back in a minute,' she said to George, glad of an excuse to escape the old man's distress.

Out in the hall, she lifted the receiver.

'Milly?'

'Oh God, Pip? I don't believe it! You're back then? Where were you?'

'Oh. You know. Here and there. Milly?'

'Yes, Pip?'

'Milly, he's . . . He's dead.'

'Who – the gangster?'

'What? No, my father. My father's died. He went this morning.'

'Ah no – oh my God, I'm so sorry, Pip, I really am. But how? That's awful. I was thinking we hadn't seen him in a while. He used to be such a regular for the pensioners' Friday lunch, ah God.'

'I've just come from the nursing home.'

'You were with him then?'

'I got back to London yesterday evening and I don't know why but I decided to go straight in to see him and when I got there—'

'He was dead?'

'No. He'd had some sort of a stroke, you see. But you know people have strokes and they don't—'

'Yes, yes of course.'

'And I mean, I still didn't expect him to, you know, actually . . . He was awake, he knew me and all. He gave me his watch. We talked for a bit and then he fell asleep. And I just sat there till it was bright and I thought when he didn't die during the night – most people go at four in the morning, did you know that?'

'No, I didn't.'

'I thought . . . I thought he was just sleeping. But then, around breakfast time, his blood pressure started to sink and he just . . . he just went.'

'So it was peaceful at least?'

'Yes, that's true. I don't know what I'm supposed to do now.'

'Are you on your own – is Dom not with you?'

'Dom is away. He's due back tonight. He's on the flight, actually, from Boston. I have no way of getting in touch. He usually goes to see him on Sunday morning, the nurse said . . .'

'Oh, but he'll have to be told before then, Pip.'

'I know that.'

'He has one of those mobile phones, hasn't he – why don't you just phone?'

'I don't know the number. Anyway, it's not that simple.'

'Would you not just phone Marj then? She'll have his number.'

'I can't do that.'

'Why not?'

'Supposing she decides to meet him at the airport?'

'So what if she does?'

'Milly, he's not on his own.'

'*What?*'

'He's with this French one.'

'You're joking me!'

'Monique is her name.'

They said nothing then for a while.

She could hear the first rumbling of 'The Fields of Athenry' break out from the far end of the bar. And then the sounds of whatever pub Pip was in playing in the background, the noise vying with the sound of the pub behind her. The early-evening chatter, and the clinking bottles; the echo of Jill Dando reading the news on both television sets.

'Are you still there?' he asked after a bit.

'Yes, Pip.'

'What time is it now?'

'Wasn't that the six o'clock news?'

'Oh yeah, that's right.'

'Poor Marj.'

'Yeah, I know. I could wait at the end of his road, I suppose, until he shows.'

'In this weather? Anyway, Marj might see you.'

'Can I ask you a favour, Milly? They gave me a box of his stuff in the nursing home. Would you mind it for me? It's just books and a few papers and bits he kept over the years. Just for a while till I find somewhere to stay. I'm afraid I might lose it. Would you do that for me?'

'I will, of course. Where are you?'

'I'm up the road, in Gerry's. I'll leave it behind the counter with him.'

'Why didn't you say so? I'll come up to you now.'

'No, no don't, I'm in a bit of a state to be honest.'

'You don't sound drunk.'

'I'm not. I'm off it. Nearly a month now. Well, next week it will be. More or less. I look a right state, though – I've been up all night.'

'Oh God, Pip. What does that matter?'

She turned slightly, her hand playing with the twisted cord of the receiver. Through the tilted mirror above the phone, she could see Trish stepping back from the till, looking for her.

'Are you all right for money?'

'Yeah, I'm fine.'

'No, really, are you?'

'I'm badly stuck, to be honest.'

'Let me come down to you. I'll take an hour off; we can work something out about Dom. I'll bring you a few quid. I can take the box then, if you want.'

He didn't answer her.

'Come on, Pip,' she said after a moment, 'what are friends for?'

'All right then. Milly?'

'Yes Pip?'

'Nothing. Just – just thanks.'

'Stay where you are, I'm on my way.'

As she put down the phone, she heard the door of the office open behind her. Then Mrs Oak's voice: 'Milly? A moment please.'

'Oh shit,' she whispered before turning around.

'I didn't know you were in here, Mrs Oak,' she said as she stepped into the office.

'I did close the door, quite loudly in fact, but you didn't appear to notice. What's going on?'

'Mr Dawson's just died. That was Phil.'

Mrs Oak sat down. 'Oh I am sorry to hear it. And where's Phil now?'

'He's up the road in Gerry's.'

'Drunk, I suppose?'

'No. He's been off it for over a month. He's on his own up there – his brother is away. I don't think he has anywhere to stay. Would it be okay if I take an hour off?'

'To give him money, I suppose. Fine. Off you go. Don't be long, though, you've seen what it's like out there.'

'I won't. I'll be as quick as I can.'

She turned, ready to run upstairs to get her coat and whatever cash she had in her room.

'On second thoughts, Milly, let me deal with it. I have to go out anyway, I can drop him a few quid on the way.'

'No!' she said, raising her voice a little too loudly. 'I mean, it's okay, Mrs Oak, I won't be long.'

'I'll take care of it, Milly.'

'But he's my friend,' she heard herself say, and then blushed at how childish she sounded. 'What I mean is, I don't think he'd like to take money from you.'

'It won't be from me.'

Mrs Oak ducked under the desk then and started to fiddle around with the safe. She came back with a brown manila envelope with the word 'Philip' scrawled across the front in shaky blue letters.

'His dad asked me to hold this for him,' she explained.

'Did he? When?'

'Just before he went into that home. A few months ago now.'

'Oh, right. Well, is there . . . is there much in it?'

'Feels like a couple of grand anyway.'

'That's a lot to hand him in one go.'

'You think I should hold some back?'

'Maybe.'

Mrs Oak was silent for a few seconds and then, 'I don't like to interfere with the wishes of the departed, but . . . Well, he could blow the lot before the funeral, let's face it. Or go on a right bender. Maybe give him a couple of hundred out of it, and then the rest just before or after the funeral, what do you think – just in case?'

'Yes, just in case.'

Mrs Oak plugged in the kettle and waited for it to boil. She held the envelope over the rush of steam for a few seconds. Then, coming back to the desk, she sat down and eased the envelope open. She pulled the sheaf of notes out, counted them and removed four fifties. Then after a moment, pulled another two fifties out. 'There's seventeen hundred left – you're a witness, all right?'

She put the seventeen hundred back into the envelope, pressed the flap back into place and leaned on it with the side of her fist.

Then, reaching into the drawer, she pulled out an empty envelope, slipped the six fifties in and with one eye on the envelope marked *Philip*, copied the name out. 'Later, I can tell him there were two envelopes, one for before, one for after.'

She held the two envelopes up. 'What you think – that should do it?'

'Yes,' she said, trying not to look surprised at how easily and how well Mrs Oak had committed her little forgery.

'I didn't realise you were so friendly with his dad, Mrs Oak,' she said.

'When you're a landlady, Milly, people entrust things to you.

255

But he liked it here – he liked us. You, me, Trish. He even liked Brenda! He appreciated the way we looked after old people, the pensioners' lunch and that.'

Mrs Oak stood up then and put on her coat. She took her wallet out of the drawer and checked it for cash. Then she reached for her car keys and stood for a moment, her soft brown handbag squeezed under her elbow. 'Look,' she said, 'I know you'd probably like to see him but I feel I should give him this money in person – you do understand? I'll tell him to buzz you tomorrow, you can see him then, take as much time as you want. Saturday's a dead day anyway. Know what I heard the other day? They're selling The Lion. It's hush-hush at the moment, but your pal Gerry, he could be out of a job. Unless he buys it, of course, which I don't see happening. There's been developers sniffing around. Anyway, don't you worry about Philip, you'll see him tomorrow. Tell you what, though, I shall be glad to get out of here tonight. I couldn't bear to hear another word about that glorified psycho. Fancy a gentleman like Mr Dawson dying on the same day as the like of that?'

She didn't hear Mrs Oak come in that night and the next morning she came down late, just as they were about to go downstairs to get ready for opening. She was all dolled up, her new Burberry mac slung over her arm. She laid the mac carefully across the chair, put on the kettle and slipped a slice of bread in the toaster. Then she announced she'd be taking the day off.

'Oh, going anywhere interesting?' Trish asked.

'Just off to do a bit of shopping. I've got that bridge club lunch tomorrow and I need to buy Ena a house-warming present. I've phoned Muriel, she's on standby if you need her this morning – but I doubt you will.'

'What time will you be back?' Trish asked.

'Does it matter, Trish? It's Saturday, we close at five. As a matter of fact, I may be taking a bit of time off this coming week.'

She left them wait while she made her tea, then buttered her toast and cut it into two careful triangles. She stood while she was eating, leaning away from the toast so as not to spill anything on her pink cashmere jumper. She only took a couple of sips of tea and half of her toast when she said, 'Just to save you exploding from curiosity, Trish, I'll explain. An old pal is in London for a few days and I'm making myself available. All my life I've lived in London, time I got to see it from another perspective, see what all the fuss is about. We're going to be tourists! Who knows, we may even go away for a night or two.'

'Anywhere nice?' Trish asked.

'I don't know yet, do I? But I promise you'll be first to know, Trish – all right?'

She gave Mrs Oak a bit of a head start, then ran down the stairs after her.

'How was he?' she asked.

Mrs Oak turned and looked at her. 'Scruffy. Dishevelled, I believe the term is.'

'Was he upset?'

'He wouldn't let on to me, would he? But yeah, I'd say he was upset.'

'Did he mind that I told you? I mean, I wouldn't like him to think that I went running to you, telling tales.'

'Don't be ridiculous – how else would I have known? I told him to phone you. Sorry, I'm in a rush. I'll talk to you later.'

'Do you think he will phone me?'

'I have to run, Milly.'

'Sorry, yes, yes, you go on.'

Mrs Oak was at the bottom of the stairs now. She called down after her.

'Excuse me, Mrs Oak? If he does call, is it still all right to take a few hours off to see him?'

'Course it is,' Mrs Oak's voice trailed over the clip of her heels going down the corridor and out the back way.

She spent the morning with her ear cocked towards the phone and her eye on the door. And once, when she was halfway up the stairs, the phone rang and she nearly broke her neck getting down to answer it, only to find the milkman on the other end looking to have his bill paid.

At three o'clock, Trish asked her if she'd mind locking up.

'No problem.'

'And will you do the cash?'

'I will.'

'But don't say you did it – I don't want her thinking I'm skiving off.'

'I won't.'

'I'm off out tonight with Vera and a few of her night-school chums. Some place in Covent Garden for a bite to eat, there's music there and all. I'm going to have my hair done first and Vera's going to buy herself a mobile phone thingy – although why, I really don't know, I'm sure she can't be that much in demand. You can join us if you like? Vera won't mind, she says her new chums are good for a laugh. Their night class is on English literature. You should like that, Milly. You'll have something in common with them.'

'Ah, no thanks, I'll wait here.'

'For what – for him to phone you? Look, he's probably busy. Funerals don't arrange themselves, you know. People have to be told; there's a service to be sorted, all that. I shouldn't worry.'

'But I'm worried about him.'

'It's not your business to worry over him, though. You're neither his wife nor his girlfriend.'

'No, but I am his friend.'

'Oh for God's sake, Milly!'

'What? His father has just died and—'

'You know something? I am so tired of watching you waste your time over that man.'

'It's not like that, I told you.'

'You think you love him, but you don't. You just want to fix him, that's it.'

'What are you even talking about! We're friends, I told you.'

'You see that he's broken, and you want to fix him. Well, forget that, Milly. He's unfixable. He likes being broken. Oh, look, I can't be bothered any more. Do what you like. Get your blanket off the bed and sleep like a little dog under the phone in case he rings. Then turn yourself into a mat, so he can walk all over you.'

She was still fuming over Trish's remarks when, shortly before closing time, a man came into the bar. A stranger, she thought at first, but as he approached the counter, there was something familiar about him. He smiled at her, and she recognised him then as the man who had helped her with the tray the day before. He wasn't wearing a suit now but was dressed in brown cords and a black leather jacket.

She said: 'Oh, hello, what brings you round here again?'

'How do you know I'm not from around here?'

'I just do.'

'I was wondering if I left a pair of reading glasses here last night?'

'I don't think so,' she said, 'but hold on.'

She pulled the lost-and-found box out from under the shelf,

holding back the roll of forgotten umbrellas that were stashed behind it. In between the gloves and scarves, there were two pairs of specs: one heavy black pair that had been lying there for as long as she could remember, and a pink tortoiseshell pair that had once belonged to Mrs Rogers.

'Sorry,' she said, 'but nothing's been handed in.'

'Oh well, I may as well take a pint while I'm here. Is the Guinness any good?'

'The best that you'll find this side of the Irish Sea,' she said and he laughed. He was a pleasant-faced man, she thought, a bit grey around the edges, probably in his mid- to late forties, good teeth, nice smile, smooth face, smooth hands, a little overweight.

He surveyed the room while he waited for the pint to settle. 'Much quieter today, eh? I mean, you'd never think it was the same place – would you?'

'It used to be mayhem in here on Saturday. But not any more.'

'How come?'

'There was a sewing factory over the road, and a couple of other businesses that worked Saturdays. But those kinds of businesses, they've closed down now. And the locals are disappearing.'

'What? They're being abducted or something?'

'They're moving out. Some of them lived over shops that have been bought by developers. Or they're dying off,' she said, thinking again of Mrs Rogers. 'We close Sundays too but that was always the case.'

'I feel bad now,' he said.

'Why?'

'I'm one of those dreaded developers. That's why we were here yesterday – we were looking at a couple of buildings at the far end of the street.'

'Which ones?'

'A pub, the buildings on either side of it. The weather was so bad, we didn't get a proper look at them. Then we started drinking. I was feeling quite ropey this morning to be honest. I'm staying in a hotel in Holborn until I find a flat; I needed some air and decided to go for a walk and well, here I am . . .'

She placed his pint on the counter. 'You're not from London, then?'

'Oh yes, I am. Recently divorced, that's why I need a flat.'

'Oh right. Can you manage without them?'

'Without what?'

'Your glasses.'

'Oh yeah, my glasses, yeah, it's fine, I've got a spare pair somewhere. Will you have a drink with me?' he asked, reaching into his pocket.

'I have to clear up, do the cash and that. We close in a while.'

She could feel his earnest green eyes following her around as she wandered about, clearing up. She thought – I wonder, was that a lie about his glasses? Then she thought – if it was, it has nothing to do with you; he's sussing out the area, that's all, fishing for information. Tell him nothing, that's what you do.

As she stood at the till sorting the cash, she took a few sneaky glances at him through the mirror. He was almost done with his pint.

She turned around and he gave her a smile. Then he raised his hand to call her.

'You were saying there that you're closing soon? You don't fancy coming for a drink, do you?'

'Oh, no, sorry, I can't. I'm waiting for a call.'

'I might have known there'd be a boyfriend.' He smiled. Then he stood up and put a fiver on the table. 'Well, it was worth a shot, I suppose.'

'No, it's not like that – we're just friends and his father died, you see. I just want to see if he needs me to do anything. We could have a drink here, if you like?'

'Okay, yeah.' He smiled again and plonked himself back down on his stool.

'Just let me get rid of the last few customers and then I need to finish the cash.'

She was coming out of the office after putting the money in the safe and there he was standing in the hall by the phone.

'They're all gone in there,' he said and she thought: he knows I'm here on my own.

'I was just looking for the gents,' he said.

She thought: he knows I've been at the safe. He's going to make me open it, and then steal all the money. Oh God.

She said: 'You mean to tell me that you were here for all that time yesterday and you didn't go to the gents once?'

He laughed; the flush on his face made him look almost shy.

The way he was looking at her. Her heart was bouncing in her chest and a weakness came into her legs.

'I seem to have forgotten,' he said.

'The gents are through the bar, on the other side.'

'I'm sorry,' he said and laughed.

'That's all right.'

He put his hand out and touched her arm. She didn't move. He stroked her arm twice with the flat of his hand as if he was stroking a cat. She could feel his touch pass through her skin.

'Do you want me to go?' he asked, smiling at her again, the smile so sweet that she wondered did he practise it in the mirror.

She thought: tell him to go, just tell him to go. Then she thought, it's been such a long time.

'You could at least tell me your name,' she said.

'Matthew,' he said, or something like that, his voice so low she could hardly hear it.

He leaned into her suddenly, his hand on the small of her back, his arms tightening around her, the colour of his leather jacket spilling like ink around her. She felt a melting sensation in her lower stomach, spreading down through her groin, an aching. He pulled her to him, the feel of his prick through his corduroy trousers hard against her leg. And she thought to hell with it all, in fact, fuck it just fuck it, and she let it take her over, pressing into him and now she could feel his tongue filling her mouth, pushing every thought in her head away except for the thought of lying naked with this stranger, his full weight pinning her to the bed, and wondering how she was going to get him up the four flights of stairs before she came to her senses and changed her mind.

The sound of Trish's voice calling her name. Then footsteps at the bottom of her flight of stairs. 'Milly? You up there, Milly?'

She jumped out of bed, threw on her dressing gown and, pulling a towel off the chair, wrapped her hair into a turban.

She opened the door.

'You gave me an awful fright, Trish. I didn't know who you were!'

'Did I? Sorry. Look I came back because, well, I wanted to apologise about earlier. I had no business talking to you that way – I was way out of order. You're never going to bed already?'

'What? No, no, I'm just out of the bath.'

'Well, I'm sorry, really I am. You sure you won't come with us? It might do you good.'

'No, I'm fine. I'm going to have an early night, watch a bit of telly. I'm tired. You go and enjoy yourself.'

'Are we all right then, Milly? Do you forgive me?'

'Of course. Go on. Your hair is lovely, by the way.'

'Oh, thanks! Thanks a lot. Well, see you in the morning then. Don't forget to bolt the door after me. Cheerio. Sleep well.'

'Yes, cheerio.'

She stayed at the bedroom door waiting for Trish's footsteps to go back downstairs. Then she went to the window. She leaned forward, nose to the pane, until she saw Trish trot through the dusk, over the road to the tube station.

'I think you better go now,' she said to the man still lying in the bed behind her.

'I thought she was gone?'

'Yes, but the boss could be back any minute. If she catches you here, I'll lose my job.'

'Oh. Oh I see. Yes, well, in that case, I suppose . . .'

She stood looking out the window while he got dressed.

A minute later, he said: 'Could I see you again sometime?'

'No,' she said. 'Thanks for asking, though.'

'What, are you married or something?'

'No. Nothing like that.'

'Won't you even look at me?' he said and then after a few seconds, 'How do I get out of here anyway?'

'Go down the flight outside the door, turn right and keep going downstairs until you can go no further, then back through the bar and out the front door. Just pull it shut after you.'

She heard him open the bedroom door. 'Why did you bring me up here?' he asked. 'Why did you . . . if you can't even bear to look at me?'

'I don't know,' she said, 'I just did.'

It was dark by now. She crossed the room and switched on her bedside lamp. A condom was lying on the floor beneath it, like a small bag of snot. She stood looking at it for a moment, then covered it over with a bundle of tissues, pulled it up and stuck it in the end of her wastepaper bin. She took her time changing the bed, removing the sheets, spreading the new ones on, adjusting and fussing till the mattress looked like an iced cake. She put a new cover on the duvet and bumped up the pillows. Then she climbed into bed and slept like the dead.

In the morning, she met Trish coming out of the kitchen as she came downstairs, wastepaper bag under her arm.

'Want me to take that for you?' Trish asked. 'I'll be going down in a bit with the kitchen bin.'

'No, you're all right, I'll do both. How was your night out?'

'All right, I suppose. A bit upmarket for me. A younger crowd, too. Talking about babies all the time. I mean, is it just me or are babies overrated? Here, I don't suppose you fancy a bit of breakfast?'

'Actually, I'm starving. I wouldn't mind a fry-up, if you're doing one?'

'All right then,' Trish beamed, 'a Sunday fry-up it is! Leave the bins there till we've eaten. You do the toast and tea and lay the table. I'll do the rest. Madam's gone out already, by the way. Mrs Richards just picked her up. They're off to see Ena's new flat, then on to some fancy restaurant in Mayfair. Honestly, the money some of those old bats have. She looked a million dollars going out, I don't know how she does it. I'm ten years younger than her and I look fifteen older.'

'You do not!'

'Yes I do. I'm forty-four and I feel . . . oh, never mind. Know what time she came in last night? Same time as me. I met her coming up the stairs. That was some shopping spree, I said, you must have spent a fortune. Very funny, Trish, she said, I went for a bite to eat and a drink if you must know. Oh yeah? I said, a date was it? I wouldn't quite call it that, she said. Of course, she'd tell you nothing, her.'

'It was probably just that pal she was talking about.'

'I have my pals, Milly, but they don't make me glow the way she was glowing this morning. You know what I think? I think it's that German bloke she met a few years ago in Malta. He phoned her a few times and came to London once to see her. Ena said he was a fine-looking man, if a bit SS-looking. Still, forgive and forget, eh, Ena?'

'She's entitled to her privacy.'

'Oh do shut up, Milly, honestly, you're as bad as she is. As soon as I'm finished breakfast, I'm going round to Vera's. At least I can get my teeth into a good gossip there.'

After Trish left, she sat on for a while at the kitchen table, listening to the sounds of the empty house coming from above and below her. She thought about the man from the previous evening and wondered at her carry-on. She did and did not know what had made her do it. And now that it was over, she didn't really care, so long as she never bumped into him again, or so long as no one else ever found out about it.

A hard, cold sunlight was coming through the kitchen windows, and behind it, she could see the clouds beginning to darken and swell. It would rain again soon. She went back upstairs and looked out of the top landing window at the rise and fall of rooftops. On the flat extension roof of a house two streets away, a woman was hanging out washing even though the sunlight had disappeared by now and rain was obviously on the way. She pictured Vera and Trish sitting in her little sitting room above the shop, picking the women apart from Vera's night class, then speculating on Mrs Oak's German lover. They would probably allow a few moments of respect for Mr Greene, Vera shedding a tear about how much she missed her father. But mostly they would waffle on, two middle-aged women, making plans for outings they would probably never go on, holidays they would certainly never take, discussing things they'd read or seen on the telly, dissecting and guessing at the lives of others. Later they would probably go for a walk through the gloomy Sunday streets, in for a drink, or they might go to the pictures, then back to Vera's again for a bottle of wine and a Chinese. Getting on with it anyway, doing their best to enjoy the small comforts of a Sunday evening after a week of relentless graft. They had both, in their time, wasted hours of their lives waiting in vain for some man to phone.

The draught coming in through the cracks in the side of the landing window soothed her face, and a gentle rattle from the window panes was making her feel sleepy again. But she would not spend another day waiting. She would go out. Do something, go somewhere, get on a bus maybe, or just start walking and see where it took her.

She collected her things, put on her coat and her scarf and went down to the bar. As she pulled the lost-and-found box out and slid a forgotten umbrella from the space behind it, Mrs Rogers' pink specs caught her eye.

She walked in the rain up Clerkenwell Road to the Italian church, climbing the few steps straight off the street to the entrance where she stopped to look for the memorial Pip had once told her about. She found it mounted over the porch, starker than expected, and a little shocking. Half-bodies in the hull of a boat, arms raised or clinging to the side. It looked as if they were being gobbled up by the sea, legs first. Nearly five hundred Italian internees, Pip had said, rounded up in England during the war, then torpedoed and drowned on the way to Canada.

There was a sound of singing from inside the church and then the words of the priest speaking Italian. She pushed the door open to find herself standing at the side of the church, right in the middle of a mass. Most of the seats were taken, apart from a few pews at the back where people on their own were sitting or kneeling at intervals. She thought of all the times Mrs Rogers must have sat here, pretending to be a Catholic so she could avail herself of a coffee and cake after mass. Even if there was no need to pretend as the sign outside had said that all were welcome. Across the aisle, behind the marble pillars, were other pews, mostly vacant. She knew not to cross the front of the altar and so made her way down to the end of the church and back up again on the far side.

As she moved along, she remembered the last and only time that she'd been in here. She'd run into Mrs Rogers outside on the street and the old woman had insisted on bringing her in. 'They keep the gates open,' she'd said with a touch of pride in her voice, 'unlike most of the churches in London nowadays.'

A day in December that had been, 'with snow in prospect,' as Mrs Rogers had put it, pulling her by the sleeve up the steps and shyly pushing the door open into an empty church. She'd given her the grand tour, as if she was showing her around her own home. The statues of saints – one for every town and occasion, Mrs Rogers explained, and when they came to the crib, she'd been like a little girl pointing her toys out, her loud, excited whisper rustling on the air. The crib had been an extravagant affair going way beyond the standard holy family with a few animals and wise men thrown in. There'd been a blacksmith, a pizza maker, a brood of hens, a fire burning in a miniature brazier, a couple of angels that looked as if they were heading off to a disco. It had been like something you'd see in the window of Hamleys. The organ had started to play, a lonely, liquid sound. And two priests appeared up at the front, speaking Italian, their words dancing around on the echo. One of them had turned and, spotting Mrs Rogers, had given her a little wave. The old woman beaming with pleasure.

Mrs Rogers had not shown her the memorial in the porch that day, nor had she pointed out the marble slab inside the church with the names of all the drowned Italians etched onto it. Maybe she had never noticed them, or maybe she had only wanted her to see the happy things contained within these ornate walls.

Now, as she walked alone along the outer aisle, she saw candles flickering on a brass votive stand, a statue of an open-handed saint looking over them. She stood beside it for a moment, then lowered herself down onto the cushioned kneeler, her fore-head resting on her joined hands as though she was praying. She thought of poor Mr Greene, and then Mr Wiseman. Petey Whitty and Mrs Rogers. She thought of Pip's father and all the other people she had grown fond of, or at least used to, since moving to London. Day after day, telling her their bits of news, giving their opinions on world affairs. And then one day they just disappeared. Some dead; others, like Mr Dawson, moved into a nursing home. All gone now anyway, like the men commemor-ated on the plaque on the wall. All sunk by life.

Slyly, she tested the stand to see how steady it was. It seemed solid enough, as if fixed into the floor. Reaching into her pocket, she slid Mrs Rogers' glasses out, and bending, as though fixing her shoe, she slipped them into the small gap behind the stand

A few nights later, they were doing the clear-up while Trish debated the secret love life of Mrs Oak.

'Not that she's ever brought *anyone* back here,' Trish said. 'But she's had her little flings. I mean, who can blame her? I would too, if I got a decent offer. Of course, she could get married again. I have a feeling, you know, that she just might. I mean, imagine if it was that German bloke she's been seeing and she sold up and moved off to Germany or somewhere? Or worse, imagine if he moved himself in here? Are you listening to me, Milly?'

'Not really,' she said.

'Well, you should do. Ever wonder what will happen to us if she decides to sell this place? I mean it's all right for you, you're only in your thirties, you can start over. But it's more difficult to find live-in work at my age – wait, did you hear that?'

'What?'

'A taxi. It's her. Eyes down. Shh, Milly, say nothing. *Shhh.*'

'I wasn't saying anything.'

'Oh, hello stranger,' Trish said, 'have a good time, did we?'

'We did, Trish, we had the most. It was magnificent. The most. Unbelievable what they can do. Quite extraordinary.'

'Oh yeah?' Trish said, throwing a look over the bar at Milly.

'Tails, whiskers, the way they move. The *howling*! My goodness. I mean, you start believing that they're real—'

'You've never been to see *Cats*!' Trish said. 'Oh, how I would love to see *Cats*.'

'Good job I brought you a little pressie then, to get you in the mood.'

She reached into her handbag and took out a package. 'Music, lyrics, they're all in there.'

She put the CD down on the bar.

'I look forward to hearing it,' Trish said, obviously disappointed that it wasn't a couple of tickets.

'Well, I'm off to bed,' Mrs Oak said.

She slipped out of her slingback shoes and hooked them over her finger. 'You have to go and see it. You really do . . . I mean, the whole production, you couldn't fault it. Magic. See you in the morning,' she sighed. 'Night night, then.'

'Bloody hell,' Trish said, when she was safely out of hearing. 'What do you think? Doesn't she look like . . . ?'

'The cat that got the cream?' she suggested, and they both burst out laughing.

The day before his father's funeral, he phoned and asked if she'd meet him at Blackfriars Bridge. There had been a few calls here and there, once to check she'd collected the box from Gerry. Another time to tell her the funeral arrangements, and once just for a chat. This was the first time she'd actually seen him since he'd come back to London. He looked pale and there was a chip out of his front tooth. He pounced a hug on her, the minute he saw her. She closed her eyes. He patted her back twice.

'What happened to your tooth?' she asked, when he stepped back from her.

He brought his finger to it, as if to remind himself. 'My tooth? That happened ages ago. A little accident. It's nothing, it's fine.'

'Don't tell me – Epsom?'

'What do you know about Epsom?'

'I know that after the races, illegal fights take place.'

He grinned at her. 'Sylvester, I suppose. God, he's such an old woman.'

'I hope you won anyway.'

'Well, you know what they say about Epsom – you don't fight to win. You fight to get paid.'

They walked over the bridge in silence, cars passing on one side, trains on the other. Beneath them, the pulse of the river.

He said, 'I can't believe it's taken this long for the funeral. Twelve days since he died. The Irish are way more efficient when it comes to burying the dead. Three days tops, from last breath to grave. Or urn, as it will be, in his case. Which I have to say surprised me – he loved nature so much, I thought he'd want to, I don't know . . .'

'Go back to it?'

'Yeah, something like that.'

When they got to the far side, they climbed the short stone steps of the landing stage and stood at the iron rail looking back at St Paul's. She said, 'I can't stay too long, I told Mrs Oak I was going to buy a pair of tights for the funeral tomorrow.'

'I've got to get back too. I'm staying with Dom.'

'You moved out of the B & B then?'

'Yeah. A couple of nights ago.'

'How's that going?'

'It's a bit awkward. I keep thinking Marj knows. And that she knows I know. The way she looks at me sometimes. I was listening to her giving a singing lesson earlier and I thought I could hear it in her voice. I can't look in her in the face. They were supposed to be moving out of the house in Paddington, buying their own place, somewhere with a garden, starting a family, all that. Marj has been full of it. But at the same time, she doesn't sound convinced. It's as if she knows. And that French one has been phoning. He's in there on his mobile phone whispering away or checking it for messages. I mean she's not stupid, Marj.'

He took a deep breath. 'Sorry, Milly. You don't know how good it is to see your face.' His eyes so sad that she had to turn away.

After a moment she asked him, 'Well, are you all sorted for tomorrow?'

'Yeah, I think so. I got a new suit anyway. And shoes. Shirt, tie, one of Dom's overcoats.'

'Very nice. And what will you do, you know, after the funeral?'

'Don't know. But I'll tell you something, I think I'll never get out of Dom's house.'

'You know Mrs Oak has money for you?'

'She gave me three hundred, yeah.'

'There's more. Another seventeen hundred to be exact. You could put down a deposit on a bedsit. Get a bit of independence from Dom. Look for work. It's a start. She'll give it to you at the funeral I'd say. But Pip – promise me you won't blow it? Your father wanted . . . well I don't know really, sorry, I shouldn't be saying this.'

'No, I get it now. He wanted me to get through the funeral without having to put the hammer on Dom. Dignity, I believe it's called.'

He put his hand over hers. It seemed steady enough yet when he looked at her, she felt it was already too late, that he had started drinking again, not at full throttle, but for the moment, he was managing to keep it under wraps.

'I look forward to seeing it on you,' she said, 'the new suit.'

She laid her head against the top of his arm and stayed for a few more moments looking down into the twist of grey water and the different-shaped boats and barges nosing under the bridge. Then she straightened up and said, 'Well, I better get back, I suppose.'

In her sleep, she could hear movement at the end of her stairs. She thought she was having a bad dream and then she thought the pub had been broken into. Leaning up on one elbow, she listened for a moment, but all she could hear were the usual night sounds grumbling through the old house. She lay down again and

273

stared into the shapes of the room: the furniture, the baton of light coming from the street, her clothes hanging on the back of the door ready for the funeral tomorrow, the green-lit number on the clock telling her it was four a.m. She was wide awake now and would probably stay that way till morning. She decided she might as well go downstairs, make a cup of tea and read for a while.

Crossing the landing to go into the kitchen, she noticed a flickering light through the crack in the door of the staff sitting room. She presumed Trish had stepped in earlier when she was on her break to record something on the video, and had forgotten to turn off the television. But when she stepped into the room, there was Mrs Oak, curled up on the battered sofa, shoes and bag on the floor beside her, the good mac just fecked there next to them. She was drinking what looked like a large gin and tonic and staring at the Ceefax sign on the screen.

'Oh sorry! I didn't realise there was anyone in here.'

'S'all right,' Mrs Oak said.

'Are you okay, Mrs Oak – do you want me to turn on the light?'

'Why do you never call me Dora?' Mrs Oak slurred. 'You've been here long enough.'

'I don't really know,' she laughed uneasily.

'You don't like the name Dora, maybe? I don't blame you. It's a stupid name, really. So is Milly, come to think of it. Two stupid names like you'd give to a couple of ragdolls in a shop. Silly Milly and Dopey Dora. We should change our names by deed poll – eh?'

'We should, I suppose.'

'I wish you wouldn't always agree with me, Milly. You think I'm a cow, say I'm a cow.'

'I do not think you're a cow!'

'Yeah, well I am.'

'You know what happens to cows?'

'They get milked . . . ?'

'Oh, that is funny. You don't know how funny that is.'

Mrs Oak took a long swig of her drink, then, coming up for air said, 'You see they buried that Ronnie Kray today?'

'It was on the news, yes.'

'Six horses, all plumed. Cameras from all over the world. No expense spared, let me tell you. Honestly, I don't think Churchill got that much of a send-off. Makes you think, eh?'

'Tomorrow should be a quieter affair anyhow,' Milly said.

'What?'

'Mr Dawson's funeral?'

'Oh, I shan't be going to that.'

'Oh. I thought . . . I mean, I presumed . . .'

'I don't feel up to it, I'm afraid,' she said, and began flicking her thumbnail off the arm of the chair. 'I think I'm coming down with that flu that's been doing the rounds. You and Trish can go. I'll take care of the shop. What time is it?'

'Gone four.'

'Four! You best go up to bed.'

'Would you like anything before I go up? A cup of coffee maybe?'

'Coffee! At this hour? You saying I'm drunk, Milly?'

'No, of course not.'

'Well, I am. I'm completely pissed. Go on now, try to get a bit of shut-eye.'

'Are you sure you're all right?' she said.

'I will be, Milly, thanks. I just had a bit of a setback, that's all. A disappointment. And I don't feel like going up to the flat just yet. But don't you worry, I'll be all right. I'll be all right in a bit.'

*

There was snow on the day of the funeral: a few light falls mixed in with the drizzle. On the way into the crematorium, she saw the lower half of Pip walking under a big black umbrella, and when they moved inside, the back of his head in the centre of the front pew. He was sitting beside a young girl, maybe twelve or thirteen years old. It took her a moment to realise that of course it was his daughter, Lorraine. She thought of her own daughter, who was about three years older, no longer a child. Angie was there, sitting on the far side of the girl, then Dom, and closer to the edge, Marj and a woman with a violin.

After the service, the rain and snow held off for a while. People stood around in groups talking and smoking, hugging one another. She found him eventually, round the back of the building leaning on the side of a car, talking to his daughter. The girl was tall and sporty-looking. Her hair had lost the baby blonde colour and had darkened to the same colour as her father's. She no longer looked like Angie. And again, she thought of Flora and wondered how tall she was now, and if she played sport and who she might have taken after, her or the man who had fathered her.

As she came nearer to them, she saw the girl was standing square on her feet yet her two legs were constantly moving from the knees. Her face was flushed, and there was a look in her eyes: hope and a touch of panic, as if she was afraid that any second her father would turn and walk away. She decided to leave them be.

When she came back round the front, Trish was lighting a cigarette for Angie.

'Mrs Oak not with you, then?' Angie asked.

'Someone's got to look after the shop,' Trish said, 'and as long as it's not me, eh?'

'How is she anyway? Still keeping you girls on your toes?'

'What toes?' Trish asked. 'They fell off us years ago.'

Angie laughed. 'You never change, Trish, God bless you.'

Trish rattled on while they smoked their cigarettes.

'I've never been to a humanist service before – is that what you call it? I thought it was going to be a Catholic affair when I spotted the two priests in the audience. Who were they, anyway? Do you know, Angie?'

'No idea. I thought it was a nice service, though. Simple. I tell you, that Marj, she can't half sing, eh? And that song at the end, what was it – when I am laid in earth?'

'How do you know that, Ange?'

'I listened to the words, didn't I?'

'Morbid though,' Trish said, 'for such a lovely song.'

'Well, it is a funeral.'

'Did you drive down from Glasgow then, Angie?'

'We flew down this morning. By plane.'

'How long that take?' Trish asked, shaking the lighter and flicking at it till it came on.

'Hour and a bit. My dad paid for it – he made me come today, to be honest. I'm heading off in a few.'

'You not coming back to Dom's house, then?' Trish asked.

'What for? I mean, I liked old John, he was a nice gentle soul, but really, I'm done with that family. I'm not going back to stand making pleasantries with that bastard.'

'He's just lost his father, Angie,' she heard herself say.

'I know that. But I can't stand being in the same room as him, I just can't.'

'Well, Ange,' Trish began, 'I've known you a long time and—'

'What, Trish? *What?*'

'No need to go all defensive on me. I was going to say, he must have treated you very badly if all these years later, you can't stand to be in the same room on the day your daughter's grandfather is buried.'

'He did treat me badly,' Angie said.

'He never hit you?'

'There's worse things, you know.'

'Like what, if you don't mind me asking?'

'Like marrying someone you don't love.'

'Oh, Ange,' Trish said.

Angie pushed a long puff of smoke through the side of her mouth. 'Oh, what do I care anyway? I'm getting married again, did you know?'

'Well congratulations! That's great news. Not another boxer?'

'You're jokin' me! This one couldn't fight his way out of a paper bag. Hardly drinks either. He's a tailor.'

'Oh, that's nice,' Trish said. 'Well, I'm pleased for you, I really am. Oh look, there's your Lorraine now. She does look like him though, Angie, when you see them standing like that together. I mean, she really does. Aw, she's a lovely girl, just look at her.'

They turned to look at Lorraine, standing beside Pip at the top of the steps, holding his hand while he introduced her to different people. Marj was hugging her now. Marj's sister was waiting to meet her. Dom was making a joke.

Angie finished her cigarette, threw the butt of it down and toed it under the gravel. 'I best go up there and get her. Come with me, Milly?'

'*Me?* Why?'

'He likes you and I don't want to see him on my own.'

'Go on, Mill,' Trish said. 'That way you'll be with him when the little one goes.'

She followed Angie up the path. 'Hello, Phil,' Angie said. 'Sorry about your dad.'

'Thanks, Angie,' he said. 'And for coming.'

'Yeah. But we have to go now, we have a plane to catch. Say goodbye, Lorraine.'

'Can't we stay a while, Mum?'

He was still holding Lorraine's hand.

'No, darlin', we can't.'

'Surely an hour wouldn't kill you?' Pip said.

'She's already missed a day of school. And the flight's booked and paid for. We can't afford to throw money away, even if you can.'

'I want to go back to Uncle Dom's house,' the girl said, a slight whine coming into her voice.

'Well, when can I see her again?' Pip asked.

'You know where we are, don't you?'

'Ah come on, Angie. I know you're down here to see your dad regularly. I don't see why we couldn't—'

'Why we couldn't what, Phil? Make life easier for you?'

'No, but do you always have to make it so difficult?'

'Because it suits you now to see her, does it?'

'Mum, please,' Lorraine said and burst out crying.

'See now, you've gone and upset her,' Angie said. 'I knew you would. I bloody knew it.'

'*I've* upset her? *Me?*'

Milly put her hand on Angie's sleeve. 'Come on, Angie, this is not the place. Pip? Stop it now, both of you.'

He nodded, let go of Lorraine's hand and stepped back.

In Dom's house, she caught sight of him several times, but never with a glass in his hand. In the hallway, he stood beside his brother, shaking hands with people as they came in. In the sitting room, he sat talking to a few old men from Mrs Oak's lunch club. Later, he stood in the kitchen making tea for Marj's mother and sister. She saw him chatting to colleagues of Dom's. She saw him thanking a couple of nurses from the home. She saw him in the hall, phoning taxis to take people home. A few times, she spotted him going upstairs, and guessed that up there somewhere he had hidden his top-up bottle, eking it out, keeping everything contained and under control. Fooling most people. But not her. Even if she hadn't spotted him going upstairs, she would have guessed: by the way he was avoiding her, by the sheepish smile he gave her from the far side of the room. By the slight pout of his lower lip.

Two days after the funeral, he came into the bar. He walked down to the end of the counter and waited for her to come to him. Then he asked for a double whiskey.

He squeezed her hand when she brought it to him. 'Sorry, Milly,' he said.

'That's okay. I prefer to know.'

He nodded and then said, 'Would you tell Mrs Oak I'd like to see her?'

'She's upstairs. She's getting over the flu. We haven't seen her in a couple of days.'

'Would you ask her anyway? And listen, while you're up there – you know that box I gave you to mind?'

'Do you want it?'

'No. But would you mind taking something out of it for me? It's a book. A dark blue cover – it's called Palgrave's *Golden Treasury*. There are a few photos and a letter stuck in the pages, mind they don't fall out.'

'No problem. But first I want to say that I thought you did very well at the funeral. And that your father would have been proud of you.'

'Yeah? I was drinking there too.'

'I know. But I don't think anyone else noticed.'

'Oh they did all right,' he said. 'Those who stayed late anyway.'

'What happened?'

'Dom and myself, we came to blows.'

'Oh God.'

'Don't ask.'

'I wasn't going to.'

She went up to her room, took the box out from the wardrobe and found the book. Then she came down to Mrs Oak's flat and rang the bell. She could hear the radio muttering away inside. She waited for a moment, rang the bell again and then rapped at the door and called out, 'Mrs Oak? Sorry to disturb you, but Philip is downstairs – he's asking to see you.'

A moment later, she heard Mrs Oak on the far side of the door.

'He's looking for the rest of his money. Tell him to come back in the morning around eleven. I'll leave it on my desk, you can give it to him then.'

When she came back down to the bar, he was waiting at the bottom of the stairs.

'Well?' he asked.

'If you come back tomorrow, she'll have it for you then. Around eleven.'

'What, she wants to present it to me herself?'

'No. She said she'd leave it for me to give to you.'

She handed him the book and he checked the pages for the photos and the letter. 'Good,' he said, then kissing her on the cheek, 'See you tomorrow, Milly.'

He didn't show up till late afternoon, just as she was about to go upstairs for her break. As he passed the counter, he lifted his thumb and index finger to show a double measure of whiskey. Then he sat into his old alcove.

He took the whiskey from her with one hand, and with the other, he took the envelope. Then he patted the seat beside him and she sat down.

He said, 'If Dom comes looking for the box, you can give it to him.'

'You made up, then?'

'No, I sent him a note telling him where it is. There will be no making up, not this time. Can't say I blame him either.'

'Why not?'

'I told Marj about the other woman.'

'Oh God.'

'I know, in the heat of the row, it just . . . well, she knows now anyway.'

He bowed his head and pressed his fingers into his forehead. Then he took another swig of his whiskey. After a moment, he tore his finger through the flap of the envelope and counted the money through the open slit.

'How much did you say was in here?'

'Seventeen hundred.'

'Looks like I'm missing a few quid.'

He pulled the money out of the envelope and a few receipts fell out on the table. 'Oh, I see,' he said. 'Very smart, very smart indeed.'

He laughed. 'Jesus, I have to hand it to her.'

'What?'

'Ah, nothing. I'll tell you another time. It's a long, stupid story. Can you have a drink with me?'

'I'm on my break, so yea.'

'I'll have the same,' he said, taking a note from the envelope to pay for it.

'No, let me get it.'

She had barely poured her tonic into the glass and taken a sip when he had the second whiskey knocked back. He put the glass down with a small final clip, then he looked at her. There was something about the way he did that.

'Ah, Pip, you're not going off on me again?' she said.

'I have to.'

'Where?'

'Ireland.'

'But why?'

'Something I need to find out. It's about my father. Maybe it's nothing. I hope it's nothing, but . . . Anyway, I feel . . . I feel I have to get out of here. Away from London. I can't seem to get a hold on anything.'

'You're not making sense.'

'No.'

'Well, how long will you be gone for?'

'I might stay there.'

'You don't mean . . . ?'

'Come with me, Milly.'

'*What?*' she laughed.

'Why not? Let's just go. The two of us. Let's just walk out. Leave our London lives behind and start again, somewhere we belong. Let's just—'

He was leaning forward now, blocking everything out with his shoulders, his neck, his hair. His face so close to hers now. She had always fancied him when he was like this, drunk but not yet plastered; vulnerable and yet somehow removed from the rest of the world. She thought, if only we were alone. If there was no one else here, I would tear into him right now.

She pushed him away from her.

'Don't be so stupid,' she said, 'stupid talk.'

'What's stupid about it?'

'I can't just . . .'

'Why not?

'It's too sudden. It's too much. And what about Mrs Oak?'

'Mrs Oak? Why are you always worrying about Mrs Oak? You owe her nothing. You've worked your arse off for her – how many years? You don't actually think she gives a—'

'Shut up, Pip – keep your voice down.'

'Fuck Mrs Oak, is what I say. She's only a fucking—'

'Pip! If you say it, I'll never speak to you again. You're drunk. Did you even sleep last night?'

'A couple of hours.'

'A couple of hours. You're hopeless. You're just . . .'

'What?'

'The bloody state of you. Every time I see you, you've another bit missing from your teeth. And look at your hands, lacerations and scars all over them. And sorry, but I don't see what you have to grin about.'

'I just like it when you give out to me.'

'You come in here and expect me to just pack up and leave; ask me to do such a thing. And you *drunk*.'

'So what if I am?'

'And what happens when you sober up?'

'It's okay, Milly,' he said. 'Please don't cry.'

'I'm not crying! I'm just really pissed off with you. Speaking like that about Mrs Oak.'

'Will you stop going on about Mrs fucking Oak. Come with me or don't come with me. That's all I'm asking.'

'And I *can't*. That's all I'm saying.'

He was quiet for a moment, then he took her hand and

brought it up to his mouth. He put his teeth on her knuckle and, closing his eyes, gently bit down on it. He kissed her hand then and put it down on the seat. Then he pulled the side of her head towards him suddenly and she could feel him whisper into her hair, 'Believe it or not, I love you, Milly. I really do.'

'Well *now* I'm crying,' she said. 'Now I'm fucking well crying.'

'Sorry, Milly,' he said, and then he was gone.

12. Pip

2017

August

HE HAS MET up with Colin a few times since getting out of the clinic – always outdoors, to facilitate his chain-smoking. Colin looks like a middle-aged biker and sounds like a timid schoolgirl desperate for a friend to confide in. On the first few occasions, he'd quite enjoyed listening to the Welsh accent, the slow, poetically arranged phrases coming out through his brown-stained teeth. Or watching the red dragon tattoo on his gym-puffed arm shimmy to the rhythm of his smoking technique. By now, though, he has had quite enough of Colin and his 'little catch-ups', as he likes to call them.

The last time they met, Colin seemed a bit peeved. 'I haven't seen you at a meeting in quite some time, Philip, and I am a little concerned . . .'

'I've been going a bit further afield, Colin,' he lied. 'I feel, you know, that I'm less likely to bump into anyone that way. It's very much a neighbourhood where my brother lives. He's quite respectable, you know, and well known too. If anyone saw me slipping in or out – well, I wouldn't want to embarrass him, you know yourself.'

'Ahh,' said Colin. 'Ahh yes, I see what you mean. Well, that is good news, because I was worried, you see, that there might have been a problem. And you can always be honest with me, you can tell me anything really; we've all had our slips, you know, our little shames.'

'Thanks, Colin, I appreciate that,' he said.

'They are what sustain us, wouldn't you agree?'

'Our little shames?'

'The meetings, Philip, the meetings.'

'Of course.'

'There are those within the fraternity who find meetings a little challenging. I mean, some of the stories you hear, you'd wonder how some people are not locked up and the key thrown away! Still, mustn't judge, must we?'

'No indeed, Colin.'

He is standing outside the café on the corner of Garway Road, waiting for Colin and wondering what class of a muffin he'll get to go with his coffee. He is wondering, too, how these decisions have become so important to him when, a year ago, he hardly even knew what a muffin was, never mind that they could come in different flavours. Then his phone rings: Colin calling.

'I'm afraid I won't make it today, Philip. Sincere apologies.'

'Not to worry, we can do it some other time.'

'I'm having a bit of a crisis, you see.'

'Sorry to hear that, Colin. But look, send me a text when—'

'If you must know,' Colin persists, 'I have to . . . I have to . . . well, it's my mother, you see.'

'She's not . . . ?'

'Oh God, no,' Colin sighs. 'Very much alive. And kicking.'

'Well, that's good anyway.'

'Is it? Sorry, forget I said that. So, everything all right your end then?'

'Yeah, all good here, thanks. Well look, I'll let you go and—'

'Hold your horses a mo. This evening, Moscow Road, half past eight, there's a meeting. We could go together, have a cup of coffee and a little catch-up beforehand. What do you think?'

'Well yeah, that would have been great but I have this physio session, you see, at a quarter to five and then I have to get back to the house to help my brother with something, and between one thing and another—'

'We don't want to get out of the habit – do we, Philip? Meetings are what keep us sober, after all.'

'I haven't got out of the habit, I go—'

'So you've said, so you've said. Even so, I hope to see you later. So long then. Mind how you go.'

'Yeah, cheers, Colin. Thanks.'

A few minutes later, he is wandering down Inverness Terrace holding his takeaway coffee in one hand, and in the other, a paper bag with a muffin inside it. He is trying to hold back for the moment when, Colin-less and alone, he can sit down on a bench, release the vanilla scent from the bag and unpeel the lid from his extra hot flat white. Behind him he can hear the rattle of suitcases on wheels and two girls speaking what sounds like Chinese. And on the opposite side of the road, a young couple, also pulling wheels, are consulting their individual phones for directions. 'The Airbnb racket,' as the man in the butcher's said to him last week, 'they've all cottoned on to it, don't care in the least that it's killing the community, greedy bastards. Always the same, innit? Greedy bastards, they ruin everything.'

And he had tutted along, rolling his eyes in agreement.

Here and there along Inverness Terrace, a few grotty B & B

joints are clinging on. And he can still catch traces of tenement living through an open window or door. A makeshift curtain on an upstairs window; empty beer bottles along a sill; a stained mattress leaning against an outside wall. Even so, he can sense the Notting Hill element beginning to elbow its way in here. The single bells on some of the front doors; the SUV cars parked out on the road. Not so long ago, you'd think twice about walking down here after dark. But under the wash of mid-August sunlight, you'd never know it. Today it looks like a film set of how London likes to be seen from afar. Smooth-faced houses, shoulder to shoulder. White walls, white pillars with black door numbers painted on. Equal visual weight as far as the eye can see, not an inch off balance for the best part of half a mile. A clean day anyhow, a good day, a not-having-to-put-up-with-Colin day. He feels an energy zipping through him, a sense of freedom. Something else about the sober life that has managed to surprise him: these small unexpected bouts of feeling alive.

As he nears the end of the terrace, the black iron canopy of a small hotel begins to edge into his little bubble. And a night, years ago, blooms into his head. He was standing at the reception desk in there, trying not to heed the smirking night clerk. Smirking at the idea of the older woman paying for the younger man. Sneering at him over her shoulder, the way night clerks probably sneer at prostitutes. Not that he was a kid or anything; he was maybe thirty-five or six. No, thirty-eight – he was thirty-eight when his father died. She was, what? In her fifties anyway. He had been drunk, of course, although he could still disguise it well enough at that age. He remembers the different shades of brown, the feeling of being swamped. Dark wood all around: the desk, the stairs, the walls. Her hand going in and out of a brown hand-bag. He remembers his shame-faced self, trying to keep his eye on a carved head that was set into the wood beneath the counter. There were a few of those carved heads, as he recalls, grinning out at him – oh, the stories we could tell . . .

He sharpens his step, keeping his eye on the opposite side of the street, not wishing to be reminded of that whole sordid affair. Although the sex, such as it was, had only taken place that one time – in a small room at the back of that hotel. Had she asked for the cheapest room, he wonders now, or had the night clerk just guessed that cheap was what she wanted?

He pulls the lid off the coffee cup and, raising it to his lips, is hardly aware of the hot liquid scalding the back of his throat. He notices a slight tremor in his hand and a bilious feeling in his stomach. Why, oh why, hadn't he taken his usual route down Queensway, instead of coming down this way, past this fucking hotel? One moment of carelessness and now he has to feel like a stinking lump of shit for the rest of the day.

The traffic breaks and he darts through the gap. When he crosses to the other side of Bayswater Road, he glances down at his hand. The coffee is gone, the muffin demolished, and he is almost running.

When he comes out of the physio session, he takes a wrong turn, then finds himself at the back end of the hospital. The waiting rooms are all vacant; the clerical staff departed. On the far side of the murky windows, claws of blinding sunlight. But in here, on this narrow little corridor, the air is dull and soupy, which suits him fine.

He feels a little better. At least somewhere in his life there has been a bit of progress. The movement in his knee has much improved, the reach of his arm is almost there; the collarbone that he has no recollection of breaking last Christmas is mending nicely. All things considered, the therapist had been pleased with him. 'And the bit of weight loss has done you no harm either,' he'd said, patting his own well-padded stomach. 'You must tell me your secret.'

At the end of the corridor, a sharp turn takes him into a tacked-on annexe with a wedge of daylight showing at the end of it. A fire-exit door, he sees now, pinned back by a cleaner's trolley. He steps outside into a waft of hash – but no sign of a smoker. Crossing a yard of old, cracked concrete, he moves through a makeshift alleyway hemmed in on both sides by high wooden fencing. When he comes out at the other end, he finds himself surrounded by glass and steel: half-built apartment blocks above him; at ground level, the shells of would-be shops and cafés. Liquid black shadows and sharp white lights shift all around him. He feels bewildered, and at the same time irked: he feels like a bee trapped in an empty jam jar.

He turns and looks back the way he has come. He can't see the hospital annexe now, only another row of apartment blocks, and skeletons of apartment blocks in various stages of construction. No sign of any workers. The whole site cleared off for the weekend. He knows the canal has to be somewhere over to his right and that Praed Street must be to his left. But he has no idea how to reach either one. He can't figure out where one building ends and another begins, not with all these sheets of glass bouncing light off one another.

He pulls his sunglasses out of his pocket and fumbles them into position. The light softens, the shadows subside. And now he can work it out – he is standing on what will soon become a central plaza. They'll probably stick a fountain down in the middle of it – call it a water feature. He imagines how it will look then, after the rolls of artificial grass have been laid down, the borders all paved, the pots of plastic shrubs put into place. The glass blocks will fill up with people. Shapes behind windows swimming around, pretending not to notice one another. At the same time, the sense of being constantly watched. All very comfortable and swish inside, no doubt. But he'd rather live on the streets than live like that. Running his eye around the plaza, he spots a pleat of shadow over to the right. He makes his way to it, passes between the edges of two glass buildings and is relieved to find the canal waiting on the other side.

The dependable canal, stretching its long arm out towards Bull's Bridge Junction. He can't remember when he was last down here – not sober, anyhow – but even in his most troubled times, he has always found something comforting about walking alongside its docile water. He decides to stay with it, get off at Little Venice and walk back to Dom's from there.

Or he could go further on, as far as Ladbroke Grove, not bother returning to the house till later. He could get a bite to eat out, maybe go to the pictures. Or . . . he could take Colin up on his offer to go to that AA meeting. The last thing he wants to do is to sit in a windowless room on a late summer's evening listening to other people's regrets and excuses when fuck knows he has enough of his own to be going on with. But it would put in an hour or two, as well as get Colin off his back for a while. Besides, just about anything was better than going back to Dom's house.

It's been happening more often. He comes downstairs in the morning to find Kim perched on a stool in her red dressing gown, beaming from ear to ear. When Dom goes out to work, she hangs about and cleans up the kitchen before going upstairs to re-make the bed for the next marathon. When Dom is working nights, she pops over early and waits for him to come home. Since Max and Jenny went off to Devon, it seems she's never out of the bloody place.

He comes back to the house in the afternoon and she's standing over a chopping board. 'Oh, Phil! You gave me quite a start! I was just making dinner – it's really no trouble to add another bit on . . . ?'

He comes home in the evening, and she's curled up on the sofa, eyes glued to *House of Cards*. 'Oh heavens, Phil! It's *you*. Did you want to watch something? Don't mind me, really. I have to fix supper for Dom soon anyway. I could do something for you if you want – or have you already eaten?'

There are many things that annoy him about Kim. Or Kimmie, as Dom has taken to calling her. The red dressing gown, for a start. Her overbearing agreeability is another. But more than anything else is the way she always manages to look surprised – even shocked – every single time she sees him.

It was different before Max and Jenny headed off; they could at least knock a bit of a laugh out of it. The absurdity of her fluttering around Dom, the way Dom was lapping it all up. And, it has to be said, she's a bloody good cook – a Cordon Bleu or Blur as she says herself. But now that there's just the three of them? It's not that he begrudges Dom his little romance, it's just that he'd rather not have to witness quite so much of it.

And then there is the question of the Airbnb.

He asked Dom a couple of weeks ago: 'When do you want to put the place up again?'

'What do you mean?'

'On Airbnb?'

'Oh, right. Well, it's August, isn't it?'

'Exactly. The best month to do it.'

'It's just that August is my time off. I don't want a load of strangers clogging up the house, do I?'

'Okay, but I can still open the bookings for September.'

'Just give it a bit of time, Phil. Do you mind? Max's going to want a few days before going up to Oxford and that.'

'Yeah, fine. But it's a lot of money. For me too, obviously. As well as you.'

'I know. We'll talk about it again next week – yeah? There's something in the pipeline I need to sort out first. But in the meantime, I need a bit of space.'

'Fine. Yeah. No problem.'

Another day he came into the kitchen and Dom was sludging Kim's special pâté onto a hoof of bread.

'Want some?' he asked.

'No thanks. I'm grand.'

'You don't like her much, do you?' he asked then.

'Who?'

'Kim. You don't like her.'

'I don't know her.'

'Ha!'

'What?'

'Well, it's the stock response, isn't it? For when your mate or your brother or whoever is going out with someone you can't fucking stand. "I don't know her."'

'Yeah, but I *don't* know her.'

'Well, I like her anyhow. So who cares what you think?'

'Exactly.'

'Know why I like her?'

'She can cook?'

'No! Well yeah, obviously it's nice that she can cook. But I like that she's such a positive person.'

'Well, she certainly seems enthusiastic.'

'I get so tired sometimes of being surrounded by all this endless fucking negativity – hang on, what do you mean "enthusiastic"? Are you trying to be funny?'

'Not in the least.'

'And she's got a great sense of humour. Don't you think? Oh come on, you have to allow that much, Phil?'

'Oh yeah, definitely,' he said.

'You really should try this,' Dom said then, sliding the bowl of pâté towards him. 'I mean, it is so fucking good . . .'

As he comes to Little Venice, he thinks of the dinner party at Dom's tonight, the Ocado van pulling up outside Kim's house across the road this morning. They are entertaining now as a couple – a bad sign, Max told him, when they'd spoken yesterday on the phone.

'So they're still at it then?' Max said.

'Very much so.'

'Oh God, I don't know how you stomach it.'

'I could do without the sound effects, to be honest.'

'Do you mind? I've just had breakfast. Is he getting fat?'

'He's packing on a bit all right.'

'Think she's lining herself up to be his next missus?'

'Don't know. He likes her, though.'

'He likes stuffing his face.'

'He thinks she's got a great sense of humour.'

'Just because she falls around the place laughing at his stupid jokes doesn't mean she's got a great sense of humour.'

'How's Devon?'

'Great, yea. Jenny hates it – or keeps saying she hates it anyhow. I'll tell you all about it when I get back.'

'You do that, Max. I look forward to it.'

They didn't *not* invite him to the dinner party. But at the same time, they didn't quite invite him either.

Dom, last night: 'I don't suppose you want to come tomorrow night?'

Kim yesterday morning: 'I wasn't sure if you were joining us tomorrow, Phil? But if you could let me know a.s.a.*peee*, I would really appreciate it.'

For some reason, he said he'd be there. Maybe it was just to annoy her, or to quieten the niggle in the back of his mind that he was spending too much time on his own. But by the time he'd woken up this morning, he had gone right off the idea.

If he goes back now, he risks walking straight into the aperitif hour. Standing in the doorway with his unshaven face and his sweat-damp shirt while the room sparkles with polished glasses and bonhomie. On an evening like this, they'll probably serve the drinks in the garden, which means he could dodge that bullet, but then, he could arrive at the house at the same time as a guest . . .

He pulls out his phone, swaps his sunglasses for his glasses and carefully prods a message off to Dom. *Sorry, I should have told you earlier but I can't go tonight. I'm going to a meeting. Enjoy.*

Then he prods another message to Colin. *Looks like I can go along to that meeting after all. Coffee first? Usual spot?*

The red and white spire of St Mary Magdalene has just come into sight when he feels his phone belch twice in his pocket. A thumbs up from Colin. A smiley face, courtesy of Dom.

It occurs to him then as he walks along that he is doing exactly what he used to do as a boy – dawdling along the canal to avoid going home. He tries to recall what the route was like then. There were a few houseboats all right, with people living inside them, hippies and other oddballs. Mainly in or around Little Venice.

The boats are cleaner now and seem less narrow: neatly hung curtains and white plantation blinds; polished chimney flues and herb gardens on the cabin roofs. Some of them even have solar panels. They look like pleasant places to live, but really, how could you put up with it – people stopping to take pictures of your house, looking in at you when you're trying to eat your dinner? Or have a kip, like that bloke there, curly-topped head sticking out from the covers. Or worse again – seeing a shadow spill over that small frosted window while you were sitting on the pot?

When he was a kid, the canal was strictly out of bounds – fraught with unspoken dangers, which made it all the more attractive to him. After his mother died, he had taken to wandering around down here during the last few weeks before he was sent to Ireland. Usually, he stuck to the pound between Paddington and Ladbroke Grove. Occasionally he had ventured further into no man's land, as far as Wormwood Scrubs and beyond. He had been strangely soothed by the prospect of danger and liked to imagine the worst. He'd been an odd kid, really, now that he thinks of it. Innocent enough, too – are kids still as innocent today, he wonders? Nearly ten years of age and the dangers that had concerned his father had never crossed his mind. Not even when a man with a morose – and, it has to be said, saintly – face asked him if he'd like to come home with him for a glass of pop and a bun.

In Little Venice, then, you'd see men pissing in the canal, frothing up the water. Now you see people jogging with plugs in their ears or walking their well-dressed dogs or sitting in complete safety on benches watching the canal-side comings and goings. What he remembers are bloodshot eyes looking out of the shadows under the bridges. The atlas of ice shapes on top of the water, the occasional rubber johnny caught between the borders.

He remembers, too, a man sitting on the bank one freezing evening, fishing with an invisible rod, trousers rolled, bare feet stuck down into the greasy green water. Poor mad bastard. And once, near the Ha'penny Steps, a drunken woman with the same accent as his mother had shouted at him: 'Go home you, go home out of that, to your mother – do you hear me?'

'But I can't go home to her, can I?' he'd shouted back at her. 'She's dead.'

Her appalled face when he said that.

Discarded bicycle wheels, shopping trollies, bottles, cowls of black smoke from canal-side factories. Brown rats slithering through the reeds. A smell of sewage. That's what he recalls of the canal then. But it's all very clean and respectable along here now, he'd have to say. All very butter wouldn't melt in the mouth.

He has no idea where his father thought he was on those winter evenings. Or if he even noticed his absence. They had stopped working as a family after her death, each closing the door of his own room after a silent dinner which, more often than not, had come from the chipper. It was as if they couldn't bear to look one another in the eye.

Mr Moyse had put an end to his canal-side gallivanting, stepping out to block his way one icy evening as he'd tried to slip in through the garden gate. 'And where do you think you were till now, eh? No, on second thoughts, you keep your porkies to yourself. But let me tell you this, my son. Come home late again, and it'll be the last time. Know why? Because every day, without fail, you'll come out the school gate and, large as life, you'll find me, come to fetch you home by the hand.'

The wrought-iron bridge comes into sight, throwing a bright blue tinge down onto the water and giving it a laundry-clean look that couldn't be further from the truth. Lifting his head, he looks up to street level. Two big tower blocks awkwardly stand over the heads of trees and the discreet well-mannered houses on Delamere Terrace. On the nearer block, he can make out a row of evenly spaced pegs running up the wall; white or maybe silver, the pegs glint in the evening sun. He's been seeing these pegs on high-rises all over London. The remnants of cladding torn off in a hurry – as if that's going to make everything all right. He brings his eyes back to the ground.

A boat café, snug to the wall, sits prettily in the frame of the bridge behind it. Tables with umbrellas laid out on the quayside. Flowers gush from baskets on the upper deck. The sound of voices and laughter. He feels the need to sit down among people suddenly, even if only for a five-minute cup of tea. Turning to the steps, he begins to climb aboard. But then a glance through the window and another back to the quayside shows that no one here is sitting alone. It's all friends and families, and couples. A bashfulness comes over him. Backways, he comes down off the steps then, redirecting himself, pushes on under the bracket of the bridge to continue along the towpath.

Snout to tail, the narrowboats line both sides of the canal now, although he notices they are becoming a little more downmarket the further he goes. As if there is a different arrangement along here for people with less money. Still, they probably wouldn't have it any other way. If there's one thing he's learned after all the years of living here it's that everything about the English comes down to class: houses, people, education, work, most of their literature. Even their postal service is subject to a class system. Some of the barges are very run-down, shawled with tarpaulin and tatty old plastic; a couple of them look as if they haven't been lived in for years. And then, just at the end of the line, snagging his heart at the very sight of it, is a barge named Millie. Not new by any means, but well maintained and obviously cared for, the name painted in an arc with a careful hand, the boat itself an even navy blue with a castle-and-roses design across the starboard. Wouldn't it be something, he thinks, to have her standing here beside him? The kick she would get out of seeing her name on such a lovely boat. He paces up and down, studying it. Logs neatly stacked on each side of the cabin entrance. Mop, bucket and a folded deckchair on the roof. Two horizontal rectangular windows and a porthole in the middle. It appears to be occupied, although he can't see the owner. He looks through the first window. A cup in the sink; a glimpse of hob; the corner of a table. At the next window, the edge of a cushion and the arm of a chair. Everything in place. Like living in a caravan but on the water: a compact, easy-going life.

He lived in a caravan once, the same shaped windows, a similar set-up inside. He quite liked it, too, apart from the cold when the weather turned, having to put his shoulder to the frost-jammed door to open it first thing every morning.

He'd come down to Epsom for a fight. Bob Coyle had arranged it; they'd made money all right but the gypsies nearly left them for dead, after which, Bob went back to Ireland. For some reason, he decided to move on to Margate. He got a job working for a firm that renovated old houses. He was the decorator – weeks spent working on high-ceilinged rooms with powdery walls. One house had taken him three months to paint in various shades of green. He had found it quite therapeutic watching the turn of his wrist, the slow drag of paint. Even if he sometimes felt as if he'd fallen into a vat of pea soup.

Only mad people lived in caravan parks in the winter then. The park deserted, the shower in the toilet block blasting out freezing water. He'd had to count his way along the empty mobile homes to find his way in the dark. But he liked his little caravan. *Holivan* – was that the name on the side of it? Pale brown with rust blotches on it, like the skin of a giraffe. The smell from the kerosene lantern. That punch of sea air in the morning, seagulls jeering at his back. He can't remember much else about those few months now. Days spent painting. Nights doing his best to drink himself to death.

He passes under the Ha'penny Steps. Every surface is covered with graffiti. The iron rails on the park, walls and pillars and posts, even the bark of the trees has been scribbled all over. Only the canal water seems to have escaped. As he turns the bend, he sees another narrowboat set slightly apart from its neighbours. Three pit bull terriers on the roof, climbing playfully over one another, while somehow maintaining a balance. Two of them a burnt orange colour, eyes of a yellowish hue. The other a plush deep grey, with blue-tinged eyes. Dangerous-looking bastards for all their playfulness. He stops for a moment to look at them. They stop playing to look at him. He sees brawn, steel jaws, killer eyes. And what do they see, he wonders? A fat sixty-year-old man they could kill in an instant, then take their time slurping over his bones.

He walks on, the shadow of his left shoulder grazing the windows of offices and apartments that come right up to the towpath. Now and then he glances back. The three dogs are still watching him. A woman leaning on the side entrance to one of the offices, smoking and looking at the dogs, nods at him.

'I wouldn't want to mess with those boys,' he says to her.

A sad husky voice comes back at him, 'I come out every day on my break to watch them. They're sweethearts really.'

'Yeah, they look it and all.'

She looks at him, her face puffed up with last night's drink, her eyeballs out on sticks.

'Mind yourself,' he says, moving on.

As he comes up at Ladbroke Grove, he looks up at the old water tower, standing on the far side on its long spindly legs. Recently, he came across a photo in an old magazine about the water tower – now an apartment, the article said. Three storeys connected by spiral stairwells. All very well, but how would you get into it in the first place? It must be a good twenty feet off the ground. The places people live in. But then, you can make your home anywhere, he thinks – if you put your mind to it.

He comes up from the canal into the dust and fumes of the main road. Early evening at the end of a hot mid-August Friday. He slips into the crowd. Flushed faces and summer clothes; drinkers grouped outside pubs. A holiday feel to the evening as if the summer is only just beginning instead of coming to an end.

While he sits on a metal chair chewing on a panini outside a café on Westbourne Grove, pretending to listen to Colin, he finds himself thinking about the houseboat again.

And he sees it again during the AA meeting while a large woman with a little girl's voice stands at the lectern and begins to speak.

'I had to look after myself, didn't I? I mean, how you going to get sober if you don't look after yourself? Two problem drinkers in the one household. That's why I left. I'd never have done it had I stayed. People judge me, leaving three kiddies with my husband. Well, let them, I say. You got to look after yourself first, don't you? Put your own life jacket on before you deal with anyone else. And it was all such a long time ago now. Ten years. So much can happen.'

He thinks of the shape of the boat, the disposal system, the little roof garden. Mostly, though, he sees the horizontal windows. He considers the line of vision. From the towpath down into the narrowboat's interior. A drop of a few feet anyhow depending on the water level. Someone inside could be looking up and still stay out of sight.

'It didn't come easy, let me tell you,' the squeaky woman says, 'what I went through. But I try not to think about all that now. I have my little job that I love and my little flat. And . . . and next Wednesday, I'll be sober five years.'

Applause breaks out around him. He lifts his hands in automatic response and slaps them off one another.

Then a man dressed in an oatmeal-coloured suit stands at the lectern and forgives himself for all the violence in his marriage. He's seen this one before, at another meeting. Over the dry cleaners? No, a church. Not this one. Or maybe it was this one – who knows?

As the man rabbits on, he realises that he no longer cares about what he says. His woes, his recovery and all his little triumphs, they mean nothing to him now. Last time he saw this man, he'd had to stand up and leave to stop himself from shouting out: 'Oh yeah, poor, *poor* you – don't even think about all the people you fucked up on the way. Slapping your kids around? The old woman whose purse you nicked, who's probably too afraid of her life to go out now? Don't you give them another thought, just as long as you're all right, Jack.'

He thinks: if you were on a part of the canal that had no viable towpath, you wouldn't have to worry about gawkers passing by. The Grand Union goes as far as Birmingham, there must be plenty of stretches that are completely private. Houseboats are cheap enough to buy but still way too expensive for him, and

303

now without his Airbnb money, there's no point in even thinking about it. But he's not thinking about it – not really. He hasn't the slightest interest in living on a boat.

He hears hands clapping again, the sound of rain on a tin roof. Whatever Oatmeal Suit has said has gone down well. This time he doesn't bother joining in. He sits still, continues thinking. It's not the boat as such that keeps coming to mind, he realises now. But for some reason, the windows.

There's a shuffle of chairs and feet around him. The sound of twenty or so alcos trying not to hurry as they make their way to the table at the side for their tea and bickies, the way they used to rush up to the bar.

'Cuppa tea, Phil?' he hears Colin say.

'What? Oh, no thanks, Colin. I'll head off, I've something I want to look into.'

'Good meeting though, eh?

'Excellent, Colin, thanks.'

'You didn't speak again?'

'No.'

'Maybe next time?'

'We'll see.'

Oatmeal Suit is standing behind Colin now, edging in to say hello. He wonders how he stole the money from the old woman – if he mugged her or dipped her or just conned her out of it somehow? He moves away. 'Good luck, Colin, see you soon.'

He takes himself to task as he comes out of the church and begins up the road. Just who the fuck are you to judge anyone? It's not as if you haven't done your fair share of thieving. Money borrowed that you'd no intention of returning. From Dom, from Milly. Even from poor old Marj. At one stage, anyone who crossed your path was a target.

And he's done a hell of a lot worse besides, he thinks. But unlike the other pair at the meeting, he's not asking for, nor is he expecting, forgiveness. Even if his *mea culpa* letters would seem to hint at it. He doesn't want forgiveness – he's never wanted what he doesn't deserve.

Maybe he should stand up one of these days, make a confession, see the shock on their faces.

'My name is Philip and I'm an alcoholic. I got into a stolen car when I was pissed – actually I ended up driving it because the bloke who stole it was too pissed, my friend's younger brother. I can't even say his name without wanting to slit my own throat . . .'

He feels a bit light-headed. He stops and, taking hold of two railing spears, steadies himself. Head low, breathing deep, he waits.

He looks at his hands, his knuckles like bare bones in the dwindling light, his grip so tight it feels like they're welded to the spearheads. When he was a young boxer, he had a habit of clenching his hands. Shamie ticking him off: 'Unclench, Phil, unclench, unclench. How many times I got to tell you? You keep them relaxed until you're ready to punch, you're tiring them out, choking the life out of them. You're in charge. You tell them – fists, relax.'

He loosens, then releases his hands.

'My life is easier now that I'm sober,' the man in the oatmeal suit had said. 'I wish I had known how easy it could be. I can measure my failings, decide what's real or imagined.'

His life is not easier, he thinks, as he stands massaging one hand, then the other. It's harder than it's ever been. He feels like he's constantly trudging along on an endless country road, so dark he can't tell the road from the sky. Not a crack of light through trees that might indicate a village, a house, a phone box even.

305

After a moment, he crosses over the road to the small park in the middle of the square. The gate is locked. He walks corner to corner under the trees until he has completed the square and is back where he started. His stomach is creaking but he's beginning to feel a bit better. A shower, that's what he needs; a bite to eat, a clean bed to lie down on.

In the small late-night Sainsbury's Local, he buys two egg-and-cress sandwiches, a packet of Hobnobs and a carton of milk. Then he stands at the end of one of the queues. Under the brutal glare of supermarket light, he studies his fellow shoppers. Most of them middle-aged or older, all of them buying their few bits for a solo supper. Coming from work or – by the look of some – the pub. But going back anyhow to an empty room to face into a lonely weekend maybe. The clock behind the tills reads half past ten. Half ten! Christ, is that all? How long a day is without drink. For all the hardship it may cause, it does, at least, help to get rid of the day, and even if you don't speak to anyone, you're there under the same roof as others – you're there as an equal. For better or worse, you are part of something. Maybe that's why so many people go to AA meetings – not because they're looking for forgiveness or a way to understand the whys and wherefores of their drinking, but simply because it's somewhere to go? A place where you will be spoken to, looked at, listened to: where you will hear the sound of your own voice speaking and think, yes, that's me, I exist, I am alive.

If he ever does stand up to speak at a meeting, instead of frightening the shite out of everyone with his tale of the burning car, he could say something simple, something honest like:

'I miss the pub. I miss it more than I miss the drink. I miss walking at dusk towards the light in the window, the rush of noise and heat as I push the heavy door in. I feel lost without it.

Homeless, even when I have somewhere to stay. I feel like I'm dragging the hours around. My arms are too long, my hands too big. Nothing feels or looks right; I just don't fit anywhere. Unless something changes and changes quick, I'm that close to going back on the drink.'

He moves up the silent queue.

If he had the Airbnb to keep him busy. Or if he had his own place. If he had his own place *and* the Airbnb. Even better. A place to come home to in the middle of the day, to cook in, to clean, to put his feet up, read a book, watch a bit of telly. Somewhere to make a cup of tea in peace. A window to look out of. He shuffles up a space – only one more to go. And again, he sees the image – two rectangular windows below ground.

The young bloke ahead of him, hardly more than a teenager, is holding things up, fiddling around with coins, searching in his pockets, patting them. Dirty, frantic fingernails.

'Sorry,' the cashier says, 'but you're fifty pee short.'

He peeps over the bloke's shoulder. A small loaf of bread and a tub of margarine.

'Oh,' the bloke says, beginning to turn, 'oh, I suppose then I best—'

He takes a fifty-pence piece out of his own pocket, leans across him and places it on the counter beside the till.

'Thanks, mate, oh thanks a lot. I walked out without my wallet, see, and—'

He dismisses the thanks with a wave of his hand, then looks the other way as the bloke turns towards the door, the sole of one shoe flapping underfoot.

Outside, two beggars squat on each side of the doorway like a pair of Lombardy lions. They are waiting, as he has waited himself, for a member of staff to bring out the unsold remains of the day. From the corner of his eye, he sees the old Indian woman is already in situ across the street under the canopy of the old cinema, hooked over her wheelchair, begging bag looped onto the handle. The only people he has ever seen come near her are charity workers she completely ignores, or sentimental drunks who fill up her pouch.

He looks up and down the road. There are few people out and about now, the restaurants have all but emptied out, post-work drinkers long since gone home. He glances up at the windows above shops and offices, then at the occasional parked car or van. Someone is watching over her, he reckons, from a safe distance. Watch her well, he thinks, and then scuttles across the road.

He passes into the silence of Westbourne Gardens, all in darkness. As he nears the end of this road, windows full of light begin to show. Even at night, there is an airbrushed look about these streets, every house brought to its utmost. It reminds him of the road Dom lives on where the residents barely look you in the eye when – and if – they bother to say hello to you. And yet, they have no trouble keeping their curtains open at night so the world and his wife can gawk in at them having their dinner. And who are these people anyway, he has to wonder, sitting in there surrounded by the props of their privileged lives? With their oversized paintings on expansive walls, their marble-topped kitchen islands? That one in there, fiddling around with her elaborate coffee machine. Or him next door with his refrigerated wine cabinet on display? Or the house on the corner of Talbot Road, where he sometimes sees a frilly-capped maid open the door to the Ocado man. Just who the fuck lives like that?

Turning the corner, he looks across the street to St Stephen's church. The clock on the spire is blocked by the full summer heads on the trees. He comes closer, is dismayed to see that it's still not quite eleven o'clock. He no longer cares; in fact, fuck it, he'll be rude if he has to, but he can't walk much further and all he wants now is to lie down on a bed.

From the corner of Dom's street, he can see the house, blousy with lit-up windows, top floor to basement. As if Dom is the sort who couldn't care less about electricity bills. Coming closer, he begins to hear the sound of the trumpet sliding into the empty street. In long, precise notes, it sounds like a musical elephant calling from the depths of the jungle. Then, the tinkling of piano keys. Followed by the trumpet again. Now both. He stops for a moment, his ear identifying a version of the theme music from *House of Cards*, Kim's favourite show.

Over next door's hedge, he views the little after-dinner scene in the big bay window. A man with his back to the company sits at the piano while Dom, face puffed up like a big purple cauliflower with a trumpet stuck in the middle of it, is turned this way. An admiring group sits around; Kim standing in a long lavender dress, face in raptures. Everyone else is turned towards Dom, except for a younger woman with long black hair who sits slightly away from the group, looking down at the floor. And he feels, as he often does when he hears his brother play, inexplicably moved and at the same time wanting to laugh out loud.

He sees his advantage – as long as the music is playing, they are unlikely to hear him coming into the hall. He makes a break for it, hurrying up the granite steps, key at the ready. He ducks into the porch, sticks the key in and carefully opens the door.

Looking straight ahead, he makes a beeline for the staircase. Dom's party piece is coming to an end with an extended flourish. Then, the applause. He is halfway up the first flight when he hears the door of the sitting room open. He keeps going, hoping it's just someone looking for the loo. As he reaches the first landing and begins to turn onto the second flight, something makes him stop. He looks down into the hall. The young woman with the black hair is standing at the foot of the stairs.

She puts her hand on the banister, twists her neck and looks up at him. He feels his heart hopping. No, he thinks, it can't be. It can't be.

'Dad?' he hears her say then. 'Dad, it's me, Lorraine.'

PART FIVE

13. Milly

1999

THEY WERE UNDRESSING for bed when Matthew happened to mention that he needed something delivered to Dublin. It was a simple enough task, he said – all they had to do was bring a set of plans to a cranky old man who insisted on having all correspondence delivered by hand.

'If you ask me, he distrusts all things English,' Matthew said. 'The Royal Mail, overseas couriers, even the accent seems to put him on edge – I've given up speaking to him, I leave him to Johnny Tipperary now.'

'Johnny Tipperary – is that his name?'

'Course not, it's just what we call him on site. I'd ask him to go, but his wife's just had another sprog.'

They weren't long in from that French place in Soho; she had a nice dinner inside her, a few glasses of wine, which was probably why she volunteered herself for the job. Matthew jumped at her offer like a dog to a bone.

Before she knew it, she was standing in her nightie in his study looking down at a set of plans laid flat on his desk.

'Recognise it?' he asked, stepping back to make room for her.

She looked down at a spread of opaque grey, small black squares and rectangles of various sizes drawn onto it, a number written in the middle of each one. She thought it looked like the sky on a dull day with a row of chimney pots running along it. She shook her head.

'That's the back lane,' Matthew said. '*Your* lane. There's the pub, and see that parcel there opposite it? Old Quinlan, he's owned that since 1955 – that's what I'm after.'

'Oh, I see,' she said. 'Isn't that the old boxing club?'

'That's right. And there's the pub. And that's Piccardi's and that's – oh, who owns that again?'

'That's Stein's.'

'Yeah, Mr Steins.'

'No, Stein. Mr Stein.'

'Right. And that little plot beside it,' Matthew said, 'is a garage owned by, oh, what's the name again?'

'Mrs Morgan.'

'Morgan, yeah.'

'And it's not a garage, it's a granny flat.'

'Mews, she's calling it now. Probably reckons she'll get more money that way.'

The central heating had gone off by now. Matthew, wearing only his trousers, didn't seem to notice. She looked down past the edge of the desk to where his bare feet were clamped onto the parquet floor. No matter how many times she caught sight of his feet, she was always struck by how ugly they were: the humped forefront, the squat toes.

She came back to the plans, her hand hovering over the lane. 'And so all of this here,' she said, 'is earmarked – isn't that what you say? – for demolition?'

'Redevelopment, darling.'

'Okay, redevelopment.'

'But don't you go getting into any of that with old Quinlan. Just give him the plans and if he brings you in for a cup of tea, talk about the weather and the price of spuds.'

'Supposing he has no interest in spuds?'

'Course he has,' Matthew said, nudging her with his hip. 'He's Irish, isn't he?'

'Very funny, Matthew. Can I go by boat?'

'Boat to Dublin?' He laughed. 'Bit of a trek, that.'

'Is it urgent?'

Matthew was laying a thin sheet of plastic over the plans; he began to roll the grey paper up. He waited until he finished before answering her.

'Urgent? I wouldn't say that. But this old geezer, he'll do what he can to hold up the show even if it's just for the hell of it, so the sooner we get going on this the better; the next week or so, and I'm happy. And yes, my darling, you can go any way you like. You can ride a bike there, as long as the job gets done.'

He screwed the roll back into the cardboard tube, put a lid on it and stuck it up on a shelf.

'Could I stay a couple of nights?'

'Course you can. I'll book a nice hotel for you.'

'No, I can do it. I'll go to the travel agency in Holborn. I know the woman who works there. Mrs Hitchins – she used to run the newsagent's on Cowcross Street.'

'You really do know them all, don't you?'

'Yes,' she said. 'Yes, I suppose I do.'

She began to walk back into the bedroom, calling over her shoulder, 'You know, he's not the only one who could hold up the show.'

'Mrs Oak, you mean? Oh, she'll come round. Jake has it all in hand. If anyone can pull off the deal, he can.'

'I don't know about that!'

She was dreading Mrs Oak finding out about Matthew. They'd been seeing each other for nearly two years now. After their little afternoon up in her room, she hadn't seen or even thought about him again. Until one day, when walking past Agnesi's café, someone banged on the window and there he was, waving out at her. She'd barely nodded before scurrying away up the road. But Matthew had come rushing out, shouting her name on the street, and so she had to stop. Before she knew it, she'd agreed to go out to dinner with him. And now here they were. Mrs Oak knew there was someone but Milly had always been careful to cover her tracks and, as Matthew's accountant Jake had been dealing with her up to now, she hadn't yet joined the dots.

Matthew came into the bedroom. 'Don't you worry about Mrs Oak. Give her enough money and she'll be happy. She's not getting any younger, is she? And let's face it, the pub's barely hanging on as it is.'

'What about Trish?'

'That's up to Mrs Oak.'

'And me? What about me? I work there too.'

'Not if you come and work for me,' he said. 'Aw, come on, love, it'll be great. We can go into work together, come home together, a new start for you, a decent wage . . . Just say yes, can't you?'

'The timing's not right, Matthew.'

He stepped up behind her and kissed her neck. 'I will always look after you. Always. But you know how to make sure of that?'

'Marry you, I suppose?' She laughed. 'Matthew, we've only just got engaged – give me a chance!'

'Christ, if my kids ask me one more time, when are you and Aunty Milly tying the knot? Their mum's even making jokes about it.'

'Let's just get this business with Mrs Oak sorted first.'

She'd no sooner agreed to go to Dublin than she started having doubts. One minute she was all excited by the prospect, the next, wishing she could find a way to back out. And now it was too late: everything had been arranged. The tickets were bought, the hotel booked. And the old man in Dublin was expecting her at eleven o'clock the following morning. She was leaving today, whether she liked it or not . . .

Matthew still nagging her to go by plane: 'You'll be exhausted by the time you arrive,' he said, 'it's bloody ridiculous. Look, why don't you let me book a flight for you?'

'I'm leaving in a couple of hours, Matthew! It's all organised. Anyway, it's Sunday, you won't get a ticket.'

'I can drive you to the airport, buy the ticket at the desk.'

'Matthew, no. Let's just leave it as it is.'

'I've never heard of that hotel, what's it called again?'

'The Aisling.'

'I hope it's in a safe area. Dublin can be just as tricky as London, you know. I know a bloke had a knife held up to his throat. Take a taxi to Quinlan's house. Take a taxi wherever you go. Don't go wandering off now.'

'I won't.'

'I wish I could come with you but I'm up to here just now.'

'I'll be fine.'

He was sitting on the end of the bed, putting on his trousers. She was in bed, sipping her tea and watching him. She put down the mug, pulled herself up, did an upright crawl to him and, leaning into his back, put her arms around him. 'You are very kind. Always. But I want to go by train and boat.'

'As long as you come back safely to me.'

'I'll only be gone a couple of days.'

'It'll seem much longer,' he said. 'Call me when you arrive. Call me after you see Quinlan, call me anyway. I don't know why you won't let me just buy you a mobile phone.'

'You buy me enough things, Matthew. If I wanted a phone, I would have bought one myself.'

'Yeah, but I told you, sweetheart, I can claim it on expenses. If you come working for me, you'll have to have a phone.'

'I know that.'

'No dinosaurs in Conad Construction, you know . . .'

She dropped her arms, edged herself back up the bed, settled her back into the pillows and picked up her mug. The tea had gone cold, but she drank it anyway.

When she looked up again, Matthew was at the wardrobe, slipping into a shirt. Whenever she stayed with him, it was always the same the next morning, watching him dress, the trousers first, then the white shirt – always immaculately laundered. For some reason, it made her want sex, more – much more – than she had done the night before. Once or twice, she had been on the brink of asking him to come back to bed.

But before she ever got round to it, he'd have put the jacket of his suit on, and in an instant, she'd be gone off the boil.

He was screwing his feet into their shoes now, smiling at her from his eyes, through the mirror. But it really was a beautiful shirt.

'Matthew . . . ?' she began.

He stood up, dragged the jacket of his suit off the back of the chair and shrugged himself into it.

'Yes, my love?'

She looked at him. 'Ah, nothing.'

He tugged a sheaf of notes from his wallet and left it on the dressing table. 'Buy yourself something nice in Dublin.'

'I don't need anything.'

'Who says you have to need it?'

Then he came up beside her, pushed her legs out of the way so he could sit down on the side of the bed. He pulled her into his chest.

'Safe journey, sweetheart,' he said, kissing the top of her head. 'And thanks for doing this, I really appreciate it.'

He picked his watch up from the bedside table, and, frowning slightly, began to strap it onto his wrist. 'As a matter of interest,' he began, 'what do you want to go by boat for anyway?'

She didn't know how to explain it, to say: I want to go as I set out more than twenty years ago, by train, boat, then train again. I want to retrace the miles: London, Wales, the Irish Sea, Dun Laoghaire, Dublin. But this time without any fear. Most of all, I want to take a good look at my eighteen-year-old self, think about what's happened to her from then to now. I want to do that before I move on to the next phase of my life.

'Oh, I don't know,' she said. 'I just do.'

There would be differences. This time there would be taxis: one to take her to Euston station and another to take her from the train station in Dublin to the hotel Mrs Hitchins had booked her into for two nights.

On the way over, there had been no question of any sort of hotel. Not even one of those kippy B & Bs on the greasy inner-city streets she used to see from the bus whenever she came up to Dublin with her grandfather. She had arrived in Dun Laoghaire then with hours to go before the boat departed, and had to stay up all night. Skulking around the residential streets, her nerves in flitters and her heart jammed in her throat, ducking in and out of laneways if a car drove by, and once, she'd had to climb over the wall of a darkened house to take a wee under an apple tree, wind-fallen fruit at her feet. At first light she'd made her way down to the port, where she sat in a corner until the ticket office opened.

The last time, she'd been carrying an old duffle bag that had once belonged to her grandfather. This time, she had a case with wheels on it.

A man in uniform lifted it onto the rack and called her madam. Matthew had put the tube containing the plans into a sort of holster that she could carry over her shoulder and she held onto it now, partly because she was afraid something might happen to it, but also because she felt it gave her an air of purpose. She showed him her ticket – first class to Holyhead. Then she sat back and waited for the trolley to be brought round. No need to ask about the price of a sandwich and a coffee. She was not a teenager running away. She was a thirty-eight-year-old woman: a woman with a job and a roof over her head – a woman with the prospect of an even better job and a better roof over her head, as soon as she moved in with Matthew. She had people who cared about her, anyway. She was loved.

Sometimes, when she looked out the window and caught sight of a scene that seemed vaguely familiar – the caged ceiling of Crewe station as it sucked the train in, or the ruins of a castle in the corner of a field – she felt a weakening inside her. And as the train crossed the border from Chester, she became that eighteen-year-old girl, her hands shaking, her stomach soured from a pregnancy she didn't – and yet somehow did – know about.

It happened again when the boat began to dock into Dun Laoghaire and she saw the mountains behind the little town. She recalled how, twenty years previously, she had looked into the dull October morning as the boat had started to pull away and had imagined that they weren't mountains at all, but the bruised paws of a gigantic beast, pushing her out to sea.

Now, as the boat pushed through the freezing air, the mountains seemed so harmless – no more than hills, really. And even less than that, they seemed one-dimensional, as if they were made of cloth and could be pulled away at any moment, like the backdrop of a stage set. She thought of Flora then, imagining that she was standing beside her. She wondered how they would look to the other passengers: a mother, young to have a daughter nearly twenty years of age, pointing out the church spires and houses rising from the quaint, crooked town. Showing the daughter the country she had come from all those years ago. She imagined Flora with her eyes damp from pity saying, 'Poor Mum, when I think of all you went through just to keep me!'

And again, that awful loneliness came over her, and for a moment or so, she was full of rage and sorrow. A grief.

But that feeling passed too, and as soon as she began wheeling her case down the ramp, she became all brisk and business-like again: a woman with a leather handbag and a good coat on her back. A woman with another train to catch, a taxi to find, a hotel to check in to. In the morning, a job to do that would make Matthew love her all the more.

The hotel was at the end of the quays, where the river came into the city.

There were leaflets all over the foyer advertising millennium celebrations. There was a woman arguing with the receptionist about the prices for staying on New Year's Eve – which was, Milly realised, only a few weeks away.

'That's three times more than what I paid last year!' the woman said. 'Three times! It's ridiculous the way we're being ripped off. And I hear we won't even be able to take a taxi to the party unless we sell our very souls. What sort of a country have we become – I *ask* you?'

When she got to her room, she looked out the window. She could see the tops of gaunt trees crowded into a very small park. Beyond them, a long view of a junction that straddled the river. Beyond that, the side view of a building that looked out of place, like a museum or a small palace, all columns and balustrades and fancy stonework. It would be dark soon, and it seemed like she had a long evening ahead of her. She decided to kill an hour or two, and go out for a walk.

There were prostitutes on the corner just beyond the hotel; all bandy legs and jaded faces, and old men in the small park were swigging from bottles. She crossed the road to a wrought-iron bridge and looked downriver. She had heard stories of the changes in Dublin over the past few years, but from where she was standing, it all seemed the same. The dirty green water, the river wrack like a scabby disease all over the walls of the embankment. The gutsy odour of sulphur and yeast. The dismal Sundays.

She thought about walking towards the centre of the city, but when she looked down both sides of the quays there were so few people about and anyone she could see had an air of despair about them. She stayed where she was, looking down at a blood-orange sunset drooling light on the surface of the greasy water. The long brick wall of the Guinness brewery had turned a rosy red, and when she turned to look at the fancy building seen earlier from her room, it was glazed with pink light. She could hear noises coming from it now, similar to the noises she heard from her room at the front of the pub, and she realised that it wasn't a museum or any sort of palace, but a railway station. Outside it, an old man was rummaging through a bus-stop bin. She thought Dublin was just how she remembered it: by turn ugly and beautiful.

Back in her room, she looked at the watch Matthew had bought her. She had only been out about twenty minutes. She picked up the phone to call Matthew, but instead found herself ordering a sandwich and a pot of tea. She took off her shoes, stretched out on the bed and turned on the television.

The next day, there was no sense of danger about the place. She sat in the taxi, the plans in their tube laid carefully across her lap, and looked out at the city. It was calmer than London, everything moving at a steadier pace; some things, like the traffic, hardly moving at all. Well-dressed people, obviously on the way to work, greeted one another, and even stopped for a chat. There were barristers striding along one quay. On a side street, two women wearing rubber boots and white coats were standing having a fag. There were cranes all over the skyline, which for some reason she hadn't really noticed the night before. Now she realised that they were rebuilding the city, knocking it down, churning it up, stretching it skywards.

As soon as they crossed the river, the view began to change until there was no sense of a city, just houses squashed up together on terraces and a few run-down corner shops. Then the road widened and the houses broadened and began to step away from one another. The taxi turned left and for a moment there was a view of the distant sea, an expanse of grey flabby beach with a few isolated people and their dogs crossing over it. The taxi turned again, meandering through streets that seemed too small for the houses they were holding. Then it circled a village green, spruce shops laid out around it: striped awning over a vegetable display; a café; a hardware shop; another café. The whole area, the people she saw walking through it – they might have been driving through an English village.

The old man asked for her name and when she told him, he looked sideways at her, as if she must have made a mistake. 'Milly – is that what you said? *Milly?*'

'That's right.'

Then he asked why the bossman hadn't seen fit to bring the documents himself.

'He thought you might like a chance to look over them first. I'm his PA,' she added, as Matthew had told her to do.

'His what?'

'Personal assistant.'

'Secretary, you mean.'

'Something like that,' she said.

'You took a taxi from the airport? I'd say that set you back a bit.'

'I didn't come from the airport. I came last night. By boat.'

'Mail boat, we used to call it,' he said and for a second managed to look pleased. 'Is that a County Dublin accent I detect?' he said then.

'Near enough,' she said.

'Well, might I be so bold as to ask – above, below or beside?'

'Above.'

'That's right,' he grinned, 'tell the bastards nothin'. Have you time for a cup of tea?'

'I thought you'd never ask,' she said and moved to step into the house.

'Tell you what,' he said, not blocking her way exactly, but not admitting her either, 'you pop down to that newsagent's down

324

the way and get my newspapers for me – they're on order. And I'll have a nice cup of tea ready for you when you get back – can you do that?'

'I can.'

'Good girl,' he said.

When she came back, the door was on the latch, which she took as an invitation to walk straight in. She called into the house but there was no reply. It was a big house, stairs going up and down; he could be at the back of it, she decided, probably in the kitchen. A door leading off the hall was open and when she looked inside, she saw a huge double room with double doors pushed open to the wall.

She was reluctant to go in and sit down, so she just stood there, her handbag and the drawings hitched over one shoulder and her arms filled with newspapers. She reckoned there were about six newspapers in all; his name was neatly written in the top right-hand corner of each one. There was a small gallery of photographs along the wall of the hall. She began to move along them. One photo showed a racehorse; the other, Michael Collins; a third was some sort of text written in Irish. The racehorse was flanked on one side by a jockey, on the other by a man in a long coat and cap. She leaned in to take a better look, wondering if it could be Mr Quinlan as a younger man. Then she saw a reflection move across the glass. When she turned, he was coming up the stairs from the floor below, carrying a tray, while struggling with a walking stick. She made a move to help him, looking around for somewhere to put the newspapers. 'I can manage, you go on in, go on. Jaysus, you can't be that shy and you working for your man.'

She could taste the dust on the air as soon as she stepped into the room. There was a coffee table with letters and newspapers all over it, a bottle of pills, a couple of dirty cups, a remote control

325

for a television. He indicated with a nod that she should clear a space. She put the stack of newspapers down and took the tray from him.

He groaned his way down into an armchair. 'The oul legs, you see, they're not the best. Do you drink your tea standing?'

'No.'

'Well, you better sit down so.'

On the tray was a teapot, a carton of milk, a bag of sugar with a spoon stuck into it, a whole packet of digestive biscuits and a single mug. He waved his hand to tell her to help herself, then he reached over, pulled the *Racing Post* off the pile of newspapers and stuck his face into it.

All around her was evidence of a wealthy man: the chandeliers from the ceiling, the antique furniture and paintings on the walls. There was a big marble fireplace in both sections of the room, each with a mountain of ash in the grate, as if he'd got fed up cleaning them out and had decided to make do with the gas heater that was purring beside him like the family cat. She helped herself to the tea and then opened the packet of biscuits.

'Eat as many as you like,' he said from behind his paper.

'Thanks,' she said and pulled two out.

For some reason, she felt completely at ease in this neglected room full of expensive things. She was at ease with the man, too, his big country face, his large square hands on the side of the newspaper. She wanted to ask him if he lived alone, if he was married or had children – grandchildren, even. And for a mad little minute, she wanted to ask him if he was looking for a housekeeper. She could imagine herself cleaning this room, going down to the shops to collect his newspapers, calling him when his dinner was ready. A man who would leave you alone. She nearly laughed out loud at the absurdity of the notion.

The old man continued to ignore her for a while. Then he put down the *Racing Post* and took up the *Irish Field*. 'Have you enough yet?' he asked.

'Plenty.'

'Well tell himself, I'll be in touch so.'

She took the dismissal, put down her mug and then, standing up, looked at him again. 'I could go to the bookies for you, if you want?'

He frowned at her as if she'd made yet another stupid mistake.

'The bookies? Sure, that's all done by phone these days.'

When she got back to the hotel room, she put in a call to Matthew. He was at a meeting so she left a message with his secretary – his real secretary – letting him know that the delivery had been made. Then she stood by the window, waiting to see if Matthew would call back. She thought of the conversation they might have. He would ask her about the old man; she would give all the details, turning it into a little story that would make him laugh. He would tell her he missed her and then ask about her plans for the rest of the day. What would she say? 'My plans? Oh, I'll probably take a stroll over to Grafton Street, have a wander around the swanky shops. Go for a coffee, a ramble through Trinity College or the Green – that sort of thing.'

But of course she wouldn't be going anywhere near Grafton Street; she would be going in the opposite direction.

She wondered when the idea first came to her – was it at the exact moment when Matthew had said that he needed someone to go to Dublin? Or did the idea begin to flicker while crossing the Irish Sea?

Or was it just now, standing here at the window of her hotel room, looking across at the back of the railway station, watching the trains like snakes, slipping in and out of the city.

She didn't like to tell the porter where she was headed and so she kept it vague.

'Could I walk from here to Phibsboro?'

'Phibsboro? Oh you could all right. Though it might take a while.'

'How long, do you think?'

He began to unfold a map of Dublin. 'Well, let's see now . . . whereabouts in Phibsboro are you going?' he asked.

She peered over his arm. She could see her destination clearly marked and that nearby was the Mater Hospital.

'The Mater,' she lied. 'I'm visiting a friend.'

He clicked on his pen and drew a scribbled knot. 'Let's see now. This is where we are here,' he began, then making a long blue wavering line up the map, he finished with another scribbled knot. 'And this, this here is the Mater. The whole thing should take you about forty to fifty minutes. Door to door. And I hope now,' he said, with a fat-faced smile, 'that your friend has a speedy recovery.'

She followed the line on the map up the hill where she had seen the prostitutes the night before and then, for a while, through a series of silent streets packed tight with red-brick houses. She noted each street name, the shut-up shops on wider streets, the many pubs and churches. On a road that swept upwards, she found herself walking alongside a funeral cortège for a while. She did not allow herself to think, except to reassure herself now and then that they would probably refuse to let her in without an appointment. And even if they did let her in, he could refuse to see her. Step by step she pushed on, her breath catching on the damp air, her face numb from the cold. When she saw a group of nurses walking towards her, she knew she was almost there.

At the end of an ordinary residential street, she passed through a set of big grey pillars. There was an avenue leading up to the building, at the side a sort of Portakabin with women queuing outside it. She stood behind the last woman in the queue and asked her if she needed an appointment.

The woman looked her up and down. She was middle-aged and her face was mauve and blocky.

'For what?' she asked.

'Well, to visit someone.'

'To visit someone?'

'Yes, do you need an appointment?'

She felt the woman both sensed and resented her shame.

'Your husband, is it?'

'No.'

'Boyfriend then? Brother?'

'Friend.'

'*Friend?*' the woman sniggered.

'Yes. I just want to know if I should have made an appointment?'

The woman glared at her; she wanted her to say it. She wanted to hear her say the word.

'Do I need an appointment to see a prisoner?' she asked.

Then the other women began to fire questions at her. Was this her first time? Did she come far? Did she not bring him up anything? What was he in for? Until, finally, a younger woman stepped out of the line and said, 'Don't mind them, they're a shower of nosey wagons. You don't need an appointment.'

She was such a pretty girl, maybe twenty years old, dressed in a black leather jacket and a short tartan kilt, her face plastered with makeup.

'So, I just . . . ?'

'That's right, you just rock up and they give you a docket.'

Another woman came up behind her, pushing a buggy with a baby inside it, and a little girl in school uniform holding on to the handle, maybe about nine or ten years old.

'Do I have to go in, Ma?'

'Don't start, you – I'm warning you.'

'I hate it in there, I do.'

'And wha'? You think *I* fuckin' like it?'

The door of the hut opened and the women fell silent. The queue shifted uneasily and now it was moving so quickly she had no time to change her mind. A man in uniform was handing her a ticket, lifting his hand to direct her. She fixed her eyes on the ground. And then the big gate.

The room like a big box when she stepped inside, the dank, cave-like odour. A hand took the docket from her and pointed to a place on the end of a long bench where she was supposed to sit down. She was afraid now, her head ringing with all the noise; the steel of the doors on the way in, the clanking finality. And the awful feeling as she'd walked along a tunnel-like corridor with the silent shadows of the other women moving around her. And now the smell of this room: sweat and tobacco; aftershave and Lynx; the hefty squirts of visitors' perfume. She scanned the room. There was the long bench where the visitors sat just beside her; a long table in the middle with a splint running down the centre of it; and on the far side, another long bench where the prisoners sat. An officer, sitting up in an umpire's chair across the room, was looking at her. She perched herself down on the corner of the bench. The women from the queue outside were seated further along. The woman with the mauve face was crying daintily into a hanky held in her big, raw hand, while across the table from her, a skimpy young lad, possibly her grandson, was doing his best to ignore her. The girl in the leather jacket sat with a frantic smile carved into her face, while her husband or boyfriend, face full of resentment, talked at her without taking a breath.

She could feel her knee jumping of its own accord and her fingers pulling at one another. She put her hands into her coat pockets to steady them up. There was something small and hard inside the right pocket. She felt around it – her engagement ring. Somewhere on the way in, she had slipped it off her finger. But she couldn't remember doing that now. She couldn't remember much of anything between accepting the docket from one officer and handing it to the other. Why had she done that, taken her ring off – to spare his feelings, was it? To give herself a chance to explain first? Yes, that must have been it.

She looked up for a while at the blue-grey cigarette smoke webbed onto the ceiling. Then she looked around the room again. She couldn't see him anywhere. All of the other women had a prisoner sitting across the table from them. She was the only one with a vacant place. He wasn't here. He wasn't anywhere in this stinking, airless box. He must be refusing to see her. The bastard was refusing to see her. It had been a mistake to come, she realised now. It was madness. Imagine if Matthew found out. Matthew, who she was going to live with, work for, marry? Matthew who loved her, who had bought the ring hiding in the corner of her pocket.

She wanted to stand up, open that door just behind her, go back out the way she had come, keep going until she heard the steel gate close behind her and she was back out in the cold fresh air. But the officer who had her docket was bent over his table, and across the way, the officer on the umpire's chair was busy watching the girl in the leather jacket. Maybe if she just stood up and called out, 'Excuse me, I've changed my mind, I want to leave.' But everyone looking at her? Everyone thinking she was mad. She lowered her head and rubbed a knuckle into her forehead. Oh, why am I always so stupid? she asked herself. Why am I always so fucking *stupid*?

And then he was there. Coming through the door on the other side of the room. He was there. The door only beginning to open when she recognised him: the shape of his shoulders, his arms, his neck. And when she saw his face!

She lost all thought of anything, of the engagement ring stuffed into her pocket, the man she was supposed to marry, the house he was going to buy for her, the business she was going to help him run. All she could see was Pip.

They sat grinning at one another across the long splint.

'I can't believe this,' he said, finally.

'Neither can I!'

'I mean, what the fuck are you doing here, Milly?'

'I don't know,' she said and they both laughed nervously.

'Well, and how are you?' he laughed.

'Okay, yea, I think.'

He had a few grey hairs on him now, but she had never seen him look so well, even his teeth looked better than before.

She said it to him: 'I thought you'd be in bits. And look at you – I've never seen you look so well. It's ridiculous how well you look!'

'Must be all the clean living.'

'Even your teeth!'

'Gives me something to do, brushing them. About eight times a day.'

'Well, you seem in good form anyway.'

He shrugged. 'I'm okay.'

'But is it not terrible in here, Pip?'

'Jesus, don't let anyone hear you call me Pip.'

'Sorry.'

He smiled at her. 'The boredom can get to you a bit,' he said, 'waiting for the day to pass and that. But it's better than it used to be. I'm coaching some of the younger lads in the gym now, which helps. And I made friends with a nun, she brings books in to me. You get used to it. Remember I spent nearly eight years in a boarding school.'

'Hardly the same thing!'

'Oh, you'd be surprised. The shit food, the standing in line, lights out, even the way the laundry is run. Put it this way, I'm used to the institutional life. But look at you, Milly, you look . . .'

'What – older?'

'No, I was going to say fierce sophisticated. Polished.'

'What? Like an old pair of boots?'

'You look great. But you didn't come all the way over specially to see me, did you?'

'No. I don't think so. I mean, I was doing a job for someone.'

'What sort of a job?'

'Oh, just delivering documents.'

'Delivering documents? Are you a secret agent now?'

'There's this man, Matthew. He's a developer and he asked me if . . .'

'This man?'

'Yes,' she said and felt her face go red.

'You're seeing him? I hope he's a nice fella. Better than the last worm anyway.'

'Mylo?'

'Even the name,' he said and they both laughed.

'He is a nice man.'

'Is it serious?'

She shrugged.

'Jesus, is that why you came, to tell me you're getting married?'

She said nothing for a moment, just sat there looking at her hands, shaking her head.

'Milly? You can tell me.'

'I came because . . .'

She began to cry then.

'What's wrong? What are you crying for? I'm happy for you. Really, I am.'

'But I don't want you to be happy for me,' she said.

'Ah Milly, now what's that supposed to mean?'

Glancing down along the bench, she noticed that she wasn't the only one crying, but that apart from the little girl in school uniform, no one was paying a blind bit of attention to her.

'I'd give him up tomorrow for you,' she said, suddenly looking up at him.

'Don't be ridiculous,' he said.

'Why is it ridiculous?'

'I'm a convict, Milly.'

'Don't say that, you're not.'

'But I am.' He gave a little laugh. 'Look, this is not like before, getting banged up for the night here and there on a drunk and disorderly. This is a serious crime. You can't go offering to—'

She wiped her eyes, pulling herself together. 'No, you listen to me, Pip. Listen. You're all I ever wanted. I don't care what you did, I know you're a good man; I know it can't have been your fault. Please ask me to wait, just ask me and I'll wait.'

She could hear his long intake of breath, then a sigh.

'Milly, you're talking shite. It was my fault. All right, I didn't steal the car, that wasn't my idea. But I was driving it. I was responsible for another man's death.'

'But who stole the car?'

'He did. Bobby Coyle's kid brother. Look, we'd been on the piss for about two days.'

'Did you know he was going to steal it?'

'No, I came out of the pub, and he was already in it.'

'But why did you drive it?'

'Because he was too drunk to see in front of him and he wanted to get to his girlfriend's house and I took it on myself . . .'

He pushed his hand through his hair and shook his head. 'Oh, come on, you must have read about it in the papers.'

'It wasn't in the English papers.'

'No, but they sell the Irish papers in London – are you telling me no one brought it into the pub?'

'If they did, they didn't show me. I just heard the bones of it from Mrs Oak, who heard it from Shamie.'

'Of course.'

She waited for him to speak.

'I fell asleep at the wheel. When the car went up in flames, I managed to get myself out, but he – he went up. I couldn't get to him.'

She began to cry again. 'Oh Pip, why couldn't you have, why couldn't you have just—'

'That's what happens when you're a piss-head.'

'I want to wait for you.'

'I have at least three years left, even with good behaviour. But there's no way, I said, no way that you're going to wait for me. I may not even come back to London.'

'Oh, you're just saying that now.'

'No, I'm not.' He leaned forward a little, lowering his voice. 'I don't want you to wait for me.'

'Well, I'm waiting anyway. I have it all worked out.'

'Since when have you it all worked out – five minutes ago?'

'I have it worked out, that's all. Look, I was supposed to be leaving Mrs Oak to move in with Matthew. Well, I won't do that now. I'll stay with her till she sells the pub.'

'She's selling the pub?'

'Yes, she'll have to. It's too long a story for now but I'll stay with her, get a job somewhere else, and then . . . I'll save like mad and then, and then, I'll find a flat for us. Mrs Oak will probably have moved to Spain or somewhere by then. I know you feel the same way about me, Pip. I just *know* it.'

'Milly, calm down, will you? And you don't know anything about me. If the bloke you're with is a good bloke, you take my advice, leave Mrs Oak, move in with him, marry him, be happy. Be safe. I can't keep you safe.'

'I don't care about being safe.'

'Yes, you do.'

'But I don't even want to leave Mrs Oak. I'm happy to stay there until she's sold the place and gets settled. She's always been so good to me. She's . . . Please, Pip. Please can't you just listen to me?'

She reached her hand out to him and he drew back, shaking his head.

'But I only want you,' she said. 'I don't care about being safe or if you're a convict or anything. Oh why can't you just listen to me? Why can't you just believe me?'

There was nothing for a moment and then, quietly, he said: 'Milly, I want to tell you something. I want to tell you something that will change your mind for you. It's about me and about Mrs Oak.'

She looked at him, afraid now of the look on his face, the tone of his voice.

'What?'

'Remember that time when my old man died? Remember I had been away and had just come back from London?'

'Yes, you got to see him just before he—'

'You were supposed to meet me in that pub where the Belfast fella used to work and Mrs Oak came instead – remember that?'

'Yes, Gerry. She had money your father had asked her to mind, yes.'

'Well, her and me, we had this thing. It started around then. Lasted for, I don't know, a week, ten days.'

'What do you mean?'

'You know what I mean. You must have guessed something was going on with her, out all the time. She was with me.'

'Doing what?'

'What do you think?'

'Oh, you're just making this up.'

'I had no money, she had plenty. She paid for me. Bought all the drink, the hotel room, whatever. Even the suit. Though she took the price of it back, after I finished with her – remember? I'm telling you this so you know that not only am I not worth your time, but she's not worth your time either. She knew how you felt about me and she still did it.'

'I don't believe you.'

He slapped his hand on the table and growled through his teeth. 'For fuck's sake, will you listen to me?'

She gave a little jump. The officer on the umpire's chair turned his head towards them and she could feel all eyes on them from both sides of the table.

They sat quietly until the officer looked the other way and the conversations resumed.

He began to speak again. 'When I get out of here, there is every chance I'll go back on the drink, and no guarantee that I won't do something similar. And you know what, Milly? I want the freedom to do that – drink what I like, fuck who I like.'

He began to stand up. 'I'm not the marrying kind, and even if I was, you were never really my type. Now go, marry your bloke. Have a kid or two. Be happy.'

He nodded to the prison officer then, and within seconds he was gone through the door at the side without so much as a backward glance.

She came out at the same time as the woman with the mauve face, walking a few steps behind her through the tunnel and then out through the gate. The woman was a silent weeper – from behind you wouldn't even know she was crying but for the movement of the hanky and the drop of her shoulders. She, on the other hand, was making a show of herself, hiccupping sobs. She stayed behind the woman up the short avenue and through the pillars. When they reached the main road, she saw the woman turning right, and so she turned left.

The tears began to ease off now, coming back at intervals whenever she remembered something else that he had said to her, or an image came into her head of Mrs Oak lying in bed with him.

After a while, she stopped crying altogether. Needles and pins had spread through her body and it felt as if hundreds of worms had nested between her flesh and her skin. She kept thinking that she was going to vomit. It was almost dark by now and she had no idea where she was going. The lights from the stuck traffic showed up a steady drizzle. After a while, she noticed an overhead railway bridge that seemed familiar. She remembered, then, that the bus from the village used to pass under that bridge and that the cobbled walls beneath it were always wet. There was a sign for the airport and Belfast. She was going in the wrong direction. She turned and looked back along the long wide street. At the far end, a blur of neon lights over shops going into the distance towards the city centre. She waited a moment, then began to walk.

She chose a run-down pub on a corner. There were leatherette banquettes and red Formica tables. An old man sat at the far end of the counter, looking up at the television. Beneath the television, another old man sat and stared down the bar at her.

She slipped into the ladies where, through a mottled mirror, she cleaned her face and patched up her makeup as best she could. At the same time, she tried not to look herself in the eye. When she came out, she ordered a large brandy and asked for change for the phone. She waited for the brandy to do its work, warming her bones, bringing life back into her hands. Then she stood up and went over to the phone. This time Matthew was in.

'Hello, sweetheart,' he said. 'I've been trying to get you all afternoon.'

'Sorry,' she said, clearing her throat. 'I went out, lost track of time.'

'Diana tells me you made the delivery. How was the old geezer – all right?'

'Oh, he was fine.'

'Didn't look as if he was about to croak or anything?'

'No, he's a few years in him, I'd say. Matthew, could I ask you something?'

'What is it – you all right?'

'I'm fine, but Matthew?'

'What is it?'

'It's just that . . . It's a bit lonely here. I was wondering, well, remember you said you could book a flight for me?'

'Course I can. I can book you on a flight first thing tomorrow.'

'Could you do it for tonight, do you think?'

'Absolutely. Let me do it now, I'll phone you back in a few to let you know the details.'

'I'm not in the hotel. Could you wait a bit to call me back – say an hour? I'll jump in a taxi and go back and get packed and—'

'All right, yeah. You sure you're okay?'

'Yes, fine. I just want to come home, that's all.'

'I'll call you in an hour with the details. And I'll be waiting for you at the airport.'

'Will you really?'

'With open arms, sweetheart.'

On the plane, an old woman had already nabbed her window seat. She thought about saying something but then decided to leave well enough alone. There was an exchange of glances as she sat down, a vague nod and then the woman turned her face to the window. A short while later, when an announcement was made that take-off had been delayed by twenty minutes, she heard the woman mutter what sounded very like: 'Oh fuck it anyway.'

The woman turned to her then. 'Sorry,' she said, 'but I've been hours on a plane already and I've had quite enough.'

'Where were you?' she asked, just to be friendly.

'New York. Then we had to stop at Shannon and transfer to Dublin when I thought I'd be coming straight into Dublin before catching a flight to London. We were hanging around Shannon for hours, and I still have a taxi ride ahead when we get to Heathrow. Over an hour. I think home to bed, I'll never get.'

'I suppose you're often popping over and back?' the woman said. 'It's not such a big deal nowadays, is it?'

'Actually, this is only my first time back in twenty years.'

The woman had pale brown eyes and thick white hair pushed back off her face. Her nose was slightly hooked. Never mind her age, she looked remarkably fresh, considering.

'But you must have been very young leaving home,' the woman said, and Milly nodded. 'I suppose I was. Eighteen.'

If she expected anything from the old woman it had been pity or maybe even a touch of disapproval. But instead, she got: 'I wish to hell I'd got out when I was eighteen!'

The old woman sighed out the window. Then, a moment later, came back with a smile. 'Family, you know.' She waved a wrinkled hand. 'Still – they're all dead now, I suppose.' And then she laughed out loud, tipping Milly on the arm. 'Oh, don't mind me. I'm a bitter old bat. I had such a wonderful time in New York even if I am exhausted. I kept thinking, now why didn't I do this *years* ago? I mean, what was I doing all that time . . . ? Tell me, have you ever been to Africa?'

'No, I haven't. I haven't travelled much really – Portugal last year and Marbella a couple of months ago. But what was New York like?'

'Oh, you can read about New York in a travel book. Or see it on the television. It's just how they say it is. But Africa now. Or India – can you imagine!'

'Maybe next time you can go there.'

'Well yes, it would be nice to think so. The trouble is, I'm running out of time. Anyway, tell me about you. Are you married?'

'No. No, I'm not.'

'But you must have had offers?'

'Well, two, I suppose. One years ago. Another more recent.'

'Wait for the next offer. Live a bit first. That's what you do. Do you plan on having children?'

'I . . . Well, I don't know really.'

'Forgive me, I've embarrassed you. I'm abrupt, I know. In fact, the older I get the more abrupt I seem to become. Still, you've plenty of time.'

'I'm not as young as you seem to think!' She laughed.

'Oh yes, you are.' The woman frowned and tapped her on the arm. 'You know, even the nicest man will bend you to his will. I should know. I've been married three times. All completely different, all the exact same. They can't help it.'

'I'm afraid it's a bit late to take your advice.' She lifted her hand to show.

'Ohh, nice engagement ring. My first husband was a jeweller. You like jewellery?'

'Not particularly.'

'But that's quite a dazzler.'

'I think it's a little big, between ourselves.'

'It must have cost a packet.'

'I have no idea. It was a surprise.'

'Good job you said yes, then,' the woman said.

14. Pip

2017

September

HE WOULD HAVE been about eight years old then – before his mother died, anyway – off school and getting over a bad dose of flu, although no longer sick enough to stay in bed. He'd been playing with Dom's old Dinky cars on the turn of the stairs, ear half cocked in the direction of the kitchen – gas flint, kettle, cups, the chit-chat between his parents: those warm sounds that always made him feel safe. His father talking about the workday ahead and saying something about taking the car to Hampstead, and his mother then, 'Would you ever do me a favour and bring that fella with you before he drives me up the wall?'

He had been thrilled at the prospect of a jaunt in the car, the inevitable treats involved, the jealousy it would inflict on Dom later. He'd just wished she hadn't said that thing about him driving her up the wall when he'd thought she'd been having such a lovely time reading to him, playing snakes and ladders, answering his endless questions on this, that and life in general.

His mother coiled the navy-striped school scarf around him, then screwed his school cap onto his head. He was to keep well wrapped up, she said, he was to be a good boy and stay in the car and read his book while his father was in seeing a customer.

But a few hours later, his father was taking his school scarf from him and turning it into a pillow for a dying man. And even before that, as soon as they pulled up outside the first pub, he stepped out of the car, walked around to the passenger side, opened the door and said, 'Well, come along then, mustn't keep the customers waiting.'

There had been an old brown pub just outside the village and then another pub on the high street. A third nearer to the heath. He loved their names, like storybook titles: the Spaniards, the Holly Bush, the Old White Bear. And the old-fashioned pub fronts like the cover of a book, so that walking in through the door, you always expected something to happen.

They ate their sandwiches in the car and drank tea out of a flask. The tea was too hot for him and his father had to roll down the window and hold the cup out until enough rain fell into it to cool it down. His father told him the rain would be good for his lungs.

'Will it make things grow inside them?' he asked and his father laughed. 'Of course not. Goodness, Phil, the ideas you get!'

Later, they went into a café. His father ordered a cup of coffee. He liked the rich sound it made coming out of his throat – cup-ofcoffeepleasemiss. He asked for a glass of milk, which didn't have the same ring to it at all. His father spoke differently to his mother; not just the accent and sound, but the words he used. He said 'amongst' and 'whilst'. He said 'thereabouts'. Sometimes there was an extra 'r' sound on the end of his words. China-*r* and idea-*r* and sofa-*r*. When a bird flew down and landed on the ground, he said it had alighted.

They had toasted teacake and the waitress gave him a choc-olate biscuit on the house. He munched his biscuit and watched the rain worm down the café window. When the rain stopped, his father's large hand soared over the table and alighted on his forehead. 'What do you say, Phil,' he said, 'to a ramble on the heath?'

A November day. Kite Hill rising behind his father and winter all around: cold trees, bristling hedges, feeble light from a grey, encircling sky. Crows squawking – or maybe they were rooks. A disappointed sound, anyway: aww, aww, aww.

His father, down on one knee, black coat draped over the damp ground, head inclined over a stranger who appeared to be gasping for life.

The voice of his father like a swing. Low and kind when he spoke to the stranger. Loud, and even a little impatient, when it lifted towards him standing there petrified, a few feet away. 'Run Phil run as fast as you can find a grown-up ask them to fetch an ambulance tell them there's a man looks like he's had a heart attack.'

The dying man with his navy-striped school scarf pillowed now under his oily head.

The dying man had spoiled everything. Moments ago, they had been happy. They were standing on the hill, breath catching on the wild whoosh of air, looking down on the spread of the hazy city. His father's voice full of patience then, pointing out landmarks, encouraging him to look, to *see* (it's no good you guessing, Phil, you must learn to look, to *see*). Can you find St Paul's for me? Can you see Westminster Palace?

His eye trailing a shrunken city that had seemed to him like a scatter of broken toys on the floor. If he hadn't turned his head quite so far, desperate to find St Paul's; if he had just concentrated on the blur at the end of his father's pointing finger.

'Dad, look, look over there! That man's just fallen on the ground!'

And now, moments later, here was his father shouting at him. Angry. His father was angry! 'Get going, Philip – what the bloody hell are you waiting for?!'

He'd been standing on the spot, a few feet down the hill, bouncing at the knees, looking all around him. Big green hill in the background; smaller bald hill under the tree where the man was lying. Scrub and endless forest; the vague outline of a miniature city pretending to be London. Four hundred acres or thereabouts, his father had said a short while ago, and now he was expecting him to find a way out of it, just like *that*?

'But where, Dad? Where will I run to? Which *way*?'

Keeping one hand on the man's shoulder, his father lifted himself a little and, shooting his arm out, shouted, 'That way, go that way! Just keep going downwards till you come to a road. Knock on a door. If you see someone before you reach the road, tell them, tell them to call an ambulance. Tell them we're to the left of Parliament Hill, somewhere as you come in by Downshire Hill. Near to Saxon Ditch, I think it's called. Will you remember all that?'

'Yes, Dad,' he said, nodding keenly even if the only word that stayed in his head was Saxon.

'Go on then. Run like the devil. Go. Go. *Go*.'

Then his father turned away from him, back to the man on the ground.

As he began to run, a new, odd sort of fear came over him and he'd had to stop. All very well ordering a stranger to call an ambulance, but how was he supposed to find his way back to his father? What if he couldn't find him at all and was left wandering through the four hundred and thereabouts acres all night? What if he was caught by that Brady man Dom said had escaped from prison and was on the lookout for juicy boys aged eight to ten?

It had been a cold, dull day; now it was freezing and dusk was coming on. Soon it would be dark. There was no one about. Earlier they had come across a few people, dog walkers and a couple of pram pushers. They had stopped to talk to a fisherman. The fisherman with dirty fingernails, squeezing a worm, pinching its mouth open so that it took the double-branched hook, then edging its soft little body around the fine steel curve. He had been afraid of the fisherman, the power in his fingertips, his killer eye. He had an idea that the pond was close by – maybe on the far side of those trees. The fisherman was an adult. If he found him, he could put the whole thing on him. 'My dad asked me to find you – yes, *you*. He said you've got to telephone for an ambulance, through those trees, up a hill, that's where *you've* got to tell it to go.'

He turned to take one last look back up the hill in the hope that the man had recovered and that he would see him, sitting up now, handing the school scarf back to his father and saying, 'I'm perfectly all right now, thank you very much.'

But all he could see were the soles of the man's shoes and his father's silhouette against the darkening sky. There was something about the way his head was turned, his three fingers raised and moving slowly over the man's head: first, they went up and down in a vertical line, then sideways left to right. In the silence of the heath, his voice carried downstream to where he was standing. It was as if he was saying a poem, the words sticking on the quiet, cold air. Not English, though. And yet it sounded vaguely familiar, as if he had heard it before. It sounded like that language Dom recited to himself when doing his homework. Latin, he thought it was called.

Had he known from that moment – something quickening in the back of his mind, then in all the excitement, forgotten? Or

347

had it been a more gradual realisation? Fragments building into a whole. After his father died and the photograph had slipped out from the Palgrave's *Treasury*, it had all started to come together. The day on Hampstead Heath. And then, a couple of years later, the day they arrived at the boarding school outside Dublin when a priest had stepped forward, opening his arms to his father: John, old friend. I'm sorry for your troubles. And later, of course, the bare, bleak house in Slough that his father had moved into after he had returned to England alone, leaving them behind in school. Other images from that house in Slough, the early weeks of his first summer holidays there while he waited for Dom to arrive from his new school in Hertfordshire. He was ten years old by then and given to flights of fancy. But real or imagined, those images had remained for all those years, half developed in the darkroom of his mind.

When he remembers his father now – consciously remembers him – or even when the ghost of his father steps into his eye-line, catching him off guard, he tries to steer the memory away from that house in Slough to the day on Hampstead Heath. And the sight of a good man wearing a long black coat, down on one knee, ministering last rites to a dying stranger.

He has often found himself wondering – he wonders now as he stands in this deserted laneway, crowbar tucked under his coat – why he had felt the need to go back to Ireland after his father had died? To ask Father Joe about the photograph? But the photograph had simply clarified what he had long suspected: his father had been a spoiled priest.

And so fucking what if he was? as Dom said, only a few weeks ago, on one of the rare occasions when they had discussed it. Dom had come out to the garden with a mug of coffee in each fist, a stack of newspapers under his arm and a packet of biscuits

348

sticking out of his back pocket. They sat on the patio, drinking the coffee, half reading the papers, Dom working his way through the biscuits. He can't remember now how the subject came up, but there it was suddenly, out on the dainty wrought-iron table.

'Let's face it, Phil,' Dom said then, 'he was always a bit odd. Personally, I couldn't give a shit. I mean, all right, when I first found out, I was . . . well, let's just say I wasn't too happy.'

'When did you find out?'

'The house in Slough.'

'Did you ever say it to him?'

'God no. What would be the point?'

'Why didn't you say something to me?'

'I don't know. You were gone back to school by then and by the time I saw you again I'd put it out of my head, I suppose. We lived in different countries, didn't we? Anyway, I just presumed you knew.'

'Well, yeah, I suspected something. But until he died, and I found that photograph . . .'

'Is that why you went back to Ireland – to have it confirmed?'

'I suppose.'

'And did that make you feel better?'

'No.'

'And did it improve your life in any way?'

'No.'

'Well, there you go,' Dom said, reaching out for another biscuit and returning to his *Sunday Times.*

He hadn't attempted to explain the return visit to Dom – he could hardly even explain it to himself – the photograph had been little more than an excuse. What it confirmed or didn't confirm had been irrelevant; it was the other memories it had stirred up. Those images that had begun following him around after the death of his father – or shortly before he'd died anyway. Those last few hours sitting by his bedside in the nursing home, watching him slip away, holding his hand, and wondering whether or not he should be holding it – that had been the start of it.

He glances up and down the lane, then angles the crowbar and edges it into the side of the window next to the lock. He pries and pushes until he hears the latch pop and the bones of the window give a long, put-upon groan. A small tight shove, then a puff of dust, followed by a cluster of runaway spiders.

He looks down through the gap to a slightly clearer version of the view through the dirty window. If he goes down there, he'll be breaking the law. He will be indulging in what Dr Sunita would call his impulsive addictive behaviour. Except, this time, he wouldn't even have the excuse of being out of his mind on drink.

That day out on the patio, Dom had said Ireland was an unlucky hole.

'I mean, look what it did to you.'

'Ireland didn't do anything to me, I did it to myself.'

'Nah . . . it's a cursed place. T.B.F.A.M., if you ask me.'

'*What?*'

'To be fucking avoided, mate.'

Going to Ireland may have been fuelled by a combination of drink and grief, but it was also driven by a need to find out the truth.

He'd been hoping to learn something about his father, the sort of man he had been when the photograph had been taken, smiling and suntanned, in collar and soutane. Father Joe squinting into the blast of sunlight with a full head of hair. A small regiment of little black boys arranged in rows, standing between them. He had wanted to hear about that time; earlier times too, the years in the seminary; his father as a boy – if Father Joe knew anything about that. And later, too, as a priest in Ireland who had fallen for the school secretary, agonising between God and a woman – he'd certainly wanted to know about that.

For himself, he had wanted a mixture of absolution and blame – for what, he had no idea. He wanted to walk away from Father Joe anyway, having reached the conclusion that his own mind had become so addled with drink, it had been incapable of reading the past, or of distinguishing the real from the imagined. He'd been searching for a way to get his father off the hook, to press the delete button on the images that had been haunting him. How going to Ireland was supposed to do this, he had no idea. But he had to start somewhere.

He gets down on one knee and, returning the crowbar to the bag, asks himself what has brought all this back into his mind? Why his father, long dead, occasionally remembered, has recently started turning up everywhere. Walking ahead of him on the far side of the street; sitting down the back of every bus he steps onto. He's the old man standing in the post office queue. He's the old man looking out of a café window. He's the 'Every old man I see' from the Kavanagh poem. But he's even closer than that. He's in the mirror watching him shave. He's in the long black coat he is wearing now, bought last week in the Oxfam shop in Notting Hill. And without drink to blur the edges, it looks like he's here to stay.

He zips the bag up, lifts it and shoves it through the open window. The bag flops and clatters onto the floor below, maybe ten feet down. Then he takes off the black coat and rolls it into a ball. A good overcoat, barely worn by the look of it. Italian label, one previous owner. The things people give away. He pushes it through the window, sending it after the bag down into the basement.

He is sweating now, his heart doing ninety, but he doesn't

want to stop and think. Not about the past, not about the future, certainly not about what he's getting up to now, this minute. He's going in. He's going in and that's an end to it.

He squeezes the top part of himself sideways, through the horizontal window, then lifts one leg over the aluminium frame. Praying for his balls to survive the ordeal, he hauls the second leg over. Elbows pegged over the frame of the window, he listens to himself wheeze and gasp – and this, he thinks, is why they call us old geezers. He looks down, reckons on about a four-foot drop, then carefully pulls one elbow, then the next, over the frame, transferring his grip to his hands. He can feel his legs swing from his hip for a couple of seconds, then, releasing his hands from the frame, he hears his own voice utter the words 'mother of fuck' as he drops. He lands. Sparks shooting from the soles of his feet up through his legs, he takes to the floor like Groucho Marx, managing somehow not to fall on his face. A few steps later, and his legs come to an uncertain stop.

Not bad, he thinks, for a man of sixty.

He stands a moment and looks around the room. Now that he's in, the first thing he wants to do is to find a way out again. A bar of rich September sunlight projects from the open window onto the back wall. Otherwise, the light in here is like a basin of dirty dishwater. He looks up at the ceiling. The old fluorescent lights are still in place. He tries the switch but nothing moves. Even if it did, though, he wouldn't use those lights – he's always hated them, their stark, irritable glare. He often wondered, after, how he had never had a fit while training in here.

He walks around the outside of the ring, stops at each corner and, leaning in, gauges the viewpoints from the lane outside. Then he makes his way down to the changing room where the light dips again.

Standing in the empty frame of the doorway, looking at the row of doorless lockers, he remembers the first day he walked in here and asked Shamie how come there were no doors in the place.

'My boys got nothin' to hide,' Shamie said. 'We don't need no doors . . . besides, in here we trust one another.'

Wooden pegs on the walls, wooden crate on the floor, a long bench scarred with the names of boys, some of whom would be old men now, if not already six feet under.

Back in the gym, he goes to a small heavy table at the back wall and, bending at the knee, begins to push it across the floor, stopping here and there to put his hands on his hips and rock his spine back into alignment. When he finally gets the table where he wants it, his back is humming from all the effort. He gives it a final push to the wall, then sitting side-saddle on the edge, he pulls his leg up and climbs aboard.

It gives him a couple of feet, but it's still tricky enough.

He gets down again, takes a few steps back. If he's to make this work, he will need to find a better way in and out. Apart from the fact that he could break his neck climbing in and out day after day, the table would be visible from the window should anyone decide to look in. And those windows need to be secured. He'll have to fix the lock – no, better than that, he'll have to fit two decent locks that won't be cracked by any fool with a crowbar in his hand.

He walks to the far end of the gym out into the small hallway, where he steps up to the door and waits for his eyes to settle into the darkness. Reaching above the door, he runs the back of his fingers along the dip of the architrave. He comes back with a handful of dirt. He flicks the mat over, leans down and pats the floor. Again nothing.

Back in the gym, he steps into the alcove where Shamie used to take care of the paperwork, cursing and groaning over his desk. The desk is still there – a fancy-looking number that was a gift from the widow of a bric-a-brac man from Golborne Road. Shamie was always losing things in the pile-up: car keys, wallet, once a half-eaten sandwich. All cleared off now, apart from a hefty body count of dead flies and a thick top-coating of dust.

Reaching his hand under the desk, he feels around to see if a key has been taped on there. Then he begins to pull at the single deep drawer on the right-hand side. He tugs and pulls, but the bastard won't budge. For a moment he thinks it could be locked, but when he tries again, he can feel a little give at the bottom. Finally, it begins to surrender, and in another few tugs, he gets it to open. The contents start to spill over even as he is pulling it out, papers gliding off the top, some falling on the floor. There are old schedule forms and weigh-in cards; scraps of paper with names and old phone numbers on them; a few faded business cards. He sees tubes of Vaseline and rolls of tape, a small pair of scissors. There is so much shit in there that he doesn't want the bother of emptying it out then loading it up again, so he edges his fingers down the sides and begins to feel around the walls of the drawer for a taped-on key. Every time he moves his hand, something else catches his eye. Old invoices and receipts for items sold by the dozen: hand wraps, boot ties, boxes of swab-sticks. Rule books and press cuttings. A couple of pocket diaries.

And then a small notebook with his name on the front of it churns up out of the pile.

Hesitantly, he opens it up and begins to flick through the pages. Various venues are listed: York Hall, Battersea Town Hall. White Hart Lane. Other venues too. Names of opponents he can barely recall. Nor can he remember all of the fights – even those he had won. A note here and there. Some of the notes are just one or two words with a question mark. Weight? Footwork? Focus? Something missing? Ready? Others are short statements: Condition good. Look at left foot. Speed improved. Not ready.

The last note is another question: Albert Hall, middleweight, next May – if ready?

Whether or not he was ready turned out to be irrelevant – he had already moved to Jackie by then and was doing well enough. The first few hopeful months before Berlin tore the balls off all that.

He begins piling everything back in the drawer. Halfway through, a weight tips off his hand. Two envelopes held together by an elastic band. And there, written on the first one in Shamie's careful hand, is *key to gym door*. Marked clearly on the second envelope is *key to outside door*. We trust one another in here, he thinks.

He goes back outside to the door, feels his way down to the lock. The lock complains a bit, but gives in easily enough. He turns the key a second time and pushes the door open.

Ahead of him, the old basement staircase edges up to a dark hallway.

As he slowly climbs, each step gives a groaning sound that is almost human. Then a faint semblance of light appears, widening as he comes closer to the top.

He is in the main hallway of the building now, standing at the front door – the door leading out to the short alley off Britton Street. A shaft of pale sunlight through the fan window above the door falls down on a pathway of envelopes and junk mail meant for the two small businesses that once shared the building with the boxing club. Like a kid kicking through leaves, he makes his way along it.

The lock obeys the turn of his hand. An easy push, and he is standing looking through the little archway to the main street outside.

Quickly he steps back inside and closes the door. He waits a moment and then opens it again. He scours the back of the buildings on each side of the archway, then decides nobody will pay any attention to him unless he starts acting suspiciously.

'So stop acting suspiciously,' he mutters before slowly going back inside and closing the door behind him.

On the way back into the gym, he steps into the toilet and shower. When he turns on the tap in the basin, it responds with a spurt of water the colour of milky tea. He leaves the tap running and goes out to the gym where he pulls his notebook and pencil from the side of his bag and, walking around the outside of the ring, begins taking notes.

When he steps back into the bathroom, a good healthy flow of silvery water greets him. He washes the dust from his hands, shakes them dry and wipes them down the side of both legs. Then he goes back out to the gym, picks up his bag and takes another look around.

He inhales the dusty air, notes the rat shit in the corner. He feels a warmth spreading through his chest. Home, he thinks, or a sense of home anyway.

When he turns back down Cowcross Street, he finds it almost deserted. A few Sunday evening strays like himself, headed for the station, past closed cafés and empty offices. The warmth of an Indian summer still on the air and the evening light only now beginning to fade. He takes his coat off and stuffs it into his bag.

Sunday is definitely the best day to go at it, he thinks; no office workers about and the building sites all empty. He could chance a few evenings, too, while the September light still holds good.

He glances across the road to the pub. The downstairs windows have been boarded up, the door to the pub, the door at the side, all planked in. He turns his eyes away from it, then swinging his bag around the corner, crosses the plaza and slips in through the mouth of the station.

On the platform he sits on a bench, his bag at his feet, and considers the task ahead of him, all that needs to be done in order to make the place habitable. After he gives it a good cleaning, takes down the rats, makes sure the jacks and shower are in full working order, he will need to start buying essentials. He pulls the notebook out of his back pocket and looks over his notes. Something to cook on; something to lie on; something to see by. A good camping shop should take care of all that; maybe a trip or two to Argos. There are a few bits and pieces in Dom's shed that could come in useful. The cold will be an issue – September is almost over and Indian summers don't last forever. A decent portable gas heater should see him right. He wonders when he should break the news to Dom. On the one hand, it seems unfair not to tell him as soon as possible. On the other hand, it might be best to wait till he has the place in some sort of order, in case things get a bit awkward.

He's about to step onto the tube when he hears the jittery sound of a phone. It could be his new phone, the phone Dom passed down to him a few days ago after he'd upgraded his own. He sits down, pokes around in the bag until he locates the phone in the pocket of his coat. A missed call from Lorraine. And he feels himself fill up with both joy and dread at the sight of her name, as he always does when she calls him or whenever he is due to meet her face to face. He hates missing a call from her, in case she thinks he couldn't be bothered to pick it up. He tries to call back, but the signal is gone now and there's nothing to do but

wait till he gets out at the other end. He expects her to cancel –
he always expects her to cancel, although this hasn't happened
yet. They've had coffee several times, dinner twice – tonight will
be the third occasion. Same place and same time, Sunday night,
Côte on Westbourne Grove – a stroll between Dom's house and
the flat she's moved into beside the Porchester Spa. The place is
quiet, the menu affordable and the food goes easy on his stomach.
For much of the time, he can't look her in the face in case he
starts crying. But when he hears her voice, the things she says,
he knows that she is without spite or guile. He likes that she
spends Sunday afternoons with her grandparents. He likes that
she's a primary school teacher in Kilburn. He can't help but be
pleased that she looks like him and nothing like her mother. He
loves the Scottish burr on her accent. The way she just comes out
and says things: 'Is it much of a struggle staying off the booze,
then?'

'Yes, to be honest.'

'And do you go to those meetings like you see on the telly?'

'Sometimes, but I find them – well, they drive me mad to be
honest.'

'You say that a lot, don't you?'

'What, that things drive me mad?'

'No! "To be honest" – you say that a lot.'

'I suppose I do. Maybe it's because I want to be honest with
you.'

'Because you've told so many lies?'

'Yes.'

'And you still feel bad about that?'

'I do.'

'I do? Is that it? It's a job of work getting you to open up – as
my grandad would say.'

'I know.'

'But you feel bad anyway about my childhood and all that.'

'Sometimes when I think about it, I can't breathe.'

'Aww, don't say that, I'm just kidding you.'

'You're entitled to be angry.'

'Well, I'm not. When I was younger maybe. So long as you don't disappear on me again. Promise you won't?'

'We're not supposed to make promises, according to AA. But to hell with them: I promise.'

'Thanks, Dad.'

Thanks, Dad. If he could put those two little words in the inside pocket of his jacket.

He finds her easy to talk to, although it's early days yet, as Kim keeps reminding him with a gleeful glint in her eye.

He would love to tell Lorraine about his little venture. But when he looks for the words in his head, it just sounds as if he's completely lost it. 'See, there's this derelict building – actually it used to be the boxing club where I trained when I first moved back to London. An old boxer I know happened to mention it to me and I thought why not? I mean, I'll be dead before they do anything with it anyway. Oh, but it's great Lorraine, it is – you'll have to come round for tea some day. It's got a boxing ring in the middle and rats around the edges . . .'

The tube rattles on. Sunday evening, he looks into the gloom of near-empty carriages. Down through the train, a rocking tunnel of glass and steel as far as the eye can see, a few people at intervals, mostly alone. In his carriage, a young oriental man nods in and out of sleep. And a girl with big legs and a disappointed face tugs at the hem of a very short skirt. Further down the way, an older woman holds on to the handle of a weekend case, pushing it forward and back as if she's rocking a pram. An elderly man sitting right opposite him fidgets his hand inside his trouser pocket. At first, he thinks he's up to something; then he thinks he's trying to disguise a palsied hand, but a tiny glint catches his eye and he notices, now, the silent mumbling at his lips. The poor old bastard is only saying the rosary. He looks over the old man's head and begins reading the names of the stations on the Circle line, thinking about them as he used to do, when he was a young man, travelling from Dom's place off Praed Street to Shamie's boxing club, and back again. Five, maybe six days a week. Names that fired the imagination: Moorgate, Shepherd's Bush, Tower Hill. He finds his own stop on the line and counts the stations to go before they get there. Even though he knows the route like the back of his hand.

He turns to the centre page of the notebook and looks down at his scribbled plans. The ring will be the marker. The left side will do as a kitchen shelf. Everything else will be on the floor with the sides of the ring serving as a wall. The rear side, a wall to his bedroom – he can lay a camp bed out on the floor beneath it. The right side, not visible from the window, can be his living room, an armchair, a small table, one of those non-electric lamps. The front part of the ring he will leave as it is, just in case someone happens to come by and leans down to look in the window. He will have to keep it spartan enough – a house of empty spaces. Just like the house in Slough, he thinks now, closing first the notebook, then his eyes.

His father met him at Slough station, his first summer holidays – his first return to England since he had started school the previous January. Ten years, four months old, he was then. Ten and a third, he used to say. His father, thinner and dull-eyed since he'd seen him last.

'Let's get you home then,' he said, taking his suitcase as they began the twenty-minute walk. So no car now, he had thought.

Nor was it home. They no longer lived in Bayswater. They lived on the end of a long silent road of houses that stood two by two, glaring at one another across the street. His mother gone; Dom still away at school for another few weeks. 'No wonder the Irish are lazy bastards,' Dom would say, half joking, when he finally arrived in Slough. 'Three whole months off for summer.'

They were alone until then, just him and his father.

A bare house – a house of bare necessity. Lino on the stairs. Small toilet straight ahead, small room beside it with a bath and basin squeezed into it. Three bedrooms, one of them tiny.

There were nails hammered into the woodchip wallpaper in the hall and going up the stairs – shadows around them; shapes of pictures and other things that had obviously once been hanging there. The house so clean and bare that he'd been afraid to unpack his case. His father showed him his room; he called it a box room. He said they would have to allow Dom the bigger room because he needed the extra space for his music stand and trumpet, as well as all the other paraphernalia. Paraphenali-ar, he said. He had forgotten that about his father – the extra r.

Alone in the box room, he had looked out of the window down into the garden. The other gardens around had washing hanging on lines. There were toys and bicycles thrown about the place. The garden next door had vegetables growing; the one backing on to theirs had swings and an apple tree. His father's garden was a long narrow rectangle of concrete paving stones with a concrete shed stuck in the far corner. No grass, no flowers, no bird house, no trees, no garage.

He knew then that whoever owned this house, it wasn't his father.

He had not been all that surprised when, a few days later, he wandered into the shed and found stacked in a cupboard a load of old pictures and other regalia – the sort of regalia he had grown used to after two terms in a Catholic boarding school. Jesus with his heart on fire; Padre Pio served up on a blue plate. A couple of popes; a saint or two; a brass font for holy water and a folded cloth bearing the words 'Ad Majorem Dei Gloriam'.

After his father died, he had been tortured with nightmares. Even when he was awake, they came at him. He was a grown man, two years off forty, but had felt like a frightened child. Lying in that shitty B & B on the Gloucester Road watching the shadows close in on him. He could feel something tailing him as he walked the streets. Even while carrying on with Dora Oak, it pursued him. Sitting beside her in the booth of a late-night café or in the corner of a low-lit bar, in the passenger seat of her car watching the road come at him, he could feel it.

The nightmare was splintered. Images coming and going. Voices. His ten-year-old voice snivelling. A wrist – his small wrist. His small wrist cuffed by an adult hand. The two hands jerking up and down.

He could hear no human sounds that day on Hampstead Heath, as he scrambled down the side of the hill. Just the frantic birds and his own sharp breath and the swish and bite as he pushed himself through the dense bushes. He was lost and he was crying. He couldn't find the fisherman, or at least when he finally found a pond – if it was the same pond – there was no sign of him.

A man on a bicycle found him stumbling out on the road.

'Now calm down, sonny. Take a deep breath, start at the top.'

The bar of the bike sticking into his bony arse. He felt dizzy with the movement of it, the man breathing behind him, the smell of pipe tobacco and onions and soap.

For years he had thought it was the man who had done it, or maybe even Mr Moyse. Big hand clasped over his wrist, moving it up and down, 'That's it, that's it.'

But then at his father's deathbed, it came back to him.

His father's voice. His father's hand. The smell of whiskey.

'Harder, Phil, squeeze harder, yes, yes. That's it, that's good. Oh sweet Jesus forgive me, oh sweet Mary mother of God.'

PART SIX

15. Milly

2008

THE WOMAN WHO cleaned the building told her about Vera. Otherwise, she might never have found out.

'I'm late this morning,' she announced as Milly stepped out of the lift onto a wide band of wet floor. 'On account of a funeral. An old neighbour of mine, poor love – knocked down, she was, on Farringdon Road.'

'I'm sorry to hear that,' Milly said as she began to pick her way across to the front door.

'Coming back from a night class, she was. Can you imagine? Trying to improve yourself and look what you get.'

'Dreadful,' she'd said, hardly listening, with all her own troubles clogging up her head.

'I didn't know her all that well to be honest because we moved away, but her dad was my chemist when I used to live round there. Better than any doctor if you ask me. Saved my life once he did, according to my mum. Poor old Mr Greene . . .'

She nearly slipped on the floor she turned round so quickly. 'You don't mean Vera?'

'That's it, Vera Greene. Did you know her? You did, didn't you?

I can tell by your face. Oh, I am ever so sorry if I give you a shock.'

'I hadn't seen her in a long time. But yes, I knew her.'

She sent a sympathy card to Trish to say how sorry she was to hear about Vera. It was the first contact she'd made in over eight years after she'd left the pub with her two fingers raised and the door slammed firmly behind her.

She wondered if Trish might get in touch when the card arrived. She wasn't sure if that was something she even wanted, but in any case, she had put the address on the back of the envelope and the phone number on the end of the card. As far as she was concerned, she'd left the door open – it was up to Trish if she wanted to walk through. A week went by without a word and she began to feel snubbed. For another week or so, she had moments of disappointment, sadness and even resentment. After that, she just put it out of her head.

Matthew had still been around then, slithering about the place, trying to avoid investors, clients, employees, debtors and looking her straight in the face. In between, his old, reassuring self would pop up to the surface now and then.

'It'll all blow over, sweetheart, you wait and see. I may need to go away for a couple of weeks, raise a bit of cash so we can finish the smaller jobs. It is what it is – what can I say?'

The day before he left, he brought her breakfast in bed and told her he'd left a few quid in the safe in case she needed it.

'I have plenty in my account, Matthew, I won't run short.'

'Good, that's good,' he said. 'I'll be back in six weeks, tops.'

'Six weeks? I thought you said a couple of weeks?'

'Ah come on, love, don't look so worried. Everyone in this game is in the same boat. There's *absolutely* no cause for concern. Not the least little bit.'

'Are we in trouble, Matthew?'

He put his hands on her shoulders, looked straight into her eyes and said, 'You have to trust me, sweetheart, that's all I ask.'

But she'd seen it on his face a few nights before, as they'd watched the evening news, the revolving doors of that big glass bank on Canary Wharf, like razor blades whipping people out onto the street, cardboard boxes up in their arms.

And she'd been hearing it ever since, too, in his late-night phone calls. And even during the day now that he was at home most of the time.

'I spent millions just getting this project to planning, a fortune buying that Irish cunt out. And as for that other cow with her pub rotting under her arse. Yes, yes Jake, yeah, yeah I *know* you told me to up the offer, you don't have to keep banging on about it. She was hanging on by the fingernails, for Christ's sake! I mean she only had a few years left on the lease. If you must know, I'd been thinking of lowering the price. And if this fuck-up hadn't . . .'

And then, at three in the morning, out on the balcony when he thought she was sound asleep:

'Look, Dave, everything – and I mean *everything* – has either been mothballed or scrapped. You have to help me out here. I'm fucked, Dave, do you understand me, mate? *Absolutely fucked.*'

For the first week or so after Matthew left, there had been endless phone calls, mostly from people who worked for him. Some of them she knew socially, others were from the office. They called her from bedsits and riverside apartments all over the city; from daytime pubs and the corners of cafés. They called walking along the streets and sitting on park benches. And then they called her from the childhood homes they'd been forced to return to because they couldn't pay their rent. The only places she didn't get a call from were the offices of M. Conad Construction and its various silent building sites humped around London.

Matthew had told her what to say. To anyone from work – 'He's on it, sorting everything out. He'll be in touch soon.'

To anyone else – 'I'm sorry, he no longer lives here.'

'But why would anyone get in touch?' she'd asked. 'If they don't know me, how would they even have my personal number?'

'They'll get it.'

'But how?'

'Times like these? People always find a way.'

He'd also told her that the architects would give her no trouble but to expect a bit of abuse from foremen and suppliers. In fact, it had been the opposite. One architect had threatened to burn her out if she didn't tell him where Matthew was.

'I don't know,' she said, crying from the shock. 'I told you I don't *know.*'

'Swanning around in his Jag, I shouldn't wonder, while I have to go home to my wife and tell her we have no fucking money to pay the school fees. You people. You bloodsucking bastards, always take care of yourselves first, don't you? Well, you better watch your back, let me tell you. You better *watch* it.'

There were so many calls for the first two weeks that, even in her sleep, she found herself reaching for her phone only to discover that the ringing had been in her head. Not that she managed to sleep much. Usually, she just lay in the dark, mourning the empty space beside her and ignoring the doubts swimming around like vicious little fish in the dark. When this happened, she recalled Matthew's words: 'You have to trust me, sweetheart, that's all I ask.'

The sincerity in his eyes when he'd said that.

Gradually, the phone calls tapered off and an awkward sort of peace came into the flat. For a few empty days, there was a lot of lying around on the sofa or getting up only long enough to make her breakfast and bring it back to bed where she stayed, reading and snoozing until night fell again.

She ate no set meals, but made do with whatever she found in the local shop or what was already in the fridge and cupboards. One day she ate nothing but cornflakes and a bumper bag of chocolate buttons that Matthew kept in his study for the nights he worked late. On another evening she got drunk on an expensive bottle of Scotch he had bought for a client and ended up spending half the night lying on the floor of the bathroom, howling vomit into the toilet. She got up at odd hours and went to bed at odd hours; she watched what Matthew called 'mindless crap' on the telly. Sometimes she left the television off altogether and just lay there, staring at the ceiling.

She began taking up more and more of the bed, until one morning she woke to find herself sprawled diagonally across it, hands over her head. Matthew had been gone for almost four weeks and she had just slept for ten hours solid. It was time to get up again, dust herself off and climb back into her life.

From the sitting-room window, she studied the cut of the river within her line of sight. To one side lay dowdy Battersea Bridge; on the other, the piers of Albert Bridge like four giant insects through the early-morning haze. Behind them, the empty pillars of the dead power station. It was seven o'clock on a Sunday morning, hardly any traffic passing below. A young couple who looked as if they'd been up all night sat on a bench across the road facing the river wall, talking, smoking, kissing. In love with every inch of each other. The leaves on the plane trees, she noticed, were beginning to yellow.

Below her window lay the sunken garden which she looked down on every day but seldom entered. She had been living here for more than eight years and yet she knew so little about the area, apart from what she had seen from the windows of this flat or from the passenger seat of Matthew's car. Matthew had never been one for walks; he considered them to be a waste of time, wandering around for the sake of it without any set destination or purpose in mind. Even if a twenty-minute walk could save them from an hour stuck in traffic, he'd choose the traffic every time, touching her leg or shoulder now and then, or giving her a little wink while he talked business on his phone.

She began to take walks in the afternoon. She walked eastwards along Chelsea Embankment, keeping to the wall, the shade of the trees above her, the water below. She loved seeing the old brick buildings on this side of the river, the new glass blocks on the other: the past and the future, the river moving between them.

On her walks, random thoughts crossed her mind about Matthew.

The way he always wanted her nearby him, leaving her to wait in the car while he went to a meeting, or to wander around the shops with instructions to buy something nice for herself. Then insisting on a proper restaurant for lunch, even if they never seemed to have time to finish it. She remembered how, when watching television, his arm sometimes felt like a tightening brace around her neck. And it seemed strange to her now, as she walked along without sound or sight of him for over a month, that rather than tell him he was hurting her, she had said nothing.

One day as she walked across Albert Bridge, a feeling of lightness came over her, as if she was walking on water. It gave her a wild sense of freedom, the sort she had sometimes known as a child, running down a hill or through an open field with the high grass flicking against her bare legs. She stopped short, a cold feeling coming into her stomach. Matthew will be back soon, she thought, and this will all end.

The next afternoon, she decided to take a different route and, straying from the river, had ended up in Brompton Cemetery. It was autumn now, early October, but the weather was holding up, and the air that had felt heavy and humid out on the streets had cooled as soon as she entered the cemetery, as if to soothe the dead.

Her mother came into her mind then and stayed with her as she walked under the lime trees up a long avenue to a honey-coloured chapel. On the way back, the shadows lengthened and silhouettes of statues from headstones and monuments were thrown on the ground before her feet. As she walked across them, she began to think of her grandparents who would surely be gone by now, buried in a graveyard far from their own home. Unless the Protestant graveyard in the village had reopened for business, which seemed highly unlikely. Was her mother, their daughter, still buried in the locked-up graveyard? Or had they made arrangements to have her remains brought to rest with them, wherever they had ended up? She doubted that too, what with the expense involved, and after all the shame she had caused them. They were mean and unforgiving people and would have left her to rot alone, for eternity.

She had never regretted leaving her grandparents, nor had she ever had any desire to get in touch again. But still, it must have been hard on them, to lose a daughter that way, killed by her own hand, at twenty-one years of age.

She had no recollection of that time, nor did she remember anyone ever speaking to her about it in the years that followed. But her grandfather had let it slip when he was drunk and someone in school had confirmed it: her mother had stepped under the Dublin to Belfast train. Such a violent end. Surely she could have found a gentler way to finish her life.

When she got back to Chelsea Embankment, she sat on the bench where the young couple had sat the week before. She watched the cobbled light on the water and made herself think of Matthew. How kind he'd been to her when she'd told him about Flora. And later, the way he had paid someone to trace her when the adoption agency proved to be a dead end. Then, coming home early from work one day to break the news to her, sitting her down, putting his arm around her. 'I'm sorry, darling, I really am. She's in Australia, but doesn't want to know, it seems. Give her time, though, she could think differently in a year or two – maybe when she has a child of her own. We'll have another bash at it in a couple of years.'

He had assured her that Flora was doing well, a university student, surrounded by friends and a loving family.

Part of her had been relieved that Flora wanted nothing to do with her. If they had made contact there would have been questions about her father – who he was and how they had met. And what then? She couldn't lie to her own daughter – she had already lied to Matthew on that account, telling him that it was a lovely holiday romance with a student who helped out on the farm. She had wanted him to think someone else had loved her, even for a short while. The only one she told the truth to had been Pip. Flora's father was no tender, shy, clever boy. He was a middle-aged brute who groomed her from the time she was a child and then as soon as she turned sixteen got stuck into her, abusing her for months on end. Raping her – because really there was no other way to put it – in the cellar of his shitty little pub. How could she risk Flora finding out something like that?

They had been trying for a baby of their own at the time; they had kept on trying, but it just never happened.

'We could always adopt?' Matthew said to her after yet another year of disappointment. She'd nodded as though she agreed with him. But she knew in her heart that he was too old to legally adopt.

And even though she knew she had done the best for Flora by giving her up, she still couldn't see herself going down that route, doing to another woman what had been done to her – taking a baby still warm from its mother's arms and walking out the door with it, as if money and a big car had given her some sort of entitlement.

'You're my baby,' Matthew had said, after they'd had sex, the same night he had mentioned adoption. 'You're my baby, and I'm yours. You're my mum and I'm your dad. You're my sister and I'm your brother. We are one another's best friends. We have all we need in one another, Milly.'

His words had sounded peculiar to her, distasteful even, as if they were crawling out of his mouth.

Now that she thought of it, four years later as she stood up from a bench on Chelsea Embankment and waited in the dark to cross the road home, it had been one of the rare occasions when Matthew had actually called her by her proper name.

Matthew had been gone almost six weeks by now; he would be home any day soon. She'd cleaned the flat the way he liked it, and gone to Partridge's to stock up on some of his favourite treats: honey and lavender biscuits, and that pâté stuff that he couldn't get enough of, but to her smelled and looked like dog shit packed into a jar.

She had been thinking of how to spend her last few days.

Earlier that afternoon, she'd come across an English reading list on a college website and had passed a bit of time going through it, delighted with herself whenever she came across a title that she'd read or had on her shelves. Tomorrow, she decided, she would go to Piccadilly and buy herself a few of the books from the list. When she brought them home, she would fit them in alongside the fancy folio editions of classics that Matthew had bought for her birthday a few years earlier. Then she would set about reading them. The fact that she hadn't gone to college was irrelevant; it would be nice to own the books anyhow, to know she had read, or was soon to read, the same books as the sort of people who went to university.

It would be an optimistic thing to do – Matthew was always giving out to her for her pessimistic ways. She was looking forward to the shops anyhow – finding the books, paying for them at the till, maybe having a little chat with the salesperson about her choices, which was something that often happened in bookshops. It was weeks, she now realised, since she'd spoken to anyone face to face or even over the phone – the phones had long since stopped ringing – which was probably why she nearly jumped out of her skin when the house phone broke into sound beside her.

It was Gemma on the phone.

In her head, she still labelled Gemma as 'Matthew's wife', and often had to remind herself to stick the 'ex-' onto the front of the title. Gemma was practical, efficient and not in the least unkind. Her children – hers and Matthew's – were nice kids, not at all spoiled, although Gemma once told her that she had to fight to unspoil them after they'd been with Matthew for any length of time.

'Well, you know what he's like,' she'd said – a comment which for some reason had thrown Milly and had her asking herself all week, what is he like? What *is* Matthew like?

Gemma was also director of an advertising agency and knew how to come straight to the point.

'Look, Milly,' she began, 'I know it's not really my business but I felt we should have a chat about Matthew.'

'I don't know where he is,' she began.

'Yes, I know you don't.'

'But you do?'

'Only because he stung me for twenty grand.'

'He did *what*?'

'Never mind all that. It's gone now. And gone forever, I should imagine. That's not why I'm calling you. It's about the flat.'

'What about it?'

'You do realise that the flat's on a lease, don't you?'

'Yes, I mean, I don't know . . . I thought we . . . I thought he . . . A long lease, though, surely?'

'You thought you owned it?'

'I suppose.'

'It's on a lease, renewable every five years. It's up at the end of next month, I'm afraid.'

'How do you know that?'

'He told me. What I'm trying to say, Milly, is you need to find somewhere else to live.'

'Well, if you don't mind, I think I'll just wait for Matthew to come back.'

'Have you heard from him?'

'No, not yet, but I'm expecting him any day . . .'

'Right. You need to start looking now. Look, Milly, I'm not saying Matt doesn't love you. He does, I'm sure of it. It's just . . . Well, he needs to be successful. To be *seen* as being successful. That's the most important thing in his life. He'd rather stay away than lose face.'

'Are you saying he's left me, Gemma? Is that what you're saying? My God, you think you can just phone me out of the blue and, and, expect me to *believe* you . . . I'm his wife.'

'And I was once his wife too. You've only been married a few years; I've known him since we were teens. He's a child, he behaves like one and he hides like one when he's in trouble. I'm not speaking to you like this out of spite or because I want to cause trouble. You must know that. I'm trying to help you. You were always very kind to the children and—'

'He wouldn't leave me like this. He wouldn't leave his children. He adores those kids.'

'I know he does. That's the saddest part, isn't it? Look, take it or leave it, but this is my advice: find yourself somewhere to live and get out of there before the debtors start calling round. Oh, and anything you take out of that flat – paintings, ornaments, whatever – make sure you own them. Find the lease for the flat, and the car—'

'The car is on lease?'

'Milly, love, it's all on lease. The only thing he owns is a shitload of debts. You need to see who the car is leased from, call them and sort it out. Then phone the estate agents – but that can wait a couple of weeks, I suppose, give you time to find somewhere else; you'll just have to hope that the rent's up to date.'

She could hardly speak now, she was crying so much. 'I can't. I just . . .'

'Milly, that's not going to help. You need to look after yourself, do you hear me? All right, Christ, all right, all right, I'll do it then. Find the leases and anything else that looks as if it could come back to bite you and let me know. Did he leave you any money?'

'I have about a thousand in my account and he left five hundred in the safe.'

'Well, that's not much good to you, is it? Look, I can let you have a couple of grand – it's not much but it's something. This recession, it's affecting everyone and it's really beginning to boulder in on us here.'

'Where is he, Gemma? Tell me. I promise I won't try to follow him.'

'Hardly!' Gemma laughed. 'He's in Dubai.'

At the beginning of November, she decided to sell her clothes.

Matthew had never left her short of money; she could have bought – and sometimes did buy – her own clothes. And yet, when she walked into the dressing room – the room that had once been earmarked as a nursery – and pushed open the door of her wall-wide wardrobe, nearly everything she could see had been bought for her by Matthew. That camel coat a few winters ago, hardly worn. The soft black leather jacket the first year they started going out together. The Burberry mac. How she hated that mac – it made her feel swamped, boxy and clumsy. She could remember saying so, or attempting to say so anyway, in that shop in Bond Street: I don't like it on me, Matthew, I'm too pale for it and not nearly tall enough.

But he had cut across her: 'Darling, don't fuss now, it's lovely.'

The six-foot-tall Russian beauty serving them had of course agreed with Matthew, closing her eyes for a second and raising her thumb and middle finger in the shape of an O as if she'd never seen anything so exquisite in her whole born life as this oat-coloured mac on this oat-coloured, five-foot-four Irish woman.

'Is perfect for you,' the assistant cooed.

'See?' Matthew said, winking at her and reaching for his wallet. 'Is perfect.'

'Well, she would say that, wouldn't she?' Milly said now, her words in the silent room sounding bitter and strange. She pulled the mac out of the wardrobe, carried it through to the sitting room and flung it on the sofa with the rest of the pile. She hadn't thrown most of her old clothes out, or given them away – they were in the spare room, hanging in a wardrobe. Bit by bit, she had simply stopped wearing them. Not because Matthew had criticised or in any way sneered at those clothes, but because he never admired her in anything unless he had picked it and paid for it himself. It had taken her a while to notice that. It had taken her a while to notice a lot of things about Matthew.

On the edge of the sofa, she sat looking at the clothes for a while. An orgy of unworn or rarely worn designer clothes; handbags that were too heavy to carry, shoes too high to wear. A gold pair of strappy sandals that didn't look like shoes at all, but weird skimpy lingerie designed for feet.

After a while, she stood up and began arranging the coats along the back of the sofa; one overlapping the other with the labels sticking out. Then she laid the dresses out on the floor. She made a row of handbags and a row of shoes. She picked up her phone and began to take photos. She selected the best ones and then pressed send.

A few minutes later the phone rang.

'Hi, Milly? Hi, yeah so thanks for sending on those pics. They give us a much better idea of what we're talking about here. We'd love to take a look. Why don't you bung the lot together and come and see us at the shop?'

'Yes, I can do that.'

'Let me just check the book for an appointment. Back to you in a tick.'

She was still on hold when the intercom rang. Since Matthew left, she'd been ignoring the intercom, mainly because he had instructed her to do so.

'They can't serve a summons on you if they can't see you, now can they, sweetheart?'

She could hear a long buzz going through the building a second, then a third time, as if the caller was intent on trying every bell in the house until someone let them in.

The girl in the vintage shop was back on the phone talking to her again. 'This afternoon suit?' she asked. 'Say around four? It's quiet then, we can give it some time. That work for you?'

'Yeah, that's fine. Thanks. Four o'clock. Thanks.'

'Lovely. Looking forward to seeing your pieces.'

'My what?'

The bell on the door of the flat was buzzing at her now.

Then a rap of a coin and a voice on the other side. 'You in there, Milly? Milly? You in there, love?'

'Look, I better go,' she said, 'there's someone at the door.'

It had always been the way whenever she saw Trish outside of the pub; even in the old days when she bumped into her out on the street, she would have to think – is that Trish? She always seemed slighter somehow, in more ways than one, as if the pub was giving her substance. Eight years on and she more or less looked the same, though her hair was a bit blacker, her makeup a bit heavier, and her teeth a little too white.

'Well, you leaving me to stand like a politician on the doorstep or what?' Trish asked.

Milly opened the door full width. 'Come in, come in. It's just that it's . . .'

'A long time, that's what it's been, little Milly. How've you been, girl?'

'Okay, thanks.'

'Yeah?' Trish said, looking her over. 'You're a bit scrawny-looking, if you don't mind me saying so.'

'I was about to say the same thing to you.'

'We should have been supermodels!' Trish said and they both laughed.

Trish looked through the open door to the sitting room. 'You having a clear-out, or have you just gone really, *really* untidy?'

'A clear-out. I was really sorry to hear about Vera.'

Trish nodded, reached out and touched her arm. 'I can't talk about it, Mill, I just can't.'

Then she looked away and walked to the end of the hall, peeping through the gap of the door into Matthew's study. She swung around then, smiling. 'It's pretty swish though – eh? Like something out of a magazine, is what it is. Mind if I have a gander?'

'Help yourself.'

Trish came back up the hall, walked into the sitting room and straight over to the windows. 'Oh, but you got some view here, Milly, my goodness. Look at that, the river right below you. You could go fishing from here with the right rod.'

She walked to the far end of the window and pointed at the balcony. 'Wouldn't I love this? Sitting out here on a summer's morning, having my breakfast.'

'Except you don't eat breakfast.'

'True. Having my morning fag then.'

She followed Trish in and out of the rooms where, every now and then, Trish turned to look at her and pulled a face of approval, or laughed at the wonder of it all.

'I tell you what, Milly, you're well set up here.'

'You think so?'

'I'm almost afraid to ask if I can smoke.'

'You can smoke, Trish, of course you can.'

'I can stand out on the balcony if you prefer?'

'Not at all. Come on, we'll go into the kitchen and I'll make us a cup of coffee.'

Trish followed her into the kitchen. 'I love your dinky kitchen – very Gary Rhodes, it is, and all your lovely stuff. It's ever so efficient-looking, the way it's laid out. You do all this?'

'No. No, it was like that when I moved in. Look in the press there, you can use a saucer or bowl or whatever.'

'I wouldn't like to spoil anything; it all seems a bit top of the range.'

'Don't be silly. Take one of the saucers, they're never used anyway.'

And then the kitchen filled up with the old familiar scent of Trish's purple Silk Cut and Milly felt as if a wall had come down. She laid the cups out, then took down Matthew's lavender and honey biscuits even if she knew already that Trish wouldn't like them.

'What you do all day?' Trish asked, pulling a chair out and sitting down. 'Put your feet up and wait for hubby to come home? Don't you work, Milly?'

'I do. I did, I should say, in one of his offices.'

'Doing what?'

'Ordering supplies, answering the phone, just the usual office stuff.'

'Oh, you must have enjoyed that.'

'Sometimes. I mean, I don't know, I often felt . . . resented, I suppose. Or stupid.'

'Not stupid, Milly, you were never stupid. The way you picked up the job and you without a clue when you started. Best barmaid I've ever worked with, smartest too.'

'I don't know about that,' she muttered, filling up the coffee pot and putting it on the hob.

Trish continued to puff on her fag, eye roaming around the kitchen.

'Imagine you owning this place, Milly – the way things turn out, we never know, do we?'

'I don't own it.'

'You're married – what's his is yours,' Trish said, pointing the cigarette at her.

'He doesn't own it either. I thought he did – I thought we both did, but then again . . . I thought a lot of things. I thought he was an honest man.'

Trish put down her cigarette and looked at her. 'What's happened?'

'He's done a runner.'

'He's what?'

'He's been gone about twelve weeks now. Twice as long as he said he'd be.'

'With someone else?'

'No. I don't think so. It's the recession. Everything went belly-up and, I don't know, he's gotten himself into some sort of trouble.'

'Oh, he'll be back, Milly, don't worry.'

'No, he's not coming back. His ex-wife told me.'

'Ex-wife? You don't want to pay no attention to her – probably just sour grapes.'

'She's not like that. He was in touch with her to borrow money. Apparently, he could go to jail if he comes back. He's in Dubai.'

'He's *where*?'

'He owes money left, right and . . . and the lease in this place runs out in a few weeks.'

'Yeah, but Du-fucking-Bai – I mean, come on! He can't be slumming it out there.'

'I don't know what I'm going to do, Trish.'

'Oh, Milly. Oh, I am sorry, my poor Milly.'

She began to cry.

Trish put out her cigarette and stood up. 'Oh, don't cry, it'll be all right. Don't go tearing your heart over him. Poor little Milly.'

'That's not why I'm crying,' she said. 'I don't seem to care about him any more. I mean the humiliation of it, the anger, there's that. But I don't want him to come back now. I'm crying because . . .'

'Because what?'

'My name.'

'Your name?'

'Hearing you say my name. I was so used to hearing it in the pub, you know how it is, everyone calling out to you, wanting a drink or a chat. And I only realised it lately, when I got to thinking about Matthew, that he hardly ever called me by my name. It was like I wasn't here. I mean, I was, but it wasn't *me*. Or it didn't feel like me – it was like I'd lost my identity or something. Sorry, Trish. You must think I'm a right eejit.' She pulled a lump of kitchen paper off the roll, wiped her eyes and blew her nose. Then she took the pot off the hob and began to pour the coffee. Trish was lighting another smoke. 'Could I have one of those?'

'Course you can.'

She took the cigarette from Trish's hand and played with it for a bit before lighting it. 'I met this woman on a plane once, an old woman, I've been thinking about her a lot. She told me all men try to control you, even the nicest ones.'

'Well, she's got a point there.'

'And Matthew was – is – a nice man.'

'Oh yeah? Leaves his wife, drops her right in it, that's nice all right.'

'He missed his kids so much when he split up from his wife. They're great kids, Trish, they really are. Do you know, I sometimes think, well I think that I was some sort of a substitute child. He was always trying to improve me: choosing my clothes, my food, my friends . . .'

'And where are they now, Milly, all your new friends?'

'Well may you ask.'

'You never had any kiddies then?'

'We tried, but it didn't happen.'

'Oh, Milly.' Trish nodded sadly, then picked up a biscuit.

They sat quietly for a moment, then Trish patted her on the back. 'The girl with no name. We didn't half miss you, Milly.'

'What – even Mrs Oak? I don't think so.'

'Oh yes. Mrs Oak more than anyone. Oh, don't start crying again! Aww. Well, cry if you must. Let it all out.'

Trish took a bite of the biscuit. 'Bloody hell, what are these made of – soap?' she said and dropped it back onto the plate.

Afterwards, they stood in the sitting room looking down at the clothes. 'You got some nice clobber here, Mill,' Trish said. 'It should fetch a few quid.'

'That's what I'm hoping. I have to find a new flat. Get myself a job.'

'Why don't you come home?'

'What do you mean?'

'Come back to Mrs O. I've left, you know, moved in with Fred.'

'Fred? You finally put him out of his misery.'

'Yeah, bless him. I don't think we'll bother getting married or anything. We're living over his old shop. Remember that place, the stink out of it? Anyway, it's a café now, he rents it out to a couple of Lebanese boys. We're all right, me and Fred. We're comfortable. She didn't take it too well, me leaving. But business was so bad, some weeks I got no wages. Anyway, I go and see her every day on my way home from work, bring her a bit of dinner and that.'

'Where are you working?'

'I've got a part-time job in the Moorfield clinic – you know, off Old Street. The eye hospital. Making tea and toast for patients after they've had their eyes done. It suits me. No night-work. Not much standing about. My good legs, they're destroyed now from years of bar work.'

'How is she, Trish?'

'She's not great, to be honest. I told her to sell up when she had the chance. I said, you could be living in the lap of luxury instead of sitting here in the freezing cold, hoping for a few customers to wander in. She had it in her head that she'd get more if it was a viable business – well you know what she's like, no talking to her really. And now look! But Milly – the price of rent! She'll give you a roof over your head, you'll be there on your own terms. You could do something else. Make a few quid elsewhere. Help out a bit in the bar at night. She only opens Tuesday to Friday now and closes by nine o'clock. Most nights she's done and dusted by seven. I don't know how long she can keep that up, to be honest. Go and see her anyway, what harm will it do? You were a long time with her, Milly. You have to admit, in her own way, she was good to you.'

'I know that, but after the last time? The things I said to her.'

'You had your reasons, she knows that. I don't think she meant to hurt you, though. After all, you reminded us often enough you and him were only friends. I never believed that, but maybe she did. Oh, who knows, eh? But I think she just got lonely, Milly. And he did have something about him, you have to admit. Sorry – it's not my place, and what does it all matter now anyway? But I'll tell you this: I never saw her so upset after you left; made her ill, it did. And she's not in great shape now – banging on for seventy, oh yes. She often speaks about the old days. Wonders how you are and that. Come back with me today, I'll go with you to see her, take the edge off things.'

'I have an appointment this afternoon, I can't.'

'Well, think about it. Think about going to see her anyway. She's not been too well.'

'Okay, but if you think she's going to kick up, you will let me know in advance?'

'I will. But she won't. Well, best be going – Fred's waiting for me down in the car. He drove me here.'

'What? He's been sitting down there in the car all this time? You should have brought him up.'

'He wouldn't dream of it. You know what he's like, odd as a third ball. You know I only found out his mum was Spanish two years ago? He's got two sisters living over there, nieces, nephews, the lot. Oh, I am glad I came to see you, Milly. I wasn't sure at first but I thought, well . . . life is short. Look at poor old Vee. Gone, just like that,' she said, clicking her fingers.

A few days later, she was standing at dusk on Oakley Street, looking at the statue of the dolphin and the flying boy. She had seen this statue many times in passing, from the bus or from Matthew's car. The dolphin solid and strong, its snout poised and determined as it pulled the boy upwards. The boy had always appeared fragile from a distance, utterly dependent on the dolphin to keep him from falling on his face. Standing beside them

388

now, though, it seemed to her that the boy was the one in control. He wasn't clutching the dolphin's fin, but resting his hand on it. He could lift his hand and fly away when, and if, he wanted to. He could abandon the dolphin. The statue was set in front of a showroom of Mercedes cars. The lights from the showroom and the flawless glass flickered around the statue and the paved area outside. The boy had a cruel mouth, she could see now, whereas the dolphin looked like a simpering fool.

Later she would wonder if it was the name of the road or the statue itself that had given her the final push back towards Mrs Oak. But in the end, she decided it was neither. She had stopped and given her mind a few moments' rest from all her worries. There had been the daubs of light from Albert Bridge and the showroom and the cars passing by. There had been the boy and the dolphin. She had been with them underwater for no more than a few seconds. Long enough to clear her mind, and allow Mrs Oak to cross it.

It was dark by now, the traffic hardly moving, the air damp and cold. The worst time to travel across the city. She thought: I'll go back to the flat, get something to eat, put a warmer coat on, head out later. Or I'll go in the morning; that makes much more sense. Or I'll phone Trish and ask her to come with me on her day off. But even as these thoughts came in and out of her head, she was walking away from the flat, up the King's Road towards Chelsea Old Town Hall and the number 19 bus stop.

There were five customers in the pub when she pushed the door open. Two old women sitting under the big window. Two market men, one each end of the counter. And Jerome, somewhere between the two.

Mrs Oak was standing behind the bar, at the end of the room, stuffing a cloth into the mouth of a glass. She lifted her head when the door opened and watched her as she walked in. She knew Mrs Oak recognised her at once, and yet she just stayed put, turning the glass in her hand.

She thought: she's either going to ignore me now, or she's going to give me a load of abuse.

She waited for Mrs Oak to put the glass back on the shelf, fold the cloth and place it beside the sink. The flap in the counter lifted, and Mrs Oak came through, turned and began to walk slowly across the open floor.

She looked thin, Milly thought, and she looked old. Her hair was cut short and was more grey than ash blonde. Her face looked worn. She was coming closer to her now and still Milly couldn't read her expression or guess what sort of a reception she was about to get.

She would be expected to speak first, she supposed. Well, she would not speak first. She would not.

'Hello, Mrs Oak,' she heard herself say. 'I don't know if Trish mentioned . . . ?'

'She mentioned,' Mrs Oak said.

As they stood looking at one another, it all came back to her – the last day, the terrible row they'd had, her own cold voice as she'd delivered her well-rehearsed spiel: 'I'm leaving, Mrs Oak. I'm getting married, to Matthew Conad – you know, the developer, the man who wants to buy you out? Oh, and by the way, I heard all about you and Phil, that little fling you had. A bit young for you, in my opinion, but you're welcome to him now, you're welcome to one another. You only have another few years to wait before he gets out of prison.' After that, all she could remember was Mrs Oak losing her temper, screaming at her, then dragging her by the arm and physically throwing her out the door onto the street.

'Well, I just thought I'd drop in and say hello,' she said. 'How have you been?'

Mrs Oak gave a short, dry laugh. 'How do you think I've been?' she said, glancing around at the empty bar stools, the vacant tables and seats.

For another few seconds there was nothing, and she almost walked back out. But then Mrs Oak's face dissolved and she opened her arms wide.

'Milly, dear Milly,' she said. 'Please say you've come back to me.'

16. Pip

2017

October

HURRICANE OPHELIA IS showing on the television when he breaks the news to Dom. A little sooner than intended, but as it turns out, he doesn't have much choice in the matter.

He arrives back on Sunday evening, after a day spent working on his cave, to find Dom in confrontational stance by the kitchen island. Also on the island he sees the banana box he nabbed from Mr Parekh's shop last week, with the few bits inside that he's been squirrelling away.

At the garden end of the kitchen is the debris of a boozy Sunday lunch: smeared plates and dirty serving dishes, several empty or near-empty bottles of wine. Eight people, he reckons. Two roast chickens – skeletons now, each with a whole lemon stuck up its hooter. Figs and honey, Greek yoghurt. There's a small pumpkin sitting in the middle of the table with bunches of grapes draped around its base. In honour of the season of mellow fruitfulness, he supposes, Kim being fond of a theme. But no sign of Kim now. No sign of anyone but a fuming Dom, doing his best to appear cool, calm, collected and sober.

'Do you have something you'd like to share with me?' is his opener.

'Like what – a bar of chocolate?' he says, turning his eyes to the small television perched awkwardly on a half-moon table at the side. Both television and table, if he's not mistaken, used to be in Airbnb room number two.

'If you could spare me the quips,' Dom says, 'and just answer the question?'

He keeps his attention on the television. Ophelia is dancing wildly over the Azores. He isn't sure if this is happening in the here and now, if it has already happened or if it's a foretelling of what could happen if she decides to head in this direction.

'Well?' Dom asks.

'Well, what?' he mumbles without taking his eyes off the screen.

From the corner of his eye, he sees Dom's hand reach out, pick up a remote control and kill the television. Then his hand returns to the box. 'What I mean is this, for example,' he says, lifting a Disneyland cup out and holding it up. He begins to lift the rest of the items out of the box, holding each one up scowling at it before dropping it back down again. 'This. And this. And – fuck me! What about this?'

The last one is an old-fashioned hooked tin-opener, the top of which has been forged to resemble a monkey's head. He's like a schoolmaster who has just discovered a desk full of mortal sins: cigarettes, dirty pictures, maybe a couple of French letters. Except in Dom's case, it's an old teapot, a saucepan, a few bits of cutlery, two plates – and of course, the tin-opener.

'They were in the back of the shed; I didn't think you'd miss them,' he says.

'That's hardly the point, is it?'

'Actually, that tin-opener isn't yours, I bought it on Portobello Road, so if you're going to confiscate the other stuff, I'd appreciate it if you left that behind.'

He notices the black plastic sack on the floor then: duvet and towels, the bulge of a pillow pressed down over the top.

'In fairness, that stuff there,' he says, pointing to the bag, 'does belong to you, but you told me to dump it after we replaced all the linen for the Airbnb – remember? But of course, if you've changed your mind and prefer to keep it now, you only have to say.'

Dom looks at him for a couple of seconds, then leans his hands on the corner of the counter and glares into the marble. His face is a greyish colour with a red blotch at the centre of each cheek. His breathing sounds a bit choppy. He thinks Dom may have worn himself out, but then he straightens up, ready to go again. This time, he doesn't hold back.

As his temper begins to rise, so the colour scheme on his face alters. The red blotches spread and the pallor lessens, until his face, jowls and neck, the lot, has deepened into a dull purple colour.

Dom is shouting by now, calling him a variety of ungrateful, sneaky bastards and pricks. 'Back to your usual tricks, I see. What was the play then? Sneak out in the middle of the night, toodley-pip and fuck you very much?'

'Toodley-pip? I don't think so . . .'

Dom snarls, making a short move towards him, as if he's thinking about throwing a punch.

'For Christ's sake, Dom, would you calm down?' he says. 'I've found my own place, that's all. I had every intention of telling you.'

'When? When were you going to tell me?'

'When I had a chance, you know, when I got you on your own.'

Dom says nothing for a moment, then he goes to the sink and pours himself a glass of water. He takes a few gulps, then holds on to the edge of the sink. After a moment, he reaches into the

394

overhead cupboard and takes out a box of bicarbonate of soda. He edges a good lump of it into the glass, plucks a teaspoon out of the cutlery drawer, then stirs the mixture. He lashes it back, clenches his teeth and shudders.

He turns around, an expression on his face as if something is just beginning to occur to him. 'Is this because of that story I told at dinner last week?' he asks.

'What story?'

'When Max was home, that story I told at dinner.'

'Max wasn't here last week.'

'The dinner the night before he went up for noughth week.'

'North week? I don't know what you're talking about, Dom.'

'To uni. Before he went up to Oxford.'

'That was three weeks ago. And I don't remember any story you told. Or any in particular. There's usually quite a few.'

'It is, isn't it?' Dom raises his arms and shakes his head in disbelief. 'You were always a touchy bastard, you. Taking offence at the slightest . . . you were always.'

'What story?'

'About that filthy old man you brought to Monique's party.'

'What? Why should that make me want to move out? Cop on, Dom, would you? It was just a funny story.'

'I didn't see you laughing too much.'

'That's because I was trying to remember it. It was years ago and I was on a binge at the time. Look, Dom, the time has come, that's all. I've been here long enough.'

'Are you back on the drink?' Dom says then. 'Is that it? It is, isn't it? You want to get plastered in peace.'

'For Christ's sake, you're being completely unreasonable. I'm your brother, not your wife. I don't need a big reason to move out. I just need my own space, a bit of privacy, that's all.'

'You have privacy here.'

'Have I, though? How come my box of stuff is sitting there then, did it make its own way downstairs?'

'My stuff, if it comes to it.'

'Except for the tin-opener.'

Dom sits down on the stool again and blinks at him. 'If you must know, I went up to check the fuses on account of this hurricane warning, and there it was sitting under the fuse box in the loo. I knew you were up to something anyway. I'm not exactly stupid, you know.'

He grows quiet again, one hand on the counter, the other on the rim of the box, as he just sits there, staring at nothing.

'Come on, Dom. Be reasonable. I'm doing you a favour, as it happens. You and Kim, well . . .'

'Kim? What's it got to do with her?'

'You'll have the place to yourselves. She can move in with you now.'

'Kim move in? Kim move in here? I don't fucking want her moving in here. Why the fuck would I want that?'

'I don't know. I just presumed, I mean . . .'

'Oh, did you?' Dom says. And he's on his feet again. 'She has a mother to look after over there. In a wheelchair. I suppose you think she should move in too? And bring her stupid fucking cat too, while she's at it? Is that the big favour you're doing me, then?'

'I didn't even know she had a mother.'

'Course you didn't. Know why? Because your head is so far up your own arse looking for something else to pity that you don't see anyone else – do you?'

'I just thought, you know, if I'm not here, it would give you two a better chance of, I don't know, making a go of it.'

'I'm trying to get rid of her, not make a go of it, if you must know.'

He waits for a moment and then sits down again. 'And what about the Airbnb? You just going to abandon it now, I suppose? Fucking typical, that is.'

'You're the one who abandoned it.'

'I only wanted to take a break from it. I had my reasons.'

'What reasons?'

'I had something in the pipeline. Doesn't matter now, it didn't work out.'

'You could have said something – what was it anyway? And how come it didn't work out?'

'None of your fucking business,' Dom growls. Then he pulls in a breath, gives a long, low belch as the bread soda kicks in. Then, with a single decisive pat of his hand on the counter he says, 'Right then, go if you're going. Go on. Don't let me keep you.'

'What?'

'You heard me, fuck off. Get out.'

'You mean now? I have to go *now*?'

Dom stands up. 'Yeah, now would be good, save me from having to nail down the contents.'

'Come on, a few bits of crap you didn't even know you had.'

'You were always the same, biting the hand that fed you. I don't know why I expected any different.'

Dom begins to walk down the kitchen towards the French doors.

'Well, is it okay if I wait till tomorrow?' he calls after him.

'What's wrong with now?'

'It's dark.'

'I can see that, yeah,' Dom says, as he begins to open the doors.

'I've no electricity.'

'You'll just have to put up with it till they switch it on then, won't you?'

'No, I've no electricity at all. There's none.'

Dom turns and looks at him. 'You're moving into a place with no electricity? You are priceless, Phil. You are one priceless fucking moron. What is it, a squat or something? A tent?'

'Right. Well, I'll just go and get my stuff from upstairs, if you've no objection?'

'Fire away. Fetch them down. And be sure to take your fucking banana box with you when you leave. There's a little torch in the drawer there somewhere, I think. Max used to play with it when he was a kid; it came out of a detective set, far as I know. You can take that, if you like. Stop you being scared of the bogeyman. The other grown-up torches stay here, in case of a power cut. And leave the keys in the hall, would you? I don't want the trouble of changing the locks. I'm going outside now to secure the chairs on the terrace, put a few things away in the shed. I expect you'll be gone when I come back in.'

'You know what you are, Dom, you know that? You're—'

'Yeah, yeah, yeah,' Dom says, opening the door and stepping out to the garden.

'A bollix,' he shouts after him. 'A complete and utter shit.'

On the far side of the front door, he puts the banana box down, then reaches back into the hall and drags his hold-all and the plastic sack of bedclothes out. He clips the door shut, then he lifts the flap of the letterbox and drops the keys into the dark hallway. He considers leaving the stuff that he's taken from Dom's house, but the last thing he needs at this point is to be left with a bare bed to lie down on, and no cup for his tea while Hurricane Ophelia is outside running amok.

Down the granite steps, he juggles the load and then, resting

398

the box on the spear-tips of the railing, opens the gate. His heart and head pumping with rage, he lumbers up the road, the hold-all across one shoulder, the box in his arms, the bag of bedclothes slapping off his knee with every step he takes.

By the time he reaches the corner, he is surprised by how quickly he has calmed down. He sits on the dicky seat under the bus shelter and thinks about Dom, his short fuse and sharp bite, the way he works himself up into a frenzy and then moves on, seemingly unaware of any damage caused. But there was something different about the way he lost the rag tonight, although what that is, he can't figure out. In any event, sitting here now, he feels neither anger nor resentment towards his brother, which seems a little odd. He reaches into his pocket, takes out his phone and toys with it for a moment. He thinks: I'll give him a few minutes to batten down the hatches, give him a chance to cool off, then I'll give him a call.

While he waits, he begins, absentmindedly, to scroll down his phone, rechecking messages already read. From Lorraine last Saturday: a photo of her leaning on the wall of a hump-backed bridge in Venice. Another photo, sent Wednesday, this time with a bloke beside her, their faces raised to the camera for an ear-to-ear selfie. They are sitting on a café terrace under the blazing light of Florence. He expands the picture, examining the bloke. A cheesy bastard by the look of him. Not that he's any right to start getting protective now.

Havin a ball, Dad. Hope all well. Milan tomorrow. See u Sunday week usual spot? Or maybe an Italian? Am expert in spaghetting now! Xxx L

And from Max last Monday:

Home last w/end of month. Wd Lorraine come for supper?
I'll cook if u get rid of Kim! Deal?

He clicks into Dom's number, is about to call, but then chickens out. He decides to send a message instead. He knows what he wants the message to convey – that he's sorry without saying he's sorry. That he doesn't want to have to tell Lorraine he's fallen out with her Uncle Dom again. That he doesn't want to lose contact with Max. Or fuck it, that he doesn't want to think he'll never see Dom again.

He prods in a few words, deletes and prods again. Then he looks up the road. There's no one about. A trace of light from the back rooms of closed shops in the row up ahead, or in blurts from the few cars passing across the open end of the cul-de-sac, or from a window here and there along the street. He feels an unfamiliar sense of ease. After a moment, he closes his phone and puts it back into his pocket. Then he stands up, gathers his worldly goods together and turns back up the road to the house.

He dumps his things behind the hedge inside the gate and goes up the steps to the front door where he spends the next few minutes either ringing on the bell or banging the knocker. He knows that Dom has to be back in the house because the light in the hall is on and it was off when he left a few minutes ago. He could shout in the letterbox, but decides against that – Dom would not appreciate the neighbours hearing his business. He gives it another minute or so, then goes back down to the garden gate. Unzipping his hold-all, he pokes around until he finds his Airbnb copybook, then he returns to the steps and sits down on the top one. He takes a pen from his inside pocket, unfurls the copybook and opens it at the last page. By the light of the porch, he writes:

I don't want to leave it like this, Dom. I really don't. You've been good to me. I know that. Look, if you want, I can still do the Airbnb. No problem. I can come in every day. Think about it anyway, and send me a text if you change your mind. Sorry for the trouble I caused.

Phil.

And thanks for everything.

He tears the page out, folds the note, pushes the letterbox open, then slips it in. He's about to let the flap fall down again, when something makes him hesitate. A shadow, like a large stain on the wall of the first landing at the top of the stairs. He pushes the flap in as far as it will go and tilts his head. The stain moves. And now he can hear a thudding sound. A thud, then a pause, and now another thud.

He calls in through the letterbox, 'Dom? Dom, are you up there?'

A third thud and then – the apparition of Dom, sitting on a step at the top of the flight. From there, like a massive toddler descending by the seat of his pants, he begins to literally arse down the stairs, one step, one thud, at a time.

His face large and beige, his right hand over his left arm, his mouth opening and closing, trying to say something.

'Dom, Dom, it's me. Can you open the door? Can you get down the stairs?'

Hand on the banister, Dom tries to lift himself up, sways a little and falls back down.

'Okay, okay. Don't move. I'll go round the back.'

Dom lifts his right hand slightly to show that he has already pulled the iron bolt across the back entrance.

'Okay. I don't think I'd be able to kick this door in – it's a big bastard. What about Kim – she has keys, hasn't she?'

Dom lifts one finger and makes a sign that means 'No Kim'.

'I'm calling an ambulance.'

Again, Dom raises the 'No' finger.

'Fuck that, Dom, I'm calling an ambulance. Then I'm asking Kim about the keys. Don't worry, I won't let her come over. Is that okay?'

Dom puts a fist over his chest and gives a feeble nod.

The minute he opens his mouth, Kim freaks out and tries to push past him.

'It's okay,' he says, 'the ambulance is on the way, I just don't want him worrying about the door being left open all night if they have to force it. I've no keys, you see.'

'It's my fault! It's all my fault,' Kim says. 'We quarrelled. Oh, why did we quarrel?'

'I've no idea.'

'He must have been so . . . it's my fault.'

'The keys, Kim. I need the keys.'

'Yes, yes of course.'

'And would you have an aspirin by any chance?'

'An aspirin? You have a headache?'

'Not for me, for Dom. In case it's his heart, it stops any clots forming. Apparently.'

'Oh yes, yes, of course.'

Kim runs down to the kitchen.

From a door at the side, the wheels of a wheelchair roll into view, followed by an old woman sitting in it. He watches while she manoeuvres herself into the hall and turns the chair, so that she is facing him from a distance.

He nods at her, opens his mouth to apologise for disturbing her and goes to step in.

'Not another step,' she says, 'else I'm calling the police.'

Kim comes rushing up from the kitchen. 'Stop, Mummy – that's Phil, Dominick's brother.'

'I don't care who he is, I don't like the look of him.'

'She doesn't mean . . .' Kim begins to explain as she hands him a packet of aspirin. 'I'm coming with you,' she says. 'I just need to put her to bed and then—'

'There's no time for any of that.'

'Bringing hardened criminals into my house,' the old woman says.

He reaches out and lifts the keys from Kim's hand.

Dom is still sitting on the stairs, doubled over now, his breathing so laboured that it sounds as if something inside him is trying to claw its way up through his lungs.

'The ambulance is on the way, Dom,' he says, running past him down to the kitchen where he grabs a bottle of mineral water off the counter.

He says it again as he kneels down beside him, holding out the aspirin and the bottle of water. But Dom can't seem to lift his hands.

He presses the tablet between his brother's flaccid lips, then pokes it further in, easing it along his plump wet tongue towards his throat. He places the bottle into Dom's mouth. 'Take a sup of this, Dom, help it go down.' The water dribbles straight down his chin. He puts one hand behind Dom's head, another on his chin and tilts. 'Okay, just swallow it, Dom, go on, just a bit. Now you have it. That's it. Good.'

Dom pulls his head away and begins to grimace, stretching his jaw.

'What is it? Is your jaw at you?'

Dom nods.

'The ambulance will be here any second,' he says, and despite everything, Dom manages a sceptical, 'Huh.'

'No really, they know, they'll be here.'

Dom slumps to one side, holding his chest.

'You'll be all right, Dom. If push comes to shove, I know how to do CPR.'

Dom closes his eyes and then opens them again.

'Sorry, I shouldn't have said that. And anyway, I didn't mean the kiss of life or . . . or anything.'

Dom slumps a bit more.

'I'm sure it won't come to that,' he says while at the same time trying to figure out how he's supposed to administer CPR with Dom lying on the stairs, never mind holding his nose and breathing down into his open mouth. In any event, they are both literally saved by the bell as the ambulance blasts into the street. Within seconds, the hall is filled with a pulsing blue light.

And it all happens so quickly then, the crew trotting in the door, pushing him out of the way, then Dom on the stretcher, gliding past him out the door and sliding up into the back of the ambulance.

'Can I go with him?' he asks. 'I'm his brother.'

A voice comes from inside: 'Hop in.'

For a while, he doesn't know what's going on. He can't see Dom's face behind the white coats and machinery. He can hear voices.

'Can you tell me your name? Tom, yes, Tom, you're fine now, mate. I'm just going to give you a bit of oxygen now, okay, Tom? Is that okay, mate? Just to give your lungs a bit of help. And now something to make you feel a bit better.'

Then another voice on the phone to the hospital arranging to have Dom met at the other end.

A medic comes up beside him and asks for personal details. He has to think for a moment before he can remember Dom's date of birth.

'Medical history?'

'I don't know. Blood pressure, cholesterol. He takes pills.'

'Family history, any heart trouble? Father, uncles, anyone?'

'I don't know.'

'Meds, then – do you know if he's on any other meds?'

He thinks about, but decides not to mention, the Viagra that Max told him he'd spotted sitting on his father's bedside locker.

'I gave him an aspirin a while ago,' he says. 'I did this course, you see, and—'

'Good. Anything else?'

'His first name's Dom, not Tom.'

He lurches with the ambulance, his head numbed from the siren wailing on the far side of this little capsule, the controlled urgency of the voices around him.

'Will he be all right?' he asks.

'We'll be there in a sec,' the paramedic replies.

Twice he is told to go home. The first time, by a nurse who looks about twelve; the second, by a doctor who looks marginally older. They both say more or less the same thing: Dom is okay, his condition has stabilised; they will know more in the morning.

'There's not much point in hanging around here though, is there?' the nurse says to him with an apologetic look up and down the deserted corridor, as if she thinks he was expecting a cocktail party. 'Come back in the morning, that's what you do.'

He nods and thanks her and stays where he is.

The doctor has a bit more information: 'Oh, he'll need surgery all right. I don't want to say any more until we have the results of the tests. Someone will give you a call, let you know what's happening. Meanwhile, you should go home, get some rest.'

He nods and thanks him and stays where he is.

He tries calling Max again. Then he sends him another text message. He replies to Kim's many missed calls with a text.

No change. Stable and sleeping. No one allowed in. Better leave the phone free, in case Max calls.

She shoots back a message:

Shall I call him?

He's sleeping.

No, Max I mean. Shall I call Max?

No ta. I'd rather tell him.

Sure? It's no problem.

Kim, don't call Max. Please.

At half two in the morning, Max finally calls. He's drinking his third vending-machine coffee at the time. For a second, he loses control of the wobbly cup and, for once, is grateful that the coffee is tepid as he watches it slop out all over his hand onto his inside leg.

Max sounds pissed or stoned or probably both. 'What's with all the calls?' he asks in a lazy, nonchalant voice.

'It's your dad, Max.'

'Yeah?'

'He's had a heart attack.'

'Are we surprised, though?'

'Max, it's serious. I'm in the hospital now. It looks like they're going to operate tomorrow.'

'Oh shit. Oh right. Yeah, em . . . what should I do? Do I just come down? Oh fuck, the last train's gone, isn't it? I could borrow a car? I don't have a full licence, but . . . or I could ask my mate, his mum sometimes lets him—'

'Don't even think about getting into a car. You can get the train in the morning. I'll call you as soon as I know what's happening. This time, leave your phone on, will you? I've been trying to get you for the past couple of hours.'

'I always have my phone on.'

'Then why didn't you answer?'

'I couldn't hear it, could I?'

'Well leave it where you can hear it, then. And Max, try not to worry. He'll be okay.'

Max doesn't reply and it crosses his mind that he may have fallen asleep, but then he hears a mumble: 'Yeah, sure, yeah, I know, okay then. See you tomorrow then, Uncle Phil. Yeah?'

'Yeah.'

After he speaks to Max, he leaves the hospital. Outside, he hops into a taxi, grateful to find the driver is a taciturn Sikh who prefers listening to a Chopin nocturne played low on the radio to sharing his opinions of the world at large. He fully intends spending what remains of the night at Dom's place, but as the cab pulls up outside the house, he finds he is reluctant to go in without

Dom's say-so. And besides, he has the feeling that the minute he steps through the door, Kim's hand will be on the doorbell. He asks the driver to wait, then ducking behind the bush inside the gate, he comes back up with the box, the plastic sack and the hold-all in his arms. If the taxi man finds anything strange about this, he keeps it under his turban.

Between worrying about Dom and waiting for the hurricane to make up its mind, he's unable to sleep. And lying in his skimpy camp bed, whiling away the turgid hours, it occurs to him that whatever pleasure there was to be gained from this little venture has – like most of the little ventures in his life – been mostly in the planning: cleaning the place up, gathering together whatever bits he needed, sneaking the hoover and the cleaning gear in and out of Dom's house. And yes, getting one over on his brother definitely had something to do with it. But now that he's actually moved in, now that he sees what it's like to be here in the dark, he has only one question to ask himself: what in the name of fuck possessed him to leave a comfortable room in a house of every modern convenience for this underground cave on a forgotten laneway in the armpit of EC1?

When he closes his eyes, he sees Dom; his lizard-grey face and the fear. That's what had been different about him, he realises now – Dom had been afraid. He can see the clammy texture of his skin; his large frame dwarfing the ambulance trolley, the pearls of sweat on his forehead. He opens his eyes. But Dom finds him anyway, his face like a big grey balloon floating aimlessly about in the dark.

In the end, he gets up, switches the camping lamp on, puts on his trousers and shoes. He can taste the damp on the air, the dust too, even though he's spent the past couple of weeks doing nothing but cleaning. Outside, there's an uneasy silence, and on a poster stuck onto the back wall, Henry Cooper, eerie in the inadequate light of the lamp, is watching his every move.

He makes himself a cup of tea, taking some comfort from the dainty blue flame of his little Primus stove and the warm fart of gas it lets off now and then. He walks about the room, sipping the black tea. Then he stops by the window and looks up into the silent laneway, not a stir of wind crossing it. His eye begins to make out the shape of the buildings on the opposite side, the walls and back entrances of vacant premises. And then he sees it – above the glass-fanged back wall of Mrs Oak's pub, inside the upper left corner of the house, a single bulb of light. He reckons Mrs Oak left it on to scare off intruders before she moved into the nursing home. Or maybe it has been there for some time, dangling from the ceiling, unnoticed and forgotten since Milly moved out to get married. It calms him, anyhow, just standing there drinking his tea, looking up at it: this little beacon to his past.

When he finally goes back to bed, he tries to elbow all thoughts of Dom out of his mind by recalling the worst kips he has lived in over the years: labourers' rooms with four men to a bed and four more on the floor. Rooms where you cooked on a gas ring set into a plank that pulled down from the wall; walls so full of stains they looked like they'd been pissed against; trains passing in the night, rattling your teeth. And then there were the hostels – or hostiles, as the residents sometimes called them. This isn't the worst place, he decides, not by a long shot. And even if it is far from ideal, there's probably no going back now. Not until Dom recovers anyhow, and even then, not without considerable crawling. And he has done all the crawling he wants to do for what remains of his sorry life. He stretches out as best he can and settles the pillow under his head. At least down here, he'll be left alone. And he won't have to sleep with his coat on either, nor pin his boots to the floor with the legs of his bed to stop them from being lifted.

He wakes to the sound of the phone purring in his earhole and then an Australian woman is telling him that Dom has had surgery earlier this morning, that he's all right and is recovering well.

'Why didn't anyone call me? I would have gone back.'

'Oh, I have no idea, dear.'

'What sort of surgery – a bypass or something?' he asks.

'Oh dear me, no. Nothing like that. An angioplasty, and he's had a stent fitted. He's back from ICU and everything.'

'Will I be allowed to see him?'

'*Of course*, my dear – you're family, isn't that so?'

'I'm his brother.'

'Yes indeed, you are. It will be nice for him to have you there when he wakes. He's been sedated, so he'll be snoozing on and off. Doctor Harris will fill you in later. If he's not around, one of the team will speak to you at some stage. But there's nothing to worry about, all righty?'

He texts Max. Max texts back telling him that the train is just pulling into Paddington and that he'll see him at the hospital.

Next, he sends a message to Kim with an update, mentioning that, for the moment, no visitors are allowed. He sends her a second message, explaining that he can't call her because his phone is almost out of charge, which is not a lie – even if it feels like one.

When he finds Dom's room, Max is already there, precariously balanced on the edge of a chair with his upper body draped over the end of the bed and his head tucked into the fold of his arms. He thinks Max is crying and, placing a hand on his shoulder, opens his mouth and begins to say, 'He'll be all right, Max, don't worry.'

410

Max jumps to his feet; his hands fly up like he's ready to do a few karate moves. But instead, he just stands there blinking out of his bloodshot eyes and gobbing like a fish. He sees now that, rather than weeping, Max has been sleeping off his hangover. He gives him a nod to come outside.

'You better go home, Max, and get some kip,' he says. 'Go on, off you go now.'

'But . . . but I've come all this way,' Max begins, his voice rising and falling, hoarse on the downturn, squeaking when it goes up. 'What if he dies, Uncle Phil? What if he dies and I'm not here?'

'He's not going to die. I was talking to the nurse earlier and she said he's doing fine. But if he wakes, and sees you in this state – well come on, Max, it's not going to do his blood pressure any good. Go home, there's a good man. I'll stay here till you come back. I'll tell him you're on your way. And I'll call you if there's any change.'

Max falters. 'Well, can I have a hug before I go?' he asks, like a little boy.

'You can of course,' he says, averting his face from the oncoming blast of sour wine, hash and kebab.

Back in Dom's room, he looks along the wall until he locates a socket under the window. He pulls his phone out of one pocket and from the other unravels a charger and cord and plugs it in. Then he takes the chair Max has just vacated and slowly allows himself to look up along the bed, to his brother.

He's like Gulliver lying there, trussed up by the Lilliputians. His hair, longer at the back, is slightly spread out on the flat pillow, and wires are pinning him to the bed. Machines bleeping and blinking all around him. His colour has improved at any rate; in fact, he looks at complete ease – a state he can't ever remember associating with his brother, until this moment.

411

A nurse pops her head in. 'Are you next of kin?' she asks.

'I'm his brother. His son has just left.'

'Oh right. I was trying to find out about the history of heart trouble in the family. Did your father, for example, have heart problems?'

'Right. No. Nothing like that.'

'Anyone else in the family?'

'I told them in the ambulance: I don't know any other members of the family. I don't know anything about my parents' families at all, now that I think of it.'

The nurse nods and then, throwing a glance at the phone in the wall, says, 'No mobile phones in here.'

'Sorry, yes of course. I'd no electricity at home and in case people want to know how he is, work and that.'

'What does he do for work?'

'He's a trumpet player.'

'Oh,' she says and then, stepping around the door, walks across the room, lifts the chart from Dom's bed and makes a note.

'Is that important?' he asks.

She puts the chart back and smiles at him. 'Keep the phone off. Go outside if you need to use it or you can always go down to one of our caffs.'

For the rest of the morning, nurses pass in and out, checking Dom's blood pressure and fiddling about with the machinery while Dom continues to sleep like a baby.

After a while, he sees Dom's hands move, then his head. A slight groan and now his eyes are open and looking straight at him.

'I'm sorry, Phil,' he slurs.

'Nothing to be sorry about,' he says.

'I love you, brother, you know?' Dom adds and he thinks, Christ, Dom, don't saddle me with that.

412

'Don't worry about anything, Dom,' he says. 'Just rest now. Relax.'

The next time Dom wakes, he's a lot brighter.

'So how are you, Phil?' he asks.

'How am *I*?' he laughs. 'Grand, thanks. How about yourself?'

'Been better, I'd say. Don't remember much to be honest. Where am I?'

'Hammersmith. They've put a stent in your heart. You're going to be fine.'

'I'll be all right to play then?'

'Oh yeah, I'm sure you'll be fine.'

'Because you play the trumpet with your entire body, Phil, you know – not just your lips and your chest. Your entire body. They know I have private health insurance?'

'What do you think?' he says, sweeping his hand over the room. 'It's like a hotel in here.'

'They must have found the card in my wallet. Nice to get a bit of value out of it anyway.'

He goes quiet for a minute and then, 'Such dreams as I've been having, you wouldn't believe.'

'Yeah?'

'I was dreaming about Mum. I was a baby, and she handed me to a monkey and he clambers off with me in his arms, up onto the roof.'

'That's mad; I mean, a while ago, I was thinking you looked like Gulliver lying there.'

'Gulliver?' Dom says. 'What's Gulliver got to do with it? Oh yeah, he used to read it to us, fuck me. The monkey, yeah. Does Sheila know I'm here?'

'Who's Sheila?'

413

'You better let her know. She'll take care of everything. Is my phone . . . ?'

'No, it's back in the house.'

'Look her up. She'll sort it all out. Sheila.'

'Who is she?'

'My secretary, who the fuck do you think?'

And then he goes back to sleep again.

The next time he wakes, he's asking for someone called Sam.

'Sam? Who's Sam?' he says. 'Someone else you work with?'

'My son.'

'Max, you mean?'

'Oh yeah, of course, Max.'

'He's on his way.'

'Do you remember the first day we went to that school in Ireland?'

'I remember.'

'He drank a glass of whiskey. Do you remember, Phil?'

'Yes.'

'Never touched a drink before or after. He was a strange one, though – a fucking weirdo, if we're to be honest. A real loner. I mean, no friends, no family. He loved us, though. He loved *you*. Golden boy.'

'You think?'

'Hey Phil?'

'Yeah?'

'Phil, you know if I croak it?'

'I had a chat with the nurse earlier, you won't be doing any croaking. We're stuck with you for another while yet.'

'No? Well, even if I don't, my solicitors . . . I can't think of the name of the company, they changed it last month, you see. But you'll find a letter in my desk somewhere with the address. You ever heard of a thing called a discretionary will?'

414

'No, can't say that I have.'

'Well, you go see my solicitor, Bea. She'ı.

'Explain what?'

'The time has come – she knows, I told her.
hold it against me. Him neither. He loved you, you k.
thought it was for the best.'

'I don't understand.'

'Well, you were always a bit thick, weren't you?' Dom smₗes
and then, 'Here, where do you suppose I got the name Sam from?'

'You wanted to call him Sam when he was born.'

'Did I? Yes, that's right, I did. I did! Why did I call him Max,
then?'

'Monique.'

'Oh, her,' he says and drops off again.

While Dom sleeps, he thinks about that time in Dublin. Two
boys, one almost ten, the other just gone thirteen. A silent father.
They were trudging around trying to find the digs they were staying in that first night. Dom constantly complaining and calling
everyone and everything they came across, thick. The stink of
the Liffey like a thousand farts as they stumbled on the cracked
pavement beside the river wall. His bare knees aching from the
cold as he'd lagged behind, holding his nose. Their suitcases had
been waiting in the guesthouse when they finally found it and
he couldn't understand how that had come about, but he hadn't
liked to ask in case Dom called him thick again. The sheets were
nylon with the whiff of old sweat on them. Two single beds; a
black wardrobe like an upright coffin; a big, bare wooden cross
on the wall.

He shared one single bed with Dom, who spent the best part
of the night heeling him viciously because there wasn't enough
room. The other single bed was tucked into the wall opposite.

ıer lay down on top of it and fell asleep with his clothes still on. But he had stayed awake himself for much of the night, keeping watch, afraid that, like his mother, his father might die in the night.

The next day, a train. A country walk, an avenue. This time they dragged their suitcases with them. A dark brick spread in the middle of nowhere. It looked less like a school than a place where things were manufactured; a factory, maybe. There were long goalposts in the distance, arms shot up to a low, dark sky. The grass was clogged with soft ice.

The priest stepping towards his father with his arms out. 'John, my friend . . .' Dom and himself looking at one another, wondering who he was and how come he knew their father's name.

They said goodbye to him in a square room, a big square table in the centre with a bowl of fat red flowers on it. The chairs were placed away from the table, around the walls. The light in the room was dim and everything looked as if it had been polished: the table, the lino, the picture of Jesus with his heart on fire, the priest's shoes. He can remember being ashamed of his own shoes, his father's, Dom's. He can remember how scruffy they all looked compared to the priest – Father Joe – who looked as if he'd been ironed all over: hair, clothes, smooth cream-coloured hands. He gave them biscuits and a glass of milk. His father saying, 'No thanks, Joe,' to the glass of whiskey. But the priest gave it to him anyway, taking his two hands and wrapping them around the glass. He held it for ages and then he just knocked it back.

The strange nasal accent of the priest: 'And what are the boys interested in, John?'

'That one likes to box,' his father said, pointing to him. He tried to catch his eye to tell him – no I don't. I don't care about boxing at all.

416

'And the other one,' he said, nodding at Dom, 'is keen on the trumpet.'

He puts his head in his hands and listens to the soft beeping machine monitor his brother's heartbeat. He feels an urge to tell Dom about the incident with his father in the house in Slough. But he knows he can't do that. When he was a child, he used to close his hands over his mouth whenever he had a secret that he couldn't share but nonetheless wanted to hear expressed. He wants to do that now, to whisper into the crib of his hands: I saw him drinking another time, Dom; I saw him drunk in the house in Slough. He molested me there, that's how much he loved his golden boy. He molested me.

The light in the room is beginning to fade – prematurely, he can't help thinking. Could be there's rain on the way. He gets up and walks to the window but it shows only the side of another building across a narrow covered courtyard. In the frame of one of the windows, a lean black man is swaying back and forwards like the pendulum on a clock. He appears to be dancing. He wonders if that could be a ward for the mentally ill over there. He is enjoying watching the man anyhow, his loose movements and steady rhythm. He sees the man lift something then, which turns out to be the handle of a mop. The man looks up suddenly and their eyes catch. The man gives him a cautious upward nod. He nods back.

Dom is in a deeper sleep now. He feels the need to get out of the room for a while; to get away from the sound of the machines, the rise and fall of his brother's chest. The next time a nurse comes in, he says to her, 'I have a few calls to make, and wouldn't mind a cup of coffee – do you think it would be all right to . . . ?'

'Of course, my dear,' her Australian voice replies, 'you go right on ahead, he's right as rain with me here.'

Downstairs, the coffee shop is about to close and the girl directs him to another café in a different part of the hospital. On the way there, he switches on his phone. A text from Max forwarding Sheila's number.

He lets Max know that his dad is doing well and is sleeping peacefully.

Max replies: *Phew. Just grab a shower and b there soon.*

Sheila keeps him on the phone for a while, listing everything that she's cancelled or rescheduled and asking him to pass on this information to Dom. He feels like saying, 'Look, why don't I just tell him that he's nothing to worry about, that you have everything under control?'

But she seems to be the type who likes to be specific, as if she's afraid to make a mistake. Or maybe she just knows what Dom's like.

He phones Kim next and has a long, convoluted conversation, most of which involves trying to keep her away from the hospital. Then he switches off the phone, orders a ham and cheese toastie and a large coffee, picks up a copy of *The Times* that's lying there and settles down for a good twenty minutes.

When he's done, he takes his time strolling back to the ward. He goes to the loo, drops into the shop to buy a pack of chewing gum and a copy of today's *Guardian* to while away the time until Max arrives.

As he turns onto the corridor where Dom's room is located, he sees a group of people outside his door. Two doctors and three nurses. His head tells him that it's just the doctors doing their afternoon rounds. His gut notes the defeated looks on their faces. They walk away from him towards the other end of the corridor, the two doctors leading, the three nurses behind. Then they turn the corner and disappear. He stands still, afraid to move. He stands until he sees the Australian nurse come out of Dom's room. She spots him and begins to walk towards him, biting her lip.

'I'm so sorry,' she says, eyes full of pity.

He shakes his head.

'I'm afraid so. He had another heart attack, poor love. We did everything we could. I tried calling your phone but I couldn't get through. Would you like to sit down for a bit and I can take you in to see him in a while?'

He shakes his head again.

'I think you should sit down, really I do. You've had a shock. Look, why don't you let me take you into the office, get you a cup of tea?'

He resists her hand on his arm, then clears his throat. 'His son,' he says, 'my nephew, he'll be here any minute. I better go outside and . . .'

'Yes of course. Would you like me to go with you?'

'No, no, you're all right. Thanks though.'

He hardly knows where is he, but he notices the peculiar light of the outside world as he walks down a corridor, towards the front entrance. A clock on the wall tells him that it's gone half past three. Through the window, it appears to be almost nightfall.

Across the street, people are standing with their phones raised to the sky. Others stand around the hospital railings talking to one another and glancing upwards now and then. A sepia-tinted sky, as if a dirty orange dusk has descended on London.

He stands at the railings and waits for his nephew. On the far side, schoolkids in blue uniform are arguing about the light.

'It's the end of the world, innit?' one of them says.

'It's not the end of the world, it's pollution, is what it is.'

'It's not pollution, a factory's gone on fire.'

'What you talkin' about, a factory?'

'I don't know, do I? One that makes orange stuff.'

'What orange stuff?'

'Like cornflakes or something.'

'Or orange squash!' another one yells.

'Or Ben's hair!'

The harsh laughter of the kids, like dogs yapping.

'It's the Sahara Desert,' one of the boys says, swinging out of the railings, 'I just heard a woman say so over there. It's dust from the desert that got blown over here by that hurricane.'

'That's rubbish that is, the hurricane didn't come.'

'Yes, it did – it just didn't bother with London, that's all.'

A man comes from around the back of the hospital and walks through the gate. He has a guitar case over his shoulder. The man pauses at the railings and looks up at the sky. He recognises him now as the man he saw earlier mopping the floor through the window of the adjacent building. His hand on the railing is long and elegant. After a moment, the man moves away. He watches him cross the street diagonally, his walk slow and relaxed. He sees Max then, standing on the kerb on the opposite side of the street, also watching the man. Max turns his head suddenly and sees him standing there, looking through the hospital railings. Their eyes meet. The kids continue to argue and jostle.

PART SEVEN

17. Milly / Pip

2017

November

SHE CAN'T SEE the day from here, only a grey distortion of the yard outside. Through the punty-glass of the window, there's a swipe of colour from the Whitbread bar-towel left hanging on the clothes line. Once it was a deep maroon with the name of the brewery and the logo of a fawn picked out in gold thread at the centre. A pinkish rag now, after all the months left out in sun and rain, the occasional bout of vicious weather.

A few weeks before she moved into the nursing home, Mrs Oak, standing at the window on the upper landing, had called over her shoulder that she wanted the towel removed. It was getting on her nerves, she said, her voice high and tight, showing a rare trace of doubt. She'd been halfway down the second flight when Mrs Oak called out again, 'On second thoughts, leave it. We don't want one of those yellow-backed vultures looking down from his perch and noticing that it's gone, now do we?'

When she'd looked back up the stairs at Mrs Oak, she could see how frail she was; death passing for a moment across her face.

She steps down into the porch. Then, placing both hands on the back door, listens. The jackhammers have fallen silent, the snarling machinery, the broken glass flying down plastic chutes from upstairs windows. A phlegmy sort of sound that always makes her think of her village childhood: old men in an afternoon pub.

The builders are on their lunch break. Between their going and their coming back is her time to slip out, returning after dark.

Now that winter is here, it's become a little easier to orchestrate her movements. The builders, working to daylight, take shorter lunch breaks and are gone by dusk, meaning at least she doesn't have to spend quite so much time hanging around the nursing home.

When Mrs Oak was still here, she used to go out more often, sometimes twice or even three times in one day. The post office to collect Mrs Oak's pension, or to buy some bread and milk. Occasionally to the pawnshop with another of her trinkets or a so-called heirloom dragged out of the junk room. Sometimes, she just went out for a breath of air when she felt the walls closing in on her. But always she went out safe in the knowledge that Mrs Oak would be here to let her back in. A quick text message in advance and the back gate would open before her. No need for all that fumbling and fear in the laneway. Mrs Oak on the far side of the wall – the strength of her.

She lifts the iron ring from the hook by the door, fiddles for a moment with the keys dangling off it and considers her route.

It used to be through Benjamin Street. More building site than street and clouded with dust then, there was less chance of running into anyone she knew. But a few months back, the hoarding was extended to block access to and from the lane. Mrs Oak cried with rage when she found out. 'Trapping us,' she said, 'that's what they're doing. Trapping us before they send in the ferrets.'

Since then, she's had to take her chances, turning right and leaving by the far end of the lane, straight into the lunchtime crowds.

She opens the hemp carrier bag. The two cardigans for Mrs Oak are neatly folded inside, one yellow, one green – or primrose and mint, as Mrs Oak had described them, handing her the keys to the upstairs flat like she was giving her the keys to Buckingham Palace. On top of the cardigans sits a pair of Mrs Oak's fancy sunglasses found at the back of a kitchen drawer. At the bottom of the bag is the lunch she made earlier, wrapped up in several plucks of serviette paper.

She settles the handle of the bag onto her wrist, releases the bolt and waits for the long rod to shoot up. Then, poking the key into the lock, she gives it a good hard twist and cautiously pushes the door away from her. A crack of white sunlight comes into the porch. She pushes again, the crack widens and now she can see the bones of broken old beer crates stuffed into the corner of the yard, the trio of steel-brushed barrels the brewery forgot to collect and, stacked against the side wall, the familiar bank of empty bottles.

She scans the small section of the skyline that is visible from here. Rooftops and chimney stacks crowd in like they're peering over one another's shoulders to get a good look at her. From Faulkner's Alley and White Horse Alley and beyond, the crests and dips of more distant rooftops, squeezed back towards Clerkenwell. No sign of a yellow hat.

She stays at the door. Her mouth feels dry and there's a throb in the centre of her throat. She leans her forehead into the back of the open door, grinding the dull ache out of it. 'I've done nothing wrong,' she whispers, 'nothing. So why do I always have to be so afraid?'

Last night it was a noise she'd heard outside. She was in the yard having her bedtime smoke; there was no wind, and it was a movement too solid and awkward to belong to a cat. When she came inside, she found the light in the upstairs landing was wasted. She nearly vomited with fear, trying to get herself up the stairs to bed. She knows now that it was probably just one of those urban foxes she heard, mooching around in the back lane. And just because a light bulb runs out doesn't mean to say there's something up there lurking in the shadows. Small things in daylight turn to terror in the dark.

She buttons her coat, settles her scarf around her shoulders, then takes the list from the bag and looks at it. For herself – carton of milk and small sliced pan. For Mrs Oak – bar of Bournville and bar of Dove soap; copy of *Hello!* magazine. About to slip the list into her pocket, she remembers the light bulb for the top-floor landing. She doesn't want to have to go back inside to look for a pen, but it doesn't matter – after last night's carry-on, she won't forget the bulb.

She wonders where to have her lunch. Postman's Park, maybe, if it's not too cold out? Otherwise she'll be eating it sitting upstairs in the back of the bus.

Every weekday she sees them, the men in yellow hats – or the yellow-backed vultures, as Mrs Oak sometimes calls them. Vultures or hawks or gulls. And any time she looks out a window, it seems another one is crawling on a nearby rooftop, and another old house is caged in iron. They've been steadily working their way up from both ends of the street, drawing nearer to the bend where the pub stands. And it can't be too much longer before they begin crawling all over the building next door, and then and then . . . For years after the collapse of Matthew's firm, they had been left in peace. Even after the bank had closed in on Mrs Oak, there had been a long remission between one developer going bust and another taking over. This latest crowd, though, they don't hang about: buying up alleyways and laneways, squeezing apartments and offices into every available orifice, replacing old shops and pubs with franchises. For the past six months or more, they've been hard at it.

'They'll have to shoot me first,' Mrs Oak used to say to her dwindling audience of customers, and continued to say, even after she closed up shop altogether and there was just the two of them rattling around in that great empty barn of a pub.

'Shoot me in the head before I give up my home, my life. Let them send who they like – bank, council, bailiff. The tosser you married, who, let's face it, started the whole ball rolling. The other tosser who's looking to turn my lovely pub into a boutique hotel – *a boutique hotel!* – whatever that is when it's at home. The police, let them send the Queen's Cavalry for all I care. Let me tell you something, my girl – they may have forced us to live like squatters in our own home, but not an inch, do you hear me? Not an inch will we give.'

It had been upsetting to see Mrs Oak in such a state, spitting and ranting without dignity, effing and blinding, on occasion going all the way up to the C word. You'd hear her sometimes, on one of the landings, muttering and cursing as she looked out of the window, and once even in the middle of the night, there was the sound of her ranting like a madwoman up in the flat. At the same time, she had quite liked hearing Mrs Oak refer to it as 'our own home'. Like they really were in it together, like this really was her home. And she had felt safe enough, as long as Mrs Oak was there. But that day now is gone.

She keeps her eyes down, until the light opens out at the end of Peter's Lane, a flutter of shadow and movement passing across it. She is always startled by the first sight of this street in daylight, all the more so after a weekend. As if all this life has been poured into it overnight. And it startles her too, on evenings when she gets back late from the nursing home, to find it's all been drained away again. Transient people. They work around here but live elsewhere. Sometimes they hardly seem real at all. Like extras in a film. And yet it is here, at the mouth of this laneway, that the loneliness really hits her. Just standing here, watching the lunchtime horde pass back and forwards. Girls in twos and threes, drinking coffee and eating lunch on the go, sharing their 'he said, she said' weekend stories. Young men in suits that seem too small for them. Arty types with tattoos on their hands or crawling up their necks. Deliverers of lunch cycling bikes with grubby-looking containers strapped to their backs. She stands for a while, watching them all: bland faces and worried faces; earnest faces attached to phones. Handsome and pretty; plain and pug-ugly. Black, white and all tints of brown.

It's something she really misses about working behind the bar, the faces. Watching the life behind each one, without anyone really noticing that she's watching them. Now she has to be content with this occasional parade of passing strangers.

She steps out of the lane, turns right and, keeping close to the wall, begins up the street.

'Watch out for the locals,' Mrs Oak used to say – and still says from the safety of her nursing-home bed while sucking on a square of chocolate. 'They'll squeal and they won't even know they're squealing. And someone is always watching, believe you me.'

But she sees no familiar faces now. She can't remember the last time she did. She sees no one at all now, apart from Shamie and Beth, the odd time she crosses the great divide of Clerkenwell Road to pay them a visit.

At the phone box she has to step back to allow two young men to pass. And then she has to step back again to yield to a yellow hat. His face, lowered over his phone, lifts for a second and then cocks sideways as he pulls the hat off and tucks it under his arm. She recognises him from the new office block that is beginning to sprout over a flat roof on the far side of the back lane.

She gets a kick out of this – the way she can tell the builders apart: the turn of a shoulder, a particular stance when deep in concentration, or from the way a cigarette is smoked. While at the same time, she can walk right by and not a one will recognise her – and why should they? So long as she's careful coming in and out, there's nothing to connect her to the pub. She crosses the street.

As she comes to the plaza in front of the station, she counts five, six yellow hats standing at the concrete bollards. Busy hands fiddling with their phones. Here and there a spare hand reaches out for a coffee cup balanced on a bollard, or to lift a sandwich or a smoke up to his face. Mostly, though, it's all about the phone. Every last man is holding one. Staring down into it. Not a word of conversation passes between them.

Years ago, you'd hardly see a yellow hat unless on an architect or a council official. Nor would you see construction workers down on the ground during the day. You'd hear them all right, voices drifting downstream to the street. Lighter voices then. They tended to be Irish or West Indian: joking and laughing through all the banging and dust, singing, whistling or wolf-whistling – do men still wolf-whistle, she wonders? They started earlier, ate on the job, kept at it so that come dusk they could get to the pub and have a good go at it. Nothing would stop the day's work, only snow and ice – or the rain when it was heavy enough to make a roof too slippy to walk on.

Mrs Oak loved them, her Irish boys. She cashed their cheques for them on Fridays, took a good chunk of it back before the night was over. Still, she often threw something up for them – sausages left over from lunchtime, the occasional unsold sandwich or ham and egg roll. 'Eat up, boys, you've got to keep your strength up.'

These East European lads, they don't go in for talking much. You might hear the rumble of short conversations first thing in the morning or instructions being passed back and forward. They make plenty of other noise, though, with their fancy machinery, a racket that would cut through your head. They go down to the street to eat their lunch, pop over to Barclay's to cash their cheques, drink their liquor straight and out in the open.

She walks through a mingle of fast-food odours: burgers and what she supposes to be Japanese curry – if she's to believe the sign painted outside the café. It makes her feel sick and at the same time hungry. The Japanese place is part of the old sewing factory – the front office, if she's not mistaken. The building next door was the factory itself. Once it was all part of the same building, a plain brick façade with little windows upstairs that opened in warm weather, the buzz of sewing machines when you passed by, and the girls singing along to a radio. Now the walls are made of smoked glass. Creatives, is what they call the people who work in there, somebody told her.

Two young women are walking towards her, laughing and talking. She waits to see if they'll stand aside, or even allow her a few inches – just enough to squeeze by. But it's clear that they'd just as soon plough her down. Maybe they can't see me, she thinks as she hops down off the kerb onto the road. Maybe I am already dead and I just don't know it.

The girls pause, one of them wanting to make a point.

'But no seriously, I mean, seriously, was he joking or what? That's what I'd seriously like to know.'

And then they swagger on by. Long open coats, bare legs on display despite the fact that this is November. Strong white teeth beneath designer sunglasses; teeth that look as if they could bite through bone.

She steps back onto the kerb, sticks her hand down into the hemp bag, pulls out Mrs Oak's sunglasses and guides them onto her small face. The world turns a watery mauve. The shape of herself reflected in the office windows. She studies it for a moment: is this coat hanging off me? Am I gone too thin? Does my head look too small? Do these sunglasses make me look like Elton John? Am I an old woman yet?

* * *

He stays with Max for a few days after Dom's death. A considerable amount of this time, Max spends upstairs in his old room puffing on a joint. He pretends not to notice this, even if the house smells as if the walls are sweating cannabis. He keeps Max fed, shouting up the stairs to let him know when a meal is ready. Breakfast is usually ignored, although it's clear from the mess he finds every morning in the kitchen that Max has been up during the night, indulging his munchies.

In the evening, Max always comes down and eats rings around himself. Sometimes he barely speaks, but other evenings he talks his head off for a good hour or two before going back to bed. They discuss the funeral arrangements for Dom: who should be asked and how it's going to be paid for. They discuss it ad nauseam and, in the end, the only concrete decision they come to is to leave it all in Sheila's capable hands. He is surprised that Max wants the full Catholic extravaganza – at one stage he even mentioned the Brompton Oratory. But when Sheila comes back with the Musicians' Chapel in Smithfield, he seems happy enough with that.

And they talk about Dom. Max is keen to talk about his father – what he was like as a boy, teenager and young man. He gives Max the abridged version: how Dom was always clever in school; how he challenged the teachers, often catching them out; how he excelled at music and maths or anything really that he chose to throw an eye over. He omits the bit about Dom being bullied in the primary school in Bayswater, his arse like a pincushion from all the compass-needle stabs he received, mainly because he was such a prat. Nor does he mention how, in turn, Dom often brought the bullying home and took it out on his younger brother.

He tells Max about the trumpet – the day in the attic when he'd swapped the labels – and is pleased to see how much he enjoys this story.

'So you mean to say, my dad might have been a boxer?'

'Maybe . . .'

'And you – you might have been a trumpet player?'

'Yeah, except I'm crap at music. But your dad, yeah, I'd say he could have developed into a boxer; he had the right mentality anyway.'

Kim drops over a couple of times, but Max doesn't want to see her. He isn't too pushed about seeing her himself, but manages to be a little more polite about it. Twice he leaves her at the door, mumbling at her from the hallway. On the third evening, when he opens the door and she is standing there with a casserole dish in her hands, he finds himself stepping back and letting her in. Max comes downstairs and says a few words to her. But when she starts sobbing and carrying on about how the whole thing is her fault, Max says, 'That's a form of grief appropriation, that is, trying to own my father's death. Well, you don't own it, you were only with him a few months, it was coming to an end, anyone could see that. Going on as if you're his widow or something.' Then he walks out of the room.

She clings to him, weeping, as he walks her back across the road, the mother waiting at the open door, firing daggers looks from her wheelchair.

'It's probably better if she stays away for a while,' he says, 'she's upsetting Dom's son.'

He expects the old bat to berate him, but she nods, reverses her chair and tells Kim to take hold of herself and get back inside.

When he gets back over the road, he promises a red-eyed Max that that's the last time he will let her in. Then, to their shame, they both sit down and mill into the casserole.

There has been no mention of Jenny Wren and he doesn't like to ask. But he does think that Max could benefit from the comfort of a woman, even if that woman happens to be his mother.

A few days after Dom's death, she phones the house.

'Max is not answering his cell phone,' she says. Not a word about Dom, not the smallest condolence. Nothing. He thinks about Marj, Dom's first wife, how kind she's been to him and Max, calling around, sitting with them, offering to help with the arrangements.

'Oh hello, Monique,' he says. 'He's asleep.'

'So early?'

'He's exhausted. I told him to turn the phone off.'

'Well, can you go and wake him, please?' she says, with a weary sort of patience as if she's speaking to a child.

He waits a few seconds and then says, 'It's the first proper night's sleep he's had all week, so no, I can't wake him.'

She gives a little laugh. 'Tell him I'm coming the day after tomorrow. I will stay with him until the funeral and later until everything is settled.'

'I'll let him know.'

'Are you staying there?'

'I told him I'd stay till the funeral.'

'There's no need, I'm sure.'

'I'm not leaving him alone.'

'But you are not living there?

'No, I'm not.'

'Good. Then I won't have to tell you to move out.'

'Oh, sorry, I didn't realise it was still your house.'

'Who owns the house is irrelevant; it will have to be sold. There are debts.'

'And what about Max?'

'He is almost twenty years old. He is not a child.'

'I didn't say he was. But he has to have somewhere to live.'

'Why don't you let me worry about Max. I'm not going to leave him walking the streets, am I now?'

After he hangs up the phone, he goes into the sitting room and sits on the armchair behind the piano. The curtains are open and the streetlamps throw a watery light over the room, bringing a transparency to everything it touches: the grand piano, the two sofas, the fireplaces, the armchairs, the pictures on the walls. His hands. He thinks of Monique and the night she made a pass at him. She'd had a few drinks on her when she came in after an evening out, and coming up behind him while he stood at the kitchen sink in his bare feet, she said, 'Feet of Christ.' Then, placing her hands on his hips, she nipped him on the back of his shoulder with her teeth. He hadn't hesitated for a second before pushing her hands away and telling her to fuck off.

Afterwards, she'd treated him like dirt, behaving as though he'd been the one to make a pass at her. He never told Dom about the little incident, not even after they'd split up.

He looks down at his hands. In the frail light they seem detached from him. They begin to tingle, softly at first, then a more insistent pins-and-needles sensation. He is seized by an irrational fear that they are beginning to dissolve before his eyes. He will be a man with no hands. He needs to get them to do something; he needs to lift them off the arms of the chair and give them something to do. He imagines a glass then, a good glass, weighted, the tawny light of whiskey inside and his hands cupped around it, lifting it up to his mouth.

In his mind he hears the whisper: 'Who would think badly of you in your time of grief if you had one – just one, to steady the ship?'

He looks behind him; the cabinet is empty. The booze, he remembers now, is still up in Dom's study. But he can't seem to bring himself to climb the stairs and go in there. Somewhere else then. It's early enough. But if he goes out now, he won't come back. And so fucking what – who cares? Max does, he thinks. Max and Lorraine. *I* do. I care.

Shaking his hands out, he stands up abruptly and goes out to the hall. He reaches for his coat hanging on the end of the stairs, takes his phone out of his pocket and scrolls down to Colin's number.

'Philip?' Colin says. 'Everything okay?'

'I'm . . . Well, I don't know. But I feel a bit, you know?'

'Course you do, it's only to be expected.'

'It's a bit late, but by any chance, is there a meeting anywhere, do you know . . . ?'

435

'Hold one moment. Don't go away. Not even for a second. Don't think of anything, keep your mind blank as you can.'

Colin comes back to him. 'Now there's one in Islington, I see. Already started but if we hurry up, we should make the second half of the show. That suit?'

'Yeah, okay. Good.'

'I'll take the bike out, pick you up then in five.'

*   *   *

She inspects the edges of the black-out curtains by the light of the street, tugging them gently at the corners and checking that the double-sided tape is still holding fast to the frame.

Mrs Oak uprooted these curtains from a crate in the junk room after the Final Notice to Quit. 'They did the job during the war,' Mrs Oak said, 'they should do the job now.'

She wasn't sure if Mrs Oak meant that these actual curtains were used during the war, or just that they were fit for purpose. She had hated them anyway, big heavy velvet yokes – the stink of them, the way they had thrown the kitchen into an instant and permanent darkness. She's gone way beyond noticing such things now.

She turns on the light in the kitchen and looks through the cupboards. A few cans and jars; three mini boxes of cereal; condiments that should really be thrown out. On a shelf above the cupboards is a couple of giant catering tins of dried soup – Cream of Country Veg and Oxtail – that have probably been there since Terry's time.

She opens the hemp bag, takes out the carton of milk and the sliced pan. Then she removes a small tissue-wrapped bundle. Every day Mrs Oak slips her one of these bundles before she goes home. She hates the way she does it, reaching into the locker, then winking and tipping her nose before backhanding her the little bundle.

The day before they put up the curtains, they'd had to hide in the cellar while the authorities came in and checked the building over. From seven in the morning till after four, they took cover behind a false wall that Mr Oak had erected back in the forties.

'To keep the cash safe,' Mrs Oak explained. 'You see, you wouldn't put it in the bank during the war, well not all of it anyhow. And to hide his black-market whatnots I shouldn't wonder. He could be a bit tricky that way, my Terry. Of course I wouldn't have known him then,' she had quickly added.

They had been up that morning since the crack of dawn. Mrs Oak made her strip her bed, pack her clothes into the old suitcase and drag it all downstairs to the cellar. 'All trace of human habitation must be removed,' she'd said as she'd emptied her own flat out. 'No toothbrushes, no loo roll, no nothing.'

They brought a flask of soup and sandwiches with them, two pillows to sit on, the duvet to cover themselves over.

'It's like being in the war again,' Mrs Oak had said, settling down as if she was quite enjoying herself. 'Not that I'd remember, I was just a babe in arms. But I would have been through it just the same.'

Then she sprinkled peppermint oil all around them and placed a raw onion on each side of their little alcove. 'For the rats,' she explained, 'they hate these smells apparently. My mother used to swear by them.'

'Rats! *Rats!* Oh Jesus. Will it work, though? Will it work?'

'Calm down, Milly. I don't know, do I? But we'll soon find out.'

They could hear footsteps overhead, doors opening and closing. The voices of men. Finally, there was a banging noise that sounded as if it was coming from the bar. That went on for about twenty minutes. And then silence. When they finally crept back up the cellar stairs, most of the daylight had gone out of the bar. All they could see of the summer's day outside were a few slits of light, like steel blades coming through the wooden boards that had been hammered over the windows outside.

Mrs Oak went to the main door and tried to open it. Then she went out to the hall and tried the side door.

'They've only barred that too,' she said. 'Bastards. May they rot in hell, the lot of them.'

She opens today's little bundle and lays it out on the table: three foil-covered pats of butter, a sachet of mustard, a triangle of cheese, a pack of two plain biscuits and another pack of Cheerios cereal. Sometimes the bundle includes one or two small plastic pods of marmalade, and every now and then, a small KitKat. She'd been hoping for a KitKat.

She used to worry that the nurses would notice Mrs Oak's petty pilfering. Now she knows it probably wouldn't even cross their minds. A few weeks ago, she got talking to a woman at the coffee station down the corridor from Mrs Oak's room. Walking in and finding the woman crying, she'd thought, another middle-aged child worrying over a parent. But it turned out to be something else.

'They're all loaded in here, you know,' the woman said, giving her nose a sharp angry blow. 'My mother . . . my mother, my bloody mother. We've given this place – what? One hundred and sixty thousand already.'

'Oh?' she said. 'I thought it was the NHS here.'

'You are joking?' the woman said. 'The NHS! That's a laugh and a half. One hundred and sixty *thousand*. And no sign of an ending. God knows how much longer she'll last. I'll have to re-mortgage the house *again*. My entire inheritance is in that house. I'll end up selling it just to keep her alive. And you know what?' the woman said then, lowering her voice. 'She doesn't even *want* to be alive. She wants to die. That's the truth of it. I'm spending all that money keeping her alive against her bloody will.'

She gets on with it, buttering two slices of bread and then warming the triangle of cheese in her hand before attempting to spread it. She cuts her sandwich into four pieces, then sticks on the kettle and sits down to wait for it to boil.

After the curtains went up, they had sat at this table and looked at one another. 'We're barricaded in,' Mrs Oak had said, 'but at least we can get out the back way. Well, you can at any rate, my old pins are no good now. And I'll be spotted the second I stick my nose out.'

'And I suppose I won't?' she had said.

'Come on, Milly, you'll be better at blending in. You're younger, for a start. More fit. You can scurry off if you notice anyone. My eyesight's not what it was. And my pins, as I've said. We'll be all right. We have my pension. You have your dole. They've cut the electricity off downstairs, but we can keep the one going up here because it's always been in a different name and they've not copped that yet. We'll get through it. What – you're not speaking to me now, is that it?'

'How are we going to manage, Mrs Oak? You can barely get up and down the stairs as it is.'

'It's that car smash I had years ago. It's come back to haunt me. Well, that and my age.'

'I can't live like this any more; I just can't. Always waiting for the knock on the door.'

'You can leave me if you want, Milly – you'll get another job somewhere, I won't hold it against you.'

'And where am I to go – with pubs closing down left, right and centre?'

Mrs Oak began to cry then.

'I'm not going to leave you, Mrs Oak; you know I'm not,' she said.

'You're a good girl – you're like my own daughter, you know that? Look, I can move into Trish's old room, then if I need to go downstairs, there's only the one flight. I know what you're thinking, Milly.'

'Do you?'

'You're thinking I should have taken the offer when I had the chance. But I just couldn't roll over. I just couldn't do it. And your husband . . . ?'

'My ex-husband.'

'Your ex. Well, I just didn't trust him – and was I right?'

When she's made her tea, she brings it into the little sitting room and switches on the television. It's the only place in the house where she feels completely safe, in this windowless room, in the centre of the house, with its bockety furniture and the television Mrs Oak bought after she'd moved into Trish's room. She flicks through the channels, stares at the news for a moment, moves on again and finally settles on a cookery programme. A man is deboning a duck: he lays it on a marble slab, places the palms of both hands on its back, 'Look at this beautiful bird,' he begins, almost caressing its bald white body. Then he says, 'Now for some *butchery*.'

She watches him turn the duck this way and that, making his decisive incisions, pulling the legs off, dragging the tip of the knife down its backbone, trimming the fat off, then scoring it. As the duck breast hits the sizzling pan, she thinks of Mrs Oak sitting up in bed with a summer cardigan around her shoulders, asking the nurse to turn down the heating when she comes in with her bedtime tea, scone, butter and jam. While here she is, sitting in her coat by a dirty two-bar fire, eating a shitty sandwich. Tight as a drum, Mrs Oak has always been, making them do without so she could keep up her top-grade health insurance. And she thinks, and then says out loud, 'Well, I hope it keeps fine for you, Mrs Oak, you cute old bitch.'

She stands up, walks out to the hall, listens to the whistle of wind through the gaps in the worn-down window frames. She is about to turn in to the kitchen with her plate and mug when it hits her that she has forgotten to buy the bulb for the upstairs landing. 'What is *wrong* with you?' she says. 'How could you be so fucking stupid?'

She feels it all pressing down on her as she sits at the kitchen table. Fifty-six years of age and back to square one; no job, and no home – or at least not for much longer. Two agencies have as good as told her that she's too old for a full-time job as a barmaid. And if she wants accommodation, she needs to be full-time.

After a while, she stops crying. She wipes her eyes with her fists. She won't think about any of that now. And as for the light bulb? Even if she had remembered to buy one, it would be too dangerous to fit it at night, standing on a chair at the top of the stairs in the pitch dark. Tomorrow she will get up, go out and buy a bulb, bring it back and fit it in daylight before she goes to see Mrs Oak. It will mean leaving the house twice. But at least tomorrow night she will be able to climb those stairs without fear.

She places her hands on the kitchen table, pushes herself up off the chair and goes downstairs for her nightcap.

It was a ritual she went through with Mrs Oak until even one flight of stairs became too much for her. She lifts the box torch from the end of the counter and switches it on. Standing at the customer side of the bar, she looks at the hanging row of optics, the diminishing line of each bottle. She thinks of the night Mrs Oak had stood here, leaning on the counter, her eye roving over the bottles. 'Know what I'm dreading, Milly?' she'd said. 'I'm dreading the day I look over that bar and see the whole row is drained. The finality of that. Oh well, I'll probably just fill the vodka and gin bottles with water, take the bad look off it – eh?'

She turns the torch, aiming its light at the far side of the counter. Then she goes round, picks up a glass and pushes herself out a drink. She takes her drink and one cigarette from the pack she keeps at the end of the counter. Then she picks up Mrs Oak's old fur coat from the stool and drapes it around her shoulders. Following the beam of torchlight, she goes down to the back porch and lets herself out.

In the yard, she lights up her smoke. No sound comes from the far side of the wall tonight. Not a cat, not a fox, not a squeak.

*   *   *

He intends staying with Max until after the funeral but five minutes with Monique and he changes his mind. Two more days just seems too long a time to be under the same roof as her snotty face and her snide remarks.

'I'll be at the other end of the phone,' he says to Max, 'if you want to meet, go for a walk, coffee, whatever.'

'But you'll come back here before the funeral? I mean, I'd like you to be with me when we leave here.'

'I'll be here. Lorraine too. We can have breakfast together first. I'll text when I'm on the way.'

'Is there anything you need?' Max asks then. 'There's a load of food still in the fridge and now that Mum's here . . .'

442

'No, you're all right thanks. Unless . . .' He opens the fridge door and is pleased to see the large two-litre plastic milk container is still there, an inch of milk in the end of it.

'I'll take this.'

'There's a small carton of milk in there unopened, why not take that?'

'It's the container I want.'

'What for?'

'An experiment.'

'Oh right, yeah,' Max says, as if that's a completely plausible reason for wanting the container. Spoken like a true toker, he thinks, and pats Max on the arm.

Max walks him to Royal Oak station and talks little on the way. They say goodbye just before the entrance. He turns to watch Max rising on the hump of the little bridge, and he is so like his father at that age, it hurts just to look at him. He sees Max stop then and pat around his pockets. A moment later, he moves off again, sending a waft of marijuana back on the breeze.

While he waits for his tube, he sends Max a text.

Maybe cut down on the dope before the funeral?

A few seconds later Max's reply comes in the shape of a maple leaf, a rocket and a smiley face.

And now here he is, standing in the old boxing gym again, as dusk turns to darkness, his first time back since the day of his brother's death.

He pulls a torch out of his pocket. Drawing it around the walls and over the floor, he is dismayed to find the place even worse than he remembers. He walks around the outside of the ring and goes into the changing room. Removing the plastic milk container from his bag, he pours the remaining inch of milk into a cup for his tea later on. Then he washes out the container, fills it with water, puts the cap back on and dries the outside of it. He brings it back out to the gym, stopping at the corner of the ring where Mr Parekh's banana box sits. He pulls through wires and screwdrivers and all the other bits he had thought might be useful. He finds the headlamp he removed from Max's old bicycle. Carefully, he pulls it out and straps it to the plastic container, with the bulb of the lamp facing inwards into the water. He switches on the headlamp and the plastic container blooms into light.

He's not sure where he got the idea for this makeshift lamp; maybe from an old Scottish vagrant he shared his tent with years ago on the Rame Peninsula. At least, he can't think of anyone who would have been more inventive. He's pleased with it anyhow, the compact glow, much better than the useless lamp he'd spent over twenty quid on in the camping shop. He could make a few more of these homemade jobs, he thinks now, brighten the place up a bit. He could put one in the changing room, turn it into a kitchen area. He could put another in Shamie's old alcove, drag the desk out and turn it into his sleeping quarters. He could buy himself a decent mattress instead of the one on the skimpy camp bed that feels as though he's sleeping on a big slice of bread. He could do a lot of things, he thinks. He could, he could. So he could.

He takes the reading light out of the box, clips it onto the next page of his book and drops it on the bed. Then he takes another walk around the room. He stops at the window. Looking up, he sees Mrs Oak's house is in complete darkness. The bulb has blown since last he was here. He feels a dip in his stomach. It's as if he has lost something. Not keys or a wallet, nothing as disruptive as that, but a small childish keepsake that doesn't mean that much to him, until it's gone. And now, apart from a couple of slivers of streetlight leaking through the shoulders of buildings on Cowcross Street, the laneway – his laneway – is all in darkness.

He had never been that far up into the house, now that he thinks of it, although he'd always known that Milly's room was up there. Behind a skimpy, badly hung door, at the top of a narrow staircase. He had watched her open the door a few times while he'd stood on the landing and waited for her to come back down. Once, when he was half frozen to death, she'd run up to fetch him a jumper borrowed from him years ago that she'd forgotten to return. He couldn't remember lending it to her, nor did he recognise the jumper when she gave it back to him, smelling of herself. He'd got the impression that she'd been wearing it in bed. Mostly, though, when she went up to her room on his account, it was to lend him money.

She had sneaked him into the pub many times, after Mrs Oak began taking sleeping pills or was off on holiday somewhere. But for some reason, he had been kept away from her room at the top, even if it was the one place where they were unlikely to be discovered. Maybe she had thought it would look too deliberate, inviting him to come upstairs, the bed on view as soon as you entered the room, the presumed intimacy. And maybe it had suited him too, avoiding all that. He regretted not seeing her room just the same: how she moved within it, her things around the place, what she saw when she looked out the window.

The junk room once, on the floor, glued together, wrapped in an old red velvet curtain that stank of ancient cigarette smoke. And a few times in the small lounge out the back, she had sat across him on the red leather banquette. Afterwards, sleeping like children, heads together, his body facing one direction, hers

445

the opposite. She had always evicted him just before daylight: wake up, Pip, come on now, it's time to go. If Mrs Oak was away, she would blame Trish. But he knew that Trish already knew – that she had always known – the dirty looks she would give him in the bar later, the snap of his change on the counter.

'Come on, Pip, wake up, it's time to go, it won't be long before Trish is up.'

Often, he would pretend to be asleep for a few seconds longer, just to hear her voice, feel her warm breath on his face.

He steps away from the window, walks back across the old gym and stops by the poster of Cooper. Standing before him, southpaw to southpaw, he says, 'I don't know about you, 'Enry, but the balls I've made of some things in my time.'

He lowers himself down onto the bed and looks at his phone again.

No new messages. Then he picks up the book, reads half a page and drops it on the floor. Closing his eyes, he pulls *The Waste Land* into his mind – the first part of 'The Fire Sermon'. Then, word by word, line by line, he follows it into a damp brown landscape.

*   *   *

She can't remember ever buying a light bulb before, which seems a bit odd. Mrs Gupti used to keep them in the broom cupboard, along with stacks of serviettes and toilet rolls. And Matthew – well, nothing ever ran out when she was living with him. Except Matthew himself, of course.

She crosses Charterhouse Square. Once, there would have been plenty of places around where you'd find a bulb; grocers that doubled as hardware shops, throw in a bit of haberdashery while they were at it. Now it's a supermarket or forget it. She will have to go as far as the Tesco Express on Aldersgate Street. The day is hard and bright, and sorry now that she hadn't thought to bring Mrs Oak's sunglasses, she squints at the light as she waits to cross over the road into Carthusian Street.

At the far end of the shaded street, she sees a funeral cortège crawling across the T-junction. A glint of black cars: hearse, limo, then several black cabs following after. A musician's funeral, probably, or maybe a conductor's, making a last procession past the Barbican.

On the way back, she goes down Newgate Street to buy envelopes for Mrs Oak. As she comes out of the shop and near to the Old Bailey, she remembers the Guildford Four. Gerry Conlon, the day he made his speech out on the street outside the courts. A fine-looking fella though, he really was. She'd been upset when she'd heard he died a few years ago. Poor man. So strong and powerful that day, in his shirtsleeves, like a young bull coming out to the crowds. He had reminded her of Pip, she recalls now. The hair, the wild eyes Pip sometimes had when hungover. Pip! Christ, but it was a while since she'd let him darken her mind.

She shakes her shoulders, tightens her scarf and pushes on against the chilly breeze. The Old Bailey is quiet today, no crowds, just two plump barristers waddling up the road ahead and a few young smokers sitting on the concrete frames that were built to contain flowers. No flowers now, not at this time of the year. She crosses the road, back into the harsh winter sunshine. A sound emerges from behind the traffic, low and long; it settles into focus as she steps onto the pavement.

It's coming from the church, drifting towards her, a sound that seems to rub against the air – a brass instrument, a trumpet. She stops outside, looking through the railings. It's coming from the Musicians' Chapel. A strange and beautiful sound. She feels as if she may have heard it before. She thinks about going in, but to intrude on a funeral? And besides, she has to get back, fit the bulb and out again, in time to see her ladyship. She waits for the last note to lift and travel through the walls, the railings, and hover over the noise of the traffic. She moves away from the chapel and continues up Snow Hill, her eyes damp and pinned to the ground.

* * *

He brings Max and Lorraine back to the house after the funeral reception. Dragging him out of the taxi and, with the help of Lorraine, getting him up to bed. Max, as pissed as he could possibly be without actually passing out, asks him to stay. 'Don't leave me, Uncle Phil,' he says. 'Stay, ah please, will you stay?'

'Let me walk Lorraine home first,' he says, 'then I'll come back and we'll see how you are.'

Lorraine is also the worse for wear, but nowhere near the same level as Max. He enjoys listening to her rambling on in her soft Scottish accent as they walk along, the fact that she calls him 'Dad' every few minutes, and clings onto his arm like she'll fall down without him. She tells him about her boyfriend, her holiday in Italy, the time she was sent home from a Girl Guiding trip for smoking. In between she throws a few questions at him, one or two of which land like a punch to the gut.

'Did you love him though, Dad, your brother? Will you miss him, do you think?'

'Well, he was my brother. Of course I did. If you'd asked me that question five years ago, I'd have given a different answer, but yes, I'll miss him.'

'What will you do with yourself now? Where will you go? Where *are* you living, by the way? No really, where? You're being cagey enough about it. Can I see it? Why not? Och, it's like talking to a stone, trying to get anything out of you!'

He kisses her on the forehead and watches her walk into the building, then he waits till she's in the lift and again until he sees the light go on upstairs. She comes to the window and sticks her head out.

'Away you, you old perv, before I call the polis.'

He laughs, gives her a wave and goes.

When he comes back up the garden path of Dom's house, Monique is standing at the open door, taking off her shoes and speaking French to a woman who was at the funeral earlier.

He stays in the doorway. 'I just came back to check on Max,' he says.

'Max is all right.'

He turns to go then adds, 'You better put a basin or something on the floor beside him, in case he throws up.'

She curls her mouth as if to say something bitchy, but then seems to change her mind. 'I'll see to it,' she says. '*Bonne nuit*, Philip.'

'Good luck.'

'Oh, Philip,' she calls after him, 'who is that woman – Kim, is that her name?'

'Kim? Oh, she was Dom's girlfriend.'

'His girlfriend? I didn't realise . . .'

'Oh yeah, he was really into her. As a matter of fact, he was thinking of, you know, asking her to marry him. Very sad really. Well, goodnight again.'

He stands in front of Our 'Enry, eating a large bag of crisps.

Out of nowhere he begins to remember the story Dom had told at dinner about the old Irishman he'd brought along to

Monique's little soirée, maybe twenty years ago. Not just the story but the incident itself, which Dom, of course, got arseways.

They had walked through the door half-pissed; the man behind him, unshaven, yellow-toothed. A Dublin man full of his own opinions. Bottles of good French wine laid along the table, platters of canapés, the geometric shapes of cheeses on a board. He can see the man now, his dirty hands and gappy grin, taking in the room before sitting down on a chair upholstered in yellow silk. He poured a whiskey for the man, then went over to the far side of the room to hear what he would come up with.

'Fifty-seven years here, I am. Never lost me accent either. Do you know why? I never speak to the English. No, nor listen to them neither.'

'Well, you're speaking to them now,' a man in a tweed dicky bow had pointed out.

'They hurt me when I come over, treating me like shite, and now they can fuck right off with themselves.'

Dom came over, drew him aside. 'Where did he crawl out of?'

'I met him in the pub.'

'Yeah, well, I gathered that much.'

There had been a girl called Rosie there – a nice girl, as he recalled, a gentle sort.

'Oh, sorry to hear that,' Rosie said, 'but you know we're not all the same.'

'Yes, you are. Superiority – it's bred into you from day one.'

Dom turned his back to the company and whispered through the side of his mouth, 'Get him out of here.'

'Ah, he's harmless. Let him get a bit to eat, I'll bring him then.'

'If you ask me,' the old man was saying now, 'them Muslim youngones are the best of the lot. See that snow last winter? They knocked on me door with a few messages for me. And the boys, too, always very respectful. Not like some of the English yokes that are going now, Jaysus but they'd piss in your ear. Out for themselves.'

Then suddenly he'd turned and looked at Monique. 'You,' he said, 'for example. Have you ever gone out of your way to help anyone in your life?'

'No,' she said, 'I don't suppose I have.'

'See . . .'

'But of course, I'm not English.'

'No? Well you fuckin' should be.'

'I think you should go home now,' Dom said.

'Home? I haven't been home since me mother died.'

In the story Dom told to Max and Jenny, he'd been made out to be a drunken, misguided but big-hearted fool, who had pitied an old man and brought him home, like a boy might bring home a mangy stray dog. But the truth was, he had known the old man would cause ructions, embarrass Dom, spoil Monique's little evening. He knew there would be a row after it, that he could show his disgust for their snobbery and lack of charity by walking out and throwing in his lot with some old man whose name he no longer remembers. That is, if he ever knew it in the first place.

He walks around the room, still thinking about the old man, listening to the sound of his heels on the concrete floor and the crisps crunching between his teeth. When he comes to the window, he stops. He looks up for a second, then puts the bag of crisps down, steps back and looks again. He double-checks to make sure that he is looking at the right building. He is. He is looking at the back of the old pub; he has the right house, he is certain of it. He climbs down off the bench and looks again. The light on the left-hand corner is on. The light on the top landing. It was off last night and now it is on again. He can think of only one explanation for how that could come about.

He brushes the crisp crumbs off his hands, then picking up first his homemade lantern and then his keys, he goes up through the house and out into the street.

In the dark laneway, he stands at the steel gate and listens.

On the other side, a cigarette is being smoked. He can smell it and he can hear the small intake of breath as smoke is being inhaled. He waits, he feels she knows he's there, that she can sense him, the same way he can sense her. He lifts the lamp so that the light shows over the gate. He hears a gasp now, the sound of feet scurrying to move. He raps on the steel door.

He says, 'Milly? Milly, it's okay, it's okay, Milly, it's me.'

18. Milly / Pip

2017

December

THE DAY MRS Oak was transferred to the hospice, Milly was waiting outside. She stood at the entrance in a slant of icy rain, holding the umbrella high over her head, so that when the doors of the ambulance opened, her face would be the first thing Mrs Oak would see.

'There you are, Milly!' Mrs Oak had called out gaily, as the attendant wheeled her down the ramp. Then, throwing a glance over her shoulder, she dismissed him with a 'Thank you, but my girl will take over from here.'

A short while later, she was wheeling Mrs Oak down the corridor to her new room – or 'the Departure Lounge' as she'd insisted on calling it. It was still only November then, but the Christmas decorations were already in place, and at the end of a dimly lit corridor, a poinsettia plant blazed like a small fire in a watchman's brazier. Matt Monro was warbling a carol over the PA system and there was an air of serenity about the place, smiley people saying hello, some of whom seemed way too young, or even too healthy, to die.

When they reached Mrs Oak's room, the door was already

open, a pleasant-faced nurse standing behind it, to welcome them in.

Mrs Oak slowly scanned the room, then she exhaled a weary but satisfied sigh – the sort of sigh she used to give at the end of a busy night, as if to say, 'Well, that went well, but thank God it's over.'

Since then, every day, with the exception of the past three Sundays, she visits Mrs Oak. Mrs Oak hasn't asked why Sunday is no longer a day for visiting, nor has she offered her an explanation.

She comes after breakfast when Mrs Oak is at her best. They chat, sometimes go outside for a turn around the garden. If it's too cold for outdoors and Mrs Oak is in a sociable mood, they might wander around the hospice and mingle with the other residents. If Mrs Oak doesn't fancy that, then they sit at the window and look down at the garden. She is thinner and often in pain. Her bones are frail and her mind goes off on tangents or for long winding rambles back to the past, but at least here, and against all expectation, Mrs Oak seems to have found peace.

She helps with her lunch, then settles her down for her sleep. When her head is on the pillow, Mrs Oak will begin talking. She talks herself round in circles until, eventually, she will have talked herself to sleep. Often, she nods off mid-sentence. Milly knows that, apart from waking for short intervals for her meds or a cup of tea, she will sleep for the rest of the day and on through the night. They have both agreed there is not much point in her hanging around. Just the same, she likes to allow half an hour's grace in case Mrs Oak wakes again.

Milly is standing by the window one afternoon, Mrs Oak soundly sleeping behind her. She is watching an elderly man down in the garden smoke a cigarette. The man has an oxygen prong stuck up his nose and appears to be smoking in slow motion, as if this is a last-request cigarette and he wants every second to count. She is completely absorbed by the man and his smoke, when Mrs Oak's voice breaks into the silence, giving her a start.

'Expecting someone?' she says.

'Me? No!'

'You look like you're waiting for someone. A bloke, maybe?'

'Sure where would I get one of those, Mrs Oak?' she says, brushing it off. At the same time, she has to laugh; Mrs Oak may be on the way out, but there is nothing wrong with her powers of perception. As Trish used to say, she could count the thoughts as they pass through your head.

Outside, Pip is always waiting. Under the same plane tree at the same corner, down the road from the hospice, she will find him.

'Well,' he asks, 'and how was it today?'

'Oh, you know,' Milly says, taking his arm. 'Were you waiting long?'

'Just arrived,' he always says.

As they walk along, they don't say very much; he pats her hand sometimes, and she looks up at his face. She would like to touch it. She would like him to put his arms around her too. But she maintains the distance. They both do. Without saying it, they are letting each other know – we won't have things spoiled by any of that old carry-on.

It takes them two buses to get back to Farringdon with a good walk in between stops. Usually, they take the first bus and walk the rest of the way. While they walk, they sometimes wander off-grid. They have coffee, a bite to eat, and end up wherever they end up. Or they might pick up a takeaway and bring it back to the pub. They never take the tube, even though it would take less than half the time. He suggested it once, and she shook her head, and he never mentioned it again.

There are days, like today, when he takes one look at her face and says, 'Why don't we just have coffee in that place down the road, then go straight back afterwards?'

And she knows this is because he can see how tired she is, worn down and weary from playing handmaid to Mrs Oak's death.

Through the window of the bus, she looks down on the high streets of London villages: trees and shop windows done up to the nines for Christmas. In the reflection of the glass, tiny white lights shift around her head and her face beneath it, pale and still.

Behind her reflection, his profile, thick grey hair, the slope of his nose, the width of his shoulder. Her tired heavy head. It begins to veer towards his shoulder. She pulls it back, leaning her head against the window instead. And she thinks of her hours in Mrs Oak's dying room, what was said and how it made her feel. Later, she will tell him about it – or some of it anyhow – but not now.

Today, it had been all about the funeral. The music, the service; what clothes she'd wear; jewellery, makeup, all that. Her eyebrows! And then the reception afterwards – she'd got herself into a state about that. Fretting over someone called Charlie Clarke and what if he's not available to play at the sing-along later, or if the piano itself is in need of a tuning. 'Because if it's off,' she'd said, wagging a distraught finger, 'Charlie – well, you know what he's like, he'll slap down the lid and walk away. And what sort of a do would that be then? Not even a sing-along to see me off.'

'I will take care of it, Mrs Oak,' she had said, taking her skinny hand for a moment. 'You don't worry about a thing. I will take care of everything.'

He tells her he would like to cook for her this evening, instead of getting a takeaway. He says it shyly, as if he's afraid that she might find it too much, him cooking dinner for her in Mrs Oak's kitchen. She notices, then, the big bag of messages at his feet. She says, 'Oh? Well, yes, thanks – that would be lovely,' and is touched to see how pleased this makes him.

They go upstairs to the kitchen and he sends her in to watch the telly, put her feet up, read her book, whatever.

She gets a fright when the smell of the food reaches her. Then she becomes emotional, although why, she has no idea.

It's just a bit of dinner, she tells herself, what the hell are you crying for – just because someone is making you a bit of dinner?

She gets up and begins tidying around the place, then after a few minutes goes into the loo and washes her face. On the way back out, she stops to watch him. He is making mashed potato, grinding the masher down into the pot. Strong, patient, his serious face. She turns abruptly away and goes back into the sitting room.

At the table, she watches him serve out the dinner. He is both clumsy and cautious. 'This looks great, Pip,' she says and then tells him about Mrs Oak.

'Today,' she says, 'was all about the funeral.'

'The funeral – her funeral?'

'Oh, she has it paid for. Years ago. The burial part of it anyway.'

'She's not being cremated?'

'No.'

She watches him plop the mashed potato down on her plate. Then a tumble of carrots and peas.

'Which would you go for?' she asks him. 'Burial or cremation, I mean?'

'Burial.'

'Why not cremation?'

'I'm afraid of fire.'

'Really?'

'Yes, really,' he says, sticking a fork into a piece of steak and wobbling it towards her plate. 'And someone has to feed the worms.'

Milly smiles. 'Anyway,' she says, 'it's the details she's worried about. What she should wear, what *I* should wear, the reception. She wants smoked salmon and a free bar – she wants to pay for it with her sapphire ring, which I'm supposed to sell. There's a list of people I'm to invite.'

'I'm sure I'm top of it,' he says.

'Oh you are all right,' she laughs.

He sits down, holds out a milk jug filled with gravy and she nods.

'Did you ever hear of someone called Charlie Clarke?' she asks him then.

'The piano player?'

'Yea, that's him.'

'I knew his son, Jamie. Years ago. Why?'

'She wants him to play the piano after the funeral. The thing is – we don't have a piano.'

'You don't have a Charlie either. He's been dead about thirty years.'

'Oh God,' Milly says. 'Poor Mrs Oak.'

'Poor Mrs Oak,' he agrees, raising his glass of milk.

Afterwards, he stays for a while and they watch telly together. He throws his coat over her legs, then sits on the far end of the sofa.

When it's time for her bedtime smoke, he goes out to the yard with her.

'You can have your nightcap, you know,' he says. 'I won't start banging me head off the wall or anything.'

'It's just a habit, really, something to mark the end of the day. Anyway, I have a new habit now.'

'What's that?' he asks and she almost says, 'You.'

'A smoke, a cup of tea,' she smiles, 'and I'm happy out.'

When she's finished her fag, he puts his cup down on the top of the silver barrel. 'Well, better be off so.'

She unlocks the back gate; he picks up the plastic container from the side of the door. He kisses her on the cheek. 'Will I see you tomorrow?'

'If you want, yea.'

'Usual time – around two?' he says, then switches on his mad little lamp. She steps out and watches the soft white blob of light disappear up the lane.

On Saturday mornings, Trish always phones from Marbella to see how Mrs Oak is doing. Then they chat for a while.

'The weather here, Mill, I swear. I have to keep reminding myself it's winter. I mean, I'm looking out at the sea and I'm blinded by diamonds. You should come over after, you know, after – when it's all over, I mean.'

'I'll have to get a job, Trish, then find somewhere to live. I won't have much time for holidays, I'm afraid.'

'No, I mean for good. There's plenty of bar work round here. You'd get a job. Fred would see to it – he knows them all over here. Oh, it would be nice to have the company too. He's not much of a one for chit-chat, and otherwise, it's his sisters and their kids yakking on about whatever it is that Spaniards yak on about.'

'I couldn't, Trish.'

'You got something better lined up then?'

'I just can't see myself leaving London.'

'Oh well, if you won't leave London . . . Still, the offer's there. I can lend you the fare, a few quid till you're sorted. So, what else is new then?'

'They started work on another new office block on Albion Place.'

'Oh yeah?'

'And Pip has resurfaced.'

'Get off! When did this happen?'

'A couple of weeks ago.'

'You never said, you sly old thing.'

'It's not like that. He's been a great help – a good friend. And that's all I want.'

'Just good friends, eh? Let's see how long that lasts then.'

'Ah, we're too old for all that other nonsense.'

'Just the same.'

'Just the same what, Trish?'

'You mind yourself, miss, you hear me?'

On Sundays, they walk through the parks: Hyde Park, Green Park, St James's. They come back to Farringdon along the Strand and down by the river and then he goes off to meet Lorraine. She wonders if he remembers the night, their first night together, when he carried the sandals across the bridge and up the hill. Or the time they stood on the landing stage at the opposite side of the river, the day before his father's funeral, and he lied through his teeth at her? She doesn't remind him. They don't talk much about the past, not if they can help it. They stick to the present. And as for the future – they certainly won't be going anywhere near that.

The first Sunday, he asks her if she'd like to join him and Lorraine for dinner in some place over in Bayswater. She says,

'Thanks, Pip, but this is your time with Lorraine. I'll give it a skip.'

The second Sunday he asks her again, and again she says no.

The third Sunday, he says, 'Max is coming,' before quickly adding, 'I'd like you to come, Milly, I think you'd enjoy it.'

She opens her mouth to say no, but at the last second finds herself saying: 'Yea, okay, why not.'

They are the first to arrive. While they wait, she looks around the room. There's a bar that takes up most of the side wall and empty tables in the middle. The few diners are seated around the other side of the room and all of them are solitary. A man here; another man there. One of the men gets up, counts out a few notes, pins them under the salt cellar and walks slowly to the top of the room. At the coat stand, he shifts himself into his overcoat, then pulls a cap out of his pocket and settles it onto his head. When he leaves, the draught curtains over the alcove give a little billow. A woman about her own age eats with her back to the room.

And that's where I should be, she thinks, tucked into a corner, eating on my own. Or gone through the curtains and out the front door, back to the sitting room for a plastic cheese sandwich and an episode of *Morse* on one of Mrs Oak's old DVDs.

He is quiet and she can see that he's nervous; his hands fidgeting with the menu, his eyes darting around. She wonders if this is something that happens to him when surrounded by drink or faced with an occasion where drink will be laid out on the table.

She says, 'I think it's very nice of you, by the way, asking me along to eat with your family.'

He looks at her, puzzled.

'What? What did I say?'

'Nothing,' he says and then rises to his feet as a woman in her thirties and a lanky young man, both with long black curly hair, pop out from the curtains and come smiling across the floor.

'Family,' she thinks. It's the word family. He's only just realised what it means.

He stops being nervous as soon as Lorraine and Max sit down. After that, it becomes a bright, chaotic table. In the middle of all the passing of plates, the laughing and joking, the telling of stories, she feels the absence of Flora. What would it be like, she wonders, to have her sitting here, a part of this little group? It's like a burning in her stomach, this longing for a thirty-seven-year-old woman she's never really met. But then Max says something or Lorraine says something or Pip catches her eye, and she is pulled back to the table.

They say goodbye out on the street. Max gives her a hug and Lorraine a kiss on the cheek.

Max says to Pip, 'Sure you don't want to come back to the house? Your old room is waiting . . .'

'No, I better get this youngone home,' he says and then, to her embarrassment, Max and Lorraine start whooping and cheering.

'And don't forget to make an appointment to see the solicitor, Uncle Phil,' Max says then. 'And you still okay about helping me go through Dad's things?'

'Of course. You just let me know when you feel up to it.'

'You could maybe stay a couple of days.'

'Yeah, well, we'll see.'

'And don't forget that other thing either.'

'What other thing?'

'What other thing,' he says. 'What other thing? Christmas, of course!'

'Oh yes, that.'

On the way home, she asks him why he needs to go to the solicitor.

'I don't know actually; something to do with Dom's will, probably.'

'Do you think he left you something?'

'No. He didn't have anything other than the house, and that's for Max. Maybe he's asked me to be executor. He was on about something before he died, so I imagine it's some sort of trust for Max. Although I'd be surprised if he entrusted me with anything like that.'

He points out the road where he lived as a child. Then he points back to the school he used to go to before his mother died. She would like to see them up close – the house, the school – she tells him.

'Yeah,' he says, 'sure. Sometime, but not now.'

Then he asks her if she'd mind if they took the tube back – 'I know you don't like the tube,' he says, 'but it's a direct line, no walking under the ground.'

'Of course.'

For the rest of the journey, she does most of the talking, asking him questions about Max, about Lorraine, about Dom. Discussing the food in the restaurant, the Brexit situation, Trish in Marbella. Anything and everything that comes into her head. Filling the air up with the sound of her voice.

But it will not be drowned out. It hangs, heavy and awkward between them: the Christmas word.

It's a relief when he finally puts it to her, a few days later when they're walking home from the hospice. 'Did I tell you, Lorraine is going to meet the boyfriend's family in Hampshire for Christmas. Then they're coming to London for a few days.'

'So you'll meet him?'

'Looks like it. I think they want to get married.'

'How do you feel about that?'

'I don't know yet. I mean, even if he's the greatest shit in the world, I can hardly say anything, can I?'

'No, you can't. But I'm sure he won't be.'

'Look,' he begins and then stops on the street. She looks at him, waiting.

'Max has asked me to spend Christmas Day with him and we were wondering . . . Well, we were wondering if you'd like to join us. We'd cook, of course. He has friends that have invited him to stay and his mother wants him to go to Paris, but he doesn't want any of that. He wants to keep it low-key and stay at home. He's in mourning, of course, even if he doesn't realise it. Anyway, it's another ten days or so; no rush deciding, but we were just wondering, like . . .'

'Oh right. Well, that's very nice of you. But I don't think so, Pip.'

'What will you do?'

'I'll pop up to see her ladyship. I'll be fine.'

'Would you not stop by afterwards? We won't eat till the afternoon.'

'No. Thanks all the same.'

'It would mean a lot to me and Max, two old bachelors, no one to show off in front of. Go on, it'll be good.'

'I'm sure it would be lovely. But I'm not really into Christmas. Never was. I'd prefer to keep it downbeat. I used to make a bit of an effort for Mrs Oak and that. Marks and Sparks readymade, and the Queen's speech. And Matthew – he used to go the whole hog.'

'And you didn't enjoy that?'

464

'Not really. I found it, well . . . a bit forced. The two of us sitting in a posh restaurant somewhere – or worse, at home: well, isn't this nice! Well, isn't that nice! I couldn't wait for it to be all over, actually, and by the time it *was* all over, I used to nearly hate him.'

He laughs. 'There must have been something you liked about him?'

'Matthew? Oh yea. There was plenty. I just can't remember anything now. Except his shirts. I do know I liked his shirts.'

'His shirts?'

'Yea, I have a thing about men in white shirts.'

'Have you now?'

'Do you remember when the pub became a fashionable spot for a while for the City boys? Summer evenings, they'd come down in white shirts, those skinny ties.'

'I can't say I noticed, no.'

'People used to slag them off, but I thought it looked quite attractive. Romantic, you know? Oh shut up you, laughing at me. What about you and your Rod Stewart syndrome?'

'My what?'

'That's what Trish used to call it. Look at him, she'd say, he's like Rod Stewart – one after the other, every girlfriend looks the bloody same.'

'You mean it *wasn't* the same girl?' he says. 'No wonder I used to get confused.'

For the next few days, when Milly arrives, Mrs Oak is still in the bed and showing no interest in getting out of it.

On the third day, Milly tries to persuade her: 'We could have a wheel about the place, see who's around, maybe have coffee with some of the others?'

'I can't be bothered with that lot. Like a load of big children, that's what they are. Infantilised. Know what happened on Sunday? This fool comes round dressed as Father Christmas, lumps of cotton wool dangling from his chin. Do you think I'm stupid or what? I says to him, this is a private room, now kindly hop it, and take your rotten bath salts or whatever that is with you. The others, that lot out there, they loved him, they did. Ooh, I've been a good girl, I swear I have. What are you grinning at, Milly – what's so funny?'

'I'm just happy to see you're still well able to give out stink.'

'Yeah, well,' she smiles, then, 'I liked it best when there was just the two of us, Milly.'

'Are you in pain?'

'No more than usual.'

'Would you sit by the window then? I've brought your chocolate.'

'All right then, let's do that. Pick us out a nice cardie, the pink – might take that ashen look off my face, eh?'

Milly helps her into the chair, cloaks the cardigan around her shoulders and wheels her to the window. 'I don't feel like the chocolate today, Milly. Do you have a boiled sweet?'

They sit together sucking boiled sweets and looking out at the winter garden. Mrs Oak takes a ramble back to the past. Her childhood in Hoxton, her brother who died in the war, the air-raid warnings howling all over the city. She speaks about the early days when she first took over the pub, recalling people and shops that mean nothing to Milly.

'That bloke Trish went off with.'

'Fred – did you know he was Spanish?'

'Ferdinand, you mean. Oh yeah, Fred's just the English version. His mother was the Spanish one, she came over during the Spanish Civil War. There's a story attached to them, can't

466

remember it now. There's a story attached to everyone, isn't there? Otherwise, we'd all be cut-out dolls.'

'Would you like some water?'

'Is it time for my pills yet?'

'Not yet.'

'His father was very good-looking.'

'Whose father?'

'Fred's, Milly. Fred's. Don't know what happened to poor Fred. They had a shop on Saffron Hill. Lived over it.'

'It's still there. Fred lets it out.'

'Good old Trish. But what's she doing in Marbella?'

'His family is from there.'

'I didn't think they had real Spanish people living in those sorts of places,' she laughs.

She falls silent for a while and then says: 'I met him at a dance, you know, my Terry. First proper dance I was ever at. And I was only allowed to go because my sister and her fella said they'd watch me. I was eighteen years old – same age as you when you came to me first. I'll never forget the sight of Terry pushing his way across the dance floor to get to me. I only agreed to get up with him to give the rest of the girls a giggle. But what a good dancer he turned out to be, for a man his size, flipping me around like I was a pancake. He left me some diamonds, you know. Five little diamonds in a black pouch. That's how I paid for the nursing home. Don't go telling anyone that – or do, if you want. What difference does it make? I'll be dead and buried.'

She winces as though a pain has just hit her.

'Are you all right, Mrs Oak? Do you want me to call the nurse?'

'I'm okay.'

'You sure?'

'Yeah. What time is it anyway?'

'Just gone eleven.'

'Is that all? You mean eleven in the morning? Oh God. Do you know, I think I might take a little nap?'

She puts her back into the bed and settles her down.

'You know, straight off, I knew Terry had something,' she says. 'He had a bit of go in him. When I was young, I was always looking to the future – after the war, I suppose – and the things I used to see! I knew we would build something together, and I mean, look at our beautiful pub – still standing, mind you. Still standing,' she repeats, lifting a knobbly, defiant fist.

'You always know from the start, don't you, Milly?'

'Do you?'

'Yes, you do. You know you do.'

Mrs Oak closes her eyes; a few tears begin to roll down the side of her face.

'What's the matter? Are you all right?'

'Nothing really. It's just, well, I still feel bad, about what happened between him and me. I didn't do it to hurt you, I hope you know that. I just lost my head for a while. I mean, you miss having a man around the place, don't you? Not just in bed, but someone to sit at a table with, go places. Have you forgiven me?'

'Of course.'

'You sure, Milly? I need to know.'

'Yes, absolutely.'

Mrs Oak gives a little sigh and turns her head into the pillow. 'I shan't be sorry to go, you know,' she says.

'Oh please, don't talk like that now, please.'

'No really, I mean it. I'm ready, I am. Looking forward to a nice long lie-in. I'm sorry I couldn't look after you better.' She opens her eyes again. 'I'm sorry I turned into such a selfish, stubborn old woman.'

'It's all right, Mrs Oak, I'll manage.'

'Course you will. We've always managed, haven't we, Milly?'

She nods.

'Go on then, give us one of those nice Irish smiles. That's it. That's my girl. You're like a daughter to me, you know that?'

* * *

He feels a sort of anguish sometimes, walking beside her, knowing that he can't tell her how he feels, even if he could find the courage to do so. Nor can he risk telling her how sorry he is for all the times in the past when he let her down. The years – because if you put it together that's what it would surely amount to – of turning up, then disappearing again; feeling so close to her that he'd had to back away. Time and time again, blowing hot and cold, so that she never knew how she stood with him.

And yet, he had always thought she must have known how he felt about her. Even if they couldn't be together, for whatever reason – he was married to Angie or was with someone else or too busy drinking. She was going out with some bloke, or they had decided it was better to just be friends. He would feel her watching him from the far side of the counter; she would turn and catch him looking at her through the mirror. Or even – and not to put too sloppy a point on it, fuck it – when he kissed her. She must have known then.

He comes along Leather Lane, fish and chips bundled under his coat, burning one side of his belly. He pushes past commuters, legal and general, scurrying towards Chancery Lane. He veers around groups coming from Christmas parties going on some-where else: girls with light dresses hanging off them, blokes with no jackets, drunk and blissfully unaware that they are staggering through one of the coldest nights of the year.

And he asks himself – what's wrong with seeing her every day? Talking to her, eating chips with her, having her walk beside you holding your arm? Ask for more and you risk losing the lot.

But he wants to protect her; he wants to look after her; he wants to tell her he loves her. He wants all the stupid old-fashioned strings that tie a man and a woman together. But he is not much of a man now at sixty years of age, living in a cave, barely enough money to get by. It's not that he'd be difficult to resist. Even so, he can't seem to stop himself hoping.

He gets to the top of the lane, pulls out his phone and presses send on the text he's already written.

Just there.

Her text comes back:

OK.

The lane so dark, he has to take out the torch. Keeping the beam low, he follows it across the broken concrete and bits of stray rubble.

He knows they are pooling their grief. His for Dom, hers for Mrs Oak – even if Mrs Oak is still hanging on. When she goes, everything will change. Milly has already told him: 'I can't leave this house while there's a breath left in her; but when she goes, I won't be able to bear staying a minute longer than I have to.'

And then what? He'll move out of his cave and back to Notting Hill until Max sells the house. And Milly? She'll call him one day to tell him that she's found a job in a bar outside Swansea or somewhere: eight quid an hour and all the jam you can eat.

In the silence of the deserted laneway, he hears the low clink of the padlock and chain. He feels the first splatter of rain on his face. The gate peeps open, and there she is.

She doesn't notice the rain, she's so delighted with the chips.

'Oh thanks, Pip! It's just what I need. Quick now, before they get cold.'

They step into the porch and she pulls the bolt over.

I could say it now, he thinks. I could just come out and say it.

But she opens his coat and takes the bag from him, mutters something about the plates being warmed in the oven as she turns away from him, briskly moves along the hallway and begins to trot up the stairs.

Later, when they come back down for her goodnight cigarette, the rain is pelting down. Rain and hail. They can hear it crashing off the glass roof of the porch and bouncing off the top of the steel barrels outside.

'I'm not going out to smoke in that,' she says.

'Smoke it here, Milly, what difference does it make?'

He sees her hesitate, then nod. She lights her smoke and they stand in the light of her torch, the smoke straying every now and then from her mouth to his face. She fans it away from him with her hand.

'It's okay,' he says.

'You don't mind?'

'I don't mind anything you do, Milly.'

She looks at him for a second then quickly turns away.

After a moment she says, 'God, it's a desperate night. You should stay. It won't take me a minute to make up the bed in Trish's room. Seriously, Pip, is it not better than catching your end in that damp cellar on your little skimpy bed?'

'How do you know what sort of bed I sleep in?'

She gives an embarrassed little laugh. 'I looked in the window and saw it sticking out from behind the boxing ring.'

'Oh, so you were spying on me, were you?'

'No! I was looking for you – if that's all right? You could move into Notting Hill, couldn't you? Has Max not asked you?'

'I could, and yes he has. I'd prefer to stay here.'

'Why, for God's sake?'

'I want . . .'

'What?'

'I want to be near you.'

There is nothing then until he hears himself say, 'I must have moved it, the bed, when I was cleaning, and forgot to push it back into place.'

He shuffles beside her for a bit and then comes out with it: 'If I stay, there's only one bed I want to sleep in.'

She says nothing.

When her smoke is finished, she pushes the bolt and opens the door. Then she flicks her cigarette end out into the yard. 'Don't start that shite now,' she says.

'I'm not starting any shite. I'm just trying to be honest.'

'Well don't bother!' she snaps. 'I don't want your honesty. You can stuff it.'

'Sorry, I know. I know how you feel.'

'Oh do you now? Well, that's a first. Do you not think I have enough going on just now? Quite enough without you . . .'

'I'm only telling you what I'd like to happen – what I *hope* will happen.'

'Don't waste your hope on me. I'm not going back there. I don't want it. If you can't keep it as friends, then forget it.'

'Why can't we be both?'

'Do you have to do this now?'

'What do you mean?'

'Try to make it more than it is; trying to make it like—'

'Like what – love?'

'Don't say that word to me. Don't you fucking dare say that word to me.'

'Milly, please just listen to me.'

'No. I won't be manipulated by you. I won't! Making me go to dinner with your family, asking me to spend Christmas . . . I don't want to be the adopted aunty. Or your temporary plus-one for family events. Standing on the outside looking in. I don't want that. And anyway, what happens next year, Pip, when you decide to make off again? What about the year after? I don't want something that I can't have for more than five minutes.'

'Milly,' he says, 'will you stop and calm down. There's no need to be so upset. I'm sorry. I am. I'm sorry.'

'Yes, well, all right,' she says, her head jerking around like a chicken.

He puts his hand on her arm. 'If you married me, it would be permanent.'

She looks horrified, then with a hard laugh says, 'No thanks all the same and very good of you to offer, I'm sure. But you're, you know, just a little bit late. Say around thirty years too late? I'm different now. After all I've been through, I'm not the stupid little . . . Look, you better go now.'

He goes out into the yard, pulls his lamp up from behind the barrel where he's left it and with his sleeve tries to dry the rain from it, the hail pebble-dashing his face and hands. He feels shaken and a bit nauseous because he knows what she's going to say next.

'Listen, maybe you should just stop coming here for a while.'

'Is that what you want, Milly – really?'

'Let's just leave it for a bit, okay?'

She pushes the gate into the lane and steps back, making room for him to pass. He walks out and straight into a puddle.

He can feel her watching him as he walks down the lane.

Then her voice comes hurling after him: 'Fuck you anyway, Pip. Just fuck you.'

He turns and sees her there, standing in her slippers, the rain bending to the shape of her body. 'Go inside,' he shouts back at her, 'before you catch pneumonia.'

Then, the loud clanging sound as the gate smashes shut.

PART EIGHT

19. Pip / Milly

2017

December

HE DECIDES TO stay with Max for a couple of days while they go through Dom's things. The first day, they blunder about from his study to his music room with no plan and little progress, until it occurs to Max that they should probably call on Sheila to help with the work-related effects. Within a few hours, Sheila is in situ and has divided Dom's life into three stacks. Music, finance and personal, while sniffling her way through a box of tissues. She insists Max remains in the room with her at all times. 'There are things that would be appreciated by various academies,' she says, 'but once they go in, they won't come out, so I need you to be certain you're happy to let them go, Max.'

He makes himself useful meanwhile, making tea and coffee and going around the house, gathering items for Sheila's stacks. She reminds him of the Irish nurse in the clinic, the all-knowing efficiency of the woman. 'Now, Phil, if you come across anything financial – bills, receipts or letters from people in the music world – you're to bring them straight down to me.'

'And what about the stuff in his bedroom?' he asks. 'His clothes and whatever?'

'Oh, that's *personal* personal,' Sheila says, 'and nothing to do with me. You two can take care of that.'

Max puts his hands over his face. When he takes them away again, he looks distraught.

'It's okay, Max,' he says, 'I'll do it. I'll start on his bedroom in the morning.'

They stay at it for most of the day and on into the evening. Sheila goes home around nine o'clock. They order a Chinese takeaway, which they slurp away at without much conversation, before falling upstairs to bed.

He lies on his old bed and looks at the night sky through the Velux window. Scraps of black through raggy clouds, the lights of the city drowning out the stars. He remembers school at this time of the year, the stars bristling against a blue-black canvas and the names that used to fill up his head then. Betelgeuse and Rigel, Castor and Pollux. Cassiopeia dancing to fiddle music from a poem they'd read in class. The things he used to know then, about stars, about nature.

He knew the shape of the countries of Africa, the names of their rivers. He could draw a map of the section of night sky that showed through the big dormitory window over his bed: pathways and canals, the various constellations. Now, he knows nothing much about anything.

He sends Milly another message.

Just checking to see how you are?

Then he looks at his previous message sent earlier today, and as yet ignored.

Staying with Max for a couple of days, if you need me for
anything just shout – P.

He stares at the phone for a minute then begins to write.

Milly, I'm sorry. I should have kept my feelings to myself.
I love you. I always have.

He gets a fright when he sees the message he's just written. He pulls his hand away from the phone. Then he brings his index finger back and quickly deletes it.

He has to leave Dom's bedroom a number of times, take a walk around the garden; sometimes he goes out and walks to the end of the road. Then he goes back and faces into it again. It's a strange sort of intimacy – on a par with the intimacy they had as boys. The smell of Dom's shoes when he opens the wardrobe door; his dirty clothes in the laundry basket. His sheets.

He finds a photograph taken when they were kids, the day he started primary school in Bayswater. The little fat face on him, grinning ear to ear, completely thrilled at the prospect of big-boy school. And Dom, leaner and taller, smiling in a forced and defiant way, as if he wants the world to know how much he resents being told to say 'cheese'.

On top of the wardrobe, he comes across a large manila envelope. He turns it upside down and various papers slide onto the bed. Two school reports from Dom's school in Hertfordshire. One when he was fourteen years old, not long after he started there.

Disappointing start. Hope he may settle in better in the

coming term. Needs to apply himself and make more of an effort socially, as well as in the classroom.

The second report is from Dom's final year and glows from start to finish.

We expect great things from our former star pupil!

There are a number of letters which, apart from the date and signature, he doesn't read. Four of these are love letters from Marj from both before and in the early years of their marriage. And then, to his shock, he finds the press cuttings from his boxing days that used to be in his father's cardboard box.

In these couple of days, he gets to know his brother. In some ways he learns more about him than he would have done had he lived for another twenty years. He now knows he bought Christmas cards from a charity for the disabled and that he donated money to a donkey sanctuary in the Hebrides. He knows that he was nervous about lectures he had to give, writing last-minute notes before he went to sleep, crossing them out, writing them again. Most of the notes seemed to be directions to himself. Pause here. Look around here. Give example here. In the margins several NB marks, a red line leading back to his text. Listen to Sinatra breathing (play example). Long tone exercises (example). Slurs and single tonguing exercises (wait for sniggering to stop before continuing).

There are only two books in his room, both well thumbed: *Song and Wind* and *Secret of Technique Preservation*.

Finally, he finds an envelope with an old Irish stamp on it. Inside is a birthday card he sent to Dom for his fourteenth birthday with a picture of a burly footballer on the front, although he can't remember ever seeing Dom kick a ball in his life.

Inside, a corny-card verse:

> *To my dear brother, there is no other,*
> *you will always be my friend,*
> *until the very end.*

Underneath are two careful words written in fountain-pen ink: *From Phil.*

When he comes out the front door, he finds Max sitting on the steps, smoking.

'We know now why he didn't take up the position in the States,' Max says over his shoulder.

'What position?'

'He was offered a gig for a year in a college over there – didn't he say?'

'He mentioned that there'd been something in the pipeline, but that it fell through.'

'Yeah, because he failed the medical. Poor old sod knew he was in trouble.'

He sits down beside Max, pats him on the leg. 'It'll get better,' he says.

'Will it?'

'Yes, son, it will.'

'You'll let me know how you get on with the solicitor?'

'I will. Before I forget, I've left two wedding rings and three watches in a box on his bedside locker. Oh, and a really good pen you might like for college. Look at them when you feel up to it. I've got his clothes ready for the charity shop. No point in sending his shoes, I'll have to throw them out.'

Max gives a short laugh. 'God, his shoes. How did he get them into that state – I mean, it's not as if he walked all that far?'

'I have no idea. There's a load of stuff to bin, I can do that tomorrow. I'm going to a meeting.'

'Really?'

He laughs. 'Yeah, afraid so. I can come back and stay tonight if you want.'

'Why don't you just stay? Move back in. Save yourself the rent.'

'I'm not paying rent.'

'You're living with Milly, then?'

'No, unfortunately not. I'm living near her.'

'Why haven't you moved in with her?'

'Well, she's sort of squatting – that's one reason.'

'Squatting!' Max starts to laugh. 'You two, you're like wayward teenagers or something. She could always move in here with you? I'm off after Christmas to Devon, then back at college. I won't be back here till mid-March. You can keep an eye on the place.'

'It's not like that between us.'

'No? You could have fooled me.'

'Anyway, I'll see you later.'

He puts his hand on Max's shoulder and pulls himself back onto his feet.

'I treated her badly over the years, Max. And now she doesn't want to know.'

'Can't you make it up to her?'

'It's no use. Believe me.'

'You could try, though?'

'See you later, Max.'

He's at the gate when Max comes after him.

'I was hoping you'd come and see the bank manager with me. I've made an appointment, a week from today – the nineteenth?'

'About selling the house?'

'Well, that's the thing, Uncle Phil, I don't want to sell it. I love this house and, come on, if I sell it, well, I'd have way too much money even after I paid off the mortgage. Can you imagine how I'd fuck myself up with all that cash at my fingertips?'

'How much is left on the mortgage?'

'A bit. But there's insurance, too. Sheila reckons when all is settled there'd be a mortgage of about five hundred k.'

'And how do you propose to pay it?'

'I'd have to earn some money, then, wouldn't I?'

'You don't want to jack in college, surely?'

'Oh no, I like it there. I intend going the whole hog – master's, the lot. I was thinking of getting the house to earn money for me – do you see what I mean? And that's where you come in, Uncle Phil.'

It seems strange to think of all the times he has passed by this solicitor's office, and somewhere up there, in a small panelled room smelling of dust and old paper, in the back of a green dented filing cabinet, a document with his name on it has been sitting for over twenty years.

It takes him a while to get his head around it.

'So you're *not* Dom's solicitor?'

'No, Bea Adams is his solicitor; we are acting for your father.'

'My father?'

'Mr John Xavier Dawson.'

'Yes, that's him.'

The solicitor is tall, thin, pale as milk. He looks out at him from dark, bewildered eyes. He is also the first official he's come across in a long time who appears to be older than he is.

'And how does my brother come into this again?' he asks him.

'He was the executor of your father's will. The custodian, if you like.'

'And this is not about Max?'

'No, Mr Dawson. Max is the beneficiary of your brother's will and he will deal with your brother's solicitors. As I said, we act for your late father. You are what's known as a discretionary beneficiary. Would you like me to go through it again?'

'If you don't mind.'

'Really, it's nothing to worry about. Your father wanted to leave you a sum of money when he died back in 1995. He wanted it to be equal to the amount he left your brother. May I be candid?'

'Please. Be as candid as you like.'

'At the time of his last will, your father had reservations about the wisdom of leaving you with a sum of money. He felt it could hinder rather than help you.'

'And he would have been right there.'

'He made your brother custodian of this money until he deemed the time to be right, or until your brother himself was deceased. As it happens, both events occurred. Your brother had given us an order to release the funds a week before he passed away.'

'Oh. Oh right. Oh well now. I don't know what to say.'

'Would you like to know the amount?'

'Yes, I suppose.'

'The net sum is ninety thousand pounds.'

'You're fucking joking me? Sorry, excuse me. It's just the . . . well, the shock.'

'That's quite all right,' the solicitor smiles. 'All you really need to know now is that I am authorised to sign that sum over to you today. Would you like me to transfer it to your account, or would you prefer a cheque?'

'I don't know. I don't know. I just . . . Could I come back in an hour? Let you know then?'

'Of course – or you could give me a call.'

He stands up, puts his coat on and walks to the door. Then he turns round and comes back to the desk.

'Actually, I don't need an hour. I know what I want to do.'

He takes off his coat again and sits back down.

'Can I have it in more than one cheque? You know, split the amounts?'

'You can have it any way you want.'

'Good, that's good.'

He can hear the shake in his voice. He thinks he would probably be better going out to the jacks for a few minutes, pulling himself together. At the same time, he's worried that if he takes his eye off this lean lanky streak he'll disappear into thin air.

'I'd like a cheque made out to Lorraine Dawson – she's my, you know, my daughter.'

'Very well.'

'Yes, so that's forty thousand pounds to my daughter, Lorraine Dawson.'

'Yes . . . and?'

'Ten thousand to myself.'

'Ten thousand?'

'That's right.'

'And the rest?'

'The rest to Millicent Edwards.'

'So, that's forty thousand to Millicent Edwards, forty thousand to Lorraine Dawson and ten thousand to yourself. Is that correct? And you are certain about this? You don't need a little more time to think it over?'

'Not another second.'

* * *

A week before Christmas she arrives at the hospice to find Mrs Oak has bounced back. She's sitting up in bed grinning all over her face. 'I'm on steroids!' she yells as Milly walks in the door. 'They pump them into you to give you a blast of energy. Wish I'd known about them before. I'm on a right buzz, feel I could dance all night, I could. Had my hair done and all, and my nails – what do you think?' She tilts her head and holds her hands out to show.

She has that handbag with her, the one she bought years ago in Malta when she went with the bridge club ladies. The pudgy brown leather with the dark pink lining that always makes Milly think of a big gummy mouth whenever she opens it.

She pats the bed for Milly to sit down beside her. Then, lowering her voice, she looks from side to side. 'The minute I snuff it,' she says, 'you take this with you, don't let anybody stop you – you hear me now?'

'I told you before, Mrs Oak, I don't want to take it. They'll think I'm stealing it on you.'

'Course they won't, silly girl!' she said. 'But just to keep you happy, I've put a letter in there, giving my permission. It says, "I, Dora Oak, wish Millicent Edwards to have this bag and all its contents." Milly, all that I own is in that bag. Soon as I go, promise you'll take it.'

She grips Milly's sleeve. 'Promise me. You have to promise.'

'Yes, all right, I promise.'

'There's a few quid, a couple of bits of jewellery – should fetch a bit, though far from enough, my love. I'm sorry. But it should be a bit of a help. I'll keep the pearl earrings just so I look nice. And don't forget my eyebrows! I don't want people looking at me in the box with these skimpy things on display.'

Every day since they had the row, she checks her phone as

soon as she leaves Mrs Oak's room. She reads his message walking down the corridor and, even though she has no intention of sending a reply, finds a degree of comfort in it. When she gets outside and crosses the road, she finds herself checking the vacant space under the tree on the corner where, for the previous few weeks, he has stood in all weathers, waiting for her.

On Thursday afternoon, her screen is blank. She remembers him saying something about the solicitor and thinks that's probably where he is now. Either that or he's left his phone down somewhere. Then she thinks: what do I care? What do I care if I never hear from him again?

The next day, she finds herself checking the phone while she's still in the room, slipping it into the pocket of her jeans and pretending she needs to use the bathroom in case Mrs Oak cops what's she's at. The screen is still blank.

And now she is beginning to feel it; the slight gnawing in her stomach, that loneliness that only he made her feel.

Fuck him anyway, she thinks.

She is coming out of the hospice on Saturday afternoon when the receptionist calls her back to the desk.

'A man left this for you,' she says, handing her an A5 envelope. 'He wouldn't hear of me disturbing you. Nor would he give me his name.'

'It's all right, thanks. I recognise the handwriting.'

She doesn't open the envelope until she gets onto the second bus. Inside she finds two smaller envelopes and a folded note.

Milly – if you wouldn't mind reading the letter in the brown envelope first. It was written when I was in the clinic and I meant to give it to you months ago. The other contains

487

*a cheque. I've come into a bit of money from my father's
estate and I want you to have this. I hope it will help you
get back on your feet. It's my way of asking for forgiveness,
so please accept it, even if you never want to see me again
– Pip.*

She immediately phones him. 'What's this nonsense about?'

'Did you read the letter?'

'No, I haven't opened the envelopes.'

'Why not?'

'I don't want to.'

'Look, my father left me ninety grand.'

'*What?*'

'Yeah, I know. And I want to give you a few quid.'

'I don't want your few quid.'

'You need it, Milly. I've given forty grand to Lorraine and forty
to you.'

'Forty? You mean forty—'

'Just take it. Don't give me a hard time now.'

'I'm not taking forty grand off you!'

'Milly, I owe you money from over the years, all the times
you—'

'Not that much!'

'I owe you so much more than money. I really . . . I mean, it
would make me happy if you'd just take it.'

'Maybe I don't feel like making you happy – ever consider
that?'

'Oh, now you're just being childish.'

'You can stick your forty thousand quid up your arse as far as
I'm concerned.'

Then she cuts off the call.

The bus is packed with Christmas shoppers, standing, seated, swaying and jolting to the movement of the bus. She feels squeezed in by the large man sitting legs spread beside her; trapped by the push of tired bodies in the aisle and at the space just beside the stairwell. All listening to her conversation (*I'm not taking forty grand off you – you can stick it up your arse!*). Even her ears feel as if they're blushing, she's that embarrassed. She decides to get off at Rosebery Avenue and walk the rest of the way.

She comes through the porch and into the bar, takes off her wet coat, shakes it out and hangs it over a stool. Then she pushes herself out a Scotch, lights a cigarette and begins to read Pip's letter by the light of the box torch. She takes it upstairs then and reads it again in the sitting room.

Staring into the black screen of the television set, she finishes her drink. In its reflection she looks like a spectre trying to make contact from beyond the grave.

After a while, she gets up, takes out her phone, goes into the kitchen and calls Trish.

'She hasn't gone, Milly?' Trish says.

'No, not yet. She's been in great form for the past two days actually.'

'Steroids?'

'That's right.'

'Yeah, they do that. Gives them a last blast of energy before they kick off. How long are they saying?'

'A few days.'

'By Christmas Day?'

'She'll go before then, I'd say.'

'Aww, Milly, the end of an era, eh? Is he still around, that Phil?'

'Oh don't talk to me about him.'

'What's he done now? Drinking again, is he?'

'He's trying to give me forty thousand quid.'

'Forty thousand what? He's definitely drinking again.'

'No, it exists all right.'

'His brother, was it?'

'No, his father's estate, I think.'

'Oh my God! So what strings are attached?'

'No strings, it would seem. But it doesn't matter, I'm not taking it.'

'You bloody are!'

'No I'm not. I mean, for Christ's sake, you can't just go taking forty grand off someone you're not even . . . you know . . . with. Or anything.'

'Oh, I see. You mean you'd like there to be a few attached strings – is that it?'

'Shut up, Trish.'

'Has he stayed off the drink?'

'Almost a year.'

'So how much did his old man leave, then?'

'Ninety. He took ten for himself and split the rest between me and Lorraine.'

'His daughter Lorraine? Well, that's not bad. It does show he wants to make amends.'

'But I could never be sure of a man like him – could I?'

'You can never be sure of any man, if it comes to it.'

'I want to be independent. Mrs Oak left me with nothing. Nothing! After all these years. A few rings in the end of her hand-bag . . .'

'They'll fetch you something, Milly. And with the forty grand, you won't be too badly off.'

'Yea, but it's not *my* forty grand. Anyway, why are you sticking up for him all of a sudden? You think he's a womanising, useless drunken bastard. How many times have you said that to me?'

'I know. But he's not a drunkard now though, is he? And Milly, he was never a predator. No really, he was a passive womaniser.'

'What does that mean?'

'You know what it's like – you see everything from behind a bar counter, and I can tell you, he never chased women, they came to him. Well, you know what some of them are like, especially when it comes to boxers.'

'Is that supposed to make me feel better?'

'Oh I don't know, you must do as you want – that is, if you know what you want.'

'I want to be independent, I said.'

'I see. Milly, can I call you back in a few? I want to run something past Fred. I might be able to help with one of your dilemmas – it won't sort you out, but it might give you a couple of options.'

The next day, Mrs Oak is sleeping. She stays sleeping for the whole day and for two days after that.

Those silent days; they are the longest days. Milly walks the room, sits down, stands up, tries to read whatever book she has picked out off the shelf in the residents' lounge. Sometimes she stays at the window and looks down at the bare winter soil. She wanders down the corridor now and then, maybe falls into a bit of chat at the coffee station or in one of the lounges. Mostly, though, she stays by Mrs Oak's side. Waiting for her eyes to flicker, a shifting of the lids. Or the rare gift of a few seconds when she opens them altogether, looks right at her and says something daft like: 'Don't tell me – I'm *still* bloody here.'

Sometimes when she wakes, she says nothing at all, just smiles right into Milly's eyes. Then she slips off again, leaving her alone with nothing to do but think and remember and regret.

On the shortest day of the year, she sends him a text.

Pip – I want to give you back the cheque. Can we meet? Tomorrow evening? I don't mind where, just not the pub.

About an hour later he replies.

OK. 7 p.m.? Piccadilly? Outside Hatchards?

The clock on the spire of St James's Church tells her she is fifteen minutes early. She remembers Pip once telling her about this church; how he would come in out of the cold, sit in a pew and just think. He said it was one of the few places where someone with no shelter could go and not feel as if they were being watched. It's only a couple of minutes to Hatchards from here and so she decides to kill the time by going inside. There are two old men, one on the far side of the aisle from where she is sitting, the other at the top near the altar. Both of them are wearing too many clothes and carrying plastic bags stuffed with what she guesses are sleeping bags. At the altar, music stands are being laid out in preparation for a concert. The light in the church has a pale bronze hue to it and the man across from her, she sees now, is reading a book by the standard lamp set into his pew. The man is elderly. It could be Pip a few years down the road. She thinks of all the other homeless people she's got used to seeing over the years in London. Sleeping in doorways and lining up at soup kitchens; the man who comes and sets himself up in the doorway of Leon every night, curled into a sleeping bag, smoking his sweet-scented vape, reminding her of Alice's caterpillar.

And she remembers the time she was on a bus coming through Charing Cross, when she thought she saw Pip down on the street. On a winter's evening, snow on the air, she jumped off the bus and went looking for him along the narrow street at the back of the station, groups of homeless people queuing for food; some of them standing around chatting while they ate out of cartons, others so mortified they put their food on windowsills of closed offices and shops and turned their backs to the street. She hadn't succeeded in finding him – if it had been him in the first place. I have done so little with my life, she thinks. Just stood there and let it happen; I took so few risks, even with Flora – I didn't fight hard enough, just waited, hoping for a miracle, until it was too late.

She thinks of Sunday-school lessons when she was a child. She loved to go, even if there were only three or four kids from a dwindling population. There was a bun afterwards, a glass of milk, supplied by that Quaker family who owned all those cafés in Dublin. Shortly after her mother had gone, a guest vicar came in to give the lesson. '"Do not be afraid",' he said, 'these words appear in the bible three hundred and sixty-five different times – that's one for every day of the year, children. Do *not* be afraid.'

She can't see him anywhere. She sees crowds, bulky in dark winter coats. Gloved hands holding the fancy turquoise packaging of Fortnum & Mason. Or, less obvious, the brown paper packages squared off with the Hatchards emerald-green ribbon. Through a cluster of moving limbs, a band of white. She is only five minutes late and he is usually so punctual – annoyingly early, in fact – it occurs to her that he has been delayed. She takes her hand out of her glove to check her phone for messages. The iced air bites her fingers on contact. There are no new messages. She looks again, between the row of taxis in the rank and the shoppers pushing in and out of the bookshop entrance. That white again, more of it this time – wider, longer, moving towards her. And there he is suddenly, standing right in front of her. He has no coat on and is wearing a white shirt and dark skinny tie.

She covers her face with her hands and shakes her head. She can hear him laughing and saying her name. When she doesn't answer, his hands come to her wrists and gently take them away from her face. She knows she is laughing but that she's also close to crying. She says: 'You big fuckin' eejit – what are you *doing*?'

'Well, I thought it was worth a shot,' he says, 'seeing how nothing else seems to impress you.'

'You're supposed to iron the creases out of the shirt before you wear it,' she says. 'Don't you know that?'

She reaches out, touches his sleeve. 'My God, you're freezing.'

Now she looks at his face, blotched with cold, his lips have a blue tint to them.

She puts her arms around him, feels his cold skin against her face.

'Where's your coat?' she whispers into his ear.

'It's in the bag.'

'Well put it on you, then – you're not much good to me dead.'

His arms tighten around her, and he says into her hair, 'Thank God you said that, because I am actually fucking freezing.'

In the Caffè Concerto across the road, she tells him about Trish's offer. His head goes down and he looks at the floor as she speaks.

'There's a flat above the café, you see – the tenants are Greek and they don't want to stay here on account of Brexit. The café is

494

let out to someone else downstairs. But anyway, Trish says that if I want I can have the apartment at a low rent, if I keep an eye on things downstairs, organise insurance, maintenance and all that. It's a one-bed – sitting room, bathroom, small kitchen. Quite nice actually.'

He's nodding, but he doesn't say anything.

'Of course, it would need to be done up. I mean, I can't bear the idea of sleeping in a bed someone else has slept in.'

'No,' he says, tapping the coffee spoon off the side of the cup.

'So a new bed would have to be bought for a start.'

'Yes,' he says.

'What I'm trying to say here is that I'll accept your money.'

'Good, it sounds as if you'll need it.'

'On one condition.'

'What's that?'

'That we buy a double bed. And that I get to sleep on the left side.'

He says nothing. Then abruptly stands up and walks away. She thinks he's leaving her sitting there, but then he goes down the stairs to the toilets.

When he comes back, his eyes are red. He sits beside her and takes her hand.

'Pip? Oh God, I'm sorry, I didn't mean to upset you.'

'That's okay,' he says and clears his throat.

'They're not moving out for another three months – the Greek lads.'

'We can stay in . . .' He begins crying again.

'In Dom's house, were you going to say?'

He nods.

'Max won't mind?' she asks.

He shakes his head.

'But after Mrs Oak dies,' she says.

He nods again, clears his throat again and says, 'Milly, I wish I could tell you, I wish I could . . .'

'It's okay,' she says. 'Pip, it's okay, it's okay.'

When Mrs Oak dies, it's the middle of the night and there are four people standing around the deathbed: two night nurses and a chaplain Milly has never seen before.

She is sitting right up beside her – just as she promised she would.

Earlier in the day Mrs Oak had come round for a few moments. She turned and looked out the window – 'Is that a moon I see out there?' – and Milly had agreed that yes, it was. Even if there was nothing out there but a flabby grey sky. Mrs Oak knew she was going and was so brave about it all that Milly had hardly been able to look her in the eye. Right from the start she'd been brave; the way she had accepted the cancer, phoning the remaining members of her bridge club before packing her bag and waiting for the ambulance to arrive.

The chaplain says his few words and one of the nurses leans over and presses her eyelids closed. Then the matron comes in, writes something on the chart and says the doctor will sign the death certificate when he comes in at nine o'clock. And then, one by one, they all creep out the door as if they're afraid Mrs Oak will wake up and they'll have to go through the whole rigmarole again.

It's bright by the time the Jamaican nurse comes back in. She switches off the lights, opens the venetian blinds and the room turns into a cage of yellow light. On the way out, she squeezes Milly's shoulder and tells her to take her time. Outside, she can hear her voice thick with tiredness as she greets the day nurse: 'That's another one left us last night, Lord be good to her.'

The day nurse replies, 'Mrs Oak? Oh, now that is a shame, two days before Christmas and all. Sad for her family and friends.'

And then both voices fall away.

She can hear the sound of doors opening and closing, the shuffle of feet towards breakfast, the turning of a wheelchair. She can hear Matt Monro begin his daily loop of 'When a Child Is Born.'

She straightens the crease in the coverlet, places Mrs Oak's hands out and across her chest so that the manicure shows on the counterpane. She takes her little makeup bag out of the mouth of the locker and rummages out an eyebrow pencil, then carefully she scratches the colour in. Then she puts a bit of blusher on her dead face and, opening the door of the locker, takes out the brown handbag.

It's late morning when she comes back to the pub. She turns on her phone and finds several missed calls: Shamie, Trish, Jerome. Three calls and two messages from Pip.

She texts him back:

She's gone. I can't talk just now. I'll be ready to leave around 7 this eve.

He comes back straight away:

I'm sorry, Milly, for your loss. I'll be across the street. Text me when you're ready and I'll come round the back. Call if you need me before then xxx

She puts the brown handbag on the bar counter, opens it up and examines the contents. A sample vial of Chanel N°5. Two lipsticks and a half-bar of Bourneville. The funeral list. A roll of cash bound with an elastic band; a watch, three rings and a bracelet. She counts the cash – eight hundred and twenty-five quid. Then she rolls it back into the band. She looks down at the roll and the jewellery and thinks: a whole lifetime I am holding on the palms of my hands.

She walks through the downstairs rooms, dust bouncing ahead of her. She passes in and out of the front and back bar, pauses for a while in the lounge, walks back and forward behind the disused counters. She sweeps the floor, buffs up the bar taps, washes off the slop trays. Then she climbs up on the footstool and polishes the mirrors.

In the afternoon, she makes her calls. She starts with Trish, then moves on to the old biddies from the bridge club. She phones Jerome and then Shamie. Most of the conversations are more or less the same. Except for the call to Shamie: 'If you're thinking of coming to the funeral,' she says, 'please don't give Phil a hard time. We're together now. It would mean a lot to me if you could at least be civil.'

'Of course, Milly love,' Shamie says. 'I understand.'

She goes into the ladies and gives the toilets a one-by-one flush. And then with the sound of crashing water echoing behind her, she pulls out the hoover and clatters her way up the stairs, unconcerned by any noise she might be making. She goes into the kitchen and yanks the curtains off the windows, then tidies and cleans all around. Finally, she goes upstairs to her room, crawls fully clothed into bed and sleeps for a couple of hours.

When she wakes, she gets up, goes down to the bar, pours herself a nip of whiskey, takes a cigarette and goes outside.

It's dark in the yard. There's the sound of distant traffic and, closer to hand, the rumble of trucks, like army tanks heading into

Smithfield market. And she remembers how vast she thought this city when she came here first nearly forty years ago. The shock she would get when out on an afternoon walk and turning a corner, she'd find the likes of St Paul's heaped up in front of her. That sense of history! Or on longer walks on her day off, standing on one of the bridges, looking down at the muddy water with the buildings stacked on both sides; some of them there from the start, others gone and quickly replaced, brick to glass. But always magnificent: a steadfast front line for the endless city sprawled behind it.

On the way back up the stairs to her room, it comes at her: a cold, terrible doubt. He won't turn up. She pushes the doubt away as she reaches under the bed and slides Terry Oak's old suitcase to her. She opens it out and looks down at the baby clothes. 1989, the year she finally stopped buying a birthday outfit for Flora. Gently, she lifts each item out, folds it and slides it into a plastic bag. She takes her own clothes out of the chest and puts the plastic bag into the top drawer, easing it shut. She keeps the baby gown and the little pink bootees and puts them into the case along with her own clothes.

She thinks it again: he won't come. He has changed his mind and is already halfway to Scotland or Devon or wherever it was that he used to flee to, when things got too much for him in the past. She has left the lights blasted on in the kitchen, the windows are naked and he isn't even coming.

But he loves her – that much she does know. But maybe it's not enough, she thinks now. Or maybe it's just too much.

After a moment, she runs downstairs and stands at the door of the kitchen. Then slowly she makes her way to the window with her eyes lowered. When she gets to the window, she closes them completely. She remembers the Christmas Eve when she was a girl, standing upstairs looking out and wishing with all her stupid little heart that he would come along, look up and see her in Mrs Oak's fur coat.

'If he's not here, he's not here,' she says aloud. 'I'll just have to get over it. I have some money; in three months' time, I'll have a flat. I'll manage. I always manage.'

She opens her eyes and looks down on the street.

Acknowledgements

THE AUTHOR WOULD like to thank the following and acknowledge their assistance and/or advice:

Christy O'Gara, London
Mickey Delaney, Dale Youth Boxing Club, London
David and Valerie McDonald
Clare Reihill, the T. S. Eliot Foundation
Rick Jones, The Waste Land walking tour
British Library Archives

For their invaluable editorial input,
Denis Hickey
Niall MacMonagle

PUBLICATIONS:

An Unconsidered People: The Irish in London, Catherine Dunne
Getty Images: 1960s–1990s
Nairn's London, Ian Nairn
Vintage 80s: London Street Photography, Johnny Stiletto
The Unofficial Countryside, Richard Mabey

501

Portobello Road: Lives of a Neighbourhood, Julian Mash

I've Lived in East London for 86½ Years, Martin Usborne

The Heath: My Year on Hampstead Heath, Hunter Davies

Willesden Local History Society, various journals

The London Compendium: A Street-by-Street Exploration of the Hidden Metropolis, Ed Glinert

London's Street Trees: A Field Guide to the Urban Forest, Paul Wood

The Secret Lore of London: The City's Forgotten Stories and Mythology, ed. John Matthews with Caroline Wise

On the Cobbles: The Life of a Bare-Knuckle Gypsy Warrior, Jimmy Stockins with Martin King and Martin Knight

Gypsy Joe: Bare-Knuckle Fighter, Professional Golfer, Joe Smith

The Hardest Game, Harry Carpenter

Kenny Egan: My Story with Ewan McKenna

The Hurt Business: A Century of the Greatest Writing on Boxing, ed. George Kimball and John Schulian

Randy: The Final, Complete Biography of Randolph Turpin, Peter McInnes

A Hurting Business, Thomas Healy

Henry Cooper: A Hero for All Time, Norman Giller

Joe Bugner: My Story with Stuart Mullins

A Smell of Burning: A Memoir of Epilepsy, Colin Grant

No Fixed Abode: Life and Death Among the UK's Forgotten Homeless, Maeve McClenaghan

Proved Innocent: The Story of Gerry Conlon of the Guildford Four, Gerry Conlon

Unlocked: An Irish Prison Officer's Story, David McDonald with Mick Clifford

A Bit of a Stretch: The Diaries of a Prisoner, Chris Atkins

The Profession of Violence: The Rise and Fall of the Kray Twins,
    John Pearson
The New Cambridge Companion to T. S. Eliot, ed. Jason Harding
T. S. Eliot: A Life, Peter Ackroyd
The Imperfect Life of T. S. Eliot, Lyndall Gordon

. . . and, of course, *The Waste Land* by T. S. Eliot, which was a
guiding light throughout the making of this novel.